BANNON BROTHERS: TRIUMPH

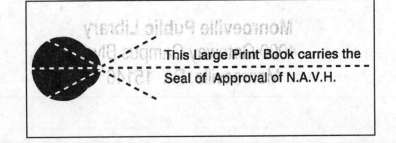

Bannon Brothers: Triumph

Janet Dailey

THORNDIKE PRESS
A part of Gale, Cengage Learning

GALE
CENGAGE Learning·

Detroit • New York • San Francisco • New Haven, Conn • Waterville, Maine • London

GALE
CENGAGE Learning®

Copyright © 2013 by Janet Dailey.
Thorndike Press, a part of Gale, Cengage Learning.

ALL RIGHTS RESERVED
Thorndike Press® Large Print Basic.
The text of this Large Print edition is unabridged.
Other aspects of the book may vary from the original edition.
Set in 16 pt. Plantin.

LIBRARY OF CONGRESS CATALOGING-IN-PUBLICATION DATA

Dailey, Janet.
  Bannon brothers : triumph / by Janet Dailey. — Large Print edition.
    pages cm. — (Thorndike Press Large Print Basic)
  ISBN-13: 978-1-4104-5828-5 (hardcover)
  ISBN-10: 1-4104-5828-8 (hardcover)
  1. Brothers—Fiction. 2. Conspiracy—Fiction. 3. Large type books. I. Title.
PS3554.A29B345 2013
813'.54—dc23   2013014043

Published in 2013 by arrangement with Kensington Books, an imprint of Kensington Publishing Corp.

Printed in the United States of America
1 2 3 4 5 6 7 17 16 15 14 13

BANNON BROTHERS: TRIUMPH

CHAPTER 1

Kelly Johns smoothed her suit, waiting for the countdown in her earbud mic as a news cameraman a block away focused a zoom lens in her direction. Seventeen stories of concrete floors towered behind her, open to the wind and weather, with a view of downtown Atlanta in the distance.

The city sparkled. This part of it didn't. A huge crane and flatbed trailers still half-loaded with rusting rebar completed the picture. The construction project had been idled months ago, its dirty-money financing gone and the site locked down by the feds. The empty streets around it were silent, ideal for taping.

"Three, two, one."

The cameraman's voice in her ear made Kelly straighten and look his way. She hoped her long blond hair would cooperate and not blow across her face. Her dark maroon suit was wrinkleproof and the color conveyed seriousness and warmth.

Kelly took a breath. She'd memorized her opening lines en route to filming the segment.

"Another scandal-ridden project shut down by the authorities," she began, gesturing to the unfinished building. "And millions of dollars — your tax dollars — lost to kickbacks. When will it end?"

She maintained an expression of heartfelt concern until Gordon spoke again. "And . . . cut. Thanks, Kelly," the cameraman said. "Good take. Sound was solid. Laura wants to get a look at it, though. Give us a minute."

Kelly barely registered his request. She saw Laura Ruskin, the segment producer, come out of the station's unmarked van and talk to Gordon.

Turning, she looked around at the building and construction site, searching for a different visual, knowing there would be several more takes, here or elsewhere. There was no point in removing the wireless lavaliere mic clipped to her lapel or the earbud.

Everything they shot today would be digitally edited at the news studio and used as an intro for her previous reportage and interviews. Hours of tape got whittled down

8

to five minutes when the subject was corruption in the construction industry. Far from thrilling, totally unglamorous, but definitely the kind of feature story that might garner a community award or two if she could manage to make it interesting.

Or so said Monroe Capp, the news director. She wasn't sure if her boss was on her side or not. Monroe had promised the feature — her first for WBRX — would run at some future date during the evening broadcast she now anchored, but everyone knew breaking news came first.

Everything but the intro was complete. It was an important story, she told herself. Atlanta was growing faster than ever, crowded with gleaming skyscrapers and world-class hotels. The sprawl threatened to overshadow the quiet, idyllic suburbs surrounding the metropolitan hub.

Kelly looked around again. No one lived around here anymore. Formerly residential, there were only a few boarded-up houses left of the neighborhood. Small lots had been bought up and fenced off into large parcels by developers waiting for the right time to build. Or not.

She looked at her watch. Kelly was expected back at the station for hair and makeup at least an hour before the evening news. Laura had decided to tape the intro in the afternoon, hoping for dramatic shadows, enlisting Gordon at the last minute and taking out a van without signing for it.

At least the segment producer was gung-ho. Laura had discovered the abandoned construction site last week and connected with someone in charge who gave her the keys to the padlocked gates. The building had no specific connection to the planned story and anything identifiable would be cut from the final tape, but the location had the look Laura wanted.

Grim. Deserted. Lonely.

Supposedly there were security guards somewhere around. Not where Kelly could see them.

She ignored a faint tremor of unease as she reached into her pocket and took out her laminated press pass. If anyone stopped her, it would come in handy. She walked through the half-built structure, her high heels echoing on the dusty concrete, going around supporting pillars and avoiding the deep, shadowy pit for the elevator shafts.

Kelly stopped for a second, wondering why the perimeter hadn't been blocked off. There were no safety cones around it and no yellow tape, and she couldn't see the bottom from where she was standing.

She caught an unpleasant whiff of damp earth from the bottom of the pit. With a shudder, she moved on, going past a concrete-slab staircase with no rails, not tempted to go up for a better view. Kelly glanced upward at a raw ceiling stained by water damage, thinking that she should have worn a hard hat. The rough walls were stained, too, but completely free of spray-painted tags and scribbles.

It was odd that there were no graffiti anywhere. And not so much as a crushed cigarette butt or snack wrapper marred the concrete floors, which were covered with an undisturbed layer of dust.

Someone was keeping the riffraff and the taggers out. Maybe a maintenance company — Laura must have gotten the keys from them. Owners of abandoned properties usually disappeared without bothering to secure their properties, with disastrous results. Squatters. Fires. Violence.

Kelly could see clear through to the back of the site, green with tall weeds. Here and there a tossed beer can gleamed against roughly gouged tracks made by bulldozers, long gone. The huge crane in front was all that was left of the heavy equipment. Kelly continued toward the open area, peering out and up at rickety scaffolding that had pulled away from the building in back. She stopped before the unfinished floor did and surveyed the scene, her arms folded over her chest.

"Kelly?" The cameraman's voice crackled in her earbud. "Where'd you go? We can't see you."

"I walked to the back," she answered. "It doesn't look like anyone's been here for a while, but the building hasn't been trashed. There aren't any footprints other than mine."

"Great. That makes you easy to follow. Stay there. We'll find you."

"Okay."

She heard a slight commotion, then Gordon's voice came in again. "Laura wants another take, different setting, same lines. Anything visually interesting where you are?"

"Maybe." Kelly didn't elaborate, suddenly noticing a luxury car on the other side of the chain-link fence behind the weeds. The car was the sole occupant of the parking lot, a wasteland of cracked asphalt and litter.

The expensive vehicle's dark-tinted windows and gleaming black finish seemed out of place in the desolate setting. There was no sign of a driver or passengers, but the slanting angle of the afternoon light might hide both.

She heard Laura and Gordon enter and follow her trail, their sneakered footfalls quiet on the concrete. Kelly turned toward them. The segment producer was carrying Kelly's bag and her own, and some of Gordon's equipment.

Laura, a short brunette in no-nonsense jeans and jacket with the station logo, stopped several feet away when the cameraman did. Gordon was a burly man with thick hair drawn back in a ponytail. Going out as a team, they got teased about the short hair on her and the long hair on him, but neither seemed to care.

He hoisted the camera and looked through the viewfinder at Kelly. Then he put on a pair of glasses and took his time about adjusting the lens.

Gordon liked to do things right and he didn't take crap from anyone. Kelly wasn't going to tell him to hurry up. He wouldn't.

Most days Kelly believed in picking her battles. She'd seen Monroe Capp and the cameraman get into some doozies more than once. Gordon Lear was the best in Atlanta and the head of the WBRX camera team, two things Capp didn't seem to care about.

"Nice pose. Hold it," Gordon ordered. "Let's get a light balance and a sound level," he said to Laura.

Kelly said her full name twice and waited. The assistant producer and the cameraman seemed too preoccupied with what they were doing to notice the car on the other side of the fence — or the faint noise of its doors opening and closing.

She was curious. Kelly shifted on her feet. "How much longer? These heels pinch."

The ploy didn't work. Gordon glared at her. "Stay still. I mean it."

With a sigh, she obeyed. The cameraman had read her body language right: she had been about to turn around.

No question there was someone in the black car, possibly more than one person. So what? A late-model luxury car like that wasn't going to be filled with teenagers. No one would sneak into the background to make faces and wave, hoping to get on the evening news.

All the same, Kelly hated the feeling of not knowing what was going on behind her back. But they were inside the building's open walls. Protected, more or less.

"Kelly, you with us?" Gordon said loudly. "Let's get this over with. Ready for your close-up?"

14

That old joke. As for the rest, the cameraman didn't mince his words. Which meant he got on her nerves sometimes. Especially when he caught her in a moment of inattentiveness.

"Yes," Kelly said. "That's why I'm standing here."

Laura frowned and shook her head. "Wait a sec." She craned her neck to get a glimpse of the viewfinder that jutted out from the video camera. "Gordon, do you want that parked car in the background?"

He squinted. "Nothing but a black blur. Not a problem. We can edit it out if need be. Kelly, we're rolling. Three, two, one —"

"Hold on. Who are all those guys?" Laura demanded. "Wait, there's a woman too. In the other car."

Kelly whirled around. A second car, a near twin of the one she'd seen, pulled into the parking lot behind the chain-link fence. Two men in dark suits had gotten out of the first car and stood behind the open rear doors, as if they were shields.

A woman gestured from the rolled-down passenger side window of the second car. Kelly picked up details automatically: pale lipstick, a patterned scarf, wavy red hair. But the woman's eyes were hidden behind sunglasses. She was speaking, but Kelly couldn't hear her words.

None of the men moved.

Instinct made Kelly step sideways and back into the shadows.

"What are you doing?" Gordon asked, concentrating on the task of taping. "I can't see you there."

"And neither can they," Kelly hissed, easing along the wall toward him and Laura. "Let's keep out of sight, shall we?"

"Why?" The cameraman looked up at her, baffled. He'd moved his glasses atop his head. Kelly doubted he could see more than a foot in front of him without them. He peered into the viewfinder again.

Kelly kept on coming, filling it. "Something tells me they're not here for a church picnic."

"What makes you think that? They didn't bring a pie?"

"Just stop taping and go!"

She reached him and grabbed for the camera. Gordon hung on to it as Kelly saw Laura's eyes widen, taking in whatever was happening in the parking lot. Laura's mouth opened in a wordless gasp.

A male roar shattered the silence.

"Get down! Down!"

Not Gordon's voice. Much deeper. Urgent. Kelly spun, too startled to figure out

16

more. She heard a muffled crack and the faint, unmistakable zing of a bullet.

Someone shoved her behind a pillar and held her there.

She couldn't see his face. Strong arms pinned her between his chest and cold concrete. Kelly tried to jerk free and hit her head. The man's breath felt hot against her hair. He was taller than she was, a lot taller. And unquestionably stronger.

"Let me go!" Kelly struggled to get the words out. The pressure of his body made it hard for her to breathe.

"Not yet. Sorry," he growled.

Dimly, she realized that thugs didn't usually apologize. But she wasn't out of danger. Her nose was crushed against a holster slung to the side of his chest under a thick leather jacket. The man moved a fraction of an inch. Kelly dragged in a raw breath that hurt her throat.

"Who are you?" she whispered.

"Your goddamn guardian angel," he muttered, looking warily to the side, the cords in his neck straining against tanned skin.

She made a mental list of what she could see. Strong jaw. Definite cheekbones. Dark hair. Somehow . . . familiar.

He moved back another fraction of an inch, but she was still pinned. The exchange of gunfire coming from the parking lot stopped — then started again. She struggled to free herself without success. Long, muscular legs on either side of her own withstood her kicking.

Suddenly the man let her go. Kelly looked around wildly and saw Laura crawling through the dust toward her, dragging their bags, followed by Gordon in a crouch, still clutching the camera.

"Get out of here, all of you," the man growled savagely. "Now!" He reached into his holster and drew a gun, heading toward the weeds and the fence, his back to her. Kelly didn't wait to see why.

She hauled Laura up off the floor and they ran together, headlong, scrambling through the gates and racing up the block to the news station van. Gordon got behind the wheel and floored it, making a wild swing into the cross street.

Kelly clutched the handhold and switched her gaze between the rearview mirror and the side mirror. As far as she could tell, they weren't being followed. At least not by the cars from the parking lot.

"Oh my God. We could have been killed." Laura cowered on the backseat, looking up after a minute when Kelly told Gordon sharply to pull over.

"There's a gas station up ahead." She pointed. "Use the pay phone and call in a shooting."

"Why?" he asked in disbelief. "Don't you have a cell phone?"

"I don't want my number recorded on the 911 database. And I don't want to sign autographs at the gas station."

He went faster. "So I get to be the fall guy? I'm not volunteering. We walked right into the middle of a gang war, and you know what they say. No one loves a snitch."

"No one followed us, and you don't have to say who you are!" Kelly grabbed the steering wheel and the van swerved into the next lane.

Cursing, Gordon pulled over by a concealing hedge and left the key in the van's ignition as he got out, slamming the door. Kelly clambered from her seat and slid behind the wheel, jamming on sunglasses as she drove over a low curb into the side lot of the gas station. The maneuver got a sidelong glance from a passerby, but nothing more. The place was busy. Without the WBRX logo, the plain white van didn't draw attention.

"We have to call. It's the right thing to do." Laura shrank back against her seat. "But what if the attendants remember us?"

"They're not even looking," Kelly reassured her. She rolled down her window to watch Gordon stuff coins into the slot and punch 911, barely able to hear him mutter the information but not his name. He hung up and tore around to the passenger seat she'd vacated.

"Duty done." He climbed back in and slammed the door. "Not that I want to be a hero. They usually die first."

Kelly pulled out into traffic. "Someone just saved our lives, Gordon. Return the favor."

They dashed into the WBRX station complex by the back way, shoving through the double doors into a long corridor. Kelly stopped for a moment to peer through the glass wall at shoulder height, surveying the newsroom cubicles.

Relative quiet prevailed. The night shift hadn't come in and the day shift was mostly gone, though there were still a few reporters and researchers at work inside the maze of low walls. Newsgathering was a twenty-four-hour operation.

"No one's looking. Just keep going," she ordered in a whisper. "I don't want to explain anything to anybody."

Her dull feature story was suddenly looking a whole hell of a lot more interesting. Monroe Capp might take it away from her. If there was a link between the gun battle and the disintegrating building, Kelly intended to find it. Intuition told her that there was. *Facts first,* she reminded herself.

"You might not have to explain just yet," Laura said slowly. "I — I didn't have official permission from the station manager to bring you and a cameraman and equipment to that building."

Gordon sighed. "They can't fire me for that."

"But didn't you say you took the van?" Laura countered.

"No one was using it, and you told me we weren't going to be gone long. Besides, I have my own set of keys for it."

"Stop it, you two," Kelly said. "I didn't sign out when I left. So we're all in this together. Did either of you tell anyone where we were going?"

"No." In chorus.

"Then we can worry about all that later. Right now we have to get a look at that tape. Gordon, which editing room?"

"First on the left." He led the way to a windowless room down the hall and Kelly closed the door. There were mismatched chairs in front of an array of digital equipment connected with snaking cords. He commandeered the biggest chair and pulled his laptop out of his backpack.

He connected it to the camera, fumbling with the USB jack. "Don't get your hopes up," he said to Kelly. "If you're thinking this is going to be a sensation on the evening news, starring you, forget it. After your intro, I got zip."

"I want to see it. Beginning to end."

In less than a minute, he had downloaded the digital footage and fast-forwarded past the long shot of Kelly in front of the abandoned building, and the interior close-ups. In silence, they reviewed the grainy background images of the car in the parking lot as Gordon's voice, then Laura's, intertwined with hers. There was a dark blur behind Kelly — the first car. Then a jittery few seconds of the second car, not in focus. The camera had caught a flash of something patterned — a scarf around the neck of the woman she'd seen. After that, it was all a blur, punctuated by gunshots and garbled shouts.

"Even the sound is crappy." Gordon lowered the volume and zoomed in and out of video, boosting the pixels into a shifting mosaic that revealed nothing. "This is pointless." He sat back in the swivel chair.

"No way to tell what was going on out there. If we could run this through better software, we might be able to see something."

"What kind of software? Who has it?" Kelly tapped the pause button.

"Not WBRX," he answered.

"I wonder if the men in those cars ever noticed us. I don't think the woman did." Kelly went back several frames to the close-up on the patterned scarf, then forward for a few. "She never got out of the car."

"You sure about that?" Gordon wanted to know.

"I could be wrong."

"Maybe you saw something we didn't. Laura and I didn't get close to where the floor ended. You were practically in the weeds," Gordon replied.

"No, I wasn't. And I wasn't looking out at the parking lot for very long."

"It's possible they saw you," Gordon insisted.

"Not only that. They could have recognized you, Kelly," Laura said nervously. "We have to 'fess up. What if someone comes after you or me or Gordon? The police ought to know we were there. Wait a minute — do you think the man who yelled at us to get out was a cop?"

"Maybe. Or some kind of special agent. Either way, he was undercover," Kelly added. "Do you two remember anything about him? He's nowhere on the tape." There was no doubt in her mind that their rescuer had stayed out of camera range on purpose.

Gordon folded burly arms across his chest. "Gee whiz. Sorry. I was dodging bullets."

"I wasn't trying to blame you for anything," Kelly said.

Gordon looked a little ashamed of himself for being snotty. "Yeah, I know. Forget it." The blunt words were somehow soothing. "I don't think any of us are thinking straight after what happened."

"Kelly, that man must have been watching you from the second you stepped inside the building," Laura said.

"Watching from where? I didn't see any other footprints," Kelly protested. Then she remembered the slab staircase that she'd passed. And the rickety scaffolding in back. Could have been either. She hadn't been alone in that building.

"Maybe he can fly." Gordon again. Sarcasm was his default mode. "No cape, though. Just that leather jacket. I don't know why you assume he's a good guy, by the way."

"I hope he is," Kelly replied honestly. "Anyway, we just happened to be there for the taping. If no one at the station knew where we were, how would anyone else?"

"My name wasn't on the whiteboard," Laura said.

"I assumed you'd entered mine." Gordon stared at the laptop screen as it flickered and went dark.

"I didn't."

The assignment editor listed every reporter at WBRX and where they were, hour by hour, on the all-important whiteboard. In case of breaking news, it took only seconds to find the people nearest the scene and match them up with a crew. Kelly hadn't bothered to fill in the information, short on time after she'd skipped the afternoon story meeting, not mentioning she was heading out to tape an intro with Gordon and Laura.

"I just thought of something else. The GPS unit in the van transmits to the station," Gordon pointed out. "Someone around here is going to find out where we were soon enough. And then we'll catch hell. I need a drink. A big, stiff drink."

Kelly caught Laura's worried glance. The

last thing they needed was Gordon shooting off his mouth at the bar near WBRX. "Go with him. I'll cover for both of you here if I have to."

"I don't drink, Kelly. You know that."

"Then I'll treat you to a ginger ale from the vending machine," Gordon offered, "I mean, if that's okay with your mommy."

He looked toward Kelly, who only nodded.

Shakily, Laura rose and followed him out of the editing room.

Kelly sat back and tried to think.

What, where, when — she made a mental outline. A routine location taping at an abandoned building had exploded into unexpected violence. What she didn't know and couldn't begin to guess at was *who* and *why.* Gordon could be right about it being gang warfare.

Terror had fractured her sense of time. It hadn't taken long. She'd been pinned for only a few seconds. But Kelly still tingled where the man's powerful body had pressed against hers, held her so tightly it was hard to breathe — and risked his life to give her a chance to escape.

He must have had backup somewhere in the half-finished building. Nobody was invincible. She hadn't noticed body armor under that leather jacket. Just a T-shirt.

An adrenaline rush flushed her cheeks with heat. Kelly pushed her long blond hair away from her face and wound a hand through it, avoiding the tender spot where her head had connected with the concrete pillar. She lifted the silky strands away from her neck to cool down.

Preoccupied, she listened to the bulletins coming from the emergency response scanners on the assignment desk, trying to make sense of the brief exchanges between the speakers and remember the codes. She got the gist of it — she'd had a lot of practice.

SUV rollover, entrapment reported, calling for door pop . . . Fire, first story commercial building, contained . . . Assault, perp fled scene, minor injuries to vic . . . Car versus pole . . .

Not a word about a shoot-out at an abandoned construction site.

She closed her eyes, trying to visualize the man who'd saved all of them. As the seconds ticked by, the feeling that she knew him from somewhere got stronger. Kelly had an excellent memory for faces, a knack that had been honed to a skill as part of her job. Celebrities, politicians, crooks, ordinary citizens — she had to remember them all.

There wasn't anything ordinary about her

guardian angel, and she'd gotten only a glimpse of his profile. But she was confident that his name would come to her. When she calmed down. Too bad they had absolutely no visual for him.

Gordon and Laura came back in. The assistant producer held an unopened ginger ale, but the cameraman had already cracked a coke and was sipping from it. He set another on the desk for Kelly. She murmured her thanks and left it at that.

Laura clutched her cold can of ginger ale, then rolled it over her forehead. "That man — well, I guess he wasn't a security guard either."

She seemed to be trying to pull a few facts together herself. "There was supposed to be one on the site — I had it written down." She started leafing through a notebook, but her hands were unsteady. "Somewhere. I can't find it. The pages are out of order."

"He definitely wasn't a guard," Kelly said thoughtfully.

"Not dramatic enough for you?" Gordon asked. "How about hit man? Or professional assassin? Skip the facts. Just get the story on the air and ask questions later. That's the WBRX way."

"Gordon, don't." Laura's voice quavered.

"Just thinking aloud. For sure, he was

28

nothing to mess with." Gordon rubbed his chin. "He had a helluva grip on you, Kelly."

She waved away the comment. "Oh, shut up."

The cameraman obliged. For three seconds. "So what now?"

Laura stuffed stray pages inside the notebook, giving up on organizing them. "I can take a cubicle by the assignment desk for a while and keep tabs on the scanners," she volunteered. "No one will notice."

"Thanks, Laura. I was just listening to them from in here. Nothing yet. But people around here would look at me funny if I went out there," Kelly said. In the station hierarchy, anchors ranked at the top. She'd turned reporter for a day, but some busybody would ask questions if she was seen doing grunt work.

Kelly turned her head and listened again. The constant crackle was inescapable. Law enforcement, paramedic, and firefighter communications were monitored around the clock at WBRX, and so was an Internet scanner feed that buzzed with tips coming in day and night. When a hot story broke, the newsroom swung into action.

The routine bulletins droned on. Laura and Gordon got quiet, listening too. Kelly heard the code for an MVA — motor vehicle accident — on a highway ramp.

Multiple aided. Additional EMS requested to scene.

A half minute of dead air followed. It was a slow night for Atlanta.

Attempted robbery, liquor store. Unit en route.

Still nothing on the shooting. She glanced up at the large clock on the wall of the editing room. A lot of time had passed since then.

Intuition told Kelly something big had gone down in the parking lot, something she didn't understand, and she'd gone running in the opposite direction. Why? She mentally answered the question.

Fear, plain and simple. Concern for Laura and Gordon. The instinct to save her own skin — and the uncharacteristic impulse to obey orders from a guardian angel with rough moves and lightning-fast reflexes.

Kelly was dying to know what had happened, and not just to him. It had been too long since she'd felt the thrill of being on the scene of an unfolding story, when nothing and no one else mattered.

"Listen, guys, there's something else we have to think about," Laura fretted. "We were at the scene, we saw the cars, and Kelly and I glimpsed who was in them. Um,

30

doesn't that make us witnesses?"

"Yes, it does. But you two can leave me out of it," Gordon said. "I don't make the news, I just get nifty pictures of it. Mr. Film at Eleven, that's me."

"Did you put booze in that soda, Gordon? The tape can be subpoenaed," Kelly said bluntly.

"No one's seen it besides us. I could erase it." Gordon got up as if every bone in his body ached.

"No!" Kelly's vehemence got through to him.

Without shutting the laptop down, he thrust it and the video camera into Kelly's arms. She had to struggle to keep both from falling to the floor.

"Here," he said. "Keep 'em safe until you decide what to do. I'm going home."

Kelly knew how often he stopped in at the bar the staff reporters and freelancers frequented. She couldn't ask Laura to babysit him a second time.

"No talking," she warned him, setting the equipment aside.

"No problem," he retorted. "I should have said straight home. Where I can drink in peace."

Startled, Kelly heard herself summoned by the squawk box on her desk. It was meant to be louder than the newsroom hum and the noise of the scanners, and it always made her jump. She swore under her breath.

"Great. I'm on air in fifteen minutes."

Laura's hazel eyes rounded with surprise. "Are you still going to anchor after what happened?"

"Why not?" The question wasn't rhetorical. Not coming from Kelly.

June Fletcher placed a light towel over Kelly's smock-covered shoulders and started to comb her hair.

"How come it's so tangled today?" the makeup artist asked. "Did you go for a run this afternoon?"

"Ah — yes."

June tsked at her. "Wish you wouldn't before a newscast."

"Never again, June. Believe me."

June continued the comb-out, humming under her breath.

"Kelly, did you know that the news director asked me to come up with a new look for you?"

"No." Kelly frowned at her reflection. She hated the way she looked in a smock.

Monroe Capp had been in charge of WBRX for all of six months. Cutting costs, he'd fired about a quarter of the newsroom

staff and word was that he was keeping tabs on the anchors' individual ratings. After a year, Kelly had earned her popularity with Atlanta viewers, but that didn't mean she could count on her contract being renewed.

She almost didn't care. Kelly was determined to move up to national news. Atlanta was a major local market, but it was still local.

If there was a big story brewing that she could get her name on, she could use it as a springboard to bigger and better assignments: roving correspondent, weekend anchor, anything she could get here or in New York. Kelly had her sights set on the three majors and the powerful cable networks that broadcast nationally from Atlanta.

"Any ideas?" June looked at her expectantly.

"I'm not changing my hair. Capp can go to hell," Kelly said firmly.

June giggled. "You tell him that. Anyway, we don't have time to experiment now."

She put down the comb and started to roll Kelly's blond locks around a round brush, pointing a blow-dryer down at the hair for a blast of smoothing heat. She was gentle, but Kelly flinched.

"Oops. Sorry," June said with concern.

"Did I pull too hard?"

"Not your fault. I got clonked back there." Kelly didn't feel like explaining how.

"What?" June set the brush and hair dryer aside and ran her fingers over Kelly's scalp. "You sure did. I can feel a lump. You should've told me."

"It's no big deal," Kelly said.

June shook her head. "What did you do, run backward into a wall?"

"Sort of." It had been more like running into a rock-solid chest with a rebound into a concrete pillar. "I just wasn't looking where I was going."

The makeup artist resumed brushing, avoiding the painful spot. "Well, it won't show."

She finished the styling and opened a huge makeup kit crammed with bottles, tubes, and compacts, selecting foundation first. June kept right on talking about nothing in particular.

"I know how to cover up practically everything. Did I ever tell you about the weather reporter with a lightning bolt tattooed on her neck . . ."

From here on in, June's chatter didn't require much in the way of a response from Kelly — the stylist would arrive in a few minutes with clothes, and the two of them

always liked to talk. Kelly kept her face motionless while her onscreen makeup was applied, waiting for an opportunity to mark her broadcast script. She reached into the pocket of the smock for a felt-tip pen and opened the folder in her lap, working around June's dabbing and fussing.

Kelly got through the half-hour evening broadcast without having to consult it, reading the same lines from the TelePrompTer with lively emphasis. Her producer, out of sight in the control room, murmured cues in her earbud as unmanned cameras moved in front of her, their positions determined by an unseen robo-operator using a touch screen in another room. The mic attached to her lapel transmitted straight to the audio engineer.

Nothing to it. Her voice was direct and clear, pitched as if she were explaining something to a good friend and not a camera lens.

With practiced ease, Kelly wrapped up the broadcast and exchanged the usual banter with her silver-haired co-anchor, Dave Maples, a favorite with viewers for his comforting baritone and craggy countenance. He delivered the sign-off and both of them looked steadily into the cameras, waiting for the tally lights to go dark. Lost in thought, she missed the signal that indicated they were no longer live.

She jumped when a technical assistant appeared at her side to remove the small lapel mic.

"Zoning out?"

With a smile, she handed him the earbud. "Guess I did. Long day. Thanks, Jeff."

He turned to her co-anchor as she stood and exited the set, heading quickly back to her office.

Kelly was transferring the footage from Gordon's laptop to her own. She didn't want it on the WBRX servers or her office computer. Not until she had reviewed it in slo-mo. She looked up when Laura came into her office with a mini-recorder held high.

"Got it." Laura spoke in a whisper. "The first reports came over the scanners while you were on air."

"Who else heard it?"

"The assignment editors."

"Who did they send out?"

"No one yet. Darla's making calls."

Kelly stood and peered out the door of her office. The assignment desk was part of the newsroom but separated from the cubicles by a low room divider. At a single long slab sat Darla Jackson and Lou Hart, the story assignment editors, tracking breaking news and feeds on several monitors and listening intently to the scanners. Darla used her computer and headset to call reporters and field crew, putting together a team, speaking with quiet urgency.

Of course, every other local news operation was listening to the same reports and would send out their own people. But some stations and newspapers might sit on it, waiting for official information.

The police traded exclusives for cooperation if they had to, playing favorites as needed. An ugly, out-of-the-way incident with unknown perps wasn't that important in the news cycle. A pop star's tawdry love triangle or a mama duck crossing the highway with her brood and a little help from a trucker got more interest.

Kelly went back in. Laura took a chair and replayed the digital recording of the scanner. A confused babble of cop talk poured out, peppered with terse codes that signified the worst. Kelly knew some of them by heart.

Fragments of information crackled and faded.

Tip called in, what, two hours ago?

Yeah, from a pay phone.

At a gas station, she wanted to say. Kelly felt a little guilty about making Gordon call. But there'd been no way around it.

Caller was male. No name. Gunshots, abandoned building, was all he said. Then he hung up.

Another tip came in after that. Noise complaint. Car horn wouldn't stop.

Someone leaning on it? Yeah. Someone dead.

The cop chuckled. Gallows humor. It got them through the night.

Kelly had an idea who might have called in the subsequent tip. Just not a name to go with the man's rugged profile.

The codes started up again. *Ten-seventy-one. Shooting. Ten-fifty-four. Possible dead body. Ten-fifty-five. Case for the coroner.*

The count rose abruptly in the next bulletin.

Two bodies, parking lot. As of now, John Does. Entire site perimeter secured. Additional units requested for floor-by-floor search. Seventeen stories. Hold it. Another body found, ground floor.

The ground floor — where Kelly had walked, oblivious to danger. Where the man had shielded her body with his, held her and let her go. Had he been killed or

38

injured? The thought was appalling.

The recording played on. The sound began to break up. Kelly could barely hear toward the end, but there was something there worth listening to again.

"Could you replay — ?"

"You do it." Laura stopped the tape and got up. "I feel like I'm going to be sick."

"Not in here."

"I wouldn't do that to you." The other woman's face was pale. "Okay if I go home?"

"I think you should. Laura, we know the police are there, and there's nothing else we can do."

"Guess not."

"Mind if I keep the mini-recorder overnight?"

"No." Laura gathered her things to go. "Be careful, Kelly," she said, turning around before she walked away down the hall.

Kelly waited for a few more minutes and replayed the last several seconds on the mini-recorder to make sure she'd heard right. It was a radio transmission, fished out of the air. By the sound of it, two cops at the abandoned building were talking to each other at the secured crime scene.

Hey. That guy over there — isn't he — ?

Yeah. Deke Bannon. The one and only.

This case must be big if he's on it.

It's big. Half the cops in the city are here.

Plus a swarm of feds. Never seen so many in one place.

Me neither . . .

Static interrupted the rest. But the name had clicked instantly. The third Bannon brother, the one Kelly hadn't met yet, was her man. Still standing.

Wow.

She pondered her next move. It should be simple enough to find Deke Bannon if he was in Atlanta.

CHAPTER 2

She was still at the station an hour later and getting frustrated. The first and last name together didn't bring up any local photos. There were some images of Deke Bannon's two older brothers, RJ and Linc.

She knew RJ, though she hadn't talked to him for a couple of years. But she'd helped him out with a prime-time report on the Montgomery kidnapping case — and boosted her show's ratings, always a nice plus. As for Linc, she'd provided an indirect connection that led him to a multiple murderer. Too bad he'd declined to be interviewed. The headlines were enough to make him disappear.

Unfortunately for her, the Bannon brothers tended to shun attention and had an uncanny way of keeping out of the public eye. There wasn't even a phone snap from either's wedding on social media or anywhere else online, though she did pull up a couple of press mentions.

Nothing for Deke.

Before her move to Atlanta, Kelly had been planning a no-holds-barred series about real undercover agents and special-forces types. Men and women who risked all. She'd had to shelve it. His brothers hadn't wanted to be involved, and they'd been leery about giving her Deke's number.

Which wouldn't have stopped her. A quick search through her laptop files yielded a contact list from the proposal. There was a phone number for Deke. Probably out of date.

The area code was unfamiliar — it wasn't Atlanta and not a cell prefix she knew. She dialed it anyway, prepared to pour on the sex appeal and not mention her real name.

The guy she reached wasn't Deke, not a friend of Deke's, had never heard of Deke. But he liked her purring voice and offered to take her out for a steak dinner next time she was in Kansas City. Kelly hung up on him.

Stumped, she phoned an acquaintance, a detective in the police department, and asked a favor. Only it wasn't really a favor. The new crime-stoppers hotline hadn't been ringing off the hook, according to him. If Kelly could help . . . She'd talked the evening news producer into featuring the hotline for a week.

All part of the game. The detective didn't even bother to ask why she needed information, going deep into a law enforcement database and unearthing several new numbers that might be Deke's.

"Thanks, Marvin."

"You're welcome. Thank you."

Back to business. She made a few notes. Deke had to be a special agent, if those talkative cops had their facts right. That would have been her guess even if she hadn't heard that stray conversation. RJ was a detective, Linc was a military op, and Deke, most likely federal.

Kelly took a moment to pull her hair back into a no-nonsense ponytail and kick off her shoes, taking a pair of flats from the closet where she kept some of her own clothes. The station provided her on-air wardrobe, but the stylist was in charge of that.

The maroon suit was in there, hung up carelessly. It would be taken away for dry cleaning. She suddenly thought of the press pass she'd put into her pocket, and looked for it. Not in either. Shoot. She must have dropped it at the scene. No way was she going back to look for it.

Kelly slung the jacket back onto the

hanger. She opened the can of coke that Gordon had brought for her. The first fizzy sip made her cough. The coke was warm and sour. But she needed the caffeine.

Kelly finished most of the can, then started in on the short list of numbers.

The first had been disconnected. The second belonged to someone who didn't speak English. Evidently Deke believed in changing his contact information frequently. But the third was the charm. There was a hint of a growl in the deep voice on the digital recording. Kelly smiled.

She was one step closer to Deke Bannon. She hesitated only a second before leaving a message.

"Hello, Deke. This is Kelly Johns from WBRX. We — ah — just met. I'd like to thank you personally." She gave her cell number and not the station's, and saved his contact information to her phone.

Done.

But would he call back? No way of knowing that. He had no reason to want a news crew following him around if he'd been working undercover.

Gordon had kept a tight focus on her during the filming of the intro. Deke might have seized that opportunity to get a bit closer, listen in.

He had to have spotted her from somewhere above and then inside the building as she walked through the ground floor. If he hadn't recognized her face, he would've heard her say her name.

Whatever. The encounter at the abandoned building could be their little secret for, oh, another twenty-four hours, max.

Monroe Capp didn't have to be filled in immediately. The police — that was different. Kelly figured the three of them had time to do the right thing. But until she got a chance to pump Deke Bannon for information and find out more, she wasn't going to let the news director assign what could be a killer feature to a low-level reporter.

In her experience, the response to the shootings said it all. Cops and feds didn't work a case together unless it was major, as in crimes that crossed state or international borders. Big, fat, juicy crimes.

She had nothing to lose by going after this story.

Her contract was coming up for review. WBRX Atlanta ranked near the top in the metropolitan market, but they weren't first. Last time she'd been casually summoned to Monroe's office, he'd been halfway through a stack of DVD auditions sent in by her potential competition. He'd had the nerve to ask for her opinion of the latest faces right out of journalism school and their résumés.

They both knew that a degree in communications didn't mean much compared to on-air personality. You had it or you didn't.

Kelly knew damn well that she needed to watch her back. New hires were always cheaper and new talent was always hungriest. Whatever had happened at the building could become a career-making feature, one that grabbed millions of viewers. High ratings *and* awards — she could use both.

If only she had a handle on this. Kelly bit her lip, telling herself not to get carried away. First things first. What did Deke Bannon know that she didn't, and why had he been prowling around that building?

Rattled as they had been, it was possible that she, Gordon, and Laura had missed something during the first several viewings. She enlarged the video file she'd transferred to her laptop but didn't start it, looking in her desk for her glasses.

The no-nonsense black plastic frames stood out against the white drawer. She slipped them on and looked down at the vibrating smartphone she'd set aside. The screen glowed with a name. Deke Bannon

Already? Had he been waiting for her call?

Don't flatter yourself, she warned silently. He didn't have to help her more than he had.

She picked up the phone and tapped the screen to answer. "Kelly Johns."

"This is Deke Bannon. I just got your call."

The deep voice and its hint of roughness made her draw in her breath, unsure of what to say first. It had been a while since a masculine voice made her feel so unsettled. She kept it simple. "Hello. Thanks for getting back to me. I owe you a big favor."

"No. You don't."

The brusque response didn't leave her much of an opening. Kelly realized that she might be at less of a disadvantage if this conversation wasn't taking place over the phone. "I was wondering," she ventured, "if you — well, I'd like to meet with you in person."

There was a second's pause.

"Where are you?" he asked.

"At the station."

"You didn't call from a WBRX line."

He'd checked. Kelly smiled faintly.

"That's correct. For a good reason. Deke, before we get started, I have to ask if we could keep what happened at that building just between us." There was a pause. "For now."

She could almost see him shrug.

"Let's talk," he said at last.

That wasn't a yes and that wasn't a no. "Do you know where WBRX is?" she asked him.

"I can find out."

"Okay. Call me when you're on the street alongside the building's parking lot. I'll go out the side entrance and find you. You won't have to sign in at the reception desk."

"Good. Don't introduce me. To anyone."

"I won't. Promise."

A half hour later her smartphone rang again. Kelly grabbed it.

"I'm here," he said.

Kelly tensed. She couldn't help it. Deke's low voice just got to her. "Where?"

"In the parking lot. Row C. I'm looking at the station entrance."

"I'll be right out." She wondered how he'd managed that. Security was tight these days what with all the wackos out there.

Kelly minimized the video file so it couldn't be seen and put the laptop on standby. She set it on her desk in front of her WBRX monitor, placing Gordon's laptop and camera into a deep drawer that locked. She put her shoes back on and went quickly down the corridor that led to the side exit, noting with relief that the evening receptionist had stepped away from the desk and phone console.

She paused on the other side of the heavy glass doors, catching a glimpse of Deke when he got out of a sleek black car. Her hero. But he looked a little beat up, wearing the same leather jacket and jeans. He spotted her and walked her way.

Kelly glanced backward to make sure the receptionist was still gone and pressed the electronic release to open the outer doors for him. Deke Bannon seemed even taller in the confined space of the side entryway, his shoulders broader under the jacket. Close up, she noted traces of cement dust in the leather's heavy folds. She half wanted to slip her hand inside and see if the gun was still in the holster. "Well, hello. I wasn't expecting you quite so soon."

"Hello." His voice, rawer than she remembered, echoed in the corridor.

He stared down at her as if he were memorizing her face, and she got her first good look at his eyes. They were a deep brown with flecks of dark gold, alive and questioning. The steadiness of his gaze held her where she was for a moment, a sensation that was almost physical.

She walked back with him to her office until the chatter coming from the scanners rose in volume and he stopped under an overhead light to listen. There were no more reports from the scene of the killings at the building. Moving forward, he frowned slightly, and she noticed the dark bruise shadowing his strong jaw.

The resemblance to his two older brothers was unmistakable. They were all tall with a powerful build. Deke, the youngest of the three Bannons, was every inch as masterful as his older brothers.

"Thanks for coming over." Kelly waved him into her office, shutting the door. She gestured to a chair by her desk. "It didn't take you very long to get here."

"I wasn't far away."

He didn't elaborate and Kelly changed the subject as she sat, turning gracefully to him and leaning forward slightly from the waist, clasping her hands over one knee as she demurely crossed her legs. "Mind if I ask how you got into the parking lot?"

Deke shrugged. "I flashed a badge at the guard. He raised the barrier just like that."

"I see." Kelly made a mental note to find out, one way or another, what kind of badge, state or federal. "Well, I'm glad you didn't have any problems." Deke was still standing. "Please sit down. May I take your jacket?"

There was a flash of a smile. "No. But thanks."

Deke settled himself into the chair, moving gingerly as he stretched out long, muscular legs in front of him. His grimy jeans had had most of the cement dust slapped off. He crossed one leg over the other at the ankle with a barely perceptible flinch. Kelly remembered with chagrin how hard she'd kicked him.

"First of all, I just have to say thanks," she began. "For everything. That doesn't seem like enough considering you probably saved my life, but —"

"More than probably. And you're welcome."

So much for that. He really didn't seem interested in her gratitude. And he didn't react when she leaned toward him ever so slightly, keeping her gaze open and warm. The I-am-fascinated-by-you position worked like magic for news interviews. Deke Bannon seemed indifferent to it.

She sat up straight. "So — how did you get to be a guardian angel?" Kelly asked lightly. "Isn't that what you called yourself?"

He smiled. "Figure of speech."

Deke seemed disinclined to answer the question. She didn't push it. Professionally, her method had always been to take her time, let the other person relax. Except he didn't seem to, ever. His gaze moved around the office, aware and alert as a wolf.

Dark eyes dashed with gold met hers. Kelly didn't look away. His slight smile cut a lean line into his cheek as he surveyed her desk. "A flatscreen and a laptop and a Twitter feed and — did I miss anything?"

She touched the keyboard to her office computer and the flatscreen lit up. "My official blog on the station website. The publicist writes it for me. I don't have time."

"You're connected." There was a wary edge to the comment.

"I have to be."

Even sitting down he radiated a controlled strength that was making her a little edgy. *Down, girl,* she told herself. It had been too long since a man had intrigued her the way this one did, Kelly realized. Deke Bannon was a force of nature in dirty jeans.

There was an awkward moment of silence. "I guess RJ told you where to find me," he said at last. "Didn't you two know each other back in the day?"

"Casually, yes." Kelly saw no need to get into that. "But I didn't ask RJ or Linc for your number." She didn't see a need to explain about the helpful detective. "After what happened, I really wanted to talk to you privately first. The station management doesn't know that I was even at the scene. We just heard about the fatalities."

"Over the scanner?"

"Yes." She leaned in just a little more and lowered her voice fractionally. "Can you tell me more?"

"Before this conversation goes any farther, are we off the record?" He looked down at the mini-gizmo.

"Absolutely," she said quickly. "This wasn't on." Kelly picked it up and slid out the NiCad battery, setting the gutted recorder in front of him.

"Thanks," he said. "How about that laptop?"

"On standby, but I'll shut it down." She tapped a few keys. The screen flickered to life and then went black. "Trust me yet?"

He laughed. Low and soft. "You're a reporter."

"I used to be. Now I'm an anchor. Great pay, less work, but nowhere near as interesting as actual reporting."

"So what were you doing at the construction site?"

"Ah — I persuaded my boss to let me out

of the gilded cage." She laughed. "I've been developing a special feature on kickbacks, corruption, that kind of thing. We were taping an intro. Totally routine. We went in, you showed up, and suddenly all hell broke loose." She waited for him to do a little sharing. When he didn't, she prodded. "What was that about? Why were you there?"

"I'm not authorized to comment on an ongoing investigation."

"Even if you did, a journalist doesn't have to reveal sources," she reminded him. Kelly gave him an encouraging nod, secure in her ability to direct the conversation. He might let something slip eventually. "You were in the building before we arrived, right?"

Deke nodded. He settled his length against the chair back and rested his hands on his thighs. She saw the hatched scrapes and cuts over his knuckles for the first time.

"I saw you before you saw me," he began. "I was on the scaffolding when you were reciting that little speech and the first car drove up. Then you went in and it was too late to stop you by the time the cameraman and that girl —"

"That would be Laura," Kelly interrupted him. "She's the segment producer."

"Sounds important," he said in a flat

voice. "But if you're in charge, you might want to put the feature on hold."

That was advice she'd expected and would ignore.

"I'm hard to scare, Deke. But feel free to tell me why I should be."

He shot her a look that was hard to read. "I wish I could."

She waited for a beat. Kelly believed in trying again. And again. "What was going on at that building? Who were those people in the expensive cars?"

"Criminals."

Kelly sat up even straighter, frustrated and trying not to show it. "Deke, you're not telling me anything that I couldn't figure out for myself."

There was a grim set to his jaw, although his voice was pleasant. "That's right. But you probably know about as much as I do at this point."

Kelly sincerely doubted that. She let his reply go without comment. In her experience as an interviewer, people started to talk just when you thought they had shut up permanently.

"I don't think so. But — oh, I'm forgetting my manners. Would you like coffee? It comes in five awful flavors. Take your pick." She waved at a one-cup machine on a tray with mugs and creamer. "Sugar helps."

"No thanks." He looked around her office again, studying framed photos of her covering breaking news. "Impressive. How long have you been doing this?"

"Since college." Let him figure out how long ago that was if he wanted to. "I've been with WBRX for about a year."

Maddeningly, he offered no biographical information.

"I like that wind-whipped shot. But why would they send you out in a hurricane?"

Kelly knew the photo he meant without turning around. She was drenched, her hair blowing every which way, and clutching a mic with the station logo, reporting live from the scene.

"I sent myself out. It was only a category two. But fun while it lasted."

"I bet." The dark brown eyes flashed with amusement.

Deke adjusted his position in the chair. He didn't seem to be the kind of guy who talked just to hear himself talk.

His brows drew down for a moment, and his expression changed to thoughtfulness.

She could guess which photo Deke was looking at now: the faded color snapshot of a little girl on a pony pinned to the bulletin board behind her.

His gaze moved from the photo to her face. The child's shy, gap-toothed smile didn't look much like Kelly's now.

"Is that you on the pony?" Deke asked, making conversation or just making sure. But the golden braids were a giveaway.

"Yes. At my grandmother's ranch."

Her answer seemed to surprise him. "How about that." Deke studied the old photo again. "Where was it?"

"Forty miles west of Mercy, Texas. The middle of nowhere."

"Texas? What happened to your accent?"

"I had it professionally removed. But you can still hear it if you buy me a drink."

The offhand remark was meant to be a joke, but Kelly felt a flash of pique when he didn't take her up on it. Still, she kept her professional face on. "Getting back to today —"

He shook his head. "Glad it's over."

"Can you tell me something about the people I saw?"

"No."

She was getting nowhere fast. He wasn't on his own turf. He already suspected her of secretly recording him. Kelly put extra warmth in her voice as she tried again.

"Maybe my office isn't the right place to have this conversation. We could go somewhere else. You pick."

"I'm fine with talking to you here." He gave her a level look. "Within limits."

That was a start. "I almost don't know where to begin. Oh — I remember now. There was a woman in one of the cars. What happened to her?"

"That's an interesting question," Deke said slowly. "I really don't know."

Kelly reminded herself that he had to have come here for a reason, had to have some kind of agenda. Her invitation to talk had been accepted with obvious reluctance, but even so . . . Here he was. Chatty as a clam.

Frustrated, she switched to a somewhat cooler tone. "That's not really an answer, is it?"

"It's the truth."

Kelly took off her glasses and rubbed her temples. "I feel a headache coming on." She opened a drawer and found a two-tablet packet of pain reliever, ripping it open and downing both with the last swig of warm coke.

"Hope that works." Kelly turned slightly to face Deke's steady gaze. "So. Is there anything we here at WBRX can do for you? Quid pro quo. We all know how the game is played."

He hesitated, shifting his long frame in

the chair. "Did your cameraman get any-thing?"

"Nope. It's all a blur," Kelly said with genuine regret. "We couldn't make out the voices. There was absolutely nothing we could use on the air. But Gordon is a wizard at digital enhancement. So who knows. Tune in tomorrow."

It wasn't much of an ace, but she had to play it. No doubt a federal op had access to the software Gordon mentioned.

"Wrong move. Kelly, you can guess what we're up against." He sat up straight, his injured hands clasped loosely, and leaned in. "I'm in deep on this case, and it's a big one. Right now the body count stands at three. It could go up if that tape is broadcast and someone on it is identifiable."

Things like that happened. Kelly nodded. He'd given her an opener.

"Who do you think is going to get whacked next?"

Deke's thick brows drew together when he frowned. "Anyone on the scene or with knowledge of the scene," he said with some heat. "I wish I could trust you, but right now that's impossible."

"Sorry to hear that."

"Look, it's best if you go through the usual channels. Right now the shooting falls under the jurisdiction of the Atlanta PD. The cops are handling it from here on in."

"Right now. Let me fill in the blanks. That could change."

He said nothing.

"I know you aren't a cop," she mused. "So what are you? State? Federal? I ought to ask to see your ID."

"Which one?"

Kelly made a clucking sound of disapproval. "And you don't trust me? I don't think I should trust you."

The sharp sound of a knock made her swivel around.

A balding man in a pin-striped suit opened the door without waiting for permission to enter. "Working late, Kelly?" His curious stare took in Deke, then her. "Oh. Didn't know you had company."

"This is our news director, Monroe Capp," she said, turning to Deke with a forced smile. He could introduce himself however he liked.

Deke stood, towering over the other man. "Hello there," he said quickly. "I'm Russ Thorn, from Dixiecon."

"Okay," Monroe replied after a moment of thought. "I think I've heard of it."

"Kelly contacted me for background information on her latest report. I was happy to help — she's a good friend. I'm a construction manager."

Monroe pumped the hand Deke extended and flashed a flawless smile. "Any friend of Kelly's is a friend of WBRX."

"Only station I ever watch," Deke said.

"That's because we're the best," Monroe boasted. "Was that the corruption report, Kelly? How's it going?"

Blatantly insincere. "Let me fill you in later, Monroe. Now is just not a good time," she replied.

"All right. We won't be able to chat at the club, though."

Kelly drew a blank. "What are you talking about?"

"Club Kiss Kiss. The opening is tonight," Monroe chided her. "How could you forget? Red carpet, everyone who's anyone in Atlanta, and WBRX. You're cutting the ribbon."

What with running for her life and sitting too close for comfort to Deke Bannon, she had completely forgotten about the event. She pulled up the calendar on her smartphone with a couple of taps. There was the reminder. Scheduled for midnight. She'd even added an icon of tiny scissors.

"You're right."

There was no getting out of it. The news

director expected on-air talent to make personal appearances all over Atlanta. Viewer interest went up when the anchors got cheek to cheek with celebrities. There were bound to be many at Club Kiss Kiss. The owner was a music mogul with a harem of models.

She looked down at her conservative suit. Beige wool crepe with a brown boatneck shell underneath wasn't going to cut it. "Good-bye for now, guys. I have to dash home and glam up."

"Think you can make it in time?" Monroe grinned.

"It doesn't take me long to get gorgeous."

"That's our Kelly." Her boss winked at Deke, who made no comment.

"Is there info on this club?" Kelly asked. "Who's going to be there?"

"Movers and shakers. Rich rappers. Country stars. Movie people. The filthy rich and those who would like to be. That about covers it." Monroe pointed to an unopened file folder she hadn't noticed on her desk. "From the publicist. Guess you didn't get a chance to review it. You were out this afternoon, I heard."

Kelly wondered who'd told him that.

"She was with me." Deke winged it with ease. "I was giving Kelly a tour of a new office building under construction. She wanted to know what's under the steel and glass."

Monroe chuckled and slapped him on the back. "Let me guess. Termites?"

"They only eat wood," Kelly pointed out, flipping through the folder without really looking at the material. "Just ask Russ. He likes to answer questions. Very helpful guy."

She beamed at him. Deke didn't smile back. Her temples gave a warning throb. The tablets weren't the fast-acting kind.

"Say, want to come with us, jump the velvet rope?" Monroe asked. "There's a VIP room and complimentary bottle service."

"Thanks. I can't. Sorry. Other plans."

"I understand. Well, very nice to meet you, Russ." Her boss turned to head down the hall again. "Stay tuned to WBRX."

Kelly waited a minute to make sure Monroe was gone, then got up to close the door again. She shot Deke a look. "Nice fakeout, but why bother?"

"He's never going to see me again. And I didn't get the impression you wanted him to know where you were."

She acknowledged that fact with a nod. "Dixiecon?"

"Doesn't exist."

"Russ Thorn?"

"Nobody I know. I was just trying to save your bacon with your boss, that's all."

"I appreciate it," Kelly said tightly. "Now, where were we?"

Deke watched her settle back into her chair. She knew her easy, you-can-talk-to-me pose was useless and that her body language expressed only tension. He straightened where he stood, jamming his hands into the pockets of his dusty jeans.

"I need you to step back and keep quiet."

She raised a finely shaped eyebrow. "I don't know how to do either of those things. And you haven't told me why you need me to cooperate."

"I just do."

"I think we're done talking," Kelly said briskly. "For today, anyway."

"Okay, but I didn't come here only to talk. I found something that belongs to you."

Kelly looked at him with surprise. She hadn't noticed anything missing after the mad dash to the van and back to the station. "What?"

"Your press pass." Deke handed over a flat plastic bag. "Someone stuck it into the chain-link fence and used it for target practice."

Kelly took that in, uncharacteristically silent for a moment.

"The cops missed it," he added.

"Do they know you have it?"

"No."

"Hmm." Kelly examined the pass inside without taking it out. As a reporter, she'd had to get used to occasionally dealing with aggressive, fixated freaks. They either shouted at her in public or when she was on assignment, or fired off a blizzard of e-mails. This was different. A single bullet hole pierced the laminated surface of the pass. Her face had been obliterated.

"Good aim. That wasn't a lucky shot," she said in a quiet voice.

"How do you know that?"

"When I was a teenager I used to shoot playing cards for fun," she answered. "Back at the ranch, I mean."

He glanced at the old photo, then took her in from blond hair to sleek heels, shaking his head. "And to think I had you pegged for a city girl. You still shoot?"

His gaze made her uncomfortable. "I'm out of practice. I don't own a gun." She looked at the press pass through the plastic again and set it on her desk.

Kelly lifted her head and stared at Deke for a moment.

"My guess would be that someone's after you," he said.

"Oh, I don't know," Kelly said nonchalantly. "Maybe it's just bad guys having a little fun."

"Or sending a message," Deke pointed out. "Keep away. Spelled with bullets."

Kelly frowned and leaned back a little in her chair. "Why me? No one knew we were going to be there, or why we were there. Laura picked that building at random." She studied him for a long moment. "You really can't fill me in on what was going on?"

"Absolutely not."

Annoyed all over again by his continued refusal, Kelly struggled not to show it. "As a confidential source, your name never has to be mentioned. It's not like you'd appear on camera. Let me know when you're ready."

Deke shook his head. "I'm not going to change my mind."

"Then I'll begin investigating on my own," she said firmly. "With or without you."

"Kelly —"

Stalemate. He stopped talking before she could do any more arguing. She rose from her chair and moved him toward the door by walking toward him. Her office was her domain; he couldn't stand in her way. But she almost wished he would. Kelly scooped the press pass from her desk, back in news-professional mode.

"Thanks for coming in. I'll walk you out. Let's use a different door."

In silence, she led him past a long glass case filled with news awards and plaques. Deke hung back, studying a row of golden statuettes.

Kelly turned on her heel when she realized that he'd stopped. "Those are Emmy Awards, if you've never seen one. Local Emmys. That's why the statuettes are small."

Deke seemed impressed anyway. "I never would have known. I have no basis for comparison."

"A national Emmy is twice that size."

Deke bent over the case for a closer look at the statuettes. "Outstanding Feature Reporting. Outstanding Investigative Journalism," he read aloud. "Any of these yours?"

"Do you see my name engraved on the bases?"

He straightened. Her clipped reply told him a lot. "I don't, no. Guess you're working on that."

"Hell yes." She pointed to the glass door ahead of them with the bagged press pass in her hand. "There's the way out."

"Thanks. I'll take that, by the way."

Kelly put her hand behind her back. "No

way. I'm keeping this."

"It's evidence."

"You're not a cop. You haven't told me what you are. The pass is mine."

"You can't use it."

"Oh yes, I can."

Kelly used that trick of walking toward him to maneuver him toward the door again. A beefy security guard was coming down the corridor behind her. Deke slowed down some. It was all he could do.

"With a bullet hole in it? For what?" he asked.

"An opener. It's a great visual."

He stopped in his tracks. "But —"

Deke shut up, aware that the security guard had stopped too and was eying him.

"No story, no glory," Kelly said. "I want both."

CHAPTER 3

The soft sky of a Southern evening had turned into velvet night by the time Kelly slipped out of Club Kiss Kiss, tired of the unbearable noise and the crush of people inside.

She'd showed up for the grand opening fifteen minutes late, but she'd done it in style, driving up to the red-carpeted entrance of the club in a limo provided by the station. There had been a uniformed chauffeur at the wheel and another uniform in charge of opening the rear door for her. She'd stepped out to applause and cheers.

After a frantic search, her jammed closet had coughed up an outfit that fit the occasion. Thin straps of faux diamonds twined over her shoulders, barely enough to support the handkerchief-pointed dark blue silk of the short dress. Stiletto sandals in a darker blue went well with it. Hair flowing free, real diamond studs in her ears, and she was done.

June's makeup job had been on the light side, thank goodness. Kelly hadn't had the time to take it off and start over.

She was good at landing on her feet, whether they were bare or in high heels.

With a lot of fanfare, Kelly had cut the ribbon with Monroe Capp at her side. The club's security detail had seemed more interested in getting into the pictures than in holding back the surging crowd. It wasn't all about her. The Kiss Kiss owners had persuaded or paid other local celebrities to appear.

"Be nice to the fans. It's great for our ratings," Monroe had muttered in her ear as he escorted her through the door.

Kelly had shaken lots of hands, posed with bigwigs, smiled brilliantly for the cameras, and sipped iced tea. Duty done. She wanted to get home. She'd slipped the chauffeur a twenty and a spare key to retrieve her car from the WBRX parking lot and stash it in a nearby parking garage for a quick, discreet exit.

The street in back of the new club was deserted and eerily quiet. Atlanta's renowned nightlife was mostly contained within high walls of new hotels and towers. Some venues were underground in vaulted, spectacularly lit spaces where the revelry never seemed to end.

Kelly looked down the empty street, seeing no one, forcibly reminded of the abandoned building halfway across town.

This neighborhood was far more posh. But the darkness seemed solid as concrete, slashed only occasionally with light when an unseen door opened somewhere. She walked quickly, ignoring a gleaming SUV emitting a thumping bass as it rolled past her and picked up speed. An all-night party on wheels — one of the newer Atlanta traditions.

Up ahead was the long neon sign of the garage. She was nearly there. Kelly breathed a sigh of relief. A prickle of warning and the odd sensation that she was being followed made her turn around suddenly. She saw no one.

But a sports car was racing toward her, an expensive model with slanting headlights. The blinding halogen glare hurt her eyes until the car whizzed past in a spray of dirt and gravel. Blinking, Kelly looked down and brushed at her dress. No harm done.

She straightened the evening bag on a thin chain over her shoulder and looked up at the same second as a man stepped out of the darkness and came toward her.

Instantly, Kelly unclasped the bag, searching for the slim canister of Mace she carried before he stopped a little distance away. She palmed it, hoping she wouldn't have to use it. Her well-honed reporter's skills tried to peg him.

Tourist, maybe. Staying at a pricey hotel if so. Good suit. Conservative tie and haircut. Middle-aged, going gray. Regular features. Pale-colored eyes. His face betrayed no particular expression.

"Hey there. Aren't you Kelly Johns?"

Be nice to the fans. She wasn't sure if that applied under the circumstances.

"Just making sure," he added in a polite voice.

"Yes, I am." She stepped sideways toward the street to go around the man. "But I can't chat, sorry. My driver is waiting for me around the corner —"

"Is he?" He looked over her shoulder.

She pointed and kept going with a fast lie. "He's right there —"

"Watch out!" He reached out to take her arm and stop her. His grip conveyed a strength that scared her — and made her drop the Mace.

In another second a black sedan sped by in silence, the whoosh of air ruffling her dress. The man watched it go.

"Must be one of those hybrids," he said pleasantly enough. "I didn't hear it coming, did you?"

"No. Now let go of me," she snapped, thoroughly rattled when he released her and bent down to pick up the Mace, holding the cylinder out to her.

"You dropped this." He still blocked her way. His courteous tone didn't hide the fact that he stood a fraction too close, even without touching her. She felt violated by his nearness and angry — but she took the Mace.

He moved around her and went on his way. Kelly stared after him. At the end of the block, another man, not as tall, materialized out of the shadows and joined him. Neither looked back at her before they walked quickly around the corner.

Her moment of unease before the man had stepped out of the dark came back to her with startling clarity. She had been followed. The two men must have communicated somehow with each other as she walked, moving closer until she had been unknowingly caught between them.

Kelly ran the rest of the way to the garage. She'd never been so happy to be under glaring fluorescent lights and wait in line for her car. The attendant rolled up fast with it

73

when the other customers were gone. The Lone Star decoration on the mirror was still swinging when she got in. That and the headrest-high stack of file boxes on the front passenger seat was how she picked it out from other, similar vehicles. Other than that, there was nothing special about her car.

Driving home, she kept looking into the rearview mirror, partly because she was scared and partly because she was speeding. Through her rolled-up window, she nodded to the doorman at her condo building when he stepped forward. He was a big guy. She felt fractionally safer just looking at him. He welcomed her with a tip of his hat and turned away to ring for a valet who would park her car in the adjoining multistory garage. They were good about keeping her car near the elevators. Once in a blue moon they put it on the roof of the garage where she could see it from her window high above.

Right now she didn't care where they left it. Kelly stuck an arm through the front seats to retrieve a knit poncho from the back before she got out. Yes, she was almost home, but she wanted to be wrapped in something huge and shapeless.

Yanking the poncho over her head, she made sure the key was in the ignition and got out, moving past the doorman and through the lobby before he could ask questions.

She pressed the button for the elevators to the higher floors, impatiently watching the numbers go down. Kelly prayed that no one would join her. She couldn't make small talk. The strangest day of her life was finally catching up with her.

The elevator doors opened silently and she stepped inside, jabbing at the control panel. She willed the doors to close, afraid she would see the man who'd stopped her on the street. The thick carpets in the lobby hushed every footstep, but the mirrored walls would give her a moment's warning. She stared at her reflection until the doors finally drew together.

The hush of the lobby was replaced by the faint whine of the car moving upward. Kelly watched the numbers light up, then unclasped her bag and got out her apartment keys before she got off. Once in the hall, she looked both ways.

Quiet as the grave. Not a neighbor in sight. But then there never was. She sometimes wondered who they might be. Breathing more slowly, she unlocked her door, got inside, and relocked it.

Kelly flung her bag onto an armchair and

bent down to unstrap her stilettos, kicking them into a corner. She padded across the white carpet and pulled the ceiling-to-floor drapes tightly shut. This high up, it really didn't matter. No one could possibly see in. But she didn't care.

It would be great to have someone to come home to. That hadn't been the case for quite a while. But then she didn't really think of the apartment as home.

Now that she was here, she could have something stronger than iced tea. She made herself a drink, something she rarely indulged in, and curled up on the sofa, pulling the soft knit poncho over her bare legs.

Kelly was so used to the hard work of chasing stories, she hardly thought about it. All of a sudden, this story seemed to be chasing her. After the shoot-out and tonight, she had to wonder whether it was worth it to constantly put herself in harm's way.

Adrenaline be damned. The mellowing effect of the drink was taking hold.

She'd been harassed before, threatened more than once. But not at this level. There was no telling if it would be worth it. A little soul-searching — never her favorite indoor sport — seemed to be in order. To her chagrin, Deke had kept his distance, and not only because he had his own agenda.

She wasn't sure she even knew how to talk to someone anymore without turning it into a ratings-grabbing interview or grist for the news mill. That wasn't all. Kelly didn't remember the last time she'd read a book from start to finish, gotten on a horse and rode like the wind, or just plain *breathed.*

Tough luck, she told herself. Breathing was automatic. She'd survive.

In another hour, she fell into a troubled sleep.

Deke entered his suite in a skyscraper hotel before dawn. A panoramic view of Atlanta was visible from every corner of the rooms. Vehicles cruised slowly down avenues and streets that confused everyone who didn't live here — far too many were named Peachtree Something. But from up here, the metropolitan plan made some sort of sense. Beyond the city lights was a vast expanse of black. Another hour would change that, the endless green vista of Georgia appearing out of the mist as the sun rose.

He went to a window, looking down at the city. Where was Kelly in all of that?

Deke had no idea where she lived. It was no secret that news anchors pulled down big bucks. Most likely she had a house in one of the expensive suburbs that ringed Atlanta.

What a day. First a stakeout, followed by a shootout. Then her. He'd tried not to say too much and ended up tipping his hand a little. Of course, Kelly Johns would have had to know exactly what he was up against to pick up on that.

The lithe outline of the woman who came out to meet him had been instantly familiar to Deke — the fitted suits she wore on the air were famous. And so was her blond hair, even in a ponytail. It was the black-framed eyeglasses that threw him for a moment.

Somehow she looked even sexier in them. If he had to write words under the mental picture, he would need only three. Intelligent. Ambitious. Stubborn.

He guessed she was single, very single. Too busy for a boyfriend, too serious to fool around. But gorgeous. All she had to do was give him half a chance and he'd be around.

Deke ran a hand along his jaw, feeling the stubble. He'd shave later, after he caught some sleep. He was more tired than he was willing to admit. Going back to the crime scene hadn't netted more information. He'd been in the way of the detectives and cops marking spent shells and measuring distances between the bodies at the site, and his colleagues kept him sidelined out of concern for his health.

He'd checked in with a medic. No lasting damage. Nothing to do but follow up with Kelly. She'd seemed okay. He guessed the cameraman and the other one hadn't been hurt either.

Kelly was sharp.

It was interesting that she had spotted the woman in the second car — he had told Kelly the truth about not knowing anything concerning her. No one at the scene had a clue. The bodies were all suits. Deke had seen the woman, too, but only for a second and not clearly.

Kelly would make one hell of a good investigator. He could teach her what she didn't already know, fast. The problem would be handling her. She was smart but maybe too headstrong to take direction.

He looked down again, feeling a little dizzy this time. Generally speaking, he liked to sleep closer to the ground.

But he hadn't had a choice of suites.

Deke moved away from the window to check the feed from the bug hidden in the wall. Nothing. The bug could have been disabled, but his gut told him no one was in the suite next door. He unlocked his door and exited to check and make sure.

A stocky housekeeper in a hairnet wearing a striped uniform over pants came out of the elevator, pushing a steel cart piled high with folded linens and towels. He thought about asking for extra soap and decided not to be annoying.

The housekeeper stopped the cart at a door up the hall as Deke used a master key-card to enter the neighboring suite. He flipped the inside bolt and took a moment to survey the scene. The occupants were gone. A room service tray on the coffee table held plates and cutlery covered with congealed grease and a few crusts.

Hungry, hungry hoodlums. They'd eaten everything.

Empty suitcases lay open on the carpet, the linings slashed. Deke snapped on a rubber glove he took from an inside pocket and ran a hand inside the nearest suitcase. Vinyl and cardboard. Cheap construction. No contraband. No nothing.

Still, the crime lab two states away might find microscopic evidence. He'd put in a request for techs to clear the room and retrieve the bugs in the lamps and walls. The audio would be analyzed and voice-prints made, fingerprints run through the national database.

They might get a hit or two. But the brains

behind this operation preferred mules with no police records who often didn't know what they were transporting.

The bunch in this room seemed to have figured it out and helped themselves to the goods. The body count would go up when the operation's enforcers caught up with them.

What a bust.

Deke had followed his orders to the letter, getting into the abandoned building by afternoon, doing surveillance on the parking lot pinpointed by the informant, watching for a major drop. Then everything went haywire — why, he still didn't know. Not because of the news crew.

The thugs in fancy cars started shooting at each other, not at Kelly or the two people with her. With the news crew out of the way, the real excitement began. Three dead. He didn't have what it took to feel sorry for criminals with homicidal inclinations, but like Kelly, he wondered about the unknown woman in the car, now missing. Still, it was all over but the paperwork, which Deke hated filling out.

A knock on the door made him straighten again. "Housekeeping," called a voice.

He took off the glove and snapped it into a wastebasket. There was another knock, louder this time. He went to the door and flipped back the inside bolt, then opened it.

"Good morning," Deke said pleasantly, flattening himself against the wall.

"If you say so."

Leaving the cart at the door, the housekeeper entered, brushing past Deke. She was a lot bigger when she was that close, about the size of a linebacker. A thick hand yanked at the hairnet, dragging a wig off with it and revealing a crew cut. Both got tossed on the floor.

An armchair groaned as Huxton Smith settled his bulk into it, unbuttoning the striped uniform to reveal a bulletproof vest. He scratched his sandy, gray-speckled hair.

"Whew. Glad this stakeout's over. I hate wearing a disguise. Especially that wig."

Deke laughed. "But you look great with a center part."

"Shut up. I never knew making beds was such hard work."

"How were the tips?"

"This suite, not great. Your criminal element tends to be cheap."

"They know they're not coming back, Hux."

His partner looked at the slashed suitcases. "Guess they got what they came for."

"You didn't hear them leave?"

"No. My supervisor had me cleaning room 17-B right around then. A bunch of frat boys hired strippers and sneaked in a keg."

"Whoopee."

"You got it. Quite a party. They served beer plus vodka plus a mixed assortment of uppers in a candy bowl."

Deke grinned. "You took inventory."

"While I mopped up the vomit, yeah." Hux scratched his head with both hands. "What a bunch of gorillas. According to hotel security, they trashed the furniture and started a slugfest, during which the strippers helped themselves to the loose wallets and vamoosed. Cops got called, hauled everyone in the room out and down in the service elevator."

"Where are they now?"

"The fratties are probably sleeping it off in the drunk tank downtown. The strippers went back to the Bump 'N' Grind, I guess. And here I am."

"You have it easy," Deke said dismissively, "handing out pillow mints while I dodge bullets."

Huxton looked him over. "Heard you almost took one. I can see the mark from here."

Deke glanced down at a streak in the

shoulder of his leather jacket and shrugged. "A graze. Good as a miss."

"Tough talk. Move faster next time, Bannon."

"I had to get some people out of the way. A TV news reporter and a crew of two."

"What the hell were they doing there?"

Deke sighed and leaned against the wall across from Hux. "Using the building for a backdrop. Unannounced and unexpected."

"What? I didn't get briefed on that."

"I got them out before the law arrived."

Huxton's face creased into a frown. "How come I didn't see anything on the news?"

"I talked to one of them afterward, asked her to keep it to herself and her crew. She didn't seem eager to let her boss know that they'd been there."

"And why was that?"

Deke shrugged. "She knew she'd stumbled onto a hot story and she doesn't want it taken away from her. That was my understanding, anyway. First time I ever actually talked to a reporter."

"Then watch your back," Huxton said emphatically. "Total pain in the butt, those news people. Bigger snoops than we are, and sometimes they're better at it."

Deke nodded.

"But they don't have skin in the game.

Once they ramp up their ratings or print a screaming headline that sells papers, they're done. We're still fighting it out with the bad guys." Huxton paused, narrowing his eyes at Deke. "So did you two actually make some kind of a deal?"

"I'm not sure."

Hux sighed. "Here's how it works, baby-cakes. You pretend to be her source in return for her silence."

Deke shook his head. "I'll try. I need to talk to her again."

"Lead her on. Stall. Distract her with a nice safe story about blueberry smugglers or something. Whatever it takes."

"Okay. Thanks for the advice."

"And keep her close," his partner continued. "I mean, by phone. Whatever you do, don't sleep with her. Is she pretty? I forgot to ask."

"She's beautiful."

"Then you're in trouble. Don't get stupid."

A muffled ringtone sounded from deep inside the armchair.

"Incoming. 'Scuse me." Huxton shifted heavily on the cushion, trying to get a smartphone out of his back pocket without success. He stood up and shucked the striped uniform, retrieving the phone just as the ringtone stopped.

Huxton studied the screen. "Hell's bells. Headquarters and the Atlanta PD agree for once. The chief is going to ask the media to play down the shooting. No more than a mention on the evening news or bury it on a back page. Over and out."

He put the phone back in his pocket without replying to the text.

"Guess I don't have to play mind games with Kelly, then," Deke said.

Huxton shot him a sharp look. "Kelly Johns was at the building? The blonde from WBRX?"

Deke stood up. "That's the one."

Huxton whistled.

CHAPTER 4

Kelly had overslept. The hands of the huge clock visible from every point in the newsroom were at 10:15 by the time she sneaked in.

"Kelly!" Fred Chiswick, the senior newswriter, intercepted her mad dash to her office. "Here's your copy if you want to take a look."

"Fred, please. I have to have some coffee before I face Monroe."

"Oh, right. He escorted you to that club opening last night. I saw the photos on the WBRX Facebook page."

Fred was following her down the hall. She wasn't about to give him the full report. By the first light of day, padding around her condo after a long, hot shower, she hadn't been so sure she was right about having been followed. But when rain clouds darkened the sky as she drove in, the strange feeling came back.

"Did you have fun?" he asked.

"Not really. I left before he did. He's going to want an explanation."

"Which is?"

They were out of earshot of the newsroom. "I was tired and bored and he was driving me crazy."

"Lie to him," Fred said cheerfully. The brash advice was at odds with his appearance. He looked like a tweedy little professor, his brown eyes hidden by round-rimmed spectacles.

Kelly waved him into her office and shut the door quietly, not sitting down when Fred handed her the pages.

"I could have e-mailed them, but I know you like to mark your material," he said.

She read it in silence, almost relieved to see no mention of yesterday's shootout. It was bound to come up at the morning meeting. One of the assignment editors usually summarized the scanner feeds out loud.

"Looks great," she told Fred, handing the pages back.

"No changes?"

"Not a one." She opened a desk drawer and looked for a comb, jerking it through her hair. There was no time to make coffee. No loss. The five flavors really were awful.

Fred was looking at the pages, not at her.

She wanted to roll her eyes. She liked him, but sometimes he was a nuisance.

"You like it, huh? The opening line's decent — I slaved over it. Sometimes the first sentence is the hardest to write," he mused.

"All I have to do is read it." Kelly found a tube of lip gloss and a small mirror. "If that's the problem, what's the solution?"

"Write the second sentence first."

Fred seemed awfully pleased with that bit of wisdom. Kelly Johns smiled as she slicked her lips, looking at him over the mirror in her hand.

"I'm not joking, Kelly. Take it from the oldest living news writer still working."

"You're not that old."

"I'm nearly extinct," Fred intoned in a gloomy voice. "Me and the dinosaurs."

"Newspapers are dying. TV news is next. You keep telling me the same things." She checked her teeth.

He ignored her comment. "I'm headed straight for an exhibit at the natural history museum. My bow tie will be displayed in a little glass case. It's not a clip-on, you know. I tie it myself."

Kelly put away the lip gloss and held up the mirror so he could see himself. "It's crooked."

"Can't have that." He tugged at the thick silk folds of the tie. "There. Sartorial perfection. Monroe won't pick on me."

"Stop it. You're in a class by yourself. They need someone around this station who can put together a coherent sentence."

"I still can," Fred said, looking a little smug. "But if Monroe Capp could get an intern to do my job, he would. You, however, are irreplaceable."

"Not."

Fred raised his eyebrows. "I heard you got a major bonus for that scandalous exclusive with the governor of the great state next door. I love politicians," he said gleefully. "They can't keep their pants zipped or their mouths shut."

"Former governor," Kelly corrected him absently. She wasn't going to satisfy his curiosity about the bonus. Let someone else mislead him. Newsroom gossip moved faster than the speed of light.

"I stand corrected. You did the reporting for that, right?"

"Most of it. It was a lot of legwork." She took a moment to clear off her desk, checking to see that Gordon's laptop and camera were still locked away. "Not something I want to do full-time. But sometimes I miss it."

"Why?"

"You ask too many questions," she said with a sigh. "I don't know. Maybe I enjoy aggravation. Come on. I don't want to be late for the meeting."

She walked quickly down the hall, Fred only just keeping up with her long strides.

Monroe swiveled in his chair as they entered, his gaze moving away from the window. Evidently he'd just made a joke — polite chuckles were dying away. Kelly glanced at the driving rain outside, pelting the Atlanta suburb where WBRX was headquartered. The news station complex was low and unassuming, but it was a constant hive of activity, filled with employees day and night.

Mornings were busiest. Kelly wasn't expected to attend this meeting as a rule, but sometimes she did. She enjoyed the verbal progress reports on stories in the works and liked to get a general idea of which were moving to the top of the roster.

Monroe had final say. The managing editor handed out assignments, taking questions from reporters before they went back to their cubicles or back out on their beats. The big conference table faced a large screen that hung from the ceiling for everyone's reference.

"Hello," Kelly said. "I was just going over copy for the evening broadcast with Fred."

"Glad you two could join us," Monroe said. "Find a seat."

Fred tried to act invisible, scuttling to a folding chair at the other end of the table. Kelly didn't bother. The reporters had returned their attention to the electronic devices in front of them, looking busy or trying to. She caught a glimpse of a solitaire setup on the screen next to her when she slid her laptop on the table and sat down.

Monroe leaned his arms on the table and looked around. "Okay, people. Set aside the gizmos. This is an actual meeting. Eye contact is mandatory."

The reporters complied. Most were a few years younger than Kelly, not anyone she'd worked with at other stations. She didn't remember all their names, but she smiled at the ones she did know. The newest hires were mostly from Internet sites, where they'd done byline articles or blogged. Their biggest advantage in Monroe Capp's opinion was that they were used to working super fast for nothing.

Of course, the station paid its employees fairly well — outside of Tina, the dewy-eyed intern sitting next to Monroe. But all of them had to hustle. Reporters were only as good as their last story, and there was no such thing as job security.

The news director turned to Tina. "I'm not sure if you've been formally introduced to Kelly Johns."

"No, not yet. You're so awesome," the young woman said with admiration and — if Kelly heard right — a touch of envy. "You're the reason I wanted to intern at WBRX."

The reporters exchanged looks. Even Monroe looked a little nonplussed.

"Is that right," Kelly said courteously. "Well, thanks." Maybe the intern meant well. But Kelly couldn't help thinking otherwise when she looked at Tina. She smiled anyway.

"Kelly is definitely a star." Monroe's attempt to smooth things over fell flat. "But she doesn't usually join us for morning meetings. To what do we owe the honor, Kelly?"

"Just thought I'd drop in, that's all. No hidden agenda." Besides finding out if yesterday's shootout was going to be assigned as a story and who would get it. Maybe more information had come over the scanners after she'd left. Being followed last night still had her on edge.

"A pleasure to have you with us," he said

jokingly. "Any ideas on how we can get Dave Maples to attend?"

Her co-anchor never showed. "Serve breakfast," Kelly suggested. She was regretting the lack of coffee.

Monroe turned the meeting over to the managing editor, making occasional comments to Tina in a low voice. Dutifully, the intern took notes. Reporters updated the group on their stories and floated ideas for new ones.

The assignment editors took it from there. They gave a concise account of last night's scanner bulletins and readouts, generating an undercurrent of excitement.

Monroe nipped that in the bud. "Don't get your hopes up, people. We're not investigating that shooting or featuring it. Fred can write a short line for the crawl. We might or might not run it."

"What's the crawl again?" Tina asked. The intern kept her pencil poised above her notebook.

"The banner at the bottom of the screen with breaking news and upcoming stories," Monroe explained.

He seemed to be about to pat Tina on the head. Kelly smiled inwardly.

"Too bad. Three bodies," murmured a crime reporter, regret in his voice. "That's a

94

good hook. Could be a three-part special."

"It's not going to happen," Monroe replied, running a hand over his balding head as if there were hair on it that needed smoothing. "Yes, I always say if it bleeds, it leads, but not this time."

"Can you tell us why?" Fred inquired.

"I received a personal call from the chief of police this morning, and another one from a government agency I was asked to not identify. Both want us to hold off."

"Someone online is going to scoop us," a reporter pointed out.

"Which reminds me." Monroe changed the subject. "We're losing viewers to the net. Atlanta is one of the largest markets in the whole US, but market share fragmentation gets worse every month. Too many Atlantans don't think WBRX when they think news. Which means . . . all of you need to work harder on getting exclusives."

He had everyone's attention by the last line.

"I'll spell it out for those of you who are new. Nothing to it. Develop contacts in government, take police brass to lunch, dig up great stories no one else knows about."

As if it were or had ever been that easy. Monroe had never been a reporter, if Kelly remembered right. But he was an expert at telling the WBRX team how to do it.

"Don't just rewrite a story the competition is doing," he added. "Unless they stole it from us in the first place."

That got a real laugh.

"Why can't we cover the shooting?" someone persisted. "If the powers that be don't want it out there, that means it could be a big story."

"Not necessarily." Monroe tapped his fingers on the table. "And we didn't get singled out. From what I understand, the information lockdown is across the board."

Kelly backtracked mentally to his previous remark. Government agency. Not identified. That didn't add much to what she knew about Deke.

"Besides, viewers don't care about another gang shooting. Not without blood and gore. There are no visuals," Monroe added.

Little did he know Kelly could provide them, along with an eyewitness report. Keeping her mouth shut wasn't easy.

"I bet the mayor's office put in their two cents," another reporter said. "They always complain about bad publicity."

"Atlanta's like any other big city," the news director replied. "Things like that happen here and everywhere else. Apparently there's nothing special about this incident."

Kelly knew in her bones that wasn't true. She'd known it from the moment the second car had pulled in and the men got out. What Monroe was telling everyone didn't make sense. A cover-up was being put into place.

After last night, she had to face the fact that someone who didn't wish her well must have seen her at the site — or escaping. The mutilation of her press pass hadn't been random malice. The two men that had followed her last night were a follow-up attempt to intimidate her.

"That about wraps it up. You all have your marching orders. Get going." Monroe's gaze swept over everyone in turn and stopped on her. "Kelly, I almost forgot. That corruption feature you've been developing — I think we should kill it for now."

The room fell silent. She pressed her lips together. He didn't have to tell her that in public. The reporters at the conference table looked awkwardly away.

"It's a worthwhile subject, but too serious. Bottom line, we need to goose the ratings."

"Okay," she said tightly. "I can set it aside."

"Please do. Stick with anchoring. That's why we pay you."

"Right." She didn't look at him.

"Any questions, people? Ask Vince," he concluded.

The managing editor took over again. "Okay, everyone clear on their assignments? Don't forget — the whiteboard is out there for a reason. Make sure we know where you are and what you're doing if you leave the station. Call in changes right away."

Was that a veiled reference to the way she'd played hooky with Gordon and Laura? No way of knowing. The meeting came to a close with a hubbub of scraped chairs and chitchat.

Kelly gathered up her laptop and other things, grateful that Fred was discussing something with the managing editor. She needed to be alone. She wanted to talk to Deke.

As it happened, he'd called her. The screen of the smartphone she'd left on her desk blinked with his number.

Kelly procrastinated, fiddling with the coffeemaker in her office. She sat down with the filled cup, trying to think of what to say.

She'd essentially told Deke Bannon that she was beginning an investigation whether he liked it or not, with or without him.

The adrenaline coursing through her system during their afterhours meeting had gotten the better of her.

She liked the feeling. Always had.

Now that Monroe Capp had spiked a story he knew she'd worked hard to develop and effectively closed the door on a potentially much more interesting one, she felt a second surge. Something was going on. She couldn't go it alone. She would need Deke.

The tech director poked his head in. "Have you seen Gordon?" he asked. "He signed out equipment the day before yesterday and he hasn't returned it. Usually he's in by now. I can't reach him."

"I haven't heard from him, Steve." A feeling of foreboding made her set aside the coffee. She hadn't thought to call the cameraman this morning. Or Laura.

"You and him and Laura have been teaming up on that corruption feature, right?"

"Yes. Which Monroe just killed."

"Sorry to hear that," he said without much conviction, preoccupied by his own problem. "Laura just called in sick — she didn't know where Gordon was either. Although it wouldn't be the first time he 'forgot' to return stuff."

A small pouch on his belt began to buzz.

"Maybe that's him," Kelly said. She hated lying to Steve when the gear was right under her desk. But she had no idea what Gordon needed to do with it or to it to make sure the footage wasn't retained.

"Hope so." He took out a phone from the pouch and squinted at it. "Hey — you're right." He picked up the call. "Gordon? Where the hell are you, buddy? I was thinking you pawned our best camera and went to Mexico or something."

Kelly sipped her coffee. Steve waved to her as he turned to walk down the hall. She got up and closed the door. The video camera and laptop would stay where they were until she spoke to Gordon herself.

She set the cup aside and opened her laptop, not sure whether to call Deke now or later. She might as well outline the story, even if she never got to do it. Ten minutes of steady typing got done before a soft knock on the door got her attention.

"Come in."

The door swung open and she saw one of the reporters from the morning meeting, another new hire, someone who reminded Kelly a little of herself at the same age. She was tall and slim, with dark blond hair in a shoulder-length bob.

"Hi. Sorry to interrupt. I'm Coral Reese."

"I know. What's up?"

Coral took that as an invitation to step inside the office, studying the photos on the walls before she spoke. "I love the pictures. You've accomplished so much."

"Oh yeah. My brilliant career," Kelly said wryly. "I hope it's not over."

"Of course it isn't," Coral said with genuine indignation. "I just wanted to say that I thought Monroe Capp was totally out of line. Someone should goose his ratings and see how he likes it."

The tart comment made Kelly laugh. "You'd better close the door if you're going to say things like that," she said.

"Oh, I'm not staying," Coral assured her. "I have work to do and so do you."

"Thanks for stopping by."

"I also wanted to say if you need someone to do research or anything, let me know. I'd be happy to help."

"You bet."

Coral left and Kelly returned to her outline, feeling a lot more cheerful. It was good to have an ally in the ranks. You never knew when you were going to need one. She took the initiative to call Deke and left a message when he didn't pick up.

The smartphone rang in less than a minute. Not him.

She looked at the screen with the identified number. She didn't want to take it, but she had to.

"Kelly Johns here."

"Ms. Johns, this is Lieutenant Dwight with the Atlanta Police Department. How are you today?"

Kelly took a deep breath. "Just fine, thanks. And yourself?"

"Doing great. I'm sure you're busy, so I'll get to the point. We were wondering if you could come in right after lunch. We'd like to ask you a couple of questions about the shooting yesterday."

He seemed so sure of himself she forgot to ask how he — or anyone — knew she'd been there.

"I see. I think I could stop by then. How do I find you?"

The lieutenant gave directions. Kelly wrote them down and thanked him, then hung up and bent down to check on Gordon's laptop and the camera with the raw footage. Locked up tight.

Who had talked? Had anyone seen her at the site besides Deke and her crew? Neither Gordon or Laura had called her.

Filled with foreboding, she skipped lunch and drove to the police station, waiting on a nearby street until it was time to go in.

She walked briskly over the pavement, going up the low stairs.

Through the glass doors at the top, Kelly

saw Laura and hesitated.

The assistant producer was on the other side of the metal detector, chatting with the handsome young officer who manned it. She noticed Kelly outside at the last second and made her way toward her with a guilty look.

Kelly held the door open to let Laura out and went down the stairs with her so they could talk in privacy.

"I had to do it," Laura said in a low voice. "I mean, not that we had anything to confess, besides that we were there by chance. Kelly, I didn't sleep all night."

"Me neither. But I would have appreciated a heads-up."

"You're right. I'm sorry. I should have called you."

Kelly stopped on the sidewalk. "What do they want to know?"

"Exactly what you'd expect. What we saw, when we saw it. We're not under suspicion or anything. Don't be ridiculous."

Kelly blew out a breath. "I just wasn't expecting this. What about Gordon?"

"Lieutenant Dwight said he would call him."

"So they're interviewing us one by one."

"It's totally routine, Kelly. Get a grip. We should have done it right away."

Kelly couldn't argue. She changed the subject. "I went to the morning meeting. The assignment editors summed up what came over the scanners. Monroe says we're not covering the shooting. Mysterious requests from on high. He wouldn't name names."

"Oh. Anyone ask where we were yesterday?"

"Nope. I even went to a club opening with Monroe last night. He didn't suspect a thing."

"Good. Any breaking news?" Laura asked hopefully. "Something that would get everyone's attention?"

"Nothing yet."

"What happened at the morning meeting?"

"The usual. By the way, Monroe killed the corruption feature."

"Why?"

"He didn't say. He doesn't have to."

"Do you think —" Laura began.

"I'm trying not to think too much about any of this." Kelly studied Laura for a moment. "You going home?"

Laura nodded. "I'll be in tomorrow."

"I'll call you soon." Kelly went back up the stairs, entering the building, getting more attention than she wanted. That couldn't be helped. Her full name and the station's call letters were right there on the sign-in sheet.

Lieutenant Dwight was businesslike and pleasant. As Laura had predicted, the interview was routine. But something in his tone made Kelly realize that he was controlling the conversation — and letting her talk.

Kelly would have loved to ask him several questions of her own.

Who were the victims? Any leads on the missing woman in the second car? How involved is Deke Bannon in the investigation, and what agency does he work for?

He didn't volunteer information of any kind, except for filling her in on the name of the building: Tridelta.

"I didn't even know it had a name. I thought it was abandoned."

"The site has been shut down. But legally speaking, it's not abandoned. However, it's changed ownership five times in less than two years."

She mentally added the information to her notes for The Story That Would Never Get On The Air.

"I didn't know that. We were just using it for a backdrop."

Dwight asked a few more questions and she kept her replies simple. They had just happened to choose that location. Everything had happened too fast to remember much. Yes, she was working on a feature report about corruption in the construction industry, but it didn't have anything to do with that building.

"Laura said you and she were working on the feature for several weeks. You came up with the idea, and she signed on as assistant producer, segment producer? Something like that."

"They mean about the same thing."

"When is it going to be broadcast?"

"I don't know." She didn't have to tell him her boss had her on a short leash. "The news director decides things like that. I'm just an anchor."

"Just?" The lieutenant smiled faintly. "I got requests from three of my guys to get an autograph from you."

"I don't mind."

"It's not allowed." He made a few more notes. "I think we've covered everything. Thank you, Ms. Johns."

"You can call me Kelly."

"All right. Kelly it is." The lieutenant sized her up. "I understand you used to be an investigative reporter before you came to Atlanta."

She brightened. "I was, yes. The harder

the case, the more I liked it."

He thought about that for a moment. "One last question. Were you or anyone at WBRX planning to report the shooting before the news blackout?"

"No."

"Why not? You were actually there. With a crew and a camera. Is there footage from the scene?"

"Besides my taped intro, not much. The building, of course. Inside and out. You can hear Laura and Gordon talking, but they're not in front of the camera."

"Anything on it that could be evidence?"

She thought quickly. "It's digital video, time- and date-stamped. So you could pinpoint when the shooting started."

He made a note. "Right."

"When we heard gunshots, we — we just ran for it. Into the van and back to the station. We didn't know what to do or even what had happened."

"Go on."

She waited for him to ask why they hadn't contacted the police right away. He didn't.

"The scanner reports came in after the evening broadcasts," she said carefully. "My boss — Monroe Capp, our news director — told everyone at the morning meeting today that the shooting was off-limits. He didn't say why."

The lieutenant looked through the file folder of papers underneath his notebook. "Our media liaison sent a memo asking for cooperation from news operations. Usual reasons. Risk of compromising a sensitive investigation, jeopardizing the safety of undercover officers, so on and so forth."

"I wish I could help, Lieutenant." The words were blurted out. She wished that she could take them back when she looked at his stern face.

"You can't, Kelly. Don't even think about it. For your own safety and for legal reasons that should be obvious, let the police handle this."

"I understand," she said.

The lieutenant stacked the file folder on top of others. "That's all for now. Appreciate your coming in. Guess I'll see you on the evening news."

She managed a smile. "Yes. I do have to go back and get ready. It usually takes a couple of hours of prep. It's not as simple as it looks."

"Nothing ever is." He stood and shook her hand as she rose from her chair. "I'll walk you out."

CHAPTER 5

Monroe made a point of stopping by her office when she got back. "Hey there," he said. "I was just talking to the chief of police. He said he saw you at the station going into Lieutenant Dwight's office."

Her boss had to have found out that she'd been at the scene of the shoot-out. He didn't seem inclined to make a fuss about it. They understood each other.

"Yes, I was," she said.

"Next time let me know," Monroe said. "I don't want my star anchor in a dangerous situation."

"Okay."

He headed off.

She decided to distract herself with busy-work while she waited for Deke Bannon to call. He might give her a different story than the official one. Lieutenant Dwight didn't seem like someone she could use as a source.

Her hour at the police station hadn't been wasted. She'd ducked into the office that issued press passes when the lieutenant went back to his.

The smartphone next to her was silent. She willed Deke to call, unsuccessfully. Gordon beat him to it. She knew his personal number. He didn't even bother to say hello.

"So what did you tell that cop?"

"He's a lieutenant." She filled him in on every detail of their conversation. "He wants to see the footage."

"I knew that was going to happen," Gordon groaned. "Nothing on it he can use, but I'll make him an unedited copy. Where did you hide the camera and my laptop?"

"Under my desk. I'll leave the key with the tech director so you can pick it up if I'm not here."

Another hour went by. She tried to concentrate on summaries of upcoming stories that she'd pulled up on her monitor, but her brain was uncooperative.

When the phone rang again, it made her jump. At last.

She picked up after four rings, the sweet spot between overeager and hard to get. "Hello, Deke."

"Returning your call. What's up?"

"I don't know where to begin at this point.

I'd like to see you."

"How about dinner?"

Kelly was surprised. The way he said it sounded almost like a date. She stalled for a few seconds. "It would have to be after we wrap the evening news. Like eight or eight fifteen. Is that too late?"

"No. We could meet at a hotel. I know one with an upstairs bar that has a great view. It's nice. And it's quiet. The restaurant is next to it."

"Look, we don't have to have dinner. I just want to talk to you somewhat privately."

"Okay. The bar has booths. It's really nice. Casual but quiet."

She jotted down the directions he gave her. "See you there. Thanks, Deke."

Hux walked through the nondescript warren of rooms at the government agency where Deke had taken up temporary residence. He found him by the piece of paper with his name on it taped to an open door.

Hux flipped the paper with one hand as he walked in and looked around. "Corner office?" His tone was friendly but mocking.

"Yeah. With no windows. Brooms do better. I'm thinking of moving into the janitor's closet." Deke didn't look up from his laptop.

Hux took a chair that was missing a

couple of back rails and sat down. "Don't do it. Just be grateful you don't have to work nine to five."

Deke looked up from the laptop and gestured to a toppling stack of files. "If that falls, it will kill me."

"Research, huh? Gotta do it."

"Any time you feel like volunteering to help with the grunt work, Hux, let me know."

"You bet. But I just got back from the war zone."

His partner's name for the worst part of the city. It wasn't that, but something in his tone alerted Deke that he needed to listen.

"I talked to some of my informers."

"Update me."

"They know who's moving major amounts of cash for drug dealers. Business is booming. Apparently some banks are, shall we say, accepting major deposits."

Deke shot him a disapproving look. "Are these guys you trust?"

"They need me, I need them," Hux said. "And dirtbags and weasels need to eat."

Deke made a wrap-it-up motion with one hand. "Get to the point."

"But there's other deals going down. It seems that someone has been trolling the area for a hit man."

"The trick is finding a competent one," Deke said.

"The job is big bucks. Half in advance, half after. But so far, no takers."

"Why?"

"The hit is high profile. Someone in the media."

That got Deke's total attention. "I heard about a case like that in London. A top newscaster was killed on her doorstep by a gangster."

"No one said whether the target was a man or a woman," Hux replied. "It could be a rumor. I just thought it was worth passing along."

"Kelly hasn't gone public with anything."

"Maybe she shouldn't. A snitch is a snitch. That's enough to get you killed by certain people."

"Like who?"

"To be determined. I did some preliminary research. I took a few of the guys for a ride in an unmarked and asked them to point out competent killers."

"Of course. Exactly what I would have done. Get any pix?"

"Some. I'll show you." Hux patted his pockets. "I hope I have the USB cord cable — here it is. Plug me in, buddy."

Deke took the dangling cord cable from

him and attached it to the side port of his laptop. He held out a hand for the small digital camera Hux handed him. Several shots popped up inside the photo app frame. Deke clicked the keys to view them full screen.

"I think I know these losers. You got taken." Deke stopped himself. "Wait a minute. Who's he?"

He pointed to a huge, coarse-featured man with spiked black hair in an ill-fitting suit. He'd been photographed in front of a small store with a few dusty goods stacked in the window that never got sold. The kind of place that served as a front for unsavory operations from time to time.

Hux craned his thick neck to see. "I didn't get a name. They just call him Ugly, not to his face. Because of that birthmark."

A blotch of livid dark blue spread up the man's huge neck almost to his jaw.

"That would show up on a Wanted poster. No one knows his real name?" Deke asked.

"I waved a hundred, and my best guy took me around the corner so that we could speak privately."

"And?"

"He had to decline the money — he insisted he didn't know who Ugly is. He practically had tears in his eyes. But you have to love the honesty."

Deke rolled his eyes. "So send him a thank-you note. That doesn't qualify as intel." He paused for a beat. "And he could just be scared to death."

Hux nodded. "A different gang is moving in around here. They specialize in money laundering, and — get this — foreclosed real estate. Bottom feeders, basically. But violent."

Deke sat back, a thoughtful frown on his face. He knew that street talk could be hot air or a smoke screen or the rock-solid truth. "Should I tell Kelly?"

"That's up to you, pal. I don't have proof of a damn thing."

"Even so —"

"She might try to investigate on her own," Hux said. "Reporters get paid to look for trouble."

"I don't think she understands how far this can go, Hux."

"So distract her with a safer assignment. Swear her to secrecy. And keep your eye on her and anyone who comes near her."

Kelly changed quickly after the broadcast, picking a white linen blouse and skinny jeans that made her legs look long and shapely. She slipped her feet into wedge sandals the same shade of dark denim and stood up to pull her hair into a loose knot. Glasses next — her defense against the *aren't-you* opening line. Sometimes it worked.

Once out of the parking lot, she glanced at the dashboard clock. She had about an hour, if she could remember which way Peachtree Avenue went and where it connected with Peachtree Street.

She negotiated the maze with ease, seeing the hotel, an impressive modern structure with a glass exterior and architectural stepbacks. Kelly slowed down, but she was driving under the hotel canopy well before eight.

A valet took care of parking her car. Kelly entered through gleaming brass revolving doors, looking up into a balconied atrium that seemed to be about a mile high. A massive check-in counter was to her left and a pricey-looking gift shop to her right.

She looked straight ahead and saw a sign for the bar Deke had specified, realizing it wasn't on the ground level. Kelly waited for an elevator, ignoring male glances of admiration. At least they didn't seem to recognize her.

The doors opened directly onto the bar's foyer. There weren't very many customers, which suited her just fine, and the hostess

116

seemed to have stepped away from her station. Kelly headed toward a table for two in front of a huge plate-glass window, discreetly removing the second chair so she could wait for Deke in solitude.

She settled herself, taking out her laptop and smartphone in case she needed to look busy, and propping her large handbag in front of both. Only then did she look out.

Forget great. The view was glorious. A sweeping terrace with an infinity pool lay just outside the window. The deep blue of the water was set off by half-hidden lights that cast a rippling illumination up into the bar. The far side of the pool seemed to blend into the skyline, reflecting the brilliant lights of Atlanta at night. The tinted glass of the bar window darkened the scene somewhat. She could just make out a man resting there, his back to her, still in the water but his arms folded on the edge of the pool, looking out into the distance.

"Can I get you anything?"

A cocktail waitress stood by, poised to take her order.

"Yes, thanks. A glass of white wine. Pinot Grigio, if you have it."

"We do."

In another minute she was sipping from a chilled glass and looking out at the pool again. The swimmer was coming toward her, underwater, moving with powerful strokes until he touched the side and rose up, standing at waist level, letting the water roll off heavily muscled shoulders and pressing it out of his dark hair with both hands.

She realized with a start that the man was Deke. He didn't seem to see her. The glass had to be reflective.

Dripping wet, he lifted himself out of the pool, his biceps swelling with the effort, and walked quickly toward a chaise, picking up a towel and tying it in a low knot around his narrow hips. Soaked, the towel clung to him. He grabbed another to dry off his powerful chest and back. His legs stayed wet as he walked, as muscular as the rest of him. No wonder her kicks hadn't done any damage.

She lifted her glass for another sip, silently congratulating herself for getting here early. What an unexpected pleasure.

She sensed someone looking her way and adjusted her glasses, able to glimpse him in her peripheral vision. A middle-aged guy with a linebacker's build and a crew cut — not anyone she knew or wanted to know. Kelly ignored him.

Deke walked to the side of the terrace and vanished behind a wooden wall. Kelly felt a slight pang to see him go. Other than that, the few sips of wine she'd had were making her feel awfully mellow. A brightness in the southern sky appeared. The moon rose, luminous and full.

Kelly heard hushed footsteps behind her and set the glass down, flipping open her laptop. Another man passed by, not even looking at her, talking softly to the woman at his side.

She checked the time as the screen came to life. 7:46. Deke would have to shower and dress fast, but he was likely to be right on time. She wasn't going to say anything about seeing him in the pool. No reason to. This wasn't a date.

More people entered the bar. The hostess and the cocktail waitress were both busy all of a sudden. Kelly left the rest of the wine untouched, pulling up a file to work on. The pool lights glimmered at the edge of her vision. She almost wished she could buy a bikini in the hotel gift shop and go for a dip after she and Deke finished talking.

She told herself that the pool was probably for hotel guests only, then wondered why he hadn't said he was staying here.

A tap on her shoulder snapped her out of it.

"Waiting long?"

Kelly glanced down at the time in the corner of the screen. 8:11.

"No," she lied. "Hi, Deke."

"When did you get here?" He retrieved the chair that she'd removed and sat down next to her. His hair was combed but still dark with moisture, just touching the back of the collar of his crisply pressed shirt. He wore the shirt without a tie, unbuttoned by two. Like her, he had on dark jeans.

"Um, a few minutes ago."

He'd shaved quickly, leaving just a trace of dark stubble along his jaw. And he smelled wonderful. She caught a whiff of clean male skin and a splash of bay rum.

"Did you notice the pool?"

She looked up nonchalantly. By now the reflective glass of the window showed more of the bar's interior than the glittering water beyond it.

"It's beautiful. Were you just swimming?"

"Yes, I was. Been meaning to, finally got around to it."

"Not like you're on vacation."

"No. But I can fake it." He smiled at her. He looked calm and sleek, as if the fierce animal tension she remembered in his hold had been exercised away.

He had the height to slouch a bit and still look taller than her. He rested an arm on the table, stretching out his long legs under it and looking around for the cocktail waitress before he turned his attention back to Kelly.

"What are you having?"

"Just white wine." She shook her head when he seemed about to ask if she wanted another. "This is it for me."

"I could go for something stronger," he said. "I don't have to drive."

"So you're staying here?"

"On the seventy-second floor."

Kelly laughed. "Do you dare look out the window?"

"It's an interesting sensation, I can tell you that." He motioned the cocktail waitress over and requested a scotch and soda, which was quickly set in front of him.

Deke straightened in his chair. "Okay. We have drinks. Talk to me."

She got through the events of the day as fast as she could, winding it up with her visit to the police station.

"Good to get that over with. The lieutenant is going to ask Gordon for that footage, though," he said thoughtfully.

"Do you know him? Lieutenant Dwight, I mean."

"No. But that's my best guess." He looked at her steadily.

"What?" Kelly knew her face was flushed — it didn't take much wine to make that happen for someone fair and blond — and she could feel the careless knot of hair unraveling at the nape of her neck. She wound a strand of it nervously around one finger, then let it go and pushed it back.

"I still want to see that footage. Maybe we can do something for each other."

"Like what?"

He shrugged, an easy motion that suggested the strength hidden by the shirt. "Your boss canceled your pet project, and Dwight told you not to investigate the shooting. Therefore, you need something to do to stay out of trouble."

She just stared at him. Right now Deke Bannon looked like plenty of trouble for any woman, let alone her. It had been too long.

"Deke, I know what I saw at that building and I know what I heard on the scanners —"

"Do us both a favor. Keep all of it to yourself."

He didn't add *and be a good girl.* But she got the idea. Kelly scowled at him. "Indefinitely?"

"For now."

"Do you need me to agree? I really don't

have a choice, do I?"

"Kelly, even I have to step back on this part of the case. The evidence is being analyzed and the murders fall under the jurisdiction of the police, not us. But there's another investigation going on — I can tell you that it's related to the shooting, and that's about it. Good enough?"

"I guess so."

"First of all, I'm heading it up. And I could use your help."

"I don't file. I don't type fast. And I'm a little too recognizable."

She took off her glasses and pulled at hairpins. The knot came undone and a river of lustrous blond hair poured over her shoulders. The big man at the nearby table gawked at her. Deke didn't notice, transfixed for a moment.

"See what I mean?"

"Huh. Yes. I do. Actually, that could be an advantage." He set aside his scotch and soda, smiling at her.

"I'm not following you," she said, puzzled.

"Let's take this discussion outside. There's no one on the terrace."

Kelly hesitated, then decided to listen. She gathered up her things and walked past the big man, not glancing down. She didn't need any more admirers, secret or not. The low hum of conversation and clink of glasses in the bar were shut out when Deke closed the door to the terrace behind them.

The infinity pool reflected the rising moon, which cast white light and deep shadows over the scene. Kelly stuffed her belongings into the handbag and set it on a chaise. She began to walk around the perimeter of the pool, hoping no one would come out for a night swim. Just looking at it soothed her restlessness.

"All right, Bannon. We're alone. Talk me into it."

"We've been following a trail of dirty money."

"I want to be sure I understand, so pretend I'm not familiar with the term. And keep it simple," she added.

Deke paused, searching for the right words. "Criminal enterprises generate a lot of cash, and they have to keep moving it around. They launder it, they smuggle it, they use it to finance other criminal enterprises. Drugs. Sex trafficking. Murder for hire. Following me so far?"

"Yes."

He walked by her side. "We're looking at a lot of people in the same web. Lately we zeroed in on someone you may have heard of. Gunther Bach."

"Doesn't ring a bell," she murmured.

"Bach is the CEO of a private bank here in Atlanta, and he only takes multimillionaires as clients. He may be running a pyramid scheme."

Kelly shook her head. "You know, it's really, really hard to feel sorry for people who are rich and stupid. Tell me why I should care."

"Get Bach on tape for me and you'll have first crack at a story that's bigger than anything you've ever done. I can't give you all the details right now, but believe me, they're juicy."

She stopped. "And you mentioned that it's related to the shooting."

"Did I say that?"

Kelly rolled her eyes and sighed. "You know you did. Can we stay on topic here?"

"Sure."

"How much risk is involved?"

"That's hard to predict. Some. Not much."

She didn't press the point. "I don't get what you're hoping to achieve. If I ask Gunther Bach a few questions, he's not going to confess to anything."

"You're right about that." His dark eyes held an amused gleam. "I only need a clear sample of his voice on tape. We voice-identified all the bad guys but one on a wireless intercept of a secret meeting. If we can match a voiceprint closely enough to the unknown one on the intercept, it means he was there."

"Which won't put him out of business. That's one piece of evidence."

Deke waved that away. "But important for building a case and getting a warrant."

Kelly folded her arms across her chest. Deke seemed to think he had her in the bag, judging by his expression. He didn't.

"Look, we think Bach is looking to burnish his reputation and attract new clients. He'd jump at the chance to be interviewed by you. We can rig a smartphone. Just put it on the table next to your car keys. He'd be a pushover for all the moves you tried on me."

"Excuse me?" Her tone grew noticeably cool.

"You know. The friendly smile. The soft voice. The leaning in."

"That's standard interview technique," she said tightly. "I didn't make any 'moves' on you, Bannon. Don't flatter yourself."

"Sorry. I wasn't aware I was being interviewed at the time."

Kelly stopped pacing. "I don't know. Let me think about it."

"I'll shut up while I'm ahead."

She turned to face him and tapped him lightly on the chest. "You want something else, don't you?"

He got right to the point. "The video from the shooting. It's safest to transfer it to a flash drive. I'm assuming you have one."

"You talk like this is a done deal," she said indignantly. "It isn't."

"I need an answer by tomorrow."

His reply seriously irked her. This was all about him.

"Why the urgency?"

"We've been tailing him. Bach may leave the country tomorrow. For good."

"All right. I'll call you by ten. But I'm not going to leave a message. You have to pick up." She shouldn't have encouraged him to the degree that she had. They were both angling for an advantage. Somehow she'd lost the round.

But a story was a story. She really did live for the rush. There was nothing like it.

"I'll pick up. And if you say no, it's not a problem."

Kelly snorted. "We'll see about that."

"Now how about I buy you dinner? They serve a great steak."

"No thanks." She walked back to the chaise and picked up her overloaded bag. "I'm not really hungry. I need to get home and catch up on my sleep."

He looked significantly disappointed. Tough luck. Taking the wind out of his sails was kind of fun.

"Deke — one more thing before we go any further. I think I was followed after I left the club last night. By two men. Any ideas on that?"

He straightened, serious again. The animal alertness came back. She liked that. She had nothing more to say as he walked her back to the glass doors and through the bar.

The big guy who'd been eying her was gone, and so were the affectionate couples. A new crowd of noisy singles had taken over the bar, with the women perched on the stools and the men standing by them and among them, vying for their attention.

"You sure?" he asked in a low voice when they reached the foyer by the elevators.

"I've been debating that most of the day. By now, yes, I'm sure. They didn't do anything. There was only one at first. He just — got too close. Said things that were off. And then there was a car, going too fast."

"Do you remember the plates?"

"No. It was way after midnight. I was scared."

"Could you describe the first man if you

had to?" Deke asked. He seemed suddenly very curious.

"Middle-aged. Very ordinary."

"Anything stand out? You know, like a hairstyle or a birthmark?" He watched her closely.

"Nothing like that. He was well-groomed, had a nice suit — he was polite at first. I thought he was a fan. Then he came nearer without ever touching me. I had to step back. He totally creeped me out."

If she had to guess, she would say Deke was making mental notes of every word.

"I was just glad to make it home in one piece."

"And you live —"

"In a rented condo."

"How's the security?"

"There's a doorman, day and night. Surveillance cameras. Valet parking — I don't have to walk through a garage or a lot."

"I'm driving home with you." Deke held up a hand when she began to protest. "Separate cars. Don't argue."

Her phone rang the second the door shut behind her. Couldn't be Deke, not so soon after he'd dropped her off. Kelly upended her purse on the couch and found the phone in the tumbled contents before the ringing stopped. It was Laura.

"Hi. I meant to call you." Kelly felt a little guilty that she hadn't. It wasn't like she was nursing a grudge against Laura for doing the right thing and going to the cops before she got around to it. "How are you?"

"I'm all right, I guess. I just wanted to touch base. I haven't been back to WBRX since — you know."

"The shootout." Laura could be awfully sensitive. Kelly believed in saying what needed to be said.

"It gave me nightmares. But it sort of helped me make up my mind," Laura said.

"Huh?"

"Listen, I never told you, but I got a job offer, like, several weeks ago from a non-profit gardening program. They do grow-it-yourself videos, apples to zucchini. I called them to see if the job was still open. It is. So I'm quitting, Kelly."

"Really?"

"Yes."

Kelly wasn't that surprised. "Okay. But are you sure you want to film zucchinis growing? I mean, they grow fast, but not that fast."

Laura laughed. "I'm sure. I'll stop by the station soon. We can go out to lunch or something."

"You bet. Looking forward to it."

"Take care of yourself, Kelly." Laura's tone grew serious. "I mean it."

"I will. You too."

CHAPTER 6

Getting Gunther Bach to talk to her had been as simple as calling him from WBRX. His secretary had put her on hold and Bach had picked up a minute later, inviting her to an early lunch at one of Atlanta's best restaurants when she told him — vaguely — that she was developing a feature story on finance.

She decided to drive herself to the restaurant, figuring she'd be back in plenty of time for hair and makeup before the evening broadcast. The car that the station provided for her was several spaces away and the driver was deep in a discussion of baseball with the parking lot guard.

After several wrong turns, Kelly spotted the restaurant and parked, entering through paneled doors in a rush. She was greeted at once by the maître d', an older man, short and impeccably groomed, who welcomed her with a slight bow.

"Good afternoon, Miss Johns," he said. "Mr. Bach is waiting for you. Please come this way."

He motioned for her to follow him. The crowded restaurant was situated in the lobby of an expensive hotel favored by business executives. She got noticed as she walked by but looked straight ahead, spotting Gunther Bach in a far corner.

And there was Deke, at a table set for one, absorbed in a menu. He didn't look up as she brushed past. A tiny blue light flashed in the phone earpiece he wore. She peeked in her handbag — the bugged phone he'd given her glowed briefly.

Bach rose as she approached. A few female heads turned. He was tall and seemed fit for his age — almost fifty, by her guess — with silver hair combed back from his angular face.

Kelly slowed down, mentally noting additional details.

He wore a European-cut suit, and that chunk of gold on his wrist had to be a Rolex. His hands were large and strong, as if he could blast a tennis serve or choke the life out of a business competitor with equal ease. There was something unmistakably domineering in his stance. Intelligent eyes, the color of cold steel, surveyed her.

Kelly gave him a sunny smile. "Hello," she said breathlessly. "Sorry, I'm a little late. Traffic."

"I understand."

"Have you been waiting long?" She fished the bugged phone out of her purse and set it next to her car keys on the table.

"No." He looked pointedly at the phone. "I do hope you won't have to take a call during lunch."

"I don't have to. But I like to know who's trying to reach me." Kelly tapped the phone screen twice with a pink-polished fingernail. "That takes care of that. I can see the number and they can go straight to voice-mail hell."

"I consider myself honored," Bach said dryly. He inclined his head. "Please sit down."

The maître d' pulled out a chair for her. Kelly slid into it, smoothing the skirt of her cream knit suit underneath her. She placed her handbag next to the phone and keys. Bach resumed his seat.

"I hope the restaurant meets your expectations. I find that the food is generally quite good."

His accent was hard to place. It could be Swiss or German — she'd found both listed as his nationality on the Internet, on different sites.

"I'm sure it is."

"Have you been here before?"

Kelly shook her head. "Never. I think I've been to every restaurant in Atlanta but this one."

"Your presence has been noted." That dry tone again. He warmed it up. "You are lovely, Kelly. More so in person than on the air."

"Thanks." The compliment made her feel a little awkward. The online mentions she'd found pegged him as a womanizer with several hundred million dollars to throw around. It wasn't enough to make her fall at his feet. "I guess you watch my evening broadcast."

"Occasionally, yes."

Gunther Bach didn't seem to be the chatty type. That went with the arrogance. Kelly unfolded her napkin in her lap. "I really appreciate you meeting with me on such short notice."

"You happened to catch me at an opportune time. I had nothing else scheduled for the afternoon — and I might fly to Europe tomorrow."

"Oh. Where in Europe?"

He smiled faintly. "I haven't decided. London, perhaps. Geneva. Or Milan. I do business in many countries."

"I see." Kelly left it at that. His closed expression didn't invite further questions as to his whereabouts.

A waiter offered her a menu, which Bach allowed her to study for only a minute before recommending his own favorites. From the way the staff fawned over him, she guessed he came here often. Kelly chose broiled trout. He ordered steak, ultra-rare, for himself, and a vodka martini when Kelly declined a drink.

Kelly picked up her water glass and took a sip, eying him. His gaze was still cool, almost wary. She would have to be on her game, she thought, putting the glass down.

"You must be incredibly busy. I'm so glad you could spare the time for an informal meeting," she began.

"Why did you call me?"

Bach went straight to the point, she thought. Fine. This bogus get-together would be over with sooner.

"When I started researching high-level finance, your name kept coming up. It's a perfect subject for a special report, don't you think? There's big money pouring into Atlanta these days."

Gunther shrugged. "The bank I run is not that large. But it is exclusive."

"That's fascinating. A secret world of power and privilege," she said eagerly. "Our viewers would love to know more."

He acknowledged the comment with a polite nod.

"This is off the record," Kelly assured him, "but would you mind if I jot down a few things as we talk?"

"I suppose not."

Kelly took a pad and pen from her handbag, doing more listening than writing. The conversation continued, along very general lines. Gunther Bach said nothing specific about the operations of his private bank or the hedge fund he controlled, but she didn't care. All she had to do was get his voice on tape.

With a somewhat unnecessary flourish, their entrées arrived. No doubt the restaurant manager had told the staff to treat them like VIPs. Most of the other patrons pretended not to pay attention, but she did attract a few covert looks from the people who were closest. Gunther sipped his martini and responded in a muted voice to her questions.

Several women who'd just been seated together nearby seemed to be pretending not to hear him. He barely glanced their way — but he did glance. Gunther Bach could probably take his pick of every female in the restaurant except her. She was grateful when one of the women complained to a waiter about the table wobbling, and they were moved away.

Kelly ignored the phone, which never rang. Deke had told her that she didn't have to worry about it. The screen glowed only once. Somehow, remotely, he was controlling it.

She wrapped up the interview over dessert and coffee, tucking the notepad and pen back into her handbag while the table was cleared.

A waiter appeared and used a silver-handled brush to sweep invisible crumbs into a small silver pan. She wished the check would arrive, but Bach seemed to be in no hurry. He rested his hands on the white damask tablecloth, looking at her. His steely eyes glittered with a new, slightly disturbing intensity.

Kelly swung her legs to the side of her chair, preparing to rise from the table with a minimum of feminine fussing. She didn't want to drag this out a second longer than she had to. Something had changed between them. She couldn't figure it out.

"Gunther, this has been great," she said. "The lunch and the information, which is very, very useful. Of course, it's going to take me a while to put together a proposal for a feature. Then I have to get approval from our news director before I can go ahead. You know how it is."

Her ditzy act seemed to amuse him. "Actually, I don't."

"Feature reporting takes a lot of research and lots of time. Speaking of that, I have to get back to the station." Kelly smiled brightly. She shifted her position and took hold of her handbag. "Again, it's been a pleasure."

"For me as well." He flashed a thin smile. "To be quite honest, it didn't seem like an interview."

Kelly managed a laugh. "Then I guess I was doing it right. I find it's best not to have a structured approach when I want a fresh angle for a feature."

"Is that it?" Bach's steel-colored eyes narrowed, but he kept on smiling. "Hmm. I suspect you are not being honest with me."

That was out of the blue. Kelly scooped up the phone and car keys. Never mind putting them into her bag. She stood. Game over, she thought. But she could still bluff. "I don't know what you mean."

"You barely took notes." His thin smile vanished.

"Ah — I didn't really get a chance. But I do have a very good memory," she said quickly.

"I see."

He wouldn't say good-bye and she couldn't just storm out. Monroe Capp might know this guy. She didn't want to be lectured by the news director for being rude to a mover and shaker.

"Gunther, I really have to get back to WBRX."

"So soon?"

Bach lifted his hands and — her eyes widened. There was a hotel keycard on the table. This hotel. Upstairs from the restaurant. The invitation was clear. Suite seduction. Maybe being seen with her had gone to his head. He'd had one martini. He wasn't drunk.

"I know women, Kelly," he whispered. "This so-called interview was a pretext. You want more from me, much more — I can see it in your eyes."

She stepped back abruptly, jarring the table.

"I'm not interested."

Gunther Bach scowled. He seemed surprised by her refusal and began to say something, but she interrupted him. "Don't worry. I won't quote you. On anything."

Kelly turned and headed for the paneled doors of the restaurant as fast as her high heels would take her.

She waited in her car for Deke to exit the restaurant, sliding down in the front seat when she saw Gunther Bach come out instead of him. The silver-haired financier looked around. He couldn't possibly want to apologize, she thought angrily. On the other hand, he'd given her the perfect excuse never to talk to him again. She wouldn't have to white-lie her way out of this situation.

Bach went back in and Deke finally appeared, walking casually across the parking lot, sunglasses on, his hands in the pockets of a very good suit. She sat up straight again. She wouldn't have guessed that he even owned one. Seeing him full-length, all she could think was that he looked great in it. He glanced toward her car, which was parked some distance from his, but avoided her gaze, strolling away.

Kelly grabbed the handle to open her car door, but something made her hesitate. Within seconds her phone rang. Not the bugged one Deke had given her, but her own. She saw his number and answered.

"Glad that's over," she muttered. "What a

creep. You missed the keycard reveal."

"Was that what he did? I heard the rest. I was wondering what he saw in your eyes."

"Cold fury."

"You didn't miss a beat, Kelly."

"True. Except for that one moment."

Deke didn't seem upset. But then, all he'd had to do was sit at a table by himself and have a business lunch with that thing in his ear.

"I thought the food was pretty good. So, other than being propositioned by one of the richest guys in Atlanta, did you enjoy your lunch?"

"Not really," Kelly snapped. She was almost angry at herself for underestimating Bach. "Did you enjoy listening in?"

"He was coming in loud and clear," Deke said cheerfully. "Good thing you didn't stick around. You might have blown your cover."

Kelly turned the key in the ignition and leaned her seat back. It didn't sound like Deke was going to saunter over to her car and have this conversation face-to-face. "Oh, please. I get hit on a lot. I can take care of myself."

He chuckled in an annoying way. "I don't doubt it. But that wasn't an attempt at seduction."

Kelly sighed, well aware that she might

have depended too much on her looks and her fame. "Then what would you call it?"

Deke didn't reply right away. When he did, his tone was serious. "Kelly, he was testing you. You might have been more convincing on the phone, but once you were across the table —"

"He figured out that I wasn't interviewing him. What did I do wrong?"

"Nothing. The guy's a professional con man. He's good at reading other people, very good. That's how he got started making money."

Kelly groaned. "Damn it. He had me." She flipped down the visor when she caught a glimpse of another older man coming out of the restaurant. "Wait — that could be him again." She peeked, not sure.

"I see who you mean," Deke said a little distantly. "That's definitely not him. Anyway, Bach went back toward the hotel through the lobby as I was leaving."

"Thanks for telling me. You owe me for this one, Bannon. I don't see how a random lunch with a lecher is going to get me the story I want."

"It will."

"I'm so ashamed." She wanted to howl. "Deke, I don't get conned. That's never happened to me."

"First time for everyone. Get over it."

"When Bach said I wasn't being honest with him, I panicked for a second. That's what he saw in my eyes. Then he pulled out that keycard, and I was dumb enough to believe he was putting the moves on me."

"I'm sure he wouldn't have minded if you'd taken him up on it."

"Drive over here. Right now," she commanded.

"Why?"

"So I can kill you."

"With what?"

"A high heel to the head."

He chuckled again. "Listen, you were great. There's nothing you can do about what happened."

Kelly looked in her handbag for the bugged phone. "Deke, come and get your toy. Unless you want me to drive it over to you."

"No to both. Let's go back to your place."

"How do you know we won't be followed?" Kelly eased her seat back up.

"Because I have someone following me to take care of that."

Kelly stopped with a jolt, upright. "Okay. I need to know what agency you work for and exactly what the hell you're up to. Or else you don't get your toy back."

"Not a problem. I recorded the whole thing on my phone. You were basically the transmitter," he pointed out.

Kelly thought fast. "Then you don't get the tape from the shootout."

The download was still on her laptop. Gordon must have given a digital copy to the police by now, but Deke wasn't with the Atlanta PD. He didn't have a warrant or a subpoena, and he couldn't make her give it to him.

"Deke?"

"I'm here."

"I know you want that tape," she said tightly. "And where else will you get it? Everyone knows feds and cops are famous for not sharing."

"Deal," he said, really laughing this time. "See you in fifteen."

Deke met the doorman's scrutiny with a steady look and an affable hello. Kelly breezed past, not stopping to explain. This was her apartment, not her college dorm.

They rode up in the elevator to her floor. There was no one in the hall when they exited. Deke looked up and down, as if it was automatic. He walked over a few steps to the fire stairs, glancing through the small glass window before he opened the heavy door to the landing. Then he came back.

"Looking for Gunther Bach? I thought you said we couldn't possibly be followed."

"Not my exact words. Not even close." He stayed by her side as they went down the hall to her apartment. He watched Kelly unlock her door but waited to let her go in first, pausing in the doorway for one last backward glance in both directions.

"Do you know any of your neighbors, Kelly?"

"No. Why do you ask?"

"Just curious."

She had nothing to say to that and motioned him inside, making sure the door was locked behind him. Deke walked through the open-plan living room to the picture window. "Great view."

"I hardly ever get to see it."

"Is that your car down there?" he asked. A man in a red vest was walking away from it.

Kelly came over to look. "Yes. That's the valet. They must be full up. They usually park it on a lower floor."

"Where would mine be?" Deke asked.

"In the guest area. Don't forget to tip."

"After I see if they scratched it or not," he replied.

"They're really careful," she said absently.

Deke moved away from the window and surveyed the apartment again. "You don't spend much time at home, I take it."

"I come here to sleep." Kelly had gone into the kitchen, where she set her handbag on a smooth white table, bare of any ornament except for a vase of bright flowers. "During the day I'm at the station or running around doing personal appearances — and sometimes I do those at night too. On the weekends, I sleep."

"Got it. Do you work from home?"

"Sometimes. I mean, I don't have to be at the station as much as I am. But WBRX feels more like home, I guess."

"This is a nice place, though." Deke seemed to be searching for words. "Quiet. Lots of space."

"It's too empty." Kelly frowned at the bare walls and the few pieces of furniture. "One of these days I'm going to put up pictures, buy some big ol' pillows, get my personal stuff out of storage — yeah, well, one of these days."

Deke settled himself on a beige sofa that looked brand new. "Takes time to settle in."

"You're right," she said briskly. "But you didn't come here to discuss the décor. Now where did I put my laptop? I hope I didn't leave it at the station."

There was no harm in making him think so. He looked a little too comfortable at the moment, even though he still had his jacket on. She knew perfectly well where the laptop was: in the chest of drawers in her bedroom.

"Would you like a soda or anything?" she asked, walking past him on her way there.

"No thanks."

Kelly opened closet doors and drawers, making him wait longer. "Here it is," she called. She came back into the living room with the laptop in her hands.

"Excellent. You sure no one's looked at this since you saw the tape?"

Kelly nodded and sat down by him. She put the closed laptop on the coffee table, which was as bare as everything else. No magazines, no books, no mail. Only with him here did she realize how very empty her place must look.

"Do you want to see it before I send it?"

Deke nodded.

"We made a deal," she reminded him.

He explained as best he could, pulling out his wallet and several ID cards. "I'm a criminal investigator, federal. I work on a case-by-case basis."

"You mean you freelance?"

"In a manner of speaking, yes. I have a

high-level security clearance. Agents who can't be pulled up on any government database are useful. One crooked agent or a rogue cop is all it takes to hack into an ongoing investigation, which puts everyone undercover at risk."

"Sooner or later the bad guys are going to figure out who you are."

"Hasn't happened." Deke leaned back into the beige cushions, looking out the window again. "But it will. Then I'll quit and do something else."

No wonder he looked twice wherever he went. Kelly studied him. In a big apartment with not much furniture, he seemed more at ease, with plenty of room for those long legs. She liked the way he relaxed, given the right space. He turned to look at her. The intensity of his deep brown gaze was startling. Kelly gave a little jump.

"Oh — sorry. Guess I zoned out. Let's look at this, and then you have to go because I have to get to work. It's already three-thirty."

She hadn't zoned out, not for a second. Kelly had been as focused on his physicality and strength as when she'd glimpsed him swimming in the dark water of the infinity pool.

She flipped open the laptop, bending her

head over it and letting her hair fall free to hide her blush. Kelly clicked around.

"Here's the file."

Deke sat up, looking sideways at the paused footage. "Go ahead. Play it."

There was an establishing shot of the abandoned building and a zoom to Kelly, who recited her memorized intro. Fade to black. More footage of Kelly inside the building. Gordon and Laura talking, off camera. In the background, the first car, parked, was joined by a second car, both black luxury models. Deke's voice, roaring. The first gunshot cracked. She lowered the volume nearly to silence. The images were herky-jerky and hard to see. It was over in seconds.

"Go back to where the second car pulled in," he instructed. "Then go frame by frame."

Kelly did as Deke asked. The features of the unknown woman weren't clear, but her face was the only one caught on the tape.

"Besides the red hair, nothing solid for an ID," Deke said, more to himself than Kelly.

"The sunglasses are designer, not drugstore," Kelly pointed out. "Definitely not your everyday shades."

Deke shot her a look of respect. "They could be knockoffs. Either way, which designer?"

"Ferragamo, I think. Or Miu Miu. I'd have to check. No trace of her yet?" Kelly asked.

Deke shook his head, studying the blurred images. "No. Nothing at the scene but the dead thugs, who seem to have shot each other."

"Does the ballistic evidence bear that out?"

He glanced up at her. "Rock on, girl reporter. So far, yes. Though that could change. The scene's been processed, but the analysis just got started."

A muffled cell-phone chime echoed in the bare room.

"That's yours," Kelly said. "Or at least it isn't mine."

Deke reached into a pocket for the phone and looked at the small screen. "Hux. About time he checked in. I have to take this."

"Not a problem." She set the laptop on the coffee table.

Kelly got up, going back into her bedroom. She stripped the sheets off the bed, going to the closet for fresh linens to have something to do while she listened to Deke's low voice. The conversation seemed fairly one-sided, with the other man doing most of the talking. Deke did say that he was looking at footage from the scene of the shootings, but he didn't mention where he was or who he was with.

She had a pillow in her teeth and was yanking a pillowcase over it when Deke came into the room. He leaned one arm high on the door frame and watched her work.

"That was Huxton Smith, my partner on this case. Agency op, the real deal, on staff. Basically, he tells me what to do — or tries to."

She let the pillow dangle in midair for a moment, holding it with both hands but not looking at him. On the threshold of her bedroom, Deke seemed too big for the space again. And much too hot to be standing within a few feet of a freshly made bed. It was too easy to imagine him in it.

"So what's up?" she asked him nonchalantly.

"They might get definitive ID on all three guys from Interpol. Hux said he'd call later tonight."

Kelly gave the pillow a plumping and tossed it toward the head of the bed. "And do I get to be in on this?"

"Let me find out who they are first."

She picked up the second pillow and crammed it into a pillow-case. A few downy feathers floated free as the pillow heaved out partway. Kelly punched it back into the case and flung it against the headboard. "Why do I get the feeling I'm being handed the easy stuff?"

"I have to keep you safe," he said bluntly. "You knowing too much or knowing dangerous things isn't going to help."

Kelly picked up a folded top sheet and moved away from him. She shook it open and whipped it out in high billows that made him disappear. When it floated down, Deke was on the opposite side of the bed. He grasped the edge of the sheet.

"Ready?" he asked.

They pulled the sheet taut and tucked it in. He straightened first and grinned with satisfaction. But he stayed where he was, as if he was waiting for her to say something.

"Thanks." Kelly controlled herself and motioned him out. "Now go. Like I said, I have to get to work."

"Send me that video file first. Got a pen and paper?"

She found both in the nightstand drawer and thrust them toward him. Deke jotted down a couple of lines and handed the pen and paper back.

"That'll do it. See you around."

Kelly didn't walk him out. She waited

until she heard him unlock the apartment door, then close it behind him.

She looked down at what he'd written. On the first line was his e-mail address, which didn't end in .gov. The second line made her smile.

That was fun. You're beautiful.

CHAPTER 7

The anchor set was empty. Kelly entered it from the side, holding a printout, hoping to retrieve script pages she'd left under the desk yesterday. A celebrity club brawl had sparked thousands of views of exclusive photos posted on the WBRX website. Monroe Capp wanted the six P.M. news to open with a recap and tantalizing new details of the story.

The spectacular fight had closed down the popular club, but Kelly couldn't remember which celeb had allegedly thrown the first bottle. Vital information that the public had a right to know.

She slid her hands into the hidden space right under the desk, feeling around. Bingo. Kelly came up with several sheets of paper. She found the name she was looking for and added it to her printout of tonight's script.

She stopped by an editor's desk and asked him to add the information to the script that would roll on the TelePrompTer in less than an hour. Sometimes anchors had to ad lib, but she didn't want to do it on purpose. The editor promised to take care of it and Kelly headed back to her office.

Her hair was done and so was her makeup. The facial tissues tucked into the neckband of her blouse to protect the material would be removed just before she stepped on the set with Dave Maples. Kelly pressed the tissues down to keep them from tickling her chin as she sat to read through her script, marking it up.

Kelly shook her head, preoccupied. It wasn't much of a story, but Monroe Capp had told everyone to play it up big. He wanted to see a ratings boost before Friday and try to pick up extra viewers going into the weekend when people tended not to watch the news much.

Good luck. It had been a slow Thursday, and there was nothing else exciting for her and Dave Maples to talk about. Kelly put down the script and leafed through the folder of circulating memos. The news blackout on the shooting at the abandoned building was still in effect, apparently. Not one mention.

There was a knock on the door. Distracted, Kelly looked up to see her co-anchor grinning at her. Dave Maples's collar was lined with tissues just like hers, his healthy tan supplied by June with a makeup brush and bronzer.

"What, no smile? Turn on the personality, kiddo. You're wanted on the set." His booming voice made the tissues flutter.

"Thanks, Dave. Be right there. You go ahead."

The older man left, whistling as he walked away. Kelly usually preferred to wait until a production assistant came to get her, but she decided to indulge Dave just this once. She picked up the script and left the other papers on her desk.

June was doing a last-minute touchup on Dave's face. Done, she whisked away the tissues and turned to Kelly, studying her with a critical eye and finally adding a dab of light powder to her nose.

"There. Now you're perfect."

"Thanks to you," Kelly replied with a smile.

The broadcast went smoothly. No mispronounced words, no gaffes. But then there was no important news. Finishing up with her usual sign-off and listening to Dave do the same, Kelly looked directly into the lens that stayed on her and waited for the signal that they were off the air.

The lights went off and the broadcast director called it a wrap.

"Doing anything special tonight, Kelly?" Dave asked.

After what had happened today, she wasn't sure how to take the commonplace question. It couldn't be a come-on. Dave Maples had been married to the same woman forever, as far as she knew. Kelly slid off the anchor chair as she answered. "Just heading home. A friend might come over. That's about it."

"Sounds good," Dave said affably. "Jenny and I plan to watch a movie in the den." He winked at her. "Getting old. But I like it."

Kelly relaxed. "Give Jenny my regards."

"Will do. See you tomorrow."

Back in her office, she changed the on-air suit for jeans and a casual top. She could have done it in the makeup room, but Kelly preferred her privacy. The wardrobe assistant would stop by to pick up the suit and send it out for cleaning. Magically, another outfit would appear in her closet by tomorrow.

Looking into her mirror, she used a makeup-remover pad to get off most of the matte foundation and contouring. The eyeliner and mascara stayed — June had a knack for creating sultry eyes. If Deke

Bannon came over instead of calling, Kelly was ready.

Of course, he might not do either.

She left the station and drove home. Her phone was in the cup holder where she could hear it ring. If he called, she would call him back once she was in the apartment.

The traffic going through Atlanta was relatively heavy. She got off before her exit and took side streets, arriving before ten. The phone had been silent. She checked it anyway. No voicemails, no texts.

Kelly slipped it into her handbag and left the car to be valet-parked, going directly up to her apartment but lost in thought, recalling Dave's plans for a cozy evening. What would it be like to have someone to come home to?

Someone like Deke Bannon.

She reached for her keys as the elevator doors opened onto her floor. Kelly snapped out of it, looking both ways down the empty hall before she walked to her apartment door. When she realized what she was doing, she smiled to herself.

Deke was here even if he wasn't.

The ringing phone woke her up. Kelly looked at the time on its screen, rubbing her eyes. Her bedroom was bright with morning light. She'd conked out without drawing the curtains and stayed asleep with her back to the sunrise. The phone display read five minutes after nine.

Deke Bannon. The letters of his name glowed above his phone number. Kelly told herself not to be ridiculous. That was what smartphones did. Her accountant's name and number glowed just as brightly.

But she didn't get the same thrill. Kelly took a deep breath and answered the call.

"Hello," she said calmly.

"Guess I'm not that exciting." The warmth in his voice was better than a blanket. Kelly could use one. She'd slept wrapped in the top sheet and nothing else.

She sidestepped the leading remark. A cute comment scrawled on a notepad didn't get him past the guards at the gate.

"I'm not completely awake. What's up?"

"We got the info from Interpol. They ID'd the thugs. Looks like they were guns for hire —"

"Who hired them?"

"Hux and I have a few theories. Can we come over?"

The second *we* finally got her attention. So she wasn't going to see Deke alone. Maybe the agent he worked with, Huxton

Smith, thought Deke needed babysitting. Or maybe Hux just wanted to meet her and Deke wanted to show off.

"I need coffee," she said curtly. Last night's romantic fantasies about Deke were going up in smoke. She had wanted him to call, had looked forward to being with him — but it hadn't happened. Having a crush on a criminal investigator was just plain stupid. They worked late hours. They were busiest on weekends. They would sell their souls for a juicy case that they could really get their teeth into.

Not too different from investigative reporters. Kelly knew she would have to be on her toes if she wanted to do that again. Becoming an anchor and delivering the news from a chair had knocked her off her game.

"We'll bring you coffee," Deke was saying. "How do you like it?"

"Huh? Oh — tall. Dash of cream. No sugar."

"Anything else?"

"No. But give me time to take a shower."

"Half an hour?"

"All right," she said reluctantly. If this was strictly professional, they might as well not dawdle. She was curious about the Interpol report.

Deke hung up and Kelly got out of bed,

leaving the top sheet in a hopeless tangle. She went into the bathroom, catching a glimpse of herself in the cabinet mirror.

Kelly flinched. Her hair badly needed brushing. The thick mascara and smoky eyeliner had smeared into dark circles under her eyes. So much for sultry. She looked like a raccoon having a very bad fur day.

The morning light was providing way too much information. She grabbed a hand towel and used it to conceal the mirror while she brushed her teeth. A long, hot shower washed away most of her irritation and a washcloth took care of nearly all the eye makeup. She felt human again when she stepped out, bundling herself up into a robe before she wet-combed her hair.

Blouse and jeans from last night, she decided. Good enough.

The doorman buzzed the intercom and she told him to let Deke and Hux come up. Kelly wasn't going to get a chance to dry her hair, but she didn't really care. She took the towel off the mirror. There was still just a trace of the eye makeup left and her wet, dark lashes looked better than mascara.

The knock on the door came sooner than she'd expected. Kelly padded barefoot over the carpet to open it. Deke stood there with a capped takeout cup, a thickset, middle-aged man at his side.

He was wearing that battered leather jacket today, over clean jeans and a dark T-shirt that nonetheless revealed a fair amount of muscle. Easy on the eyes. Even with that annoying grin on his face.

"Here you go." Deke held out the cup. "Cream, no sugar?"

Kelly gave him a semi-smile. "Whatever's in there, I'll drink it. I don't even have instant."

She took the cup from him and stepped to one side to let them in.

"You must be Huxton Smith," she said to the other man. "I'm Kelly Johns. Come on in."

"Thanks. Very pleased to meet you. Sorry to wake you up. He said you wouldn't mind."

Kelly waved both men toward the white table in the kitchen. "He doesn't know me that well."

She brushed past Deke as she went to the sink, setting the takeout cup down in it and carefully removing the lid.

"Did I get it right?" he asked.

She took a taste. "Yes. Thanks."

He exchanged a look with Hux, who moved to the table, putting a laptop onto it and quickly booting it up.

Kelly raised a questioning eyebrow as she turned to them, sipping the coffee. "Is that your laptop or his?"

"Neither. Government machine," Deke told her absently. He looked back at the screen. "It seemed simpler to bring it along since I can't e-mail you classified documents. The Interpol report is on it."

"Gee whiz. My first peek at something classified." Kelly took a middle chair, leaving the opposite ends of the table to Deke and Hux.

"We owe you," Hux told her. "I wanted to thank you personally for the tape from the scene. The digital forensics team is on it. We got some twists and turns to figure out. Dead perps, missing lady."

Deke settled himself into a chair and slid the laptop in front of her. "Read the profiles. Let me know if anything rings a bell."

"I barely saw those guys," Kelly protested. She skimmed, more interested in the photos than the detailed profiles. Aliases, underworld connections, crimes — there were too many of those to count.

She never would have connected the well-dressed men in the luxury cars to these mug shots. All were different nationalities. Pyotr Zaminsky. Russian. Age 31. Avery Twiller. American. Age 27. Estaban Lopez. Mexican.

Age 23. The word DECEASED was stamped in red across each face.

"We know who they are, for what that's worth," Deke said. "But not why they were meeting at that building or what went wrong."

Kelly studied the photos. "Just going by their names, I would say you're dealing with a global enterprise."

Huxton Smith nodded. "The government task force on this is huge. Exactly where to begin is the big question."

"Simple." Kelly pushed the laptop back toward Deke, who shut it down. "Go after the biggest guy."

Deke grinned. "I like the way she thinks, don't you, Hux?"

She finished her coffee and stood up, putting the empty cup on the counter. "I don't actually know if that's the right thing to do. But that would be the best story."

Hux raised a hand. "Whoa. Much as we appreciate the cooperation of the media, we're not ready to go public yet."

"You have nothing to worry about. The official news blackout is still in place, at least where I work."

"Good to know." Hux seemed satisfied with that.

"Deke, I wanted to ask you —" Kelly

turned toward him. "What happened with that voiceprint?"

"Nothing yet," Deke said a little too quickly. "We're waiting for an in-depth analysis."

"We are? What are you talking about?" Hux looked from Kelly to Deke.

A little too late, Kelly realized she'd crossed an invisible line. But why wouldn't Huxton Smith know about her lunch with Bach? It had been Deke's idea. And he'd said it was part of the case that the two men were working together.

"I'll let Deke explain," she told Hux.

Hux jabbed at the button panel in the elevator. "I know you had to get her to give up that footage, but why didn't you leave it at that? Now she's a partner in the whole investigation?"

"Not quite."

"I can't believe you asked her to sweet-talk that Bach guy. That's not what I meant by keeping her busy."

"I had to come up with something that involved an aspect of the case so I could stay with it. The contract you heard about is still on offer, right?" Deke watched the doors slowly close as Hux nodded. "You're the one who told me to keep her close."

"I wish I hadn't." Hux kept his gaze on the decreasing floor numbers. "Down we go. I hate high buildings."

"She practically volunteered, Hux. Kelly was an investigative reporter before she became an anchor. This case is heating up fast. I need someone like her."

"Reporter, anchor — you don't want her to know too much. Can you trust her to keep her mouth shut?"

Deke waved away the question. "The tape she got was excellent. I needed Gunther Bach's voice for comparison to the one we didn't know. Job done."

Hux sighed. "I bet Bach got dizzy just looking at her. She's much too beautiful to work undercover. And too well-known."

"That right there is an advantage," Deke said. "And she's a natural, particularly with men. She keeps them from thinking."

Hux rocked back and forth on his feet. "What does that say about you?"

Deke smiled a little sheepishly. "I can handle her. But thanks for your concern."

"You're welcome. There's another problem. A big one. Kelly's a civilian."

"Technically, so am I," Deke retorted. "Different rulebook. Not yours."

"What does that mean?" Hux glared at him. "That you get to make up your own rules as you go along?"

A soft stop made Huxton lurch. He righted himself. The elevator doors opened into the lobby. Deke and Hux walked past the doorman, putting their argument on hold.

Two hours later, Kelly was on her way back to the station. Her phone rang from deep inside her handbag. She ignored it. For the moment, no news was good news.

The afternoon routine at WBRX settled her down. The morning visit from Deke and his colleague had made her nervous. Huxton Smith seemed a little suspicious of her after he'd been informed that she'd interviewed Gunther Bach. And Deke had been . . . all about Deke.

She saw him more clearly now. His interest in her was professional, with a little flirtation thrown in to ensure her cooperation. Kelly pulled her car into a parking space, got out, and locked it.

Good old WBRX. Inside the station walls, she didn't have to think or worry or scheme for the next several hours. She just had to do what was expected of her — and what she was paid for, she reminded herself. She walked past the newsroom, not glancing at the cubicles to see who was in today.

A page in a blazer handed her the script for tonight's broadcast shortly after she got to her office. Kelly looked it over. The lack of hard news lately was almost alarming. Without it, the newswriters were forced to make mountains out of molehills. Whatever. She was a pro, she would deal. With the right delivery, a dull story could sound almost as exciting as one that was breaking hot and fast.

Almost.

Kelly was aware that she was craving another rush of adrenaline. Playing Gunther Bach for a sucker had been entertaining while it lasted — until the financier had played her back.

There was no role for her to play in the shootout investigation. The scene had been processed and sealed. The Atlanta PD didn't need her to double-check for clues.

On Deke's side of things, he knew much more than he was willing to tell. Knowledge was power, and he was in charge. She really, really didn't like it. But she knew there wasn't a damn thing she could do about it. Yet.

Kelly pushed a button on a computerized photo screen looking for the one that always cheered her up. She didn't keep it on the wall for a reason. Too personal. She stopped on her grandmother's beloved, sun-weathered face, smiling at Kelly the day she'd taken the picture.

It worked. It always worked.

Her gran's encouragement and pride in her had gotten Kelly further than either of them ever dreamed. But she wasn't sure that digging up dirt on criminals would have impressed Nelda Johns. Her grandmother preferred tales of good-hearted persever-ance and grit, preferably with a moral that was short enough to embroider.

Her phone rang again. Out of habit, Kelly had taken it out and placed it on her desk. She guessed it was Deke before she even looked at the screen. With a frown, she answered it, vowing to do the talking before he could coax her into doing him another favor.

"Hi, Deke. Thanks for stopping by this morning," she rushed. "The Interpol report was interesting. Never saw one before. And oh, I *liked* Huxton. You can tell him that. Oh my — here's the —" Let Deke fill in the gap. "Guess what just landed on my desk. More work. I gotta go."

There was a pause. "In a sec. I have a question for you."

He was so self-centered he didn't even

notice when she was being obnoxious. "Go ahead."

"Do you have to work all the time?"

"What?"

Deke clarified. "Do you do the evening news on weekends too?"

"No. Monday through Friday only. Why?"

"How would you like to fly to Dallas with me after the broadcast?"

"What?"

"Something big is about to go down. We track Internet chatter on money laundering, and the buzz really picked up last night. A lot of it tracked straight to Gunther Bach's ISP addresses."

"Interesting. But not surprising." Kelly found a pencil and paper to make notes.

"His so-called bank and that hedge fund require a constant supply of fresh cash, and Atlanta is getting too hot — Georgia regulators are starting to crack down on Bach and others."

Kelly stopped scribbling. "Which means — ?"

"They move on and move out. New city, new suckers. Which brings me back to Dallas. There's a gala fund-raiser for the arts this weekend. Tickets for two are going for two hundred fifty thousand dollars. Criminals want to crash the party."

Kelly leaned back in her mesh chair. "And do what? Pick pockets? Steal diamonds? No one wears the real stuff out in public anymore, Deke."

"That's beside the point."

"Just tell me what you're going to be doing."

"Watching the action. Looking for certain people on our list. Finding out who they talk to."

"And why do you want me to tag along?"

"I thought you might be interested." His bland tone gave away nothing. "I promise you it'll be a lot more fun than that lunch."

"I don't think so, Deke. Besides, I can't simply pack up and go." That was more than a white lie. Kelly had been doing just that for years.

"Why not?"

"Um, prior commitments, I think. I have to check my calendar."

Undaunted, Deke tried something else. "You know, I checked out some of your investigative pieces on YouTube. You were really something. Disguises, fake identities — there was nothing you wouldn't do to nail someone."

Kelly laughed a little. "I probably still have some of that stuff."

"Bring it."

She got serious again. "I haven't agreed to anything. Besides, I did those undercover reports a couple of years ago. I'm out of practice."

"You've got what it takes, Kelly."

She didn't answer.

"All expenses paid," he said. "Swanky hotel. Maybe even a penthouse suite."

"Do I have to share the suite with you? I hate sharing." If he thought she was going to tumble into bed with him after they'd done a little light snooping, he needed to get over that notion right now.

"I'll see what I can arrange."

Annoyed, Kelly tapped the pencil she was holding against the edge of the desk. He'd have to do better than that. But she was feeling a tingle. A sure sign she was craving excitement. She fought back by asking Deke more questions, trying not to seem interested.

He laid it out. The event had a memorable name, that was for sure. "The media are calling it the Billionaires' Ball. Come with me, Kelly. How can you resist?"

"I've been to events like that before. Sorry if I don't sound more excited. Who's the sponsor?"

"Natalie Conrad."

The name rang a bell with Kelly. "Oh — I

know her. Not personally," she added quickly. "But I met her several years ago, more than once. At benefit galas for different things — charity, the arts. She's very generous."

"She can afford to be. Harry Conrad left her everything."

"I looked him up once," Kelly said. "Megarich. Mansions and estates all over Europe and the US, controlling interests in huge corporations, et cetera. Money to burn."

"Well, his widow is keeping up the tradition. This ball is supposed to benefit a new art museum to be named after him. It hasn't been built."

"The Conrads were world-class collectors," Kelly said. She was intrigued but not at all ready to say yes. "Is she actually going to be at this ball?"

"Yes."

"That's newsworthy," Kelly mused aloud. "I remember hearing that she'd become a bit of a recluse."

Deke pounced on that. "Another reason to go — you could snag an exclusive interview with her."

"You sound like our news director. Monroe would love the all-expenses-paid angle. The bean counters have been breathing down his neck."

"Your weekends don't belong to Monroe Capp," Deke pointed out. "Can we leave him out of this?"

"Okay," Kelly said cheerfully. "Sounds like I can go as myself. If I go."

"Tell me what I need to do to persuade you."

"What will I get out of it? Who's coming to this thing? Give me a rundown." She poised the pencil over the paper, ready to make notes again.

"Besides the billionaires?" Deke replied. "They head the list and they got the engraved invitations, but there's not that many of them. Moving down, some celebrities, lots of models, second-tier socialites, and people like that were contacted online. And then we get to the attractive undesirables. I've already identified a couple of high-level con artists among the RSVPs by their e-mail addresses."

"You're such a snoop. Is that proper etiquette? I guess Emily Post doesn't cover criminal investigations," she joked.

"Look it up. Let me know. Anyway, one is a friend of Bach and the other —"

Kelly interrupted him. "How did you get an invitation?"

"In the mail."

Kelly rolled her eyes. "And I had to ask." She thought it over, still deliberating. "I'm not sure I want to waste a weekend on this."

"Remember what you said about going after the biggest guy? We think he's going to be there."

Kelly was inclined to stall, although Deke had pretty much sold her on the idea. His deep voice was a little too persuasive. "Can I call you back?"

"Make it soon. There's space available on a private jet leaving Atlanta Hartfield tomorrow afternoon."

"Now you're talking."

"That's free too. But we have to jump on it. The pilot won't wait."

"We?"

"Just you and me, Kelly."

She looked at her watch. Kelly thought some more. Deke was basically offering twenty-four hours of pure fun, no strings attached. Dallas was a great city, and she hadn't been back in ages. Flying there in a private jet was a plus. No check-in lines. No fans recognizing her at the airport. Another chance at a story that had more twists and turns than a snake on a hot rock.

"Okay. I'll go."

Kelly swiveled to face Deke in a huge chair

upholstered in butter-soft leather. Sleek built-in consoles held creature comforts behind doors that opened at a touch. Liquor. Snacks. Two wide-screen televisions.

If not for the faint vibration of the engines, she could be in a very luxurious living room. It wasn't the first private jet she'd flown on, but it was definitely the nicest.

The pilot had come aboard and was going through the preflight routine in the cockpit, not looking back into the cabin once. Someone outside on the Jetway slid the door into place. Kelly watched it auto-latch from the inside. Deke got up to check it and came back.

"Do you know how to fly this thing?" she asked him.

"No. But I know how the doors work. No flight attendants, as you can see. Just the pilot."

"Should I say hello to him?" Kelly murmured. "I can't catch his eye."

"You don't have clearance to fly out with me," Deke explained. "So you are officially invisible."

"I am?" Kelly had to smile. "I don't think that's ever happened to me. Invisibility is an interesting sensation. Very interesting."

"Thought you'd like it." Deke rocked back, taking in the cabin fittings with a look of approval.

"Is this a government jet?" Kelly asked.

"Are you kidding? No. Private all the way." He patted the upholstered arms of his swivel lounger. "It belongs to a concerned citizen of Atlanta with an interest in our investigation. Sometimes he lets one of us hop on if the pilot is flying to meet him at a different airport."

"How convenient."

The pilot flipped the last switches. A prerecorded female voice came over the speakers with the usual passenger information.

"Buckle up," Deke said. "How long since you've been back to Texas?"

Kelly searched for the ends of her seat belt. "Years."

They both leaned back as the jet began to taxi toward an open runway. She looked toward a window at the small blue lights that edged it, twinkling in the darkness. The cabin illumination dimmed.

"Do you have family there?" Deke asked softly.

"Not anymore."

CHAPTER 8

Kelly watched and listened from the other side of the lobby of the Hobart, a new hotel in Dallas that had been designed to evoke a vanished era of wealth and privilege. It boasted a spectacular ballroom — a panoramic view of it was playing silently on a widescreen above the reservation desk.

She smiled to herself. Deke was charming a front desk clerk into revealing that both penthouse suites were available. Apparently the billionaires were staying elsewhere.

The young woman hesitated, then nodded when Deke asked to see the manager. It wasn't long before he came out of the front office with two keycards and a triumphant grin on his face. The bell captain personally saw to their luggage while Kelly signed the register and offered up her driver's license to a different clerk. She assured him that she would enjoy her stay. No one asked questions. It was liberating not to be recognized.

The door closed behind the bell captain before Deke would explain.

"I showed the manager my badge, dropped a few hints about our mission, let him make a couple of calls for verification, and that was that. Nice guy. He comped everyone on the team and us," Deke said when the door closed. "This ball is a security nightmare. All he wanted to know was why we hadn't contacted him sooner."

"You're very persuasive."

He laughed, looking pleased with himself. "Anything for the lady who doesn't like to share. Go ahead, pick a suite. I don't care which one I get."

Kelly opened the adjoining door. "They're exactly the same. But — the view's better in this one." She stepped over the threshold, leaving the door open.

An hour later, traces of shower steam drifted in through the open door. The drinks and relaxed conversation they'd shared on the private jet had brought them closer — but not that close. The carpeted threshold between the suites could have been an invisible force field. In unspoken agreement, Kelly and Deke stayed on their respective sides as they conducted an off-and-on conversation without once looking at each other.

It hadn't taken her long to hang up her clothes and lingerie organizer and get her cosmetics set out. Her travel routine never changed. She took out a small zippered case she kept on a high shelf in her closet at home. There were things in it she could use tonight. Kelly wanted to look them over before she showed them off to Deke.

He'd showered in the meantime, blasting the water at full heat on his side. Kelly had done the same but finished first. After several more minutes, she heard him shut off the spray. There was the unmistakable sound of a towel snapped off a rack.

It was easy to imagine that slung around his hips. Kelly remembered Deke as she'd seen him at the hotel pool in Atlanta. Only here, there would be nothing on under the towel. She smiled. She heard Deke open something, probably a grooming kit. The items inside it rattled.

Pfft. The scent of aerosol cream alerted her to his next move: shaving. He didn't say anything for a minute, concentrating on what he was doing.

She returned to what was left in her suitcase: bagged shoes, sleepwear, a couple of magazines, and a paperback book tucked in at the last minute. Hotel rooms were where she did her reading. Kelly tossed all of it on her bed in a jumble, which wasn't like her. The spicy fragrance of his shaving cream was distracting.

"I almost forgot to ask you," he called. "Do you know anyone in Dallas?"

"Not a soul."

"So you're cool with doing this. You don't have to, Kelly. Just wanted to make that clear. Again." There were long pauses between each sentence, as if he were trying not to nick himself.

"Deke, I wouldn't have said yes if I thought there was an outside chance of running into anyone who knows me. This far from Atlanta, I'm not exactly famous."

Another pause. Another *pfft* of aerosol. She couldn't wait to see him squeaky-clean and baby-faced. "That's only a matter of time," he said. "You will be."

She heard the water running in his sink, then splashing, as she picked up an armful of garments she'd draped over an armchair before her shower.

"I'm working on that," she said, hanging up the clothes. "But thanks for the vote of confidence."

"Just keep my name out of the final story."

"You bet. Which reminds me. Are you us-

182

ing a different name tonight?"

Deke was humming to himself. He might not have heard her. He didn't answer.

She visualized him rinsing off the shave cream and patting his handsome face dry. Wrapped up in a huge towel herself, her legs and shoulders bare, Kelly sat down at a vanity table with a round mirror. Her hair was up in a loose knot. She hadn't needed to wash it. When her hair was unpinned, a touch of backcombing would give her straight locks a little oomph.

Gotta work with what you got, she thought as she studied her unmade-up face. Kelly poked around in the cosmetics on the counter, selecting shades.

Deke finally replied. "I think I'll be Russ Thorn again. Can you remember that?"

"Yes." Kelly began to apply makeup. Her shower had refreshed her and left her skin looking dewy. She decided to skip foundation and let her light freckles show. Looking different was a good idea. Dramatic eye makeup, bigger hair, and chandelier earrings would be an amusing change. She was pure Texan, after all.

She studied her reflection and applied berry-stain lip gloss, then slipped the thin tube into the zippered case. Next came eyeliner and shadow, more than she usually wore but not too much. The final result was . . . sexy. There was no other word for it, even with her hair still in the prim knot.

Her on-air look was conservative and classic, but June at WBRX had done Kelly's makeup for late-night glamour events, too, and taught her plenty of tricks.

Dallas, here I come. She rose from the vanity and walked over to the wraparound window that framed the glittering skyline. The metropolis stopped at the Trinity River, a flat expanse of shoals and shallow water barely visible at night. Around her stood the towering new buildings of Dallas's downtown, some outlined in jewel-toned lights against a black sky without stars.

She knew they were there. The light of the city made them disappear, that was all. Far to the west, high above the nearly empty country where she'd spent her childhood, millions of stars still shone.

The brisk sound of a knock from Deke's suite made her turn away.

"That's room service," he said from the adjoining room. "Are you decent?"

"Not really."

There was a pause. Kelly could almost hear Deke's indrawn breath. She smiled again.

"Okay." Not looking, he half closed the

door between the suites with an out-stretched hand. "Come on over when you are."

What a gentleman. It was almost a shame. But it was inappropriate to even think about a business relationship turning into something more too quickly.

On a male spectrum from married guys looking to get lucky to single men wanting to get wild, she couldn't really place Deke. He didn't seem like any of the other investigators, government agents, or cops she'd come across in ten years of reporting. Too many of them had assumed she was available. Once in a while, when she felt like it, she was. At least she'd never fallen in love. That would have seemed like going too far.

Deke opened the hall door to the room service waiter. Kelly listened absently to the minor commotion of the tray being brought in and set down, and the faint clang of the metal domes being removed from the plates.

"Looks great," he said to the waiter, who thanked Deke enthusiastically for what had apparently been a generous tip.

Kelly got up from in front of the vanity mirror and walked to her suitcase, taking a long, almost weightless robe made of travel jersey from an inner compartment. The tailored design featured lapels and cuffs piped in white, but the navy-blue material was on the slinky side. Wearing the robe with nothing underneath was asking for trouble.

She moved to the closet alcove and let the towel fall off her nude body to the floor. Kelly knew Deke wasn't watching — the doorway was empty and there wasn't a sound from the adjoining suite.

Rummaging in the lingerie organizer, she pulled out her favorite pale blue silk bra trimmed with lace and matching panties. Kelly stepped into the panties and pulled them up. The whisper of silk over skin was barely audible. But both suites seemed even quieter.

Bra next. He couldn't possibly hear the tiny fasteners hook together.

She found the light chemise she'd brought to sleep in. It would make another layer under the robe.

In less than a minute, she was wrapped and buttoned, the long robe providing maximum coverage. Kelly picked up her laptop for a little extra protection, holding it in front of her like a shield, and went back to get the zippered case. She gave the knotted sash an extra tug as she went through the open door connecting the suites.

Deke was sitting at the table, the room

service meal for two on uncovered plates, still hot. He wore a dark tank top and athletic pants with a stripe down the outside of each leg. He was barefoot. Wet-combed, his hair looked black. He glanced up as she came toward the table, looking only at her face.

She had to give him credit for self-control. His dark eyes never moved down. Behind him, in the next room, she glimpsed an expanse of snowy white bed with nothing on it. He'd probably thrown everything he'd brought onto the luggage rack — after he'd pulled out the jock togs he was wearing — and slung his black-tie carry-on bag onto a closet hook. Men traveled light.

It was just as well she was buttoned up. Kelly sat across from him, slipping her robed knees under the draped white table-cloth and keeping the zippered case in her lap. She put her laptop beside her plate.

"Do you always bring that to dinner?" Deke inquired.

"I thought I might get a little work done. This isn't a date."

"You look gorgeous."

She waved away the compliment. "Not yet. I'm not even dressed."

"Don't remind me."

Kelly's hand moved to check the top button of her robe. It hadn't popped out. She picked up her cloth napkin and put it in her lap. "Shall we eat?"

"I'm starved," he admitted. "How about you?"

"I was thinking I'd just pick. But this looks too good."

The cold lemon chicken she'd ordered was thinly sliced and arranged atop a fresh salad. Deke's entrée, a man-size burger on a toasted roll, was still sizzling.

They started in on the meal, not talking at first. She couldn't help noticing how smoothly he'd shaved. Deke's rugged face did look younger, but there was nothing babyish about it. The dark tank top was taut over his broad chest, his strong arms on full display.

Enjoy your dinner, she told herself. This *was* just dinner, even if he looked ready to do battle. Or make love. Oblivious to her wayward thoughts, Deke upended the ketchup bottle and gave the bottom a good whack, prepping the burger to his satisfaction.

Kelly got busy with her knife and fork. She wasn't doing herself any favors by constantly checking him out. They were a team, that was all. The story came first.

They talked about other things as they ate.

"Mmm. That was really good." She put down her fork. "But I don't want to eat too much before the party."

Deke had polished off most of his burger. She didn't know where it had gone. The tank top didn't show a hint of bulge.

"I brought a few things that used to come in handy," she said, putting the zippered case on the table.

He held his hands up in mock surrender. "Nothing that takes bullets, I hope."

"No. I told you I don't own a gun."

Kelly took out a small rectangular mirror about a half inch thick. "I had this thing custom-made. Looks like a makeup mirror — actually, it is. But it also takes photos and transmits them wirelessly."

"Not suitable for dudes." Deke looked impressed. "But I want one."

"What I would do was take it out of my purse, make a trout pout at myself, and fix my lipstick."

She demonstrated with the lip gloss. Deke seemed mesmerized, but not by the gadget.

"Snap snap," she said, pressing the mirror's rim twice.

"I didn't hear anything."

"Check your phone. I just sent a photo of you staring at me."

He reached for his smartphone and tapped

the screen. "Here it comes — oh no," he groaned. "That's worse than my driver's license picture."

"Let me see." She took the phone from his hand, laughing. "Yup, definitely not something you would send to your mother. I'll take another."

"Spare me. I get the idea." He took the phone back from her and looked at the photo again before he deleted it. "Good lens on that gizmo. The image is super clear. Does it take videos?"

"Short ones. Like a minute."

"And it fits in a purse," he said approvingly. "We're going to need it. I forgot to tell you before we left — the hotel's social director issued a ban on smartphones at the ball. No cameras either, except for a couple of designated photographers."

"Seriously? Every party and club I go to, everyone's taking and sending photos."

Deke grinned. "Which end up on Facebook. And if you're famous, the front page or the evening news. Rich men don't want to get caught with a drunken leer on their faces, staring down the wrong dress."

"Hey, what about the women? There's always one who decides to dance on a table or smooch a waiter." Kelly was mildly amused. "I guess Natalie Conrad knows her guests."

"She doesn't know all of them," Deke said. "You ready to go undercover again?" he asked, relaxing in his chair.

"Ready as I'll ever be. And I'm not really undercover. She's met me. This is another easy assignment, right?"

"Maybe for you. I don't know a damn thing about Dallas society."

Kelly had to smile. "Do I look like a former debutante?"

He finished his glass of ice water. "Yes, actually. Were you one?"

She shook her head. "Are you kidding? There wasn't a chance in hell of that happening. What makes you think I come from money?"

Deke grinned and tilted his chair back. "The way you move."

"And what exactly is that supposed to mean?" Her tone had a noticeable edge.

"You walk like you own the world and no one tells you what to do."

"You're right about the second part." She pushed her plate to the side. "Anyway, no one at this event besides Natalie is likely to recognize me."

Opening her laptop, Kelly quickly changed the subject. "If you could bring me up to speed on the investigation before we make our grand entrance, that would be great. Any new developments?"

"Some. Do we have to do this right now? I should run out and get a burner."

"Huh?"

"A prepaid disposable cell phone to hand over to the guard." He was talking about the social director's ban. "I don't want to hem and haw when he asks me if I have one. It's a prop."

"Something I need?" Kelly asked.

"I'm still going to carry my real phone. So should you. Don't worry. We won't get frisked."

"I hope not."

The gown she'd brought along had no place to hide anything. It clung. It revealed. She couldn't wait to see Deke's reaction when he saw her wearing it. Right now he looked impatient.

"The hotel gift shop might sell prepaids. Worth a try," she told him. "Okay, quick questions. Do you have an update on the voice-print analysis?"

"I just got a text on that. Done."

Kelly suppressed a sigh. He never actually told her much unless she really prodded him. It wouldn't hurt to remind him that she'd done him a huge favor.

"Did Hux let you know?" she asked. "I got the idea you didn't want him to know I'd met with Gunther Bach."

Deke ignored the dig. "The update came from the lab."

"Share it. I'm all ears."

Deke brought his chair back down on the floor and reached toward the coffee table for his smartphone, tapping the screen before he read the text aloud.

"Results inconclusive. Low probability that unsub — that means unknown subject — at prior meeting is Gunther Bach. Additional analysis to follow."

Kelly looked at him impatiently. "Spare me the tech talk. Your people obviously don't have a clue at the moment."

"Bach is still a person of interest," Deke defended. "If I didn't explain it before, voiceprints are comparisons. You never get a precise match. But thanks for trying."

She felt a little miffed. "So where is Bach now?"

"Out of the country, as far as we know. We were able to pull up his flight information. He booked a one-stop with a layover in Phoenix. Final destination, Mexico City."

"Did you —"

"No. Hux tailed him to the airport, got as far as security, and saw Bach in the VIP line.

He didn't feel like flashing his badge when we had nothing on the guy."

"Oh, I could think of a few things," Kelly said. "I feel sorry for the flight attendants. But good riddance. I can't believe I wasted a lunch hour on that creep." She got up and collected the dishes and cutlery, stacking everything on the tray like a pro.

"You can leave that for the housekeeper," Deke said with amusement.

"I don't like looking at the gruesome remains."

Kelly balanced the tray on a half-moon table near the suite's main door. She opened the door and peered outside before she bent gracefully to set down the tray on the hall carpet.

"Were you ever a waitress?" he asked when she came back.

"Yes."

He looked at her expectantly. She didn't see any reason to tell him her entire life story. Deke would have to be satisfied with the basics.

"I worked my way through college," Kelly said flatly. "And it took me a while to pay off my student loans. My own fault. I majored in You Can't Get A Job With That."

"Let me guess. English Lit?"

"That's right."

"And how did you become a reporter?"

"I talked my way into a job at a local TV station because I was good at bugging people and I could write. We had five thousand loyal viewers and three advertisers."

"Where was that?"

"Virginia. In the boonies. Which is where I went to college. Once I got out of high school, I headed east and didn't come back. Then I moved to a bigger station and kept on going from there. Eventually I became an investigative reporter and then I got the Atlanta gig. Are you done asking me questions?"

"Sorry. Just curious. Ask me a few."

"I already did my homework on you and your brothers. It's amazing how little information there is on the Bannons. Especially you."

"That's how I like it," Deke answered. There was a guarded look in his eyes.

Kelly wasn't going to grill him on his past if he intended to keep it to himself. There were safer topics, like multiple unsolved homicides.

"Let's get back to the investigation. I'm beginning to wonder why you invited me to Dallas."

"The pleasure of your company?"

That didn't deserve a reply. She glanced down at her laptop and realized that she hadn't turned it on. A minute later, she got a nice surprise. "Hey, free Wi-Fi. Is that a penthouse perk?"

"Yup."

She didn't look into the glowing screen after she tapped a few keys, just at him. "Okay, nuts and bolts questions first. Did the ballistics tests reveal anything interesting?"

"Kelly, think about how long it takes to find shells and bullet fragments in a seventeen-story building and a parking lot. They're just getting started."

Kelly positioned her fingers above the keyboard. "How about bloodstains? Spots? Spatter?"

"Same deal. Blood analysis can take weeks. You know that."

"I'm not a detective." Kelly smiled sweetly. "But you know what would make a great visual? A computerized reenactment of the shooting. Graphs, bullet trajectories, figures in 3-D."

"Dream on."

"We need something fabulous before the story goes cold and no one's interested."

"That would be the purpose of the news blackout," Deke muttered.

Kelly seized on the comment. "Really? Can I quote you on that?"

"Absolutely not."

"Deke, you have access to all kinds of inside information. You and I might have the same liaison at the police department. Who's your guy?"

Find common ground. Get the other person to believe you were on their side. She had always been good at both.

"Someone I trust."

"Another non-answer," she sighed.

"I don't have to tell you everything." Deke shifted in his chair.

She figured she might as well keep him on the hot seat. "And I keep thinking we have a deal."

Deke shrugged. "I'll answer questions as I see fit. But I can't speak for the police. They have their own way of doing things, and I'm not going to second-guess their investigation."

"Is that a nice way of saying that feds and cops don't like to work together?"

"Kelly, lay off. And don't put words in my mouth," he said in a level tone. "My dad was a cop."

"And your older brother RJ followed in his footsteps," Kelly replied. "Why didn't you?"

"I'm not good at following orders. Like you."

The corners of her mouth quirked for just a second. She couldn't really argue with that.

Deke's steady brown gaze made her uneasy. So did his next question. "While we're on that subject, what did your father do?"

Kelly was aware that she'd left him an opening. She covered.

"Good question. He took off when I was really little. We never saw or heard from him again. For all I know, he's dead." There was a sudden fierceness in the depths of her green eyes. "I'm not sentimental about him."

"No reason you should be."

Deke's blunt response made her want to get the explanation over with. It wasn't classified information. Just not something she ever talked about.

"By the time I was a teenager, I figured if he didn't want me, I didn't want him. I started using my mother's maiden name."

"Johns?"

"Yes." She braced herself for the inevitable next question. It was slow in coming and Deke asked it gently.

"Is your mother still alive?"

"No. She died of cancer when I was nine.

My grandmother raised me. She's gone too. I love her and I miss her. Can we talk about something else?"

"Pick a topic."

Kelly composed herself. He gave her plenty of time.

"What exactly are you hoping to find out tonight?" she said finally. "You gave me a general idea, but I could use something more specific. Starting with how you got the invite. Were you on the A list or the B list?"

"Neither," he replied.

There was that annoying grin again. She couldn't shake the feeling that he was one step ahead of her, for reasons he wasn't about to explain. Kelly glared at him until he gave in. Or pretended to.

"One of our undercover agents knows someone on Natalie Conrad's personal staff," he said. "This ball is going to be the first of many. She plans to host similar events in different US cities and abroad."

"She has houses all over the world. Palatial houses," Kelly added. "Maybe she got tired of decorating them all."

"Could be. Maybe she just wants to get back into the social whirl." Deke reached for his laptop. "Guests are coming from all over for tonight's shindig."

"I noticed more private jets touching down right after we landed."

Deke gave a nod. "This could be the highest concentration of rich people in one place ever. And we have more bad guys to keep an eye on than we thought. Headquarters sent a fresh batch of photos while you and I were en route. Want to see them?"

"Hell yes." Kelly's eagerness showed in her body language.

"Got the file right here. Just let me open it up and — hang on." He tapped the keyboard for a minute, then turned the laptop toward her. "I removed the identifying captions. See if you can tell our agents from the bad guys."

"Deke —"

"Good training," he said cheerfully.

Her momentary exasperation vanished as she looked at the rows of photos. He'd handed her the kind of challenge she enjoyed most. There was nothing easy about it. These weren't mug shots or freeze-frames taken from surveillance video.

No sullen stares, no scowls. No unshaven jaws on the men. No messed-up hair or streaked mascara on the women. Every single subject seemed to be well-groomed and confident, and obviously a lot more intelligent than the average lawbreaker.

Kelly studied the faces for several minutes, until she realized Deke was gazing just as intently at her.

She looked up. "Okay. Test me." She rotated the laptop so they could both see the uncaptioned photos on the screen.

"Go for it."

Kelly pointed to several male faces and one young woman. "I'm not sure on everyone, but I would guess those four are crooks."

"Right on the men. Wrong on the woman."

"Is she an agent?"

"Yes. But it's interesting that you picked her out. She used to be known as the Happy Hacker, liked to break into classified databases just for the hell of it. Eventually, she was arrested and charged, but she got out of doing time by, uh, sharing her expertise."

Kelly's eyebrows raised.

"Sometimes it's what we have to do. She turned out to be one of our best, even if she doesn't like to follow the rules. So how did you pick those four?"

"Instinct. Something in the eyes, I guess. I really can't define it."

"Good work. If you can pick them out at the ball, even better. Those photos are out of date."

"But what about the others? Let me try to get all of them." There were nine other images on the screen. Kelly studied it again. "Hmm. Those two in the bottom corner are probably agents. And so is the lady at the upper left and this guy in the middle."

"Right again." He looked genuinely impressed. "Tell me how you knew."

"Those true-blue shirts and dark suits. The steady gaze and square shoulders. They look just like agents on TV," she said. "And I can see lanyards for the ID badges on the two in the corner."

Deke applauded. "Whatever works. You nailed more than half correctly. That's better than average." He tapped several keys and brought back the captions.

Kelly studied the screen with renewed interest. "Are all of them going to be there?" she asked.

"We don't know exactly which ones yet, if you mean the bad guys. They do tend to need a constant influx of cash, like Gunther Bach. Most of them aren't in his league, though. But they could steal hundreds of millions if they pick the right marks tonight."

"Just like that?"

"No," he acknowledged. "But once they get someone rich and greedy to trust them, they know how to make money disappear."

"Where to?"

"Overseas accounts. Sham funds. Churning it through banks that look the other way. Sometimes suitcases are the best way to move a lot of cash and not have it traced."

Deke tipped his chair back again and folded his arms across his chest. The nonchalant pose made her wonder how often he'd taken on assignments like this.

"Ball or no ball, this could get dangerous," she said.

"I'll cover you."

Kelly was rarin' to go. Her undercover reporting had been limited to fraud that affected the average viewer. Home-repair scams, seniors conned into giving away their savings online, lonely hearts that were bound to be broken — she'd seen and heard it all.

"I almost forgot to ask," she said thoughtfully. "Do you want me to flirt with the bad guys or hang out with the bad girls?"

Deke looked her over and laughed. "You could do both. Work the ballroom. You can't predict who's going to be standing next to you at any given moment."

"No, probably not."

"However, I can't hang around the powder room. You get to do that."

"What a thrill."

Moving to music in Deke's arms felt wonderful, even if his whispers in her ear were less than romantic. He was filling her in on some of the other guests as they whirled in slow circles on the dance floor.

The vast ballroom was packed with guests, and more were arriving every minute. The vaulted ceiling above was an exact replica of a fantasy from another age, decorated with gilt and extravagant paintings of celestial beings among clouds.

A flock of waiters in black tie wove through the crowd with silver trays, offering flutes of chilled champagne to all takers. Deke scored one for Kelly without spilling a drop and handed it to her.

"Thanks." She drank it quickly and another waiter whisked it away when she set the flute down on an empty table.

"You looked like you needed something cold."

"It is warm in here. Who are those two?" She looked discreetly in the direction of a couple stepping into the spotlight.

"The Hales," he said. "As in *the* Hales. The richest family in Dallas. And possibly the most distinguished."

A stately woman decked out in silver bugle

beads was escorted onto the dance floor by her white-haired husband. He led her into a dignified waltz.

"Bet you anything she was the belle of the cotillions back in the day." Kelly's eyes sparkled. "All white satin and long gloves and sassy as hell."

Deke agreed with a nod. "Mrs. Hale is a friend of Natalie Conrad, you know. Might even have introduced her to the late Mr. Conrad back in the day, if I remember right."

Deke did his homework. Kelly hadn't finished reading all the background material for the guests on his laptop. "Really? Here in Dallas?"

"I'd have to check."

"Where is our fabulously wealthy hostess?"

"I don't think Mrs. Conrad is actually here yet."

"How will we know? There must be close to a thousand guests."

"Beats me. Listen for a trumpet fanfare."

"Very funny."

"I'm sure she'll be announced."

His hand moved lower on Kelly's back, resting at the waist of the sage-green gown she'd brought along. The sensuous material draped perfectly and never wrinkled. The bodice was cut high, but every other part of the gown was cut low or slit up to here. She'd changed out of the blue silk bra into a backless corselette, invisibly boned for elegant support. The sensation of his fingertips on her bare skin made her shiver a little.

"You look fantastic," he murmured into her ear, his lips brushing against her flowing blond tresses. "The competition keeps sizing you up."

She glanced toward the gold-papered walls of the ballroom. The younger female guests were standing there three deep, a riot of color in bouffant dresses and sheaths, chatting with each other or their escorts.

"This isn't a pageant, Deke."

"No? Who invited so many beautiful women? I don't know when I'm going to get around to dancing with all of them," he teased.

Kelly stiffened slightly in his embrace.

"Settle down," he said soothingly. "I only have eyes for you." Which didn't keep him from returning the smile of a taffeta-clad temptress on the sidelines.

"Right."

The waltz ended and the band segued into a romantic song. Deke knew the lyrics. "My love is real," he crooned.

"Too bad the bling is fake." She stopped

for a beat and fiddled with the adjustable ring on her left hand. The "diamond" was heavy and the gold-tone band was beginning to itch.

"Can't tell from a distance. I expect the ladies think you're my wife."

"Doesn't seem to keep them from looking at you." Kelly clasped his hand again and they danced amidst the others. The elderly couple bowed out to a smattering of applause, and the younger generation got out on the floor.

"Let's act loving. Put your head on my shoulder," he instructed.

"You're too tall," she muttered into the pleats of his dress shirt.

Deke rested his chin on top of her head. "Relax. Cuddle up. Get a look around."

Kelly let her eyes close halfway and put on a blissful smile. Actually, she liked this. His arms were as solid as his chest. Black tie suited him. She nestled closer.

No one would interrupt them or cut in. From under her lashes, she surveyed the crush of people in attendance. Deke had continued to brief her while they dressed in their separate suites.

She'd already spotted two of the other agents, both male. They didn't seem to register her glance at all.

The social director's ban had been followed, as far as Kelly could tell. It was nice not to be dazzled by flashing cameras, and the glamorous guests could actually see each other without smartphones in front of their faces.

She and Deke had been asked courteously about both in the B-list line before entering the ball. Deke dropped the prepaid cell in an assigned basket, just so no one would get suspicious, and tucked the claim ticket inside his jacket.

Kelly suddenly felt Deke go tense. She took a half step back to look up at him. His thick brows had pulled together slightly over his alert dark eyes. He frowned just before he bent his head and pressed an unexpected kiss on her cheek.

"I need you to kiss me back. Right now. Sorry."

Hide in plain sight took on a whole new meaning. Kelly took a second to nuzzle the strong line of his jaw first, enjoying the fragrance of fine masculine cologne before she lifted her lips to his.

What a kiss. She was into it. So was he. When he lifted his head, she was breathless.

"Sorry," he whispered.

"Don't be. That was — great. Unprofessional, but great."

"I had to. For a second I thought I saw someone who doesn't need to know I'm here."

"Who?"

"He's gone now."

"Was he on the laptop?"

"Let's not talk about it. Dance with me." He looked down and smiled a little wickedly at her. "You need to fix your lipstick. Maybe you could take a few photos while you're at it."

"Back to business, huh?"

He drew her close again, keeping his voice low. "That's how it has to be."

The evening wore on. The guests kept arriving, providing Kelly and Deke with all the cover they needed. Introductions were made and quickly forgotten amid trivial conversations that ebbed and flowed. Kelly felt at home. Even though not everyone in attendance was from Texas, variations of the dry, warm drawl she knew so well could be heard everywhere she turned.

Deke excused himself. She didn't mind. Kelly needed to sit and collect her thoughts. She refused more refreshment from a passing server with a tray of flutes. The music and the heat and the sheer number of guests made for a dizzying combination. Kelly knew a second glass of champagne would be the equivalent of a knockout punch.

From a distance, she glanced at him occasionally. Deke stood in a corner with some of the other undercover agents, all men. Idly, she wondered where the Happy Hacker was and tried to remember the woman's real name.

Alison Powell. That was it. Alison wasn't among the crowd, as far as Kelly could tell.

Kelly intended to talk to her sooner or later. There had to be quite a story there — Deke hadn't told her the half of it. She opened her evening clutch and found a small pad with a jeweled pencil and noted down the agent's name.

Her fingers touched the tube of berry lip gloss. Taking out the mirror-slash-camera, which was tucked into a pocket of the clutch, Kelly applied a dash of gloss and pressed her lips together, enjoying the slick feel. Deke had kissed her thoroughly and well.

She looked over the mirror, surveying the legions of guests in constant motion, hoping to snap another photo of someone from Deke's laptop. Kelly had already taken several, without being able to view the results in public. Whatever. Her memory and eye for detail were just as useful.

A faint prickle of unease came over her. Someone was watching her from behind — she always knew when that happened.

Kelly raised the mirror and saw a man making his way to her. Leanly built, immaculately dressed. Silver hair. She swallowed hard, keeping her gaze on him. A minute passed. She could hear his steps over the dull roar of the huge gathering and the music.

Gunther Bach's steely eyes filled the mirror and stared into hers. A chill ran down her bare back. Kelly tucked the mirror back in her clutch and turned in her seat to look up at him. "Mr. Bach. This is a surprise."

"What are you doing here, Kelly? Do you know Natalie Conrad?"

"I met her several years ago at a gala in Atlanta."

He inclined his head in a stiff little nod. "Ah."

"Is she a friend of yours?" Kelly asked innocently.

"One might put it that way. Natalie and I were very close for years." He didn't elaborate. "When I received the invitation, I respectfully declined. I knew I would be on my way to Mexico."

"But here you are." Kelly smiled brilliantly. "Why?" She didn't mind badgering

211

him. Not after the way he'd put her on the spot in that restaurant.

"Natalie does not take no for an answer, and my new secretary gave her my itinerary. She called me when my flight landed in Phoenix and — how shall I put it? She persuaded me to attend."

His cold glance moved from Kelly to the table, taking in the fact that there was no other chair. "Do excuse me. There are other guests here who are dear friends. I would like to speak to them before I leave."

"Are you still flying to Mexico City?"

Gunther's reply was edged with venomous disdain. "That is none of your business." He moved away.

Kelly watched him go. It was as if the crush of other guests had swallowed him. Tall as Bach was, a lot of Texan men were taller. The silver-haired figure vanished. She wasn't sorry to see him go.

A rich rancher type whirled his pretty partner by in a two-step that had some of the crowd moving back and others joining in on the dance floor. Kelly started a round of applause and gave a whoop, standing up to watch and clap in time, inspiring others to do the same.

The band caught on and launched into a fiddler's tune with even faster riffs. The dancers kept going as long as they could, walking off the floor a few minutes later. The electric energy they'd generated seemed to go with them. The hubbub died down. More champagne flutes made the rounds on trays lifted high, and so did a mix of costly hors d'oeuvres.

Kelly took a few tidbits on the proffered tiny plate. She'd never been a fan of caviar, but she needed to eat something. Her dinner with Deke seemed like it had happened a week ago. She was wiping her fingertips on the napkin when a wave of fresh excitement rippled through the vast ballroom. Kelly found a place to set down the tiny plate.

Natalie Conrad had arrived.

Broad-shouldered bodyguards in dark suits led the way for the supremely elegant woman who walked behind them, acknowledging the crowd now and then with a nod. Her hair was black with a streak of natural silver in front, parted on the side and falling to her shoulders in a straight, glossy sweep. Enormous diamond drops, brilliantly real, hung from her earlobes, swinging with each step. A fitted evening suit in metallic charcoal revealed long, flawless legs and breathtakingly high heels.

She walked with grace, never stumbling

for so much as a second, a faint smile beginning to appear on her face.

The refined simplicity of Natalie Conrad's style was extremely expensive to achieve. Kelly had been in the media business long enough to know that. She had to admire how the older woman pulled it off.

Her flawless makeup betrayed no hint of her age. Only her lips seemed not quite perfect, blurred somehow — collagen, Kelly realized. The effect was nonetheless sensual.

Her head turned and her gaze alighted on Kelly. Natalie Conrad had remarkable eyes, the deep green of a northern sea, watchful and slightly weary. Kelly reminded herself that the other woman was older by several years than when they'd last met and had lost a husband into the bargain. Some changes couldn't be helped.

Natalie Conrad's beautiful eyes narrowed when she recognized Kelly. She walked on immediately, her full lips tightening into a frown of displeasure. Kelly stepped back and let the crowd enfold her.

CHAPTER 9

Kelly edged sideways through the crowd. It took her a while. No one looked at her. It was a relief.

Seeing Gunther Bach's cold eyes in back of her hadn't been fun. *Psychos in the mirror may be closer than they appear.* He'd kept on coming until he was breathing down her neck. Then they'd had that odd conversation. Kelly was surprised he'd talked to her at all.

She was grateful that all eyes were on Natalie Conrad at the moment. Kelly made her way to the open bar, stopping in front of the only bartender without a line at his station. He gave her a friendly smile. "What can I get for you?"

"Just a coke, please." The ambient noise and crush of people were getting to her. Champagne was still out of the question.

"There you go."

He served it up over ice as Kelly snapped

open her evening clutch. "Thanks." She put a tip in a crystal vase filled with bills.

The bartender looked over her shoulder and Kelly turned to see a trim, composed-looking man with a clipboard holding a thick sheaf of papers. "Miss Johns?"

"Yes?" He didn't say how he knew her name, but Kelly could guess. In less than five minutes, a murmured order from on high had been quickly issued to find out what she was doing at the Billionaires' Ball.

"May I speak to you privately?"

Other guests stepped up and got the bartender's attention. She might as well play along — but she wasn't going to let Mr. Clipboard make her feel like a party crasher.

"And you are?" she asked him.

"Neil Atwood. Assistant coordinator of the guest list. My superior asked me to find you." He fumbled for an ID badge. Kelly glanced at it. Looked real to her.

Closed-circuit cameras were everywhere. He wore an earpiece. Someone unseen must have spotted her making her way through the crowd and directed Atwood to this area. A couple moved away from the bar, fresh drinks in hand, eying her and the coordinator curiously.

"Let's talk over there." Clutch in hand, she gestured toward a brocade-padded bench in an alcove filled with dramatic flower arrangements.

"Thank you for your cooperation. I think that will do."

Kelly led the way but Atwood remained standing while she settled herself onto the bench, sipping her coke.

He riffled through the papers attached to the clipboard. "There is a media list. But you're not on it. Our oversight, perhaps."

Kelly decided to brazen it out. "I'm a plus one. I'm here with Russ Thorn."

"Ah." Atwood consulted the clipboard. "Tibbett. Thompson. There are several Thorns — and there is Russ Thorn." He took out a pen and made a note. "His name is listed with a plus-one. It seems we never received your name. Unless your middle initials are T.B.A. for To Be Announced." He chuckled dryly at his little joke.

Kelly didn't. "I know what it means." She finished her coke as Atwood reached into his jacket for a communication device. It hadn't beeped. Maybe it was wired directly into his brain along with the earbud. He pressed a button and spoke into it.

"Miss Johns is the guest of Russ Thorn," he said in a low voice. "Yes. Of Dixiecon Capital. Please fill in the blank on the master list."

How much did it matter now? Kelly didn't bother to ask. Neil Atwood couldn't be speaking directly to Natalie Conrad. More likely someone with a larger clipboard. Kelly disliked his officiousness, but she understood that it was part of his job.

"Anything else you'd like to know?" she asked brightly. She rose from the bench and handed her empty glass to a passing waiter.

"No, Miss Johns. And I do apologize for interrupting your evening — just a moment." He covered his ear to hear what the other person was saying, then talked to her. "It seems that Mrs. Conrad would like to chat with you."

"Oh?" That was out of left field.

He listened again, his expression unreadable. "In an hour. On the dais. Would that be all right?" he asked Kelly.

"Ah — yes." The chance of landing an exclusive interview with the no-longer-reclusive Natalie Conrad was why she'd come to Dallas, after all. But there was no telling why she had been summoned into the other woman's presence.

Atwood concluded the conversation with a nod. "Please meet me here in the alcove and I will bring you to Mrs. Conrad."

"Not a problem."

She watched him walk away, then turned,

almost stumbling into Deke. His warm hands cupped her bare shoulders, helping her regain her balance.

"Where'd you come from?" she asked, tugging a shoulder strap back into place when she was steady.

"I was making my way over to you at the bar, and then I saw that guy talking to you. He looked harmless. Is he?"

"His name is Neil Atwood. He's the associate coordinator of the guest list. He wanted to know who I was."

"Out of everyone here? Why?"

"First things first. I ran into Gunther Bach."

Deke didn't say anything for a few seconds. "I guess he decided to stay in the US."

"You can ask him," Kelly said. "Then Natalie Conrad and I happened to lock eyes when she made her grand entrance. Did you see her come in?"

"From a distance. I didn't see you."

Kelly smoothed her dress. "I got the feeling that she recognized me and wasn't too happy about it. So someone sent Atwood to snap at my heels."

"You should be on the guest list."

"You were, with a plus one. Not named. Thanks for not taking care of that."

"Sorry." He offered a bland smile. "Sometimes the less said, the better. If they throw water on us, we dissolve. Nothing left but the fake ID."

He ignored her silent glare, taking her elbow to steer her back into the ballroom. "There's something I want to show you."

Kelly blinked in the brilliant light. With the ball in full swing, the whirling dresses and jewels made a glittering display of wealth. "What? Money in motion?"

"No." He pointed upward. "That balcony. Want to sit there? We'd have a great view of everyone."

Kelly missed it at first. The balustered balcony projected slightly from the vaulted wall among a row of others. She realized it was the only real one. The others were masterfully painted and designed to fool the eye. From where they were standing, the illusion was perfect.

"Sure. How do you get up there?"

"There's a hidden staircase. One of the agents told me about it."

Deke took her by the hand to the other side of the ballroom, where they exited through a service door behind a caterer's station.

The hall they found themselves in had cinder-block walls that were clean and recently painted, but it was still a jarring contrast to the deluxe décor of the ballroom.

"He said to go twenty steps and then left at the second door." Deke looked down at her and smiled. "The balcony is three flights up."

Kelly made sure there was no one coming down the hall, listening for a moment for good measure. "Let's do it."

They counted to twenty like kids on an adventure and reached a door that opened into a stairwell. Kelly lifted her dress in front to climb the narrow stairs without tripping, glad when they finally stopped on the landing that led to the balcony. The music swelled and rose in waves, interwoven with the chatter and laughter of the crowd.

Deke didn't step out onto the balcony. She hung back too.

"Wow," she said softly. From high above, the grand ball was even more breathtaking. Kelly spotted Natalie Conrad on a dais with her entourage, sitting at the center like a queen at court. There was something that looked like a small house next to her. Not a doll's house — it was all jutting angles and flat planes.

"That must be the architect's model of the art museum," Kelly said, pointing.

Deke looked in that direction. "I think you're right."

"Well, that's something we can talk about. I'm supposed to meet her in about forty-five minutes," she told Deke.

He raised an eyebrow. "You didn't tell me that."

"You were being annoying."

Deke chucked her under the chin. "Don't be so touchy. Sounds like you're going to get that interview."

"Maybe. I have to lead up to it gradually." She retreated back to the landing. "I don't want her to spot me up here."

"Good point. Me neither. We're not the stars of this show."

Kelly opened her evening clutch and took out the mirror camera. "Hey, I got some interesting photos. Want to see?"

"Sure."

She pressed a hidden button and the mirror slid off into her palm. Kelly touched the camera screen. "Slide show, coming up. I believe that's Agent Two in the first shot."

"Correct." He didn't seem terribly impressed.

"And that's a waiter," she went on. "Agent Two is giving him the secret signal for more canapés. The waiter stops and — look past the tray to the left. Bad Guys One and Five are standing right there."

Deke came closer and studied the screen.

"You're right. Doing absolutely nothing il-legal. But you spotted them. Good work. I had a tough time getting close-ups of any-one."

She scrolled through the shots. Some were random. "I tried to take as many as I could. The memory card holds tons. Sometimes I just put the shutter on auto-click."

"Smart. Like sports photography."

"If fixing lipstick is a sport. I never got a chance to actually put any on. Hold this." Kelly handed him the camera part.

She found the lip gloss and applied it, us-ing the mirror in her palm. Deke occupied himself with studying the photos she'd taken a second time, scrolling back and forth. "Hey. I think you got something im-portant."

"Besides the canapés? I didn't get one of Gunther, if that's what you mean."

"I'm not talking about him. Come here. Check this out."

Kelly capped the gloss and stuck it back in her bag. "I should go. I don't want to be late for my chat with Natalie."

"You have plenty of time to get down there." Deke put himself and the camera in her way. "Real quick — watch what hap-pens."

Against her will, Kelly looked down. Deke

had pulled up a snapshot of a nondescript male guest in a gray suit. "See what I mean? He's leaning over that thirtyish woman decked out in emeralds."

"So? He wasn't on your laptop," Kelly said after studying him for a few seconds. "Or do you mean the woman?"

Deke shook his head. "No. I mean him. And he was on it. You didn't tag him as bad or good. The photo you saw was taken a couple of years ago. Looks like he's lost a lot of hair since then."

He zoomed back in until only the couple's hands were visible. The woman was nervously twisting an emerald bracelet. In photos taken seconds apart, shown quickly, Kelly saw her take it off and rub her wrist. Then the woman half turned, distracted by someone Kelly couldn't see.

Deke zoomed in as tightly as the camera would allow. The man's hand covered the removed bracelet. Deke zoomed back to show the whole scene again. The man was steps away from his victim, his back barely visible. The bracelet was gone.

"Huh. I really didn't see that happening," Kelly said with amazement. "But like I said, no one wears real jewels to an event like this."

"Send me the photos, please. I think this

woman did. I overheard someone having hysterics over a missing bracelet. The security people were trying to calm her down."

Kelly took the camera from him, pushing buttons to send the photos to his e-mail. "Really?"

Deke nodded. "I didn't see her, but I'd bet anything it's the same woman."

"Not to be cold-blooded about it, but she should have been more careful. Things like that happen," Kelly said. "But — how does it connect to your investigation?"

"That guy's got a record and more than one felony conviction. He's been out on parole for a while. If the cops can arrest him for grand theft — and I think that's what we're looking at — we might get him to talk about a whole lot of other things. He'll be facing hard time if he doesn't."

"Over a bracelet? Why would he risk prison again in the first place?"

"Criminal compulsion. Staying in practice. Just plain stupid. Take your pick."

"How come I didn't notice him in action?" she asked.

"You weren't looking for anything like that. Which is why we work in teams, Kelly. We cover each other."

"Hmph."

"Besides, crooks of his caliber have a sixth

sense about being watched. I hope we can find him before he gets away."

The mayhem at the abandoned building at Atlanta came back to her. Investigating was one thing. Dodging bullets was another. "Good luck. That's where I draw the line."

"Damn right. I'm not putting you in danger."

Kelly zoomed in on the bracelet. "Look at those big green rocks. If they're real, that bracelet could be worth close to a million."

"Put it in perspective. Gunther Bach probably steals a hundred million every year, maybe more. And he's still not the biggest guy."

"I was just going to ask you about that —"

"Later." Deke gestured toward the stairs beyond the landing. "Let's go."

Kelly walked quickly around the ballroom's perimeter, going back the way she came but without Deke. He was mingling again. The bracelet thief had to be long gone.

She reached the alcove a few minutes ahead of time. Neil Atwood was waiting for her, half-concealed by the flower arrangements. He wasn't holding the clipboard.

"Do I have time for the ladies' room?" she asked hopefully.

Atwood looked at his watch. "Just barely. Please hurry."

She dashed in. There was no one in front of the mirror and she didn't hear anyone in the stalls. The presence of a ladies' maid guarding fresh hand towels and a tray of little conveniences would limit casual chatter between female guests anyway.

Kelly set her evening bag on the marble counter, then dampened a folded hand towel with cold water and pressed it to her cheeks. Then she ran a small comb quickly through her hair, wishing she'd worn something more demure. The backless, clingy dress would look wrong somehow next to Natalie Conrad's elegant evening suit.

That couldn't be helped. Kelly left and followed Atwood through the crush of guests to the dais where Natalie Conrad still sat.

Atwood brought Kelly up the low stairs to the side, approaching Mrs. Conrad with deference. There was an attractive older man on either side of her, leaning in attentively as she spoke in a low voice. They were both impeccably groomed. One had dashes of silver at the temples and the other had snow-white hair. Natalie Conrad seemed younger than either man, but she might have been close in age to the first.

She stopped talking when she saw Kelly, rising graciously from her seat. The two men rose also. "Run along," she told them playfully. "We can pick up where we left off later."

They obeyed, nodding to Kelly without expecting to be introduced and leaving the dais. Atwood retreated to a respectful distance.

"I was so surprised to see you when I walked in, Kelly," the older woman began. "Forgive me for not smiling. I wasn't sure it was you at first. By the time I realized it was, the crowd had closed in."

"It's a wonderful ball. Thank you —" Kelly stopped. She couldn't say *thank you for inviting me.* She hadn't been invited.

"You and I had such a nice chat in Atlanta at the benefit gala — ah, it was years ago, wasn't it? But I remembered you the instant I saw you. What are you doing now? Are you still a reporter?"

"Not really," Kelly said. "I anchor the evening news. Occasionally I do a feature."

"Oh, I see," Natalie said. "I must confess that Monroe Capp let me know you'd be here." She smiled blandly.

And Kelly thought she'd escaped unnoticed. Good old Monroe. He had a way of finding out what everyone was up to and he loved to meddle. But how did he know Natalie?

"Kelly, please sit." The older woman made it easier for her by resuming her own chair. "You must be exhausted. By the way, he mentioned that you'd been shot while you were taping a report. Some sort of criminal altercation, was it? I had no idea that reporting could be so dangerous."

Kelly racked her mind for the right words to downplay her experience. "I just happened to be in the wrong place at the wrong time. I wasn't hurt."

"Even so — you had to have been traumatized."

The older woman's nervous manner and fixed stare were hard to take. Kelly looked away. "Not really. All in a day's work for me."

"My dear, I admire your courage."

"I really was just standing there. There are neighborhoods in Atlanta where you don't want to do that. I wouldn't even call the area a neighborhood. It's slated for development."

"A word that so often means condemned."

Kelly looked at her, puzzled. "Natalie, with all due respect, I'd rather not think about the incident. If we could talk about something else . . ."

"Of course." The older woman condescended to her with a gracious smile. "Are you enjoying the party? I hear you've been dancing nearly all night."

One thing was certain about Natalie Conrad: she paid extremely close attention to a lot of things — and she could pay other people to do her watching for her.

"What else can I do? The band keeps playing."

Natalie's silvery laugh rang out. "My dear, I think it is the company you keep. Is the young man your fiancé? Last time we met I believe you were unattached."

"No," Kelly said quickly. "Russ is just a friend. He's a wonderful dancer."

Natalie gave her an amused, conspiratorial look. "I don't know him, but I wish I did. Atwood had a photo — he and his team keep me informed as best they can."

Kelly had noticed that.

"The guest list just kept getting longer. We need donors at all income levels for this fund-raiser. Not everyone has a million to give away."

"I certainly don't," Kelly said cheerfully.

"So did you know I was hosting the ball when Mr. Thorn asked you to accompany him?"

"I did, yes. He made sure to tell me. He

didn't know that you and I had met before."

"Such a small world."

Kelly was desperate to change the subject again. Natalie's gaze held an inquisitive intelligence that went far beyond her ability to make small talk. "Tell me more about the art museum, Mrs. Conrad."

"Please call me Natalie."

Fair enough. Kelly didn't mind. "Is that the architect's model?"

Natalie looked proudly at the small structure beside her. "Yes. Isn't it marvelous."

That didn't seem to be a question. Kelly agreed with a nod.

"And it will cost millions to build," the older woman said thoughtfully. "I do wish you worked in Texas and not Georgia."

"I don't know if I ever told you that I'm a Texas native — does that help?" Kelly could almost feel the twang coming back. She suspected that wouldn't impress Natalie Conrad one way or another.

"Oh. How interesting. But it doesn't really matter. I know you and I would trust you to produce a feature story."

"What about the Dallas media?" Kelly asked.

"Out in force," Mrs. Conrad said dismissively. "In all honesty, an art museum benefit simply isn't their sort of story.

Nonetheless, they are here."

Kelly didn't need to look at dangling press passes. She'd spotted several reporters already, swilling champagne and eating all the coconut shrimp. Took one to know one. She'd made meals out of canapés and free drinks more times than she could count, back when she was an underpaid newbie. There were undoubtedly many more media people here tonight representing local TV, the newspapers, and the blogosphere.

Natalie's disapproving frown eased into a smile as she thought of something else. "Would a feature on an east coast station help us get national coverage?"

"Why not?" Kelly took the opportunity that had just been offered. "We've had several stories picked up by the major networks. They're cutting costs too. In-depth features, general interest — they get to go national without sending out a team of their own."

"Ah. But even so —"

"You once had a home in Atlanta, as I remember."

"Yes. I still do."

Kelly picked up on what the other woman left unsaid. Natalie owned many houses. They weren't homes, strictly speaking, since she probably didn't stay more than a week in any of them, like a lot of rich people.

"We could say you are an Atlanta resident, you know, part-time. And of course the story would be mostly about contemporary art."

As if. The average viewer wouldn't be wowed. Art with a capital *A* was a public-television topic, not a ratings raiser. But Kelly wasn't going to give up.

"With you to introduce it in a brief interview —"

"My dear, this isn't about me." Natalie Conrad's soft voice was threaded with steel. "After my husband's death, I became a much more private person."

Kelly wasn't going there. *Some say you became a recluse, Mrs. Conrad. Can you tell us about that?*

"But this project changed everything." Natalie gestured toward the architect's model. "Harry had always admired the Fisher Museum in Houston. I think ours will be a worthy rival."

She sat up, her back ramrod straight. Natalie Conrad's most striking characteristic was her pride. It put the steel in her voice and burned in her eyes as she turned her classically beautiful face to Kelly.

"I'm sure it will." Once again Kelly noted the blurred line of Natalie's lips, feeling a

233

little ashamed for thinking it was due to collagen. Tears, emotions, even suppressed anger, could give a woman that look.

"I hope to name it for him. The museum board must agree," Natalie said, looking down at the model again. Seeming dissatisfied, she turned it so that a projecting angle faced front.

Must agree? Did anyone ever say no to Natalie Conrad? Kelly told herself not to fill in too many blanks until she had more information. "I think that's a great idea," she said.

The other woman didn't answer. Natalie Conrad seemed pre-occupied as she looked at the model museum, her expression troubled. Kelly set aside the idea of an interview for the moment, sensing that the subject was effectively closed.

Well-dressed guests, a woman and three men, had come up onto the dais and seemed to be waiting to speak to Mrs. Conrad, kept discreetly at a distance by Neil Atwood and other staffers in dark suits.

The older woman barely looked up as Kelly said something about getting back to the party. She had the feeling she was about to be dismissed.

"Please stay," Natalie said suddenly. "If you decide to do a feature — and we would

234

be honored — you'll want to hear what those people have to say." She gave an almost invisible nod in their direction.

"Won't they mind if I listen?" Kelly asked.

"I don't care." Natalie's smile was less than warm. "They want something from me — their names on a wing or a gallery. And I want something from them."

Kelly didn't have to ask what that might be. The honor would cost many millions. Worth it, apparently, for those who could afford it.

"Forgive the cliché, my dear, but time is of the essence," Natalie continued. "We need to put together the museum's financing tonight if we can. Listen and learn."

Kelly sat back.

The murmured conversations with the people on the short line weren't as interesting as trying to figure out Natalie Conrad's accent. She didn't have one. Her precise pronunciation could be the product of a finishing school, probably abroad. Kelly tried to remember where Natalie was from and drew a blank, realizing that she knew more about the late Mr. Conrad than she did about his widow.

An hour passed. The private negotiations were over and deals had been struck. The money at stake was mind-boggling. And all for an unbuilt art museum with no start date for its construction, as far as Kelly could tell. She hadn't been able to glean any hard facts at all.

With pledges from ultra-rich donors secured, the bidding opened to the public: a select group of the merely wealthy seated in gilt chairs in several rows before the dais.

A roving spotlight moved over the group, stopping on each donor as names were called from an unseen microphone and the amounts announced. Huge monetary gifts were added to a running tally, accompanied by roars and cheers. Bigger spotlights began to rove over the crowd in the ballroom, ratcheting up the excitement. Kelly had never seen anything like it.

Natalie Conrad presided from the dais, encouraging the attendees to dig deeper. The final total was staggering. Between the glaring spotlights and the frenzied noise, Kelly had had enough and felt a mean headache coming on. Slipping away down the low stairs to the side, she went in search of Deke.

Finding him was an impossibility. It was after midnight and the party was deteriorating. It got worse once she was in the thick of it. A stiletto heel took a step back and nearly nailed her gown. Kelly lifted her skirt a few inches and hung on to it, pushing through loud guys and women with smudged makeup trying to be heard over the din. A large hand cupped her rear and squeezed. Kelly turned around and swung. Her closed fist just missed the jerk. He guffawed and stumbled away.

Forget it, she told herself. She needed to get to the penthouse and just chill out, call room service for some real food and something hot to drink. Deke might already be there on the other side of the adjoining door. They could trade notes, talk, relax — she wanted to do that, badly. Then a roving spotlight stopped and trapped him in a circle of cold light.

Deke was at a table with two women, having a grand old time. They couldn't see her.

Kelly recognized one of them as his fellow agent, the Happy Hacker. Mousy but cute. The other one was familiar. That taffeta dress and the come-hither smile — Deke had winked at her while they were dancing.

Was Taffy an agent too? No telling. Kelly almost didn't care one way or another. But it would have been nice to have a *complete* list of the players in advance, she thought grimly. Apparently Deke felt entitled to give out that information on a need-to-know basis.

Moving on when the spotlight did, she glided past the suddenly darkened table, noting the empty bottle of champagne stuck upside down in a bucket of melting ice.

Whoopee. The party was definitely over as far as Kelly was concerned. She didn't turn around when she heard Deke call her name. But she was whipped around to face him seconds later, his grip on her arm almost painful.

"Where are you going?"

"Bed."

"Not by yourself."

"I don't need a babysitter, Deke. I don't even need a night-light. You can party on. I've had enough."

"Stop it. Both those women are colleagues."

"I recognized the hacker." She pulled away from his hold, trying not to make a scene. Kelly made the mistake of glancing back at the table.

Deke's companions were looking at her curiously.

"The other one is also an agent." The mocking gleam in Deke's dark eyes didn't reassure her on that score.

"Of course." Her lips curved into a stiff smile of response. She was mad at herself for being jealous, even for a few seconds.

The feeling was irrational and unwarranted. The look on his face didn't make things better. Smacking him wasn't an option, but it would have been satisfying. "See you in the morning."

"Kelly —"

He couldn't stop her from heading out. Kelly walked on, keeping her gaze on an open exit to the side, the only one that wasn't swarmed with people.

Then the lean figure of a man walked swiftly through the shadowy hall beyond the doors. Even at this distance, the aristocratic profile was recognizable. Gunther Bach.

She glanced back toward Deke, instinctively seeking confirmation. He caught up with her. "Don't follow him," he muttered. "That's not your job."

"I didn't intend to."

The crowd surged, separating her from Deke. A huge man with unruly black hair and a shapeless suit stepped between them, his back to Kelly. Deke looked up at the interloper with an expression of mingled anger and surprise.

Her lucky break. Kelly went a different way without a backward look at him, going through double sets of doors with a stream of people. There was no sign of Bach in the lobby. She made double sure he wasn't following her when she stepped into the elevator that would take her to the penthouse suite.

Exhausted and preoccupied, Kelly didn't see Deke catch up again and watch her until the doors closed. She had no idea that Huxton had stationed himself on their floor for the night or that he confirmed her safe entry into the suite with a text to Deke. All she wanted to do was flop on a freshly made bed and not think.

Wire-framed fixtures with bare bulbs threw harsh light over the cinder-block walls of a corridor meant for hotel staff and catering equipment. Gunther Bach nodded to a slightly built man going in the opposite direction, pushing a wheeled cart overloaded with dirty glassware and plates. He could only hope the fellow would take him for a banquet manager or some such personage.

The man kept his head down, as if he hoped not to be noticed as well, and concentrated on what he was doing. He made a turn into the chaotic work area Gunther had already passed. A cloud of dishwashing steam drifted down the corridor when the cart rattled through the doors.

Gunther coughed and continued to walk

240

briskly, heading for an exit that led to the hotel's parking lot. Once outside in the night air, he breathed more easily. He narrowed his eyes, adjusting to the relative darkness of the parking lot, looking for his luxury rental before glancing at his watch.

He had ten minutes before Konstantin would arrive. Time enough to collect himself and rehearse what he would say. His silent partner would expect a complete report.

First, Gunther took out a silver cigarette case and treated himself to a calming smoke. Then he crushed the butt underfoot and got into his car to wait.

Soon enough, a huge black SUV rolled past him. Gunther glanced at the plates, comparing the numbers to several sets he had memorized. One set matched. The vehicle was Konstantin's.

He watched the SUV go into a parking space, getting out of his car when the brake lights went off. Gunther looked around the parking lot, which was empty, except for a few exuberant drunks who weren't likely to remember him or anything else.

The passenger door of the SUV opened with a soft click as he appeared in its mirror. Gunther got in.

Konstantin himself was at the wheel, which was unusual. His bulky body seemed too large for the seat he occupied and his black, disheveled hair brushed against the interior roof. The dark blue birthmark on his face didn't show much in the shadows. A stray glint of light revealed a heavy ring on one of the meaty, thick-knuckled hands resting on the inner curve of the steering wheel.

The man was a brute. But highly intelligent. At this stage of the operation, Konstantin ranked one level below Gunther himself.

"Good evening," Gunther said.

Konstantin growled a reply as he pushed a button. Gunther heard the doors lock.

"Where is your driver?"

"He was needed elsewhere," the other man replied. "Too many ears make problems. Now talk."

Gunther obliged in detail. Occasionally Konstantin cut him off with an impatient grunt, telling him to get to the point.

"We made many new friends," Gunther said sarcastically. "With luck, some will talk to us tomorrow or the next day. Even I have never seen so many rich people in one place — Natalie Conrad is like a magnet. Imagine paying millions to put your name on part of a building. But people do."

"Were you photographed with her?"

"No," Gunther said. "But she knew I was there. She reached me at the airport just in time. The opportunity could not be ignored."

"We were ready for you," Konstantin said simply.

He reached for a flask and unscrewed the cap. The sickly-sweet smell of plum brandy reached Gunther's nose. The other man took several swigs and wiped his mouth on the back of his hand.

"One of my men saw you talking to a blond woman. Very pretty. Who was she?" Konstantin asked the question as if he knew the answer and was only looking for confirmation.

"Kelly Johns. She is a news anchor from Atlanta. We had lunch together recently — very recently. She tried to pump me about my financial enterprises, supposedly for a feature report."

"And?"

"I thought of a distraction. My attempt at seduction disgusted her."

Konstantin laughed rudely. "For a reason. You are old."

Gunther bit back a curt reply. "But I found out what I wanted to know."

"Go on." The bulky man took another nip of brandy.

"That she was lying about her reasons for meeting with me. For a fraction of a second there was fear in her eyes."

"Always good to see," Konstantin muttered.

Gunther anticipated the next question. He took several sheets of thin paper from an inside pocket of his jacket and unfolded them on the dashboard. Konstantin squinted.

"She is not on this list. Therefore, she was not invited. Security was very tight for this event. Natalie told me that. Of course, she has no idea why I changed my plans at the last minute. I suspect she thinks I still have feelings for her."

Konstantin shook his head. "You?"

"I won't shatter her cherished illusion. She is still useful, and we need new clients with deep pockets. None of our accounts have been frozen."

"Yet." Konstantin seemed distracted. Gunther noticed him looking into the rearview mirror. There were other people in the parking lot. Well-dressed guests were waiting in the valet line for their cars to be brought.

Double-wide service doors opened suddenly. A long cart was thrust through, laden with thick, yard-high rolls of something gray. Gunther caught a glimpse of brightly colored edging. The red carpets were being removed from the ballroom.

"So much work," Konstantin muttered. Three men pushed the heavy cart, and one in front helped steer it to a storage building.

He and Gunther watched in silence as a second cart followed the first. The men handling it set the brakes to keep it from moving and went to help the others unload.

Gunther turned and looked over his shoulder. They were not that far away. He could see a dark stain spread beneath the second cart, dripping from a corner. A roll of carpet thrown on top bulged in the middle.

He faced forward again. Konstantin offered a few words of explanation. "It had to be done. And I did not want the body in my car."

"Who was killed?"

"A thief. His name is not important."

CHAPTER 10

Kelly awoke to sunlight pouring in through the penthouse suite windows. She'd forgotten to close the drapes before collapsing into bed last night. She pushed back the covers and sat up, yawning. At least she hadn't slept in her evening gown. There was a drift of silky, sage-green material over one of the armchairs. Her high heels were where she'd kicked them off, more or less in a corner.

Barefoot, she padded to the bathroom, looking for her robe. The hotel air-conditioning had been auto-set to high, and the chemise she'd slept in wasn't enough to ward off the chill. Tightening the sash knot on her way back, Kelly noticed a piece of paper that had been shoved under the adjoining door of the penthouse suites.

She hesitated, but only for a second. Kelly picked it up.

First five women to call win a free breakfast!

Deke hadn't signed it. But by now she
knew the number he'd added — it had appeared on her phone often enough. Kelly
looked at the clock. 8:46. Way too early to
activate her sense of humor. She ripped the
note in half and shoved it under the door to
his side.

She was annoyed with him, nothing more.
That he hadn't told her absolutely everything about the operation wasn't the end of
the world, and so what if she'd been startled
to see him in the spotlight with two women.
Her momentary flash of jealousy was completely irrational. Deke was an intriguing
guy, and great-looking, but Kelly had accompanied him to Texas to get another side
of a story she wanted to do. It was best to
leave it at that.

She walked to the window, gazing out on
Dallas by day. Like Atlanta, it was divided
by fast-moving highways weaving through
skyscrapers and older buildings of brick,
though Dallas was nowhere near as green.
The morning sun brought out the businesslike look of the city. The magic was gone.

Kelly turned away, looking for the room
service menu. She frowned when she saw

that another note had replaced the first on the floor. There was something else beside it — a long, green stem.

He must be enjoying this little game. Kelly walked over and stopped by the second note, reading it without picking it up.

Sorry. Talk to me. P.S. The rose won't fit under the door.

Kelly relented. She turned the lock and opened it. There stood Deke holding eleven red roses in a vase. She picked up the long-stemmed one on the floor and stuck it in the vase. "Are those a peace offering?" she asked.

"Yes."

"What for?" Her question was sincere enough. "You didn't do anything wrong."

"Good to know."

"Besides, I'd rather have coffee." She walked in, looking around some more.

"It's in the carafe. Good morning. How are you?"

Kelly gave him — and the room — a fast once-over before she replied. "I'm barely awake."

He looked a little silly holding that tall vase of long-stemmed roses, what with the stubble outlining his strong jaw and his messed-up dark hair. He wore the same tank top and athletic pants with a stripe down the side that he'd had on before dressing for the ball yesterday.

There were no signs of a passionate encounter anywhere in the suite. The couch pillows were lined up. There were no delicate underthings tossed on the floor or hanging from the chandelier. Through the bedroom door, she could see that the king-size bed had been slept in, but only on one side. The other half of the comforter was unwrinkled, still neat and square-cornered.

Done. Deke didn't even seem to notice that his suite had been inspected.

He set the vase by the widescreen TV and gestured toward the table, which was set for two. "I was hoping you'd join me."

"Look, about last night," she began, then stopped.

"I understand."

"Let me finish," Kelly said firmly. "After I left Natalie Conrad up there, I just wasn't up for meeting anyone. Call it nervous system overload. I didn't mean to be rude to your colleagues."

"They were cool with it. You did look tired."

The second comment irked her. Kelly lifted one of the metal domes on the room service spread, happy to see crisp bacon and scrambled eggs. She could use a hearty breakfast. "One of your female agents would be a good angle for the story."

"I was thinking the same thing myself."

"Really."

"They do things differently from us guys," he began.

"How?"

"I can give you their numbers if you'd like to do some interviewing. After hours, we huddled at the hotel bar, had a few drinks, caught up on business —"

"I get it." Kelly picked up a piece of buttered toast and bit off a corner. "So did you find out everything you needed to know last night?"

"I was about to catch up to you to talk about that when that huge guy stepped between us."

Kelly thought for a minute and then she remembered, but vaguely. Black hair, badly dressed. She hadn't seen his face. "Who was he?"

"No one you would want to know. I recognized his face from a photograph Hux took. Didn't expect to see him here, though. I'm not sure if it means anything." Deke pulled out a chair for her. "I'll brief you on other stuff during breakfast, okay?"

She sat, tucking her robe under her and adjusting the lapels. His suite was chilly too. "After. I need to eat." Kelly noticed that Deke didn't seem to feel the least bit cold. Worked for her. She got to admire him half-dressed by the light of day.

He looked really good in the morning. One man in a million did, and here she was with him. Being with him, about to eat breakfast with no one else around, felt pleasantly domestic — in a highly sensual sort of way.

"You spent a lot of time with Natalie Conrad," Deke said. He leaned back in his chair, munching calmly on the last piece of toast. "What's your take on her?"

Kelly searched for the right word. "Natalie? She's — intense. And hard to figure out. But this project means a lot to her. She wants to name the museum after her late husband. I got the feeling that she'd do anything to make it happen."

Deke brushed the crumbs from his hands. "The bidding frenzy was really something. Mrs. Conrad knows how to get rich people to give it up."

Kelly poured coffee for both of them. "They get their names on the museum. If it gets built."

Deke looked at her inquiringly.

"I noticed that she never mentioned a start date or where it would be located. An architect's model doesn't mean anything. You have to wonder, right?"

"That works both ways," Deke pointed out. "Pledges don't mean anything either until the money is in the bank."

Kelly nodded, cradling the warm cup in both hands as she sipped coffee. "True. Cynical, but true. So how about your investigation? Any leads?"

"The short answer is yes. The team has to put it all together. Looks like our bad guys are trying to get into Dallas and start doing business. We can request go-aheads to investigate some, do online surveillance on others, and keep talking to our informants. If big money is being moved, we move in."

"Moved?" Kelly laughed. "You mean like in a truck?"

"They do it all the time. But it's not the easiest way." Deke switched the subject. "Hey, I got the photos of the bracelet thief to the cops — thanks again."

"You're welcome. Don't mention my name if they catch him. I don't have time to chat with detectives about something I didn't see."

"No problem," Deke teased. "I'll take the

credit. Did you get any other photos after that?"

"Not once I was sitting next to Natalie. And not after. The noise, the bling, the lights —" Kelly set down her cup and rubbed her temples. "Go away, little headache. Please go away."

"Sorry about that."

She smiled at him. "I'll live. I wanted to be there. And I got something out of it."

"Is Natalie going to give you an interview?"

"That's a long shot, but I did ask," Kelly replied. "I got a polite no."

"Which won't stop you."

She acknowledged that fact with a shrug. Deke rose and went to get his laptop, bringing it over to the table. Kelly watched idly until the screen came to life.

He'd created a spreadsheet of sorts, with some of the photos he'd shown her before the ball and some new ones. Crooks to the left, likely victims to the right, and available agents in a middle column. Several names of celebrities and the socially prominent popped out at her.

The Hales were not among them, Kelly noticed. Not every rich person was an easy mark. She suspected that the dignified Mrs. Hale would think nothing of using her beaded evening bag to beat up a crook.

"Are you going to tell those people to watch out?" she wanted to know. "Besides the bracelet getting stolen, nothing happened, right?"

"Not yet. But it wouldn't be the first time we alerted banks in advance. For what that's worth," he added. "We don't always know who's on our side and who isn't."

"What about someone like Gunther Bach?"

"Not a damn thing we can do about him until a whole lot more dots get connected. We watch and wait, that's all. He may be en route to Mexico again. And from there, we don't know."

Kelly studied the faces. "I forgot to ask if you had run-ins with any of these characters before."

"Only one." He pointed to a man with a narrow face. "I testified against him a couple of years ago. That was why I had to kiss you."

The memory was potent. The suddenness of his lips on hers, the strength with which he'd pulled her body close to his — she tried not to look at Deke now. "Is that your standard evasion technique?" she joked.

"Actually, no. It's not in the manual."

Kelly could feel his gaze on her. She kept

her tone light and her mind on the business at hand. "Whatever. So you think these new developments might be related to the shooting in Atlanta?"

"It's a strong possibility. Some of what we've been hearing on the streets suggests it, and the evidence could point that way."

"Could you be less specific?"

He picked up on her sarcasm without reacting to it. "We're a long way from arresting anyone. We can't get warrants without probable cause and actual facts. There are a lot of pieces to this puzzle. This is only the beginning."

"Hmm. I like the sound of that."

"Say what?"

"This could be a series, not a one-time feature." Kelly looked up at him. "Can you e-mail me these files?"

"No."

The blunt reply didn't invite a discussion of the reasons why he couldn't. Kelly let it go. She'd wangle the information she wanted out of him somehow, promise him something he really wanted — then make him wait for it.

"Okay. Well, I should get back to Atlanta tonight." She didn't want to ask him if he was staying or going. "Is that jet available?"

"No. However, I'm authorized to buy you

a commercial ticket."

"Sweet. Go for it." Kelly sipped the last of her coffee as Deke tapped the keyboard.

He waited for an airline page to download, and scrolled through the available flights. "There's a three-ten nonstop to Atlanta with a couple of seats left in first class. Window or aisle?"

"Window. If I can look out, I don't have to talk to anyone."

"I know what you mean. You're checking a bag, right?"

"Yes." She put down the empty cup. "Before I forget, thanks for the look at your operation. Going undercover with you really was interesting."

Deke closed the files and shut down the laptop. "I guess we both got what we came for."

Looking at his broad shoulders as he turned away from her made her inclined to disagree. That wasn't all. Deke had a way of walking that would catch any woman's eye. Long legs, nice butt, solid muscle in the middle, and those *arms.* She wouldn't mind being held in them right now. Maybe messing up his disheveled dark hair even more. Kelly was regretting her ankle-length robe and ironclad professionalism.

"Yes. I should type my notes while everything's still fresh in my mind. Beats browsing at the airport bookstore."

"You have plenty of time."

Kelly made a wry face. "Just enough. I have to pack, shower, grab a taxi, and trek to the gate."

"Even so —"

"Deke, my last flight out of DFW involved the monorail, a shuttle bus, and close to a mile of walking. It's not my favorite airport."

"It is big," he admitted. "Think of it as exercise."

"Don't you get enough chasing crooks?" Deke certainly looked like he did. She wondered when and if she would get to see him showing this much muscle again.

"Not always." He clicked a final key. "Okay, you're good to go. Want me to send the reservation to your smartphone?"

"Please."

A moment later, her phone chimed, distantly, inside the evening bag in her suite. "Modern living. I love it," she said. "Thanks."

"You're welcome."

Kelly got up to go, tugging at her robe. "Deke, one more question," she said casually.

"Ask away."

"Since when does the government authorize a freelance agent to buy first-class tickets?"

"It doesn't. I used my miles."

Kelly shot him a disbelieving look. "I hope you didn't use them up."

"There's more where those came from."

She was all for hustling, but he seemed a little too eager to send her on her way. "Aren't you sweet. But that really wasn't necessary. Your next ticket is on me. I have more frequent-flyer miles than I know what to do with."

"Forget it. My pleasure. Call me when you get to Atlanta."

Several hours later, Kelly was relaxing in a comfortable first-class seat, letting her mind drift as she looked out the plane window. She had the row to herself and had curled up with a book she wasn't reading and notes she wasn't writing. Lazy clouds drifted over sprawling ranches, which changed to farms dotted with irrigation circles as they flew on. The patchwork-quilt look of the landscape was comforting. After a while she dozed off.

"If it isn't the Happy Hacker," Deke said. He tossed a duffel and a garment bag on the bed in a different hotel, a twenty-minute cab ride away from the first, in a run-down neighborhood of Dallas.

"Give it a rest, Bannon. That nickname is getting old." The young woman already in the room didn't bother to turn around to look at him. Her smooth, light brown hair was drawn back into a long ponytail that lined up exactly with her spine.

Hux entered in another minute. "She's right. Want me to beat him up, Alison?"

"That's okay, Hux. I can do it myself." Alison Powell stared into a laptop set on a rickety table that leaned against the wall. Her gray eyes gleamed blue, reflecting the screen.

"Sorry. I promise never to call you that again. What a dump," Deke muttered, looking around.

"You picked it," Alison reminded him.

Hux set a suitcase on the luggage rack he unfolded and looked around with dismay. "You couldn't find anything better?"

"It's close to the pawnshop," Deke said. "I didn't want to hang around on the street in a rented car."

"You and me both." Hux turned to Alison. "Any sign of the guy?"

"Not yet." She rubbed her eyes. "I'm sick of surveillance, I can tell you that. What took you guys so long?"

"The hotel manager wanted my analysis

259

of the ballroom security video. He let us monitor it because of the phone and camera ban," Hux answered.

"Anything useful on it?" she asked.

"Only nine thousand people went in and out of that hotel during our time frame. So, no. Not a damn thing." Hux glanced at his partner. "And after I got done with him, Deke had to get his lady friend to the airport."

"Awww," Alison said. "What a gentleman."

"I try to be," Deke sighed. He went over to Alison and bent slightly to look into the screen. "Look at that. We're right behind the counter. We can see every customer that comes up to it, full face."

"No sound, though," she said.

"Can't have everything. Great visuals. Exactly what we need. Bet the other teams on stakeout don't have this," Deke replied.

"It only took me five minutes to hack in," Alison said. "They spent serious money on their system. Digital security cams, wireless feed to new computers. Lame password, though. Typical."

"Good work." Deke walked to the grimy window and looked out at the flashing sign below. WE NEVER CLOSE. The pawnshop was a big place with metal grates over the brightly lit windows. According to his police contacts, they did a brisk business and didn't fence stolen goods. They made more money staying on the right side of the law. In return, the police patrolled the street regularly, which allowed the owners to stay open twenty-four hours a day, seven days a week.

The sound of a cell phone had Hux digging in his pocket. He picked up an incoming text. "Huh. The Dallas PD found a body outside the hotel. Rolled in a carpet, left on a storage cart. Unidentified male, thirty to forty. Removed to morgue. Anyone want to go see?"

"No." Alison had never liked the gritty side of investigations.

"Later. He isn't going anywhere," Deke answered.

Hux stumbled over something on the floor and swore. He bent to retrieve it and held it up. "Ugh. A flip-flop."

"Only one?" Deke asked absently.

"Yeah, only one," Hux said with disgust. "What, do you think we could pawn a pair?" He tossed the rubber sandal into the wastebasket.

"Don't throw it out. You could use it to kill bugs," Alison joked. "I did see a couple of big ones skittering around." She rose, stretching.

"And here come their flying friends." Hux swatted at a whining, invisible insect. "Look at all those busted screens. We're going to get eaten alive tonight."

Deke reached for his wallet. "Here's five bucks. Go buy a can of bug spray."

"You're a prince, Bannon. I think I can afford it."

Deke put the bill back into his wallet. "Then go. Now. Before the place on the corner closes."

"Okay. I can't kill mosquitoes with a handgun. They're too fast."

He slammed out and Deke took Alison's chair, looking into the laptop. "Is it possible to switch to a different camera?"

She reached over his arm and pointed to an icon on the screen. "Yes. Click that. You can keep more than one window open if you want."

Deke pulled up a view of the door, guarded by a burly guy in a bulletproof vest, who buzzed in a customer, shabbily dressed, with white hair. Deke followed the old man as he approached the clerk at the counter and unrolled the top of a paper bag with shaky hands, tipping something sparkly onto the glass.

Probably some piece of junk, Deke

thought. Poor old guy was hoping to get enough to buy a bottle of Old Overcoat. He practiced zooming in and out — and whistled suddenly under his breath.

"Hey. Am I seeing things? That looks like it."

"Seriously?" Alison came back and peered into the screen, tapping a couple of keys to enlarge the image. She glanced at the color printout of the emerald-and-diamond bracelet for comparison. "Could be. But he's going to sell it for chump change." Another tap and they both could read what the clerk scrawled on a piece of paper. "Ten bucks. Hmm. That's on the high side for costume jewelry."

"Whatever. That's not the thief we got pictures of."

"Maybe he was working with someone else."

"Not this grandpa." Deke reached for his cell phone. "I'm going to call my contact. They'll get someone in there. You can go. I'm on this."

Alison stopped what she was doing. "I can't leave now," she grumbled. "And let you get the glory if that is the bracelet? No freaking way."

Something had been slipped halfway under

her door. Kelly saw it before she reached for her keys. She opened the door and rolled her bags in, avoiding the cream-colored envelope. Then she went back to get it, absently noticing that it was heavy for its size.

She supposed it was a last-minute invitation, maybe to a Saturday-night event in Atlanta that she'd been fortunate enough to miss. Monroe Capp would have had something like that sent over by messenger, signed for and delivered by building staff.

Entering her apartment, she closed the door behind her and slid a finger under the lightly sealed flap to open the envelope. Inside was a card printed on the same high-quality stock. She didn't need to read it right away. Definitely an invitation. For some reason there were photos enclosed. She could hear thin crackly paper.

Kelly headed for the kitchen and slung her purse over a bar-style chair. She put the card on the counter, not wanting to look at it or the photos right away. Kelly stuck a large glass under the icemaker and waited for a few cubes, then poured a can of soda over them, taking the glass to the table with the card.

She pulled it and read the message on the front. Professionally printed. Unsigned.

Thank you for joining us at the Billionaires' Ball! We look forward to seeing you again.

Maybe the assistant in charge of the guest list was making amends for his rudeness — for a second she couldn't think of his name. Atwood, that was it. Or possibly Natalie Conrad had insisted that he follow up with a thank-you note, just because she and Kelly had spoken, even though Kelly hadn't donated a dime.

Why take the trouble to get an unnecessary thank-you note here before her arrival? Her plane had touched down in Atlanta only an hour and a half ago.

She opened the card and unfolded the paper that protected the photos. Several different snapshots of her were enclosed. None with Deke. Just her. Sitting at one table or another. She was walking toward the camera in one. The photos were identical in one respect.

Her face had been shot out of all of them.

A message was scrawled on the inside of the card. *Bullets for a bombshell.*

CHAPTER 11

Kelly pushed the card and photos away. A sick feeling of dread washed over her. The night-shrouded view of Atlanta from the nearby window seemed menacing, as if someone was out there who could see her now.

It wasn't possible. Her building was taller than all the others nearby, her apartment high above the darkly glittering city. But she rose and pulled the cord to close the drapes.

It didn't make her feel safer. She searched in her purse for her cell, wanting only to talk to Deke. The call went straight to voice-mail. She didn't leave a message. Maybe he was in the air right now, on his way back. He hadn't said.

Kelly drew in a shaky breath, trying to calm herself. Everything had changed. This wasn't a game. A story she had to get was turning into a story that might kill her. Asking for information on the card from the building's staff wasn't the way to go. If someone had been paid to look the other way, they wouldn't be talking.

She crossed her arms tightly over her chest and paced the carpeted floor. Soft as her footsteps were, they still echoed faintly in the sparely furnished apartment. Kelly moved from the living room to the bedroom.

Maybe the man who'd slipped the envelope halfway under her door had wanted her to think he hadn't come in. Her apartment hadn't been ransacked, but it might have been bugged. Hanging around with Deke for a day and a night had changed how she thought about things like that.

Kelly walked around her bed, looking intently at the walls, running a hand over the window frames and doorjamb. Anger replaced fear. She pulled open the folding closet door and banged it back.

Clothes. Shoes. What had she been expecting to see?

She yanked up the bedskirt and used it to drag all the bedding to the center of the mattress. Then she grabbed a mirror to look underneath the frame, seeing nothing but a few dust bunnies and a lost sock.

Kelly wasn't going to kneel and make sure there were no monsters under the bed. It didn't matter. She couldn't stay here.

WBRX had run a dozen stories on women who'd been stalked. Seven of them were no longer alive. Stalkers came back.

Returning to the living room, she found her laptop and located a luxury hotel that catered to business people temporarily based in Atlanta. The site downloaded quickly. A video tour was available. Kelly concentrated on the fine print. Discretion assured. Twenty-four-hour security guaranteed.

Not cheap, even at monthly rates. But worth it.

In less than an hour, she was checking in.

Kelly was heading to her office by ten, brushing past reporters and other employees. Monday mornings were always hectic around WBRX. Weekends were when murders, fires, and assaults spiked, a fact of life that newspeople and hospital ER staff knew all too well. Loyal viewers would be waiting for their fix of Saturday-night mayhem in tonight's evening broadcast.

Fred Chiswick popped his head up over his cubicle before she could duck.

"Kelly!"

She didn't stop. The senior newswriter was a little too happy to see her. No doubt he wanted her opinion on his segment for

268

tonight's broadcast. Kelly waved and kept moving.

"Fred! Sorry. Can't chat — later, maybe."

Later as in never. Or at least not today. Looking disappointed, Fred sank back down into his cubicle. Kelly felt only a little guilty. It wasn't possible to be nice all the time. She hadn't slept. The card and photos were on her kitchen table. Deke could take them to forensics.

As for her job, Kelly intended to go through the motions, thankful for her status as an anchor, which allowed her to hide out in her office until afternoon and her call for hair and makeup. A station page would deliver final copy before that, and the Tele-PrompTer meant she could deliver the news without thinking about it.

She turned the corner and bumped into Gordon.

"Hey," he said. "I meant to call over the weekend."

"But you didn't." Kelly wasn't inclined to swap small talk with the cameraman.

"Sorry. The playoffs were on."

She smiled thinly. "Missed 'em. I was out of town."

He matched his steps to hers. "Yeah? Where?"

"Texas."

"Big state. Want to narrow that down?"

"Dallas."

That seemed to satisfy him for some reason. Gordon slowed down, digging in the pocket of his chinos. "Wait a sec. I have something for you from Laura."

Kelly hesitated. It seemed like a very long time that they had all been together at the building site, but the shootout had happened only a few days ago. "How is she?"

"I guess you know she's quitting," Gordon informed her.

"Of course. Didn't you?"

"No one tells me anything," he grumbled. "Not right away, anyway. She left me a message and said something about going into organic vegetables. Quieter. Safer."

"It's her decision," Kelly replied. She looked at Gordon's outstretched palm. "And those are — ?"

"The keys to the building gates. She said to tell you to give them back to the guy."

Kelly plucked them from his hand. "Tell me his name and where I can find him."

"Uh — Laura told me, but I forgot."

They had reached the editing rooms. "Call her back, Gordon."

"Yeah, sure. And I'll tell her good luck with the carrots."

"Just get the information." Kelly continued down the hall without looking back at the cameraman.

There seemed to be no end to the flow of staffers. Fortunately, most of them didn't speak to her. Kelly kept her gaze trained on an invisible point on the far wall, pretending to be a very important person with too much to do.

She was almost at her office when Coral Reese, the new reporter who seemed to always be at the station, came toward her, waving a memo to get her attention. Kelly had asked her to look up a few things and Coral had jumped on it, eager to make herself useful.

"Hey, Kelly. Monroe Capp sent me to find you. Says it's urgent."

"What else is new?" Kelly asked wearily. "I just have to take care of a few things in my office before I enter the inner sanctum."

Coral laughed. No one seemed to notice. It wasn't as if the WBRX news director was popular. "I'll tell him you're here. Oh, and I found a lot of documentation on that abandoned building in city records. It is soo complicated, but I can give you the basics later if you want."

"Sure. And thanks." Kelly was beginning to like Coral. The young reporter didn't seem overly impressed by Monroe Capp's posturing, for one thing.

Coral did a one-eighty turn and went back the way she'd come, her blond bob swinging. Kelly scooted into her office, closing the door behind her. Outside of Emperor Monroe, she wasn't required to talk to anyone else. She settled herself in her swivel chair and touched a key to open the WBRX home page for staffers.

Kelly knew the drill. Stare into the screen, act busy, keep fingers clickety-clicking on the keyboard. She breathed deeply, willing herself to calm down. Out of habit, she scanned the WBRX home page. There was no breaking news to get excited about. Fractionally relaxed, she leaned back in her chair.

The desk phone rang. The jangly noise seemed too loud in a room with a shut door. Kelly looked at the caller ID screen, noticing the Dallas area code. She hesitated before picking it up. But on the off chance it was Deke, who still hadn't returned her call to his cell, she picked up the receiver.

"Kelly Johns, WBRX."

The cultured female voice that responded was the last thing she expected to hear.

"Hello. This is Natalie Conrad."

"Oh." Kelly couldn't quite hide her surprise. "Good morning, Mrs. Conrad."

"I believe I told you to call me Natalie." The reminder was crisp.

"Right. Yes, you did. How are you? The Billionaires' Ball was quite an event — and by the way, I want to thank you again for taking the time to talk to me."

True enough, as far as it went. What Kelly really wanted to know was the names of the photographers who'd chronicled the grand occasion. She had to start somewhere to find her stalker. But Natalie Conrad wasn't likely to know such a minor detail. Atwood might.

"My pleasure."

"What can I do for you, Natalie?"

"Are you busy?" The inquiry seemed pointed.

"Mondays are always busy around here — but I'm not." Kelly paused. Listen and learn. Natalie Conrad had said just that.

"I'll get to the point. The money we raised didn't match our expectations," the other woman began.

"Oh."

"The costs were extraordinary." Natalie's silvery laugh seemed at odds with her concern. "You can't penny-pinch in Dallas."

Kelly wondered what the other woman was getting at.

"I do think we might need to broaden our

efforts," Natalie continued. "Especially since we haven't purchased a site for the museum as yet."

That was something Kelly had noticed on her own. But she didn't have the nerve to ask tough questions at the moment. And she didn't share the older woman's obsession with memorializing her late husband.

Vision, Kelly silently corrected herself. Natalie Conrad had a vision. The glamorous widow wouldn't use any other word for her pet project.

"Kelly? Are you there?"

"Yes," Kelly answered hastily. "I'm sorry. I was thinking about — what you just mentioned."

"Were you." It wasn't a question but a statement. "My dear, I should apologize for calling you at work. Perhaps this isn't the best time."

Despite her elaborate courtesy, there was no mistaking the frosty edge in Natalie's voice.

Too bad, honey, Kelly thought, irked by the dismissive way the billionaire's widow said the word *work.* Without a doubt, Natalie Conrad was accustomed to people hanging on her every word and doing her bidding and being honored when she called. But Kelly just couldn't fake it right now.

"I'd love to hear what you're up to, Natalie. In detail. But I do have a meeting with our news director in five minutes."

Natalie was silent. "Oh. I see. Do give Monroe my best."

Ouch. Kelly would have to. This call was proof enough that Mrs. Conrad followed up on things. "I certainly will. And I hope we can talk again soon, Natalie."

"In person?" The older woman's voice was warm again. "Why not? I may be in Atlanta as soon as next week. Au revoir, Kelly."

Kelly said good-bye and hung up, shaking her head. She really couldn't peg Natalie Conrad. She suddenly wondered how Natalie had obtained her direct number. The receptionist didn't usually put unknown callers through to the anchors. Kelly got more than her share of unwanted attention as the WBRX blonde.

The desk phone buzzed with an internal message. Monroe was waiting.

The balding news director was leaning back in his swivel chair, his tassel-loafer-clad feet up on his desk. Kelly didn't sit down, annoyed to have to wait when he'd summoned her. The conversation — his half of it, anyway — seemed fairly trivial.

Affably, Monroe wrapped it up and

brought his chair down. "Howdy."

Kelly had never heard him say *howdy* before. One eyebrow went up in a quizzical arch.

"Don't look at me like that." He chuckled. "I knew you were going to Dallas over the weekend even before you left."

Did Monroe Capp like to read his employees' e-mail? She wouldn't put it past him. She had looked up the ball online.

"An old acquaintance of mine enjoyed meeting you again. I understand it was quite a shindig. Did you have fun?"

Shindig wasn't a Monroe word either. But at least she knew how Natalie Conrad had gotten her number.

"Yes."

"Natalie was impressed by you."

"I don't know why. Although she did pull me out of the crowd to talk to her."

"Well, a little while ago she took the trouble to call me up and congratulate me on my good judgment for keeping you front and center at WBRX."

Kelly shrugged. She couldn't think of anything to say to that, and it wasn't exactly a compliment.

"Natalie and her late husband used to live near me and my ex-wife in Buckhead, in this great big mansion. Sometimes they used it for entertaining. On a grand scale. Other than that, they weren't there much."

That piqued Kelly's interest. "I didn't know that."

"Before your time. I don't live in Buckhead anymore. When we were talking, she mentioned that she'd met you at benefit galas in Atlanta now and then."

"Yes. That's what the Dallas thing was — a massive fundraiser to build a new art museum."

Monroe nodded. "Natalie loved to collect, and Harry liked to indulge her. They didn't have any children. He was a lot older than she was." He thought for a few seconds. "He met her in Russia, I think."

"When was that?"

"Years ago. Maybe before you were born. He was in Moscow on business, buying up refineries, mines, oil fields. Not totally on the up-and-up."

"Hmm."

"Anyway, Natalie needed to feather her twenty-bedroom nest, and she and Maya used to hit the galleries together. Natalie liked to encourage young artists, if you get my drift. Some of them are making millions now. I can't say I understand modern art, but to each his own."

Kelly cleared her throat. This couldn't be

why he'd wanted to see her. Her gaze moved around the office, stopping on the pile of DVD auditions from her potential competition.

Monroe fiddled with a pencil. "That's ancient history. Am I boring you?"

"No. Thanks for sharing."

He laughed and leaned back again. "Listen, I called you in to tell you that the news blackout on that building shootout got lifted."

"Why?"

"My guess is that the cops are stumped. They need leads. Are you still hot to do some reporting?"

The question startled her. Monroe Capp was known for changing his mind on a whim, but that was a serious leap.

He moved aside the stack of DVDs and lifted a binder marked with a consultant logo she recognized. "My boss — and I do have one — hired Rivers and Oxford to analyze our ratings and poll viewers. Seems that the folks out there in TV land want more Kelly Johns."

"Really."

"Yes. And we're going to give them what they want. Which means more on-air face time for you. Not bad, huh?"

"That's an interesting development," she

said cautiously. He had to be telling the truth, at least in part. But Kelly guessed he hadn't found an SYSC who was capable of replacing her. The acronym stood for Someone Younger Sexier Cheaper, and everyone around the station knew what it meant. His offer didn't mean she was going to stop looking over her shoulder to see if anyone was gaining on her.

"The shootout seems like a good, gory story. The corruption thing you were working on with Laura, forget it. That stays spiked. No one wants to see visuals of tax returns and listen to a lot of complicated explanations."

Kelly didn't want to seem eager, and she wasn't. Receiving what amounted to a death threat had dampened her enthusiasm a little. Deke had hinted at a link between the Dallas ball and the Atlanta investigation. That card was one hell of a link.

"Let me think about it. I'm not sure what our angle should be."

"Dead gangsters, what else," Monroe said. "Cars riddled with bullet holes. I guess they mopped up the blood, but maybe you could sweet-talk some cop and score forensics photos. Put it all together and get the sound editor to add some bang-bang and screaming sirens. Special Report, with Kelly

Johns," he intoned in an announcer's voice. "How does that grab you?"

News didn't just happen, it was made and remade in the studio. Business as usual. She still wasn't sure.

"Hey, one more thing. That redhead. What happened to her? Gordon showed me the tape."

"She disappeared." Kelly was relieved that Monroe wasn't taking her to task for not being first in line to see it.

Her boss pointed the pencil at her. "That's our angle. *Cherchez la femme.* Look for the woman. Hype it to the max."

"I can't find her if the cops can't."

Monroe rolled his eyes and groaned. "Do I care? I have a seven-day schedule to fill up. If the shootout story fizzles out, we move on to something else. Atlanta is a big, wicked city. I see a lot of Special Reports starring you in the future."

Kelly made up her mind. He was offering her something she had wanted, badly. Finding out who'd sent the card or what someone thought she had to do with Deke's investigation would take weeks or months. She might never find out who'd delivered the damn thing. "Give me a day or two to get started."

"Not a problem. Just make sure that we

know where you are at all times. And, Kelly" — he pointed the pencil at her — "don't work alone. That's an order."

Kelly almost smiled. Deke wouldn't let her. Monroe didn't have to know who she would be working with.

She asked if there was new information on the building and Monroe shoved a file of printed-out material at her. "Do your homework. And you can thank Coral Reese for getting that."

"I will."

The message light was blinking when she got back to her office. She'd missed his call. Damn and double damn. Kelly grabbed the receiver and pressed the redial button.

Deke glanced around the hotel suite she'd rented for a month. "Not bad. This looks more like an apartment."

"That's the idea."

Kelly realized that he was wearing the battered leather jacket she remembered. The crease left by the bullet was hidden by his stance. She thought about asking to take it, but he seemed restless. It would be awkward if he had to tell her no.

"You were smart to get out. I'm glad you're here." He hadn't been able to leave Dallas for two days after getting her call.

He wasn't that free to come and go, not with the new developments in the case.

"It's closer to WBRX too. Which is nice if I ever have to stay late."

"Try not to. And don't come home alone. Call me."

"All right. I'm taking you up on that." Kelly ignored his look of faint disbelief and handed him a glass of soda.

"What did you do with your car?"

"Didn't even want to look at it. It's in the apartment parking garage. I took a taxi. I couldn't shake the idea of the windshield being smashed to scare me — or worse, someone waiting in it. I figured I'd just deal with it later," she said.

"Good. Let me go over it before you do anything."

"Okay. Fine." She sat down on the couch, putting her glass on the coffee table. The suite was actually larger than her place, but she still got the sensation that he was too big for it. His presence made her feel a little calmer.

"Where are the card and the photos?"

Kelly reached for her purse. "Right in here. Picked up with a paper towel and zipped into a plastic bag. My fingerprints are all over them, but maybe you can get something."

She pulled out a large, flat plastic bag and set it on the coffee table. She picked up her glass and curled into a corner of the couch, as if she wanted to get as far away from the evidence as possible. Deke sat down on the middle cushion, handling the ziplock bag carefully, moving the items so that they could be viewed without being removed. He studied the card first, then the photos.

"Bullets for a bombshell. Interesting message," he said finally.

"Yes. I'm inclined to take it seriously."

Deke turned his head to look at her, his dark gaze understanding. "Good. I'd like to compare these to the press pass."

Kelly frowned. "Oh — I left it in my desk. Which is locked."

He set the plastic bag on the table. "That's better than unlocked, but not by much. A desk lock can be picked with a paper clip."

"You and I are the only ones who know about the press pass," she said defensively.

"Look, I don't expect you to think like a cop or an investigator. I wouldn't want you to be that paranoid."

"Gee, thanks. While we're on that subject, can you test my new door for me?" Kelly pointed toward the door.

Deke got up and went out into the hall, reaching a hand around the door to lock it automatically. He pulled it shut and rattled the knob to make sure it was locked.

Silence. Then she heard the faint noise of metal on metal, no louder than a tiny animal scratching. If someone else had been experimenting, she might not have heard it at all.

In another minute, the door swung open and Deke came back in.

"That answers that." She almost didn't want to meet his eyes.

"Look, Kelly, there's no such thing as total security. You're probably safer here than you are in your apartment. You got out fast and you didn't tell anyone where you were going. And you stayed away from your car, which was smart. You did the best you could."

"Am I safe on the street?"

"If there are other people around, yes — but that's a qualified yes. Wherever you are, be on the alert. But you can't live in a bunker and never come out."

Kelly finished her soda and swirled the ice cubes around thoughtfully. "A nice, restful bunker actually sounds pretty good. But I paid in advance for this place, and it ain't cheap."

Deke looked around as if he were assessing the truth of the statement. "So long as you can swing the rent."

"I can. And I may be picking up some extra work soon." She held up a hand to keep him from asking about that just yet. "Now tell me what happened after I left."

"We broke into small groups around Dallas, thinking the bracelet would be pawned. I was stoked when a homeless guy brought in something sparkly and green in a paper bag to the place we staked out. Turned out to be costume jewelry by some designer. He got ten bucks and a ride to a shelter in an unmarked cruiser. The other stakeouts got zip. The bracelet is still missing."

Kelly studied him. "I don't believe you. You sound way too casual. What really happened?"

"That's the truth," he insisted. "But I'm getting around to the other thing. We got word of a body found outside the hotel, near a storage area, wrapped in a roll of carpet from the ballroom. Male. Gray suit, empty pockets, no ID. Middle-aged. Beaten so badly his face was pulp."

"And . . ."

"It took us a while to get in to look at him. The medical examiner had his work cut out for him. It probably wasn't a professional hit — he still had his fingers."

Kelly looked pale. "Go on."

"The morgue tech inked him. He'd been outside for a while, which speeded up decomposition, but the prints were clear enough to submit to the national database. You okay? You look a little sick."

Kelly was pressing her cold glass to her forehead. "I'm all right."

"We got a high-probability match to the thief you took photos of — I told you he had a felony conviction and did time, right?"

"Yes."

Deke stuck his hands in the pockets of his jeans and rocked a little on his feet, looking thoughtful. "End of story. Our chance to flip the thief is as dead as he is. An informer would make solving this case one whole hell of a lot easier."

Kelly gave a nod. She hesitated before she spoke again.

"Deke, do you think that whoever killed him is stalking me?"

"No way to tell at this point. But anything is possible."

Kelly picked up the ziplock bag. "Take this with you when you go. Maybe your techs can find something else that matches somebody else."

"DNA, skin cells, microscopic blood drops —"

"Let's go with the DNA. I was talking

about the envelope flap. It wasn't sealed too well, but spit is spit."

"I guess it wouldn't be yours." Deke looked almost amused. She seemed to have recovered her usual cool aplomb.

"Correct." Kelly swung herself off the couch and went to the window. "Check out my new view. Do you see what I see out there?"

Deke moved to stand beside her. The skeleton of a building rose in the distance, towering over the scattered small houses and empty lots around it. His eyes narrowed against the Saturday afternoon sunshine. "I count seventeen stories."

"I did too. How far away is it from here?"

"I'm guessing a mile and a half," he said.

"You drove here. Let's go look at it again."

"Do you have a death wish?" Deke asked.

"No. I wouldn't go there without you, and I happen to know there are undercover cops there around the clock. And we can get in without them."

He looked at the keys she was dangling. "How about that."

"Apparently the news blackout on the shootout is officially lifted. Monroe put me on the story."

"Does that mean you have to do it?"

Kelly dodged the question. "I want to. You in?"

Deke took a long time to reply. "I should say no. But I can't. Someone has to save you from yourself."

"Oh please. You help me, I'll help you. We make a good team."

His dark gaze moved over her. He didn't seem to believe the casualness of her reply, but he didn't argue with her. "Yeah. We do."

"So you'll go?"

"Give me ten minutes."

"You going to call Hux or something?" Kelly walked near the window. "Don't mind me."

"I'll go out in the hall," Deke said. "I wanted to get a look at the stairs and exits on your floor anyway. Won't take long."

He left, closing the door behind him. He walked several doors down to the end of the hall and went through the unlocked door to the stairs, leaning against the wall and keeping his voice low.

"Hux. It's me. Kelly got a sicko card with photos of her from the ball. They were shot out like the press pass. I'm bringing all of it to the lab for analysis."

Hux swore. "Doesn't confirm anything, but it changes everything."

"Yeah."

"How is she doing?" Hux asked.

"Scared and won't admit it. She's never had to deal with a stalker. Listen, did you get a chance to talk to your informers about that contract that was out on her?" Deke asked.

"All of a sudden no one even remembers it."

"Hux, when the street shuts up, you know that's not good."

"Tell me about it."

"Listen, that guy I saw in Dallas — yeah, the monster with the black hair and the birthmark — is he back in Atlanta?"

"I don't know. He hasn't been seen around that store. Maybe he got a job."

Deke shook his head. "That's what I'm afraid of."

"I know what you mean."

Deke made eye contact with an undercover leaning against an idling SUV. Forget the fresh air. The guy had come out for a smoke, which he lit up, exhaling in a gray plume. It was as good a way as any to hide your face some.

The cop was wearing an oversize Braves jersey with a matching cap pulled low on his forehead, almost resting on wraparound sunglasses. The hand that lit the cigarette touched the bill of the cap.

I see you, you see me.

Deke motioned back unobtrusively. He knew the other man was getting an eyeful of Kelly Johns into the bargain. She looked damn good in sleek jeans and that slouchy knit thing on top. It was loose, but not everywhere.

He followed her to the gate, watching her unlock it and going through behind her, surveying the scene. The heavy machinery was still on-site, stuck in the same giant ruts. High above, he could see a spiderweb crack in the center of the construction crane's window. The flatbeds loaded with rebar had been used for target practice too. Beer bottles lay in their shadow, some in shattered pieces.

"If anyone needs a poster image for urban blight, this is it," Kelly said. She'd stopped a little ahead of him, doing her own looking around.

"What were you expecting?"

"I found out that an international consortium is angling to buy the building. They want to tear it down and start over."

"Business as usual." Deke caught up to her.

The concrete floors were littered with trash. A crumpled wrapper blew past and tumbled into the deep pit for the elevator shafts. The same musty smell of damp earth still emanated from it. Deke coughed.

"Last time we were here, these floors were clean," Kelly murmured.

"The maintenance contract was paid up months ahead. Before the owners defaulted."

Kelly shot him a curious look. "How do you know that?"

"I snoop. Same as you."

She laughed and walked on, heading for the back of the structure and looking out into the parking lot. There were no cars at all. A truck rolled down the street that led into it, then went through an intersection, driving away toward the dwindling sun.

"This is where we first met," she murmured.

"Feeling sentimental?"

Kelly ignored the comment. But she turned around to look at him. The warm, late-day light hit him straight on, tracing golden lines over his rugged body. He stood there, legs apart, hands in the pockets of that battered jacket. Lit up, the folds of heavy leather looked even more battered, but he didn't. The word for him was *invincible*. It wasn't an illusion or her imagination. The more she knew him, the more she craved the strength he radiated.

She had to get a grip. Think of something else, keep it light.

"Let's see. You were there and I was here —" Kelly stopped, taking a moment to drink him in. She couldn't help it.

"Actually, you were closer. A lot closer." His deep voice echoed softly in the emptiness.

Kelly's heart skipped a beat. She had been. Without thinking, without wanting to think, she went to him again.

Deke opened his arms to embrace her and pull her against his muscular length. Something melted inside her as she pressed against him, her body supple and warm, yearning for the connection that meant so much.

Big hands slid around her waist. The heat of his touch made her tremble, longing for more. She stood on tiptoe, arched against him, tilting her face up and looking into the dark eyes that roved over her face. Gently, his lips brushed over her burning cheek, seeking her mouth. Her lips parted eagerly, desiring only his kiss.

Deke's hands slid lower. With her hips firmly cradled against his, the kiss got hotter. She never wanted it to stop.

CHAPTER 12

Kelly needed that kiss. She almost moaned when Deke broke it off — but he wasn't done. His lips moved along her cheekbone to her earlobe, and from there to the sensitive cord of her neck. With tantalizing expertise, he traced it with the tip of his tongue, then nipped. It was like being made love to by a wonderfully wild animal. But he was pure man. The powerful length of him was all the proof she needed of that.

Kelly leaned her head back, closing her eyes as he swept up her hair, pushing it away to press more kisses to the skin bared by her loose knit top. Their heated embrace made the top slip off one shoulder. He put his other hand over it in an unsuccessful attempt to preserve her modesty. The soft friction of the material between her skin and his palm was gently stimulating. Deke caressed both shoulders before he let his hands slide down her back — and inside the top at her waist.

Kelly drew in a breath. They couldn't go further than that. Not here. She put her hands over his and made him stop. Deke sighed, his jaw against her cheek and his breath stirring warmly in her hair.

"You're something else, Kelly Johns," he murmured.

"I shouldn't — we can't do this, Deke."

"We just did."

The faint sound of footsteps on the concrete floor snapped her back to reality. Kelly stiffened in Deke's arms, trying to see over his shoulder. There was a rasping cough — a smoker's cough.

"It's that cop," she whispered. Reluctantly, she stepped back. Deke's hands lingered on her for a fraction of a second and then he let her go, turning to look.

The undercover officer was alternately hidden and revealed by the rows of concrete columns as he approached.

Kelly quickly pulled herself together, adjusting her clothes and running both hands over her hair to smooth it. She knew her face was flushed. The lengthening shadows offered some concealment.

Deke smiled down at her. He didn't need fixing. But he didn't look quite the same. His gaze was thoughtful and his lips were tender. She didn't know he could get that romantic.

It doesn't mean anything, she told herself. *It won't go anywhere.* The kiss had — just happened.

They were standing a few feet apart when the other man reached them. If he thought there was anything going on, his expressionless face didn't betray it. He no longer was wearing sunglasses.

"Hope I didn't startle you," he said, extending a hand to Deke. "I'm Raf Simmons. Detective, Zone Six. My shift ends at sunset. Just thought I'd say hello and introduce you to the next guy."

"Thanks," Deke said. "I guess me and Kelly are about done wandering around. Not much to see, right?"

The question was addressed to her.

"No," she said. "It's hard to believe that there was a shootout."

"The crime scene techs searched the site and the parking lot several times over. They picked it clean," Simmons said. "It actually looks worse now."

"Did any of your officers go into the neighborhood?" Deke asked. "Someone might have seen something."

"No one lives around here, if that's what you mean," the detective said. "The developers convinced the city to condemn the remaining houses before the building started."

He turned at the sound of a car horn.

"That's Terhune. He's probably wondering where the hell I am."

"We won't keep you," Kelly said.

The three of them walked back to the front of the building and through the open gate. Kelly locked it and kept the key. Raf Simmons didn't seem to notice.

The introductions were made, but the relief, Joe Terhune, didn't get out of his car. Kelly and Deke moved to one side as the officers talked in low voices.

"Want to walk the streets?" he asked her.

Kelly looked back. The abandoned building loomed over them. This late in the day, the area seemed lonely and foreboding. Simmons was right. It really wasn't a neighborhood.

"You have a gun and they can cover you," she said slowly. "So long as they can see you, that is."

He nodded. "We don't have to go far. And there isn't that much to see. I was kind of curious about that old factory over there."

She looked in the direction he indicated. A weathered brick structure that took up half a block was within sight of both undercover vehicles. The side without windows was covered with a huge, ghostly sign that had faded away, half-paint and half-brick. Kelly made out a few letters here and there, but she couldn't read what it said.

"All right. Tell them where we're going, okay?"

Raf Simmons was already in his SUV and rolling out when Deke went to talk to Terhune. Kelly pulled her top tightly around her shoulders against the cool of the evening, rubbing her arms.

"He says teenagers hang out there sometimes," Deke told her when he came back. "There was a party there last week. They didn't set the place on fire and no one fell through the floor. So I guess we're safe."

"Good to know," Kelly said sarcastically.

"It's empty," Deke reassured her. "The cops did a drive-by and a walk-through just before we arrived."

Side by side, they headed away from the undercover cars and walked toward the factory. The skeletal shadow of the building behind them stretched nearly that far. Kelly felt better when they were clear of it.

Close up, the factory seemed solid. The high, large windows were grimy, but only a few panes were broken. Kelly realized she could make out part of the original sign, give or take a few missing letters. FINE SHOES FOR LADIES AND GENTLEMEN. A high-buttoned shoe was just visible below that. Other painted signs had been added over the years. Tattered flyers for auto repair shops and check-cashing offices were pasted over those.

The factory had seen better days, but it was still standing. Kelly had a soft spot for places like this. She noticed that a side door was ajar. Deke looked at her. "Want to take a look inside?"

"Sure."

He took her hand. The warmth of his skin brought every second of that totally amazing kiss back in force. Kelly fought a rush of feeling she didn't know what to do with. They went up a short flight of exterior stairs and stopped at the door. A longer flight continued up the side of the building and doubled back before it reached the roof high above.

Looking into the cavernous interior, Kelly couldn't see the end of the space, even with light still coming through the windows. She looked up when Deke did. The vaulted ceiling was two or three stories high. It too was hard to see in the gloom.

"Looks like there used to be a second floor," he commented.

"Maybe so. I can't imagine having a party in here."

"That's because you're not eighteen." He laughed.

"Thank God for that," she said fervently. She peered into the shadowy space again. "There's a draft coming from somewhere. Feel it?"

"Probably the cellar. There could be a broken window we don't see." Deke stepped back, wrapping his arms lightly around her. "You cold?"

"Not when you do that."

"Wear my jacket," he offered.

She hesitated, then accepted with a nod. There was no knowing when she would get the chance again. He slipped it off and draped it over her shoulders, flipping up the collar around her neck. The heavy leather had retained his body heat. It felt great. "Thanks."

The holster he wore didn't show much next to his dark thermal top. Kelly knew he could draw his weapon without fumbling for it.

"Let's go up to the roof," he suggested.

She wouldn't mind getting a bird's-eye view. The missing woman could have escaped down an alley they wouldn't be able to see any other way. But it was bound to be windy up there.

"I'm putting this all the way on." Kelly slipped her arms into the roomy sleeves and fastened the snap tab at the collar so the jacket wouldn't slip off. Eagerly, she followed him up the longer staircase.

Deke pulled himself up and over using the iron frame at the top. He looked back down at Kelly. "You're going to love the view."

"I bet it's very scenic."

She took the strong hand that reached to assist her and made it over the building edge without any trouble. The view actually was interesting, although it was anything but beautiful.

The Atlanta skyline in the distance glittered against the glowing sunset sky. The abandoned building didn't look as lonely with that as a backdrop. She could guess at the extent of the largely vanished neighborhood below from their high vantage point.

Besides the alleys, there were faint, very faint, trails through dusty lots that had once been lawns. Young children had run over them, back when kids played outside. She could imagine clothes-lines hung with washing, and mothers making small talk from one yard to another, visiting with each other before the fathers came home from this factory and others. Bygone days had left their marks before they vanished forever.

She smiled to herself. Human interest. Every newshound learned what it could do for a story. By this point, she did it automatically.

Deke was thinking along more practical lines, judging by his expression. His dark brows were drawn together and his gaze was intent, almost as if he were studying a map.

"She could have come down that alley," he muttered, talking more to himself than to Kelly. "It's the only one that connects directly to the parking lot. And it's so narrow she had a chance of not being seen."

He straightened and looked at Kelly. "You know, Kelly, you're the only actual eyewitness. Everyone else at the scene saw her through a lens or on tape."

"I only caught a glimpse of her."

"No one else did," Deke argued.

"So what? Your team analyzed the tape frame by frame. The drawing they came up with has to be better than my memory."

He shrugged, looking out over the desolate blocks below. His gaze stopped on a boarded-up house not far from the abandoned building. "She could have gotten that far and hidden for a while."

"Let the cops get a search warrant and do the looking," Kelly said firmly. She knew what could turn up behind doors nailed shut.

"I could still do ground tracking. There have to be clues all over this area. It hasn't been that long."

"There's nothing to see." She undid the snap tab at the jacket collar, enjoying the feel of the wind on her body. Being up on a roof and above it all was liberating.

"Sometimes that depends on how hard you search, Kelly." He studied her for a moment. "You look good in that."

"It's too big. But I love it." She grinned at him, hoping he wouldn't ask for it back right away.

"Keep it on until we get to the car." He chucked her under the chin. "Ready to head home?"

For a second, looking into his dark eyes, Kelly forgot that she didn't have one.

"Yes," she said. "Let's go."

Kelly took a mirror out of her desk drawer and glanced at her reflection, then winced. Her sleepless night showed. She put the mirror away so fast she thought she'd cracked it. Like she needed any more bad luck. The card and the mutilated photos were with Deke, but a faceless image of herself had appeared in her dreams.

A soft knock on her open door made her whirl around.

"Good morning," Coral said. "I was wondering if this was a good time to talk."

"Is it about the building?" Kelly asked.

"No." Coral seemed reluctant to say more.

"Close the door and come in," Kelly said. "Have a seat."

Coral looked up and down the hall, and then clicked the door shut. She settled next to Kelly in the chair by the desk. "I was talking to Laura last night," she began.

"Oh. And what did she say?" Kelly had a feeling she knew what this was about.

"There's a lot going on, and you're right in the middle of it. Are you sure that's a good idea?"

"That would be today's big question. I guess she told you about the shootout."

Coral nodded. "She just blurted it out. That's why she's quitting, right?"

"Yeah. And I won't." Kelly reached into her desk and held up the bagged press pass. "Check this out. My souvenir of the shooting."

"Is that you? But it —" Coral looked pale when she saw the bullet hole. "Oh my God."

Kelly put the pass back in its hiding place. "And I got photos of myself from a benefit ball in Dallas, also shot through the face.

303

Not suitable for framing."

"What's going on?" Coral said. "You should tell the police."

"I have." Kelly wasn't going to get into her relationship with Deke. "There's a limit to what they can do, and I haven't actually seen whoever is trying to intimidate me. Let's hope that's all they want to do." She kept her voice steady. There was no sense in scaring a junior reporter half to death.

"I had no idea." Coral left it at that.

"Laura didn't know about the pass. Can we talk about something else?"

Coral collected herself. "Sure. If you have the time."

"I could use a distraction." Not the most flattering answer, but it was the truth.

The junior reporter took a deep breath. "I also wanted to ask you — I mean, I heard talk, you know how it is in the newsroom — about Gunther Bach."

Kelly frowned. She wondered who'd seen her in the restaurant and cranked up the gossip machine. It could have been anyone from a former colleague she hadn't spotted in time to a busboy with dreams of tabloid glory. No doubt there was a smartphone snap of Gunther leering at her somewhere on the web.

Sometimes she wished she wasn't so well-known. Of course, she took full advantage of it when she needed to.

"He's a financier," Kelly said. "Super successful."

"Sounds like there's a story there."

Coral's interest put Kelly on the spot, but she didn't actually mind that much. The junior reporter was a natural — and Kelly could use some help.

"Someone told me that Bach was under government investigation, so I had an informal lunch with him," she replied. "You never know what people will say off the record. He's made hundreds of millions of dollars in the last couple of years, and no one can figure out how."

"Did you find out anything?"

Kelly leaned back in her chair. "Not much. He sidestepped my questions, but I have to admit he's intelligent. And a major creep. I ran into him at the ball in Dallas, by the way."

"Really? He could be stalking you."

"I don't think so." Although Kelly wasn't totally sure of that. "I heard he was trolling for rich Texans."

"Even so. What you get to do is exciting. I wish I got sent out of town on assignment."

"I was on my own. It had nothing to do with WBRX."

"How long did it take before you could set your own hours?"

Kelly wouldn't put it that way. She worked harder now than she ever had. "A while."

Coral looked around Kelly's office. "I'm dying to move up and out of cubicle land. No what-are-you-working-on questions from colleagues. No one looking over your shoulder."

Kelly didn't reply. Her lips were pressed together as she tried to keep from smiling. Coral turned beet red.

"Which is exactly what I'm doing to you, isn't it? I'm sorry, Kelly. I don't know what got into me."

"It's all right." Kelly laughed. "Look, I could use some help with other things. You up for extra work? But you do have to keep your mouth shut. This is between you and me."

Coral was taken aback by the blunt reply, but Kelly didn't have time to be polite. "If I can get something on the air, I'll make sure you get credited for extra reporting," she added, softening just a little.

"Oh. Okay. Yes. Absolutely."

Watching Coral go from zero to sixty for a chance to get her name on something was funny.

"Fine," Kelly said. "I'll let the assignment

editor know you're researching a proposal for me in your spare time. Just so long as they know where you are, they won't care."

"Great," Coral said. "And I won't say a word. You would know who blabbed if I did. If that makes sense."

"It makes perfect sense." They understood each other.

"When do you want me to start?"

"How about now? You can work in here for a while unless there's something you have to be doing in the newsroom."

Coral got up. "Let me get my notebook and my purse. I'll be right back."

While she was gone, Kelly moved things around, placing her laptop squarely on her desk and shoving the monitor for the station's computer to the angled section for Coral to work on.

The junior reporter came back, carrying a few things.

"Go ahead and see what you can find on Gunther Bach," Kelly said happily. She had never had an assistant as a reporter, and she hadn't thought she would need one as an anchor. But if she was going to do both jobs, this could work out fine.

"Ooh. Here's the Dallas event. The Billionaires' Ball, huh?"

"It should be extensively covered."

"Yup. Plenty of photos. And there he is. So well-groomed. And look at that silver hair. Icy eyes, though."

Kelly looked over from her laptop. "He's a shark, and there's blood in the water."

"That sounds awful. But I know what you mean." Coral studied the images, clicking through to the sites that featured them. Absorbed in her work, she didn't say more, and the office was quiet except for the mouse on the mouse pad.

Kelly kind of liked the company. And she wasn't able to obsess the way she did when she was alone. An hour went by before either spoke.

"I was wondering why the newspaper articles and magazine mentions were all so positive," Coral finally said. "Then I found this PR profile on Bach." She swiveled the monitor around to show Kelly. "Atlanta's top ad agency created it and everyone cribbed from it. Not exactly news."

"People don't always know the difference."

Coral tsked. "They should."

"You have a lot to learn," Kelly said, smiling.

"I guess. Let's see — I looked at the European finance sites in English," Coral said after a while. "Apparently Gunther

308

Bach is very good at staying several steps ahead of investors demanding their millions back. Supposedly, the risks involved were explained to all. Smart people got out early and raked in the bucks. The latecomers lost out."

Soon to be repeated in the US, Kelly thought. She wondered if Gunther Bach had gone on to Mexico after the event in Dallas. Deke had access to information like that. She didn't.

"Want all these pages copied?"

"Go for it."

Quickly moving the mouse, Coral copied articles and web pages, moving everything into a catchall file on the computer screen. "Do you have a printer in here? I forgot to ask."

"Yes I do. It even works."

"Send and . . . print. Here it comes." The junior reporter looked up at the clock. "Time for morning meeting. Gotta go. That was fun."

"Thanks. Remember, you're on the company schedule, not mine," Kelly said. "Don't fall behind on your own work."

The printer hummed and spat out pages. Kelly got up and adjusted the printout tray so they wouldn't all end up on the floor. Later, she would discuss what Coral had found with Deke.

Kelly's plans hadn't changed. The right story still could mean vaulting through the ranks to a national news slot and, yes, grabbing a golden statuette with her name on the base. Kelly didn't care if glory was fleeting.

She started looking for coverage of the shooting. Owing to the blackout, there wasn't much. But WBRX already had exclusive material to offer: live footage from the scene, which would be edited, padded out with commentary, and jazzed up with graphics and sound effects.

Kelly found a bare-bones report on the police blotter for that day and short mentions drawn from the scanners breaking the news. Additional reporting from behind the yellow tape didn't add much, but she could write her own copy. If they had to slap a feature together fast, they could do it.

Kelly printed out a few pages and left her office, looking for Monroe Capp. She figured he would be in the control room, supervising the process of putting together the early afternoon newscast before it aired.

With one hand on the doorknob, she turned it and peeked inside. She could just see Monroe, silhouetted in front of multiple screens glowing in the large, dark room.

There were at least a hundred of them, some larger than the others, displaying various elements of the show and technical information.

The director sat in the center of it all, manipulating an enormous console switcher, his hands moving over brightly colored knobs and switches arranged in rows. Not far from him was the technical director, wearing a headpiece mic with another in front of him on a thin silver wand. Other staffers were looking into screens on the side.

The producer was going over the live shots and prerecorded elements with Monroe, trying to get the right mix. He wasn't in the best of moods. Above them was an illuminated clock, its hands moving inexorably toward showtime.

Kelly closed the door softly, not wanting to get yelled at. She'd have to catch Monroe later. On her way back to her office she heard her cell phone ring and ran, hoping it was Deke. She wasn't disappointed.

"Hello," she said. "How are you? Where are you?"

"Still in Atlanta. But not for long." His deep voice was reassuring, but the words weren't.

"Oh — too bad. I was thinking we could

have dinner or something."

"Wish I could, Kelly. Sorry. I got picked to go back to Dallas, tie up a few loose ends."

"All right. Then I'll see you when you get back." She kept her tone cool, trying to sound professional.

"First thing. I promise."

Kelly just didn't want to let him go. She reached out and closed her office door. "Deke, did you take the card to your forensics lab? Anything to report?"

"I left it with the paper specialist. The card and envelope are heavy stock, with some texture, which means John might not be able to pull a latent print. But he's going to try."

"Thanks."

"The photos are totally clean, outside of the bullet holes. Untouched by human hands, John said. But he's looking at them too. Then the handwriting analyst gets a go at it."

Kelly was grateful for all the experts she didn't know and might never meet. She heard the sharp rap of knuckles on her door and opened it to Monroe, keeping the phone against her ear.

He looked at her impatiently. "Excuse me. I didn't mean to interrupt an important call," he barked. "The tech director said you peeked into the control room. If you want to see me, come to my office."

"Be right there," she said to the wrinkled back of his shirt as Monroe strode away down the hall.

"Is that your boss?" Deke asked.

"How did you know? I have to go," she told him quickly. "Call me when you can, okay?"

He said he would and said good-bye. Over and out. Kelly put the phone on her desk and gathered up the few pages she'd printed, slipping them into a folder.

Monroe threw a sour look at her as she entered, narrowing his eyes at the folder in her hand. "What's that?"

"A little research."

He groaned. "No."

"Monroe, if you want to do a feature on the shootout, a few facts won't kill us. And don't forget we have tape from the scene. A WBRX exclusive."

Monroe's eyes gleamed. "Yeah. Keep reminding me."

"But it runs less than a minute. It would be nice if we had something to say too."

"I see your point. Yap all you want. For a feature, we can do cuts in advance."

Kelly didn't bother to reply. He wasn't

wrong, just annoying.

"By the way, the director wants to see the tape when he gets out of the control room. I assume you'll want to be there."

Kelly nodded, tapping the file folder against her thigh. There was no sense in taking out the papers or discussing the side topic of Gunther Bach with her boss. When Monroe was busy, he had the attention span of a gnat.

"Anything else?" he asked.

"Nope."

"Then get outta here. I mean that in a nice way."

"Sure you do," she said. The finger he jabbed in the direction of the open door was Kelly's cue to leave. "See you later."

Summoned via phone intercom at the usual hour, Kelly walked from her office to the makeup room. Dave Maples was in the chair and wearing a smock over his suit.

June Fletcher had just stepped back and was studying his rock-jawed face, not pleased. "Yikes. There is such a thing as too tan."

Kelly's co-anchor turned to look at himself in the mirror, smoothing down the tissues protecting his snowy collar. "I would call that a healthy glow," Dave said.

June didn't bother arguing, just got busy. In another few minutes, Dave looked more natural. He got up and let her remove the smock, then made a gallant gesture in the direction of the chair. "Your turn, Kelly."

"Thanks."

She sat and closed her eyes, letting June do her magic. "So what's the big story tonight?" the makeup artist asked.

"There isn't one," Kelly replied.

June clucked with disapproval. "You mean the world isn't coming to an end?"

"Not anytime soon."

Kelly could have done the broadcast in her sleep. Her mind was elsewhere. The routine stories had called for nothing more than the usual banter and an occasional concerned frown. She slid out from behind the slab top of the anchor desks, avoiding the tangle of wires hidden from the cameras.

Dave Maples had done the sign-off tonight and now was talking about the broadcast with the director, who was still in the control room. Actually, Dave was only listening, his gaze fixed on nothing. The director was talking to him through the clear IFB bud in Dave's ear. There was nothing like feedback to make an anchor look like a lunatic.

Handing over her lav mic and bud, Kelly left the set. She went around several corners to reach the newsroom. The steady hum of the scanners reached her first. Then suddenly the chatter grew louder, voices overlapping.

Jumper. Male. Unidentified. From penthouse floor. There was a witness. Promenade sealed. Additional units requested to scene. Repeat, additional units requested.

The address was given. She knew the street and the promenade, part of Atlanta's most expensive new condo complex. She heard the assignment editor at the scanner desk yelling for someone to get out there. Kelly almost bumped into Monroe by the time she turned the last corner.

"Did you hear that?" he asked her. "Poor bastard. But he might make the eleven o'clock news."

"Deke. Did I hear you right? Gunther Bach was the suicide?" Kelly grabbed a pencil. She'd been working late at the office when his call came in. "The scanners didn't ID the jumper. Who's your source? Tell me how you know."

"That thing you're talking on? The telephone? They have them all over the country now. I got a call."

"Don't be snotty. From who?"

"Someone who shall be nameless. He also e-mailed a couple of photos from the scene. Not pretty, but it was Bach all right. I'm being called back from Dallas."

As usual, Deke seemed to possess the ability to walk through walls and talk to everyone. Right now, it aggravated her.

"On whose authority? Your handler or lion tamer or parole officer or what?"

"I like lion tamer. I should be in Atlanta by midnight."

"I assume you're going to the scene. Is the medical examiner there yet?"

"Yeah. He got dragged out of some fancy party. I hear there's quite a crowd on the sidewalk," Deke replied. "Detectives, EMTs, undercovers, beat cops, you name it. And the techs are going over his apartment, dusting for fingerprints and looking under the bed."

"Not for missing socks, I take it."

"No."

"With that much official attention, I'm guessing they suspect murder rather than suicide," Kelly said.

"That's conjecture," Deke pointed out.

"Us newshounds do a lot of that. Anything else I don't know and won't be allowed to say on the air?"

"I'm glad you know where the line is drawn," Deke said.

"You're drawing it. Not me. Is it possible it could have been something other than suicide? Interrupted robbery, followed by homicide?"

"Nothing seemed to be taken. Apparently there was an insurance inventory of the penthouse art and valuables in his desk. There was no sign of forced entry."

"So he could have been killed by someone he knew," Kelly said.

"It's a likely scenario. But it's not the only one. The scene hasn't been processed. They still have to search for a note or some other indication that he wanted to take his life — that's routine. Then there are fingerprints. Or no fingerprints."

"I don't follow you."

"If there aren't any, that's suspicious. Surfaces don't get wiped down at suicide scenes. If there isn't some trace of him on the balcony railing — smeared palm prints, fingerprints — you can draw your own conclusions. But keep them to yourself."

Kelly fell silent. She had disliked Bach, had even been afraid of him, but she wouldn't wish a death like that on anyone.

"You still there?" Deke asked. "Don't get mad at me just because I can't give you a day pass to the penthouse."

"I'm not mad. I'm just dying of curiosity. So what exactly will you be doing when you get there?"

"I'm meeting Lieutenant Dwight from the Atlanta PD. He called me in for a consult on some other evidence."

The name didn't register at first. Then Kelly remembered — he was the taciturn lieutenant who'd interviewed her the day after the shooting. "Give him my regards."

"I will."

"Is there any way I could be useful?"

Deke didn't answer for a moment. "Actually, there is something you can do that I can't. When the autopsy is over, go to Gunther's funeral."

"And why do you want me to go?"

"They'll expect some news presence, and you knew him slightly. Look sad but stay alert. Find out who shows up."

"Anyone in particular you're looking for?"

"My guess is that a lot of people would have been happy to see him dead. We know his US operation was headed for a fast meltdown and that his hedge fund was on the verge of collapse."

"That's not news."

"Let me bring you up to date. Gunther Bach was blowing through money to the tune of a million dollars a day. He borrowed a hundred million not that long ago to keep his fraud going — a personal loan from an unidentified 'friend.' With the stipulation that it be repaid promptly."

Kelly was scribbling madly. "Go on."

"Bach defaulted on the loan this afternoon. Now he's dead."

Lieutenant Dwight pretended not to notice when Deke finally ended his second call to Kelly around two A.M. The crime scene techs had cleared out of the penthouse, taking large paper bags and boxes filled with anything that could be evidence.

Tall and rangy, Dwight paced the luxurious apartment once more, his long stride carrying him swiftly through the rooms.

He returned to see that Deke was standing, taking a final look around himself. "Ready to go?" the lieutenant asked him.

Deke seemed reluctant. "Yeah. But I feel like there's something we overlooked," he said.

"I always feel like that. Sometimes I'm right and we find something. But we turned this place upside down and inside out."

Deke slipped his phone into an inside pocket of his leather jacket.

The lieutenant gave a dry chuckle. "Keeping Kelly close, are you?"

Deke nodded. "As close as I can. It's not like she follows instructions."

"You're good at working the media, Bannon. It's a necessary evil."

Deke knew the lieutenant was only half-joking. "Don't ever let her hear you say that," he replied. "I prefer to think of it as working *with* the media."

"Spin it any way you like. You know what I'm talking about. Best to say things straight. If you can't, I will. I have nothing to lose." He gave Deke a considering look. "She's not my girl."

Deke didn't answer.

"If you don't mind my asking, is she yours?" A wry smile altered the expression on Dwight's lined face.

Deke shot him a wary look. "Kelly and I are a team. Can I leave it at that?"

The lieutenant folded his lean arms across his chest. "Bannon, I don't want this investigation compromised. If you say too much, it will be."

"She's helping us, Dwight. She is seriously good at this game."

CHAPTER 13

"Come on, Kelly. How often do I ask you for favors?"

"Every day? Once a week? I can't remember," Kelly said. "You keep right on doing it."

She had him there. Monroe Capp had the grace to look a little ashamed. "I hate funerals," he said. "And I barely knew Gunther Bach."

"But you got an invitation." Unlike Deke, who'd already asked her to go.

"I have another commitment." Her boss wasn't giving up. "Come on. Help me out. You can take an extra personal day this month."

"I hardly knew him myself," Kelly protested. "We had lunch in Atlanta. Once. We had a creepy conversation in Dallas after that."

"How about this? Skip the funeral." Monroe switched to negotiation mode. "I heard it's supposed to be on the small side anyway. The memorial service invitation is for me and a guest, so that could be you."

"I wonder if any of the people he cheated are going to be there," Kelly mused. "Talk about real tears."

"That's not nice."

"Neither was he."

Monroe Capp looked almost defeated. Almost.

"Why do I get the feeling you haven't told me everything?" Kelly asked after a beat.

"Because I haven't," Monroe shot back. "Okay, here goes. Natalie Conrad is flying in the same day. Her social secretary left me a message, so it's not like it was a personal request, but Natalie wants me to sit next to her at the memorial service."

"Oh. Now I understand."

"Kelly, I just don't need the aggravation. She was a problem when we both lived in Buckhead."

"Why?" Kelly was interested.

"Natalie — ah — came over now and then when Maya wasn't around. She wasn't looking to borrow a cup of sugar, put it that way. And when I got divorced and she was widowed, I think she expected me to, you know, take care of her."

Kelly just looked at him. Monroe met her

gaze and read her mind. "Go ahead and say it. I'm not a sex god. But I'm single and under sixty and trustworthy."

She suppressed a smile, not too successfully.

"Compared to some," Monroe amended. "She knew I didn't need her money. Anyway, I was really relieved when she moved on. But I don't want to renew our acquaintance. Please, Kelly. Help me out."

There were no relatives at the memorial service, as far as Kelly knew. Gunther Bach didn't seem to have any.

A man at the lectern gave a discreet cough as mourners faced forward. No white clerical collar, no black. Just an ordinary suit and neutral tie. There was something generic about him.

"Good afternoon. As we gather to remember a colleague and friend of many here today . . . excuse me. Is this on?" The man turned to someone at the side to ask about the microphone. Judging by his opening line, he seemed not to have met the man he was eulogizing.

The problem was fixed and he droned on.

Kelly could have done better on the details. Gunther Bach had never married and had no children. Kelly had found not one mention of family online. Women, yes. Lots of those. Par for the course for a womanizer. He had wealthy friends, not that many, and innumerable business acquaintances.

"It is well to remember that death comes for us all in time. It is my understanding that Gunther Bach lived life to the fullest . . ."

The mourners filling the somber hall for the memorial service sat in rows, mostly expressionless. Their attire was just as somber, running to severe, tailored suits for both sexes.

Kelly told herself not to think like a tabloid reporter. There was no reason to expect a veiled beauty overcome with grief-stricken sobs, or the appearance of a long-lost relative. Gunther Bach's inner circle evidently didn't go in for drama. But she had to wonder what they did go in for.

The speaker wrapped up the eulogy and stepped down. No one came forward to offer something more personal.

"Sir. Madam. Sir." With muted voices and gestures, the dark-suited ushers directed the guests to rise.

Slowly, everyone filed out to a smaller hall, where a cold buffet was laid out on a banquet table draped in white damask. It didn't look particularly fresh.

There was ice water in pitchers, with coffee and tea provided by catering-company servers. Gunther Bach's funeral was definitely not the kind of send-off where people drowned their sorrows or got emotional.

People moved discreetly away from Kelly, seeming to know who she was, as if no one wanted publicity. She didn't care one way or another. Not having to engage in conversation allowed her to study the guests and commit a few faces to memory for later research.

There was a subdued commotion at the entrance and murmurs ran through the scattered group. Kelly set her glass of water aside by the cold buffet and straightened her clothes. That had to be Natalie Conrad.

"Hello, everyone."

Her voice was low but she entered like a queen, quietly acknowledging her subjects with a nod here and there.

"Natalie." A well-dressed woman lingered over the name, following up with a double air-kiss and a pat from a gloved hand. "I'm so sorry you missed the funeral and the eulogy. But it is good to see you."

Both comments held a touch of acid, Kelly noticed. Just enough.

"A sad day." A courtly older gentleman

bowed slightly to Natalie. "Yet how lovely you look, Mrs. Conrad."

"Ah, you are here at last." A heavy man with an accent spoke to her in a gruff voice. "It is good of you to come."

It was almost as if Natalie Conrad had been widowed a second time, Kelly thought absently. But as far as she knew, Natalie and Gunther had never meant that much to each other. The guests seemed to think otherwise.

Observing them all, she went back to making mental notes. She'd type them up when this charade was over and get them to Deke.

In an aside, he'd told her that she might be surprised by who showed up at funerals for victims of violent crimes. She knew what he meant, but she didn't see anyone she thought was capable of murder.

They all seemed to be rich people with reserved manners. There were no celebrities, though Kelly had half expected to spot one or two.

No one had been charged with any crime. Leaks to the media had been controlled. Gunther Bach's death had been officially tagged as suspicious, nothing more, pending further investigation.

Natalie made her way across the hall, exchanging nods of recognition with a guest

327

or two. She wore a light coat over a matching dress, subdued in color but closely fitted and trimmed with black velvet. She was heading for Kelly, but not obviously. There was a brief moment of eye contact that widened Natalie's beautiful eyes.

She reached Kelly at last and took her arm, drawing her aside. "Monroe told me you would attend in his place," she murmured. "So kind of you. You look a bit forlorn."

"I really don't know anyone here," Kelly said tactfully.

"Some of Gunther's friends are unpleasant. I do hope they aren't ignoring you." Natalie reached out to take Kelly's hands and clasp them warmly in her own.

Kelly couldn't pull away. But something about the older woman's intensity made her nervous.

"No. I'm a stranger, that's all."

Natalie sighed. "They could be more welcoming. Gunther would have insisted on it. He was such a gregarious man — with an eye for the ladies, of course. I would guess he was charmed by you."

The older woman's gaze fastened on her with a hard sparkle. Kelly thought it was possible that Natalie had been drinking. But there was no whiff of liquor on her breath.

She exuded costly perfume, nothing more.

"I couldn't say," Kelly answered. "To be honest, I hardly knew him. But I understand that you two were close."

"Yes, we were. Once upon a time. That — well, that was long over. I am so glad that I had a chance to see him in Dallas before his tragic death." Lowering her voice, she almost purred the last two words.

Kelly was taken aback, trying to figure out how a memorial service had turned into a stage play starring the eccentric Natalie Conrad. It seemed safest to agree. "It was a tragedy. I was so shocked when I heard."

"My dear, where were you at that moment?" Not waiting for an answer, Natalie spoke first. "I was in my garden, watching the moon rise. For some reason I was thinking that Gunther might be looking at the same moon far away. Strange, isn't it? But at the time, it seemed like only a fleeting thought."

Kelly realized that Natalie was talking about the hour of night when Gunther Bach had died. She searched for some reply, but was interrupted by someone who knew Natalie.

The elderly woman sidled up and edged in front of Kelly without saying *excuse me.* "Can you give me just a minute of your time, Mrs. Conrad?"

"What?" Natalie snapped out of her reverie. "May I ask who you are?"

"I'm Frances Berry. I lived in the apartment down the hall from Mr. Bach. He invited me in once for a glass of schnapps. I saw your picture — I thought you were lovely."

Natalie's expression was glacial. "Imagine that. I had no idea he had my photo on display."

The elderly woman persisted. "He told me a little about you. He'd be happy to know that you came today. He seemed to be a very lonely man."

Natalie Conrad's perfectly plucked eyebrows went up. "We are all lonely people, Mrs. Berry. Now if you would excuse us —" She reached across to take Kelly's arm, turning around with her and putting a decisive end to the conversation.

They walked a few steps away.

"What an odd little person," Natalie murmured. "I never went to Gunther's apartment. I thought for some reason that his penthouse was the only one in the building. I didn't know he had neighbors."

"I think she meant well," Kelly said softly, covering her irritation at being steered away. Natalie Conrad was putting her long fingernails to good use. She had a surprisingly strong grip for a slender — and older — woman.

"Perhaps." Natalie sighed. "I hope I wasn't too rude to her. I suppose I should mingle." They turned to face the other guests, who merely nodded if they noticed the two women at all.

"I'm sure you have friends here," Kelly replied. "It was nice to see you again, Natalie. Even under the circumstances. But I do have to leave."

"Must you?" Natalie asked peevishly. "I can make excuses to Monroe if you like. Won't you come with me to Buckhead afterward? I haven't been back to the house that Harry and I shared in ages. I don't want to go alone."

Ultra needy. And borderline nuts. Both were snap judgments on Natalie's character, but Kelly knew they were accurate. At first she was inclined to politely decline. But something stopped her. She sensed there was something to be learned by accompanying Natalie to her mansion and she would have her own transportation if she wanted to leave. She had decided on a long-term rental car for the time being. Deke hadn't had a chance to look at hers.

Natalie seized on Kelly's momentary

silence to press her advantage. "Don't worry, dear. I called ahead. I still have live-in servants on the property — the house will be ready for us. And it's not as if you're staying overnight."

Kelly was intrigued. A glimpse into the former mansion of one of the wealthiest couples in the world would be an excellent starting point for an interview — which could be linked to Gunther's sad demise if Natalie would talk about him. Kelly had broken the initial news in a brief report the day after Gunther's death.

"Please say yes," Natalie begged her.

Kelly knew an opportunity when she saw one. But she left herself an out. Natalie had just arrived. She would want to talk with other guests and she would think nothing of keeping Kelly waiting.

"Thank you," Kelly said bluntly. "I do have the rest of the afternoon free. But if you don't mind, I would prefer to wait in the parking lot in my car."

Natalie patted her arm. "I understand completely. There are far too many cold fish here — and I don't mean the ones on the buffet table. Let me chat with a few acquaintances, though."

Kelly thanked her instincts for predicting that. She would have time for a quick call to Deke, if he picked up. "Of course. Please don't hurry on my account."

"I won't be long. Then we can be on our way."

"Sounds good."

Kelly discreetly left the gathering by walking around the guests without making eye contact.

The dreary afternoon was nearly over. Even if Natalie didn't know it, she was effectively being interviewed as of now.

Kelly breathed a sigh of relief when she stepped outside. The day was overcast, but there was a fresh breeze that lightened her mood as soon as she got away from the grim guests. She glanced over her shoulder as heavy doors swung shut behind her, making sure that no one had followed her.

She headed for her rented car, turning on the cell phone she'd switched off during the eulogy and pulling up Deke's number.

He answered after a few rings. "Hey, Kelly. How was the memorial service?"

Kelly gave him a rundown as she unlocked her car and slipped into the passenger seat. Natalie's penchant for gracious conversation meant she might have to wait an hour or more. She kicked off her black pumps and leaned the seat back, getting comfortable as she talked.

"Sounds like it was worthwhile," he said. "Let's look at the rogue's gallery when you get back, see if you can find a few faces."

"Okay. But update me," she said. "Any news on what happened to Bach?"

"They still can't say for sure if it was suicide or homicide."

"No one can make an educated guess? There must be some clues."

Deke paused. "As far as his apartment, it's more like the absence of clues that we're looking at. For example, the balcony railing had a layer of city dust that no one had touched for weeks."

"And that means . . ." Stubbornly, Kelly wanted to make him go over the facts in detail. She knew Deke wasn't telling her everything with the new police investigation under way.

"Could mean a lot of things. None of the windows were open," Deke said. "And we know he didn't go off the roof because the door was locked and the soot and dust in that area, inside and out, also hadn't been disturbed."

"Got it."

"So if he went off the balcony, he didn't vault it or climb over it. Since there were no marks on the railing, he was probably thrown."

Gunther had been fit and he was tall. There had to have been a struggle. Deke seemed to be giving her a chance to figure it out. Nice of him. "It took two to do that."

"Or one man who was strong enough and tall enough to hurl him clear of the railing."

Kelly thought. "Someone would remember a man like that."

"It's a big-city apartment building," Deke said. "People who live there don't hang around in the halls. But we're interviewing everyone, starting at the top and working down. So far no one heard or saw anything out of the ordinary."

Which reminded Kelly. "An old lady who lives on his floor was at the memorial service. Frances Berry was her name — it seemed to me that she actually knew Gunther."

"Thank God for old ladies," Deke said.

"So did you talk to her?"

There was a brief pause. "She was out." He was making a note. "But we will."

"Moving right along," she said briskly, "do you have any details about the autopsy?"

Deke sighed. "I hate to cross the line and give out information."

"Do you want me to sign a confidentiality agreement?"

He laughed. "I don't have that kind of

authority. And a piece of paper isn't going to stop you."

"Just tell me. I'm not going to blurt it out on air. Dave Maples might faint. He can't stand gore."

"All right."

She guessed Deke was consulting a notebook.

"Given the condition of the body, the medical examiner had a tough time identifying subtler signs of trauma, but he's sure Bach was roughed up before he died. As far as the toxicology analysis, the results won't be back for a couple of weeks at least."

"What are they looking for?"

Deke stopped. "Kelly, I'll be straight with you. This case could tank — and the evidence made inadmissible in court — if you're all over it."

"You're in too deep to back out now," she retorted. "Believe me, I'm not typing this into a laptop and I'm not going to make a single word of this public, even though it's killing me. I keep reminding myself that I owe you."

"What for?"

"Oh, you know, saving my life. That right there could be enough to keep me in line."

Deke acknowledged that with a laugh. "All right. Drug and toxin tests are routine in an autopsy. What they're looking for is a heavy-duty tranquilizer, according to the medical examiner. Hang on. I'll give you the details."

She waited.

"New psychoactive, experimental in Europe with restricted availability," Deke reeled off. "In FDA trials here, not likely to be approved in the US."

Kelly found a pen and scratch pad and jotted down the brand name. That wasn't classified information. "If the toxicology results take weeks to come back, how do they know the name of the drug?"

"There was an intact pill stuck in Bach's throat," Deke explained. "The brand was readable. He may have been unknowingly drugged at first, then forced to swallow more."

"Why?"

"Maybe his killers wanted to make sure he wouldn't struggle or scream."

Kelly shuddered. "That's awful."

"There was a new bottle of spray cleaner under the sink. A torn rag soaked in it was found in Bach's kitchen garbage."

"How convenient."

"Not really. We sorted through every damn garbage bag in the building's Dumpster before we found one with a receipt that had his signature. Ask me how many bags we opened."

"James Bond didn't have to do stuff like that. Two hundred and five?"

"Close enough." Deke continued, "Our guess is that the spray cleaner was used to remove fingerprints, and thoroughly. The techs didn't pick up a single one, anywhere. With the exception of the balcony, the whole place was immaculate."

Kelly listened.

"The rest of the rag got stuffed down Gunther's throat, on top of the pill," Deke said tersely. "He probably didn't have the strength to fight his attacker, Kelly. But he didn't go down easy."

She was lost in thought after the call concluded, finally switching the key in the ignition so she could listen to the radio and take her mind off what Deke had told her. A rap on the car window snapped her out of her reverie.

Kelly pressed the button to roll it down. "Natalie — sorry. My mind was elsewhere."

"Completely understandable." Natalie pulled the collar of her light coat up and took car keys from an Hermès bag. "Do you want to follow me?"

"Yes. But please give me the address. I can use the GPS app on my phone just in case we get separated."

Natalie provided it and waved to indicate her car. Kelly got out and went around to the driver's side of hers, taking a long look at the sleek sports car as Natalie unlocked it from steps away. The taillights flashed twice. Their distinctive configuration would be easy to follow.

She slid behind the wheel of her car, thinking how much Natalie's must have cost. Kelly had never cared all that much about what she drove. But the sports car was definitely out of her league.

Natalie Conrad's mansion in Buckhead was old and oppressive — and totally different from the clean, contemporary look of the planned museum.

Just for the hell of it, Kelly silently counted windows on the second floor as she followed Natalie from the porte-cochère. Monroe Capp hadn't exaggerated when he'd said the house had twenty bedrooms.

She entered the carved doors with a feeling of apprehension. There was a servant waiting just inside who'd evidently opened them at the sight of Natalie's car rolling up. She seemed to be in late middle age, wearing a dark uniform dress with a white collar. She didn't meet Kelly's gaze, responding first to Natalie's sharply voiced request.

"Tea and light sandwiches in the drawing room, Finley. And be quick about it."

"Yes, Mrs. Conrad."

Natalie took off her lightweight coat and tossed it on a massive sideboard that had pride of place in the foyer. There was nothing else on it but a black marble vase.

The huge house exuded gloom. There were fabric covers over most of the furniture Kelly could see, and the drapes were closed everywhere she looked. A wide, floor-to-ceiling window in the drawing room was the exception. Kelly walked past a set of antique armchairs to get to it, drawn to the splash of sunlight.

"That's quite a view."

A plush green lawn that hadn't been mowed recently sloped down to an ornamental pond surrounded by willows. Nearer to the house were tall, shaggy hedges that almost concealed narrow paths winding through them.

"It used to be much nicer. The grounds are in dire need of landscaping," was Natalie Conrad's reply.

Kelly didn't mind the overgrown look. But she couldn't say so in those words — Natalie might take it the wrong way. She turned away from the window toward the arrangement of armchairs, noticing for the first time that the wallpaper was sun-faded, except for several large patches where it looked new, as if paintings had been removed.

Natalie, who had seated herself, seemed to expect a question on the subject. "Are you wondering where the art went?"

"I was, yes."

"Many of our paintings are on extended loan to museums," the older woman said. "They are safer there, since I so rarely come to Buckhead."

"That makes sense."

"I find it more satisfying to give these days. One can only acquire so much before it becomes overwhelming."

Kelly didn't know much about the ins and outs of the art world, but obviously a loan and a gift were two different things. It was interesting that Natalie didn't bother to draw a distinction.

"That's admirable," she said. "Will the Conrad collection go to the new museum?"

Natalie turned in her chair to face the empty wall. "Yes. Eventually. I do hope that it will be built in my lifetime. So far, the benefactors have had to use their imaginations. All I have to show them are blueprints and that architect's model." She laughed lightly. "We may be years away from approval. So many regulations, permits, forms — thank goodness I have people to see to all that. It never seems to end."

"Someday it will."

"Yes. I can't complain, Kelly. But it is a great shame that Gunther will never see the museum. He would have been so proud."

Kelly didn't know exactly what to say. The details of Gunther Bach's death weren't something she could share. "It's hard to believe that he's gone."

She paused, hoping Natalie might feel the need to fill in a few blanks. But the older woman seemed pensive. "He shall be missed."

Kelly wasn't going to mention Gunther's financial crash if Natalie hadn't heard about it — it wasn't public knowledge yet. With luck, she hadn't invested with him. Kelly assumed she had advisers and accountants by the score.

But she was beginning to get an inkling that Natalie Conrad didn't have as much money as people thought. The downturn in the economy had hit some very wealthy people hard — no one was completely immune. This house might be proof of that.

Kelly supposed there wasn't much point in keeping up a place if no one lived in it, but even so. Despite its luxurious, Old World furnishings, the darkened mansion had a faintly musty atmosphere. And so far she had seen only one servant, though there had to be others around somewhere. It would take a small army to manage a place this size. Still, there was something shabby about Natalie Conrad's house, grand as it was. Somehow Kelly had been expecting more.

But the Buckhead mansion was only one of many houses that the Conrads had owned and Natalie had inherited. If Kelly officially landed the interview — and even better, coaxed Natalie to reveal more about her connection to the mysteriously dead Gunther Bach — they would shoot it elsewhere.

A telephone rang on a lacquered desk.

"Excuse me."

Thick rugs softened every step Natalie took to answer it. She murmured a few responses to the caller and ended the conversation, moving to a set of crystal decanters and pouring herself a stiff drink.

"Would you like something stronger than tea?" she asked Kelly. "I can't imagine why Finley is taking so long."

"No thanks."

Natalie shrugged and gulped down the

amber liquid, pouring herself another before she returned to sit with Kelly again.

"That was Luc, a young friend of mine, who just called. I think he's about your age. He's an artist — I suppose you could say I collect them too." Her eyes were shining. Alcohol or not, she seemed happier.

Kelly smiled. It wasn't her job to judge.

"He's working on a new series about death and rebirth. Luc never does anything frivolous." Natalie finished her second drink and set the glass aside.

"Oh. How interesting."

Natalie sat back and ran a hand over the brocade of her armchair. "Which is why he hates this place," she said.

That was more than Kelly needed to know. She just listened.

"To think I once considered it and everything in it the height of elegance," Natalie continued. "Now, pah. If there was a fire and it all burned to ashes, I would miss nothing. Too many possessions can be a burden, don't you agree?"

For someone who had everything, maybe that was easy to say. Kelly only laughed. "It's not something I think about."

"And why is that?"

"I have what I need, but that's not much. I travel a lot and I've lived in a lot of different places. I like to be able to just go."

The arrival of Finley, the servant with no first name, came as a welcome distraction. She carried a large silver tray, laden with all that was needed for afternoon tea, including small, crustless sandwiches. Kelly hadn't eaten at the memorial service buffet, and the food looked tempting.

At Natalie's nod, the woman put the tray on the low table between the two chairs and retreated.

"How do you like your tea?" Natalie inquired, preparing to pour.

"With lemon. Thanks."

She took the porcelain cup from the older woman's hand and took a sip. It was cool enough to drink. No doubt the kitchen was some distance from the drawing room, and Kelly had guessed that Finley was on her own in it.

The tiny sandwiches were filling and not as posh as they looked. That was tuna fish in them.

The conversation continued somewhat randomly as they ate. Natalie did most of the talking. When they had finished the food, she put down her teacup and glanced out the window. Kelly saw an indistinct figure pass by.

"Dear me. I think I see — yes, that is the

landscaper. He's long overdue."

Natalie rose and looked through the glass, tapping on it to get the man's attention. Evidently she succeeded.

She turned to Kelly. "Would you mind if I stepped outside to speak with him?"

"Not at all."

Natalie walked away. Her footsteps echoed over the marble floor of the grand entrance. Kelly sat still when she heard the front door click. She didn't care to get up and look around. She didn't want to seem to be prying if Natalie returned before she could dash back.

The sudden sound of an argument reached her from outside. The landscaper's voice was so deep Kelly couldn't make out the words through the closed window. Natalie's was shrill and hectoring, nothing like the smooth, cultured tone she liked to pour on.

Kelly was forced to listen. After a minute she realized that the two weren't speaking English. The temptation to get closer to the window and see what Natalie looked like in a rage was too strong to resist. Kelly got up but stayed hidden.

The man who stood facing Natalie had his back to the window, his hands thrust into the pockets of a canvas barn jacket. He was so tall and built so broadly that he concealed her. There was the sharp crack of a slap. Natalie must have hit him because his hands stayed in his pockets. His head barely moved.

He couldn't be a landscaper. But who he was and why Natalie was so angry at him was a mystery to Kelly.

The argument died down from that point. Kelly took a step, about to go back to her chair when the man turned around. She noted the thick scarf around his neck before she registered his rough-hewn features and sullen expression. The tirade seemed to have had no more effect on him than the slap.

He saw her. His eyes were black as his hair. He looked at her intently for a little too long. Then he walked away from the window and Natalie. She came back in, alone.

She seemed more nervous than ever. Kelly didn't ask questions, just looked at her once and then away while Natalie composed herself.

"Kelly." She finally spoke. "I barely slept last night, and I suppose I have a touch of jet lag."

The flight from Dallas to Atlanta was less than two hours. But if Natalie was making excuses, Kelly didn't mind.

"Would you mind very much if I gave you the house tour some other time?"

"Not at all." Kelly had been trying to plot a graceful exit. And she didn't want to see the rest of the depressing house. "I hope I didn't wear out my welcome."

The other woman did look genuinely tired. She managed a smile. "Of course not."

A few minutes later, when Finley appeared to take the tray, they exchanged good-byes and Kelly saw herself out.

She waited until she was on the main road that would take her back to the highway running through Atlanta and pulled off at a lookout point to call Deke.

She just wanted to talk to him. The afternoon had left her with a bad feeling and a headache.

"I was just about to call you. What's up?" His voice was low, as if he didn't want someone else to hear him talking.

"Nothing. I'm heading back. I just got done having tea with Natalie Conrad at her great big gloomy house."

"Did she say anything about Bach?"

"Not really."

Deke paused. She heard street noise in the background. A siren wailed, then faded away. "I'm still here," he said.

"Are you free tonight?" Kelly asked.

"No."

She was puzzled by the flat reply. Then someone called him by his last name. He had to be working. Why didn't he just say so?

"Hang on. Let me get to where I can talk." Moments later, he spoke again. "I'm with Hux. He wanted help following up on leads." A blare of loud, thumping music drowned out the rest. "Okay. I guess this is not the doorway to have a private conversation. I'll call you back."

"You don't have to. I might as well just head home and sack out in front of the TV."

"Text me when you get there, Kelly."

"I will."

She ended the call, disappointed.

Chapter 14

Monday morning came too soon. Kelly entered WBRX at a dead run, bumping into Coral Reese. "Sorry. Overslept. Not really here yet."

Coral laughed. "Hey, I got some more info on those shell companies you were asking about. I highlighted everything I understood."

Kelly looked at her blankly. "Shell what?"

"Never mind. You need coffee," the junior reporter said. "I'll bring the folder by later. Brush your hair," she added in a whisper, moving on.

The newsroom was humming. Kelly glanced at the clock that ruled them all.

Gordon appeared out of nowhere. The burly cameraman stopped, blocking her way. "Morning meeting in half an hour."

"Do you mind, Gordon?" She tried to get around him. "It's not like you have to be there."

"Us camera people are always out in the fresh air and sunshine, reporting the good news," he said dryly. "How are you?"

"Fine."

"Oh yeah? What have you been up to since we were dodging bullets together?"

"Lots of things. I have to go."

"Come out to the van and see me sometime," he called after her.

She would be on time for the morning meeting. Monroe would want updates, assignments would get handed out — and she heard him coming down the hall.

"There you are," he said. "How was the memorial service?"

"It was strange. And Natalie Conrad is a piece of work."

"Told you."

"She invited me to tea afterward."

Monroe's eyebrows went up. "Lucky you. You made the inner circle."

Kelly went into her office and slung her tote bag over the back of her chair. "I really don't need a new best friend, thanks."

"But she's rich and influential."

Kelly shook her head firmly. "I don't care. She acts like she owns everyone and everything."

Monroe laughed. "Let me break it to you gently. She actually does. We could do a feature on her, you know. *The Ten Most Powerful Women in Atlanta.*"

"I don't think she's lived in that Buckhead house for years. And it's not really Atlanta, is it?"

"So we bend the truth a little. So what?"

"I'm beginning to think that maybe it matters." Kelly went to the coffeemaker, grabbing a bottle of water from her desk to fill the reservoir. She dropped a filter packet of coffee into the basket, but it split open.

The day went downhill from there.

That night she finally saw Deke. The front desk at the hotel called her before they let him up. The place had decent security. Whether it was good enough to keep her safe remained to be seen. Kelly opened the door to his knock.

He must have given the staff cause for suspicion. His dark hair was scruffy and his strong jaw was shadowed with stubble. The leather jacket was even more creased, as if he'd slept in it somewhere.

"Come on in," she said. "Stakeout over?"

"It wasn't really a stakeout." Deke gave the place an automatic once-over. "I know I look like hell. You don't have to tell me."

"I wasn't going to. Can I get you anything? I have cold cuts and bread and mayo. How about a beer?"

He shook his head. "No thanks. Me and Hux hit every dive bar and back alley in Atlanta."

"Excuse me?"

"Not to drink. To get information."

Deke settled himself on the couch, stretching out his long legs. As an afterthought, he leaned forward and slid off his jacket.

"Would you mind telling me what's going on?"

"That's why I'm here. Look, Kelly, an informer tipped off Hux to a contract on offer. For a hired killer," he added, catching her baffled look. "It's related to the shootout."

"Gang feud? Revenge?"

"We almost wish. The payoff is huge, but no one wants it. The target is too well-known."

Kelly nodded, but not in encouragement.

"Hux came to me with the rumors and his initial legwork. We followed through. Seems that our usual suspects turned the job down right away. Which means it's likely to be a new thug on the block."

"Let me guess. He's not in your laptop," she said quietly.

"He might be by now. Tonight we got a slew of pictures on the sly. Looks like there's a new gang moving in on Atlanta."

"Nice to know."

"There may not be an organized effort behind this, Kelly. We could be looking for just one or two people. At first all Hux could find out was that someone in the media was targeted."

"There are lots of us in Atlanta," she said quietly.

"Yeah, well, we finally found the one dude who knew a little more about the proposed hit. Not who would do it or who's behind it, just who was supposed to get killed. You."

Her eyes flashed with anger. "Why am I singled out? Other stations picked up the Bach story and the newspapers reported the shootout."

"You were the only eyewitness to it. That's my reasoning. Hux agrees."

Kelly walked away from him into the kitchen. She looked into the refrigerator even though she knew there was hardly anything in it. She settled for a glass of cold water from the outside dispenser, took a sip, and put it down on the counter. Her tense throat made it hard to swallow.

"You know, in my business, you do sort of get used to maniacs."

"Nothing like this," he countered.

"I know several reporters who get death

threats," she said. "If you do investigative stories or crime-watch features, that comes with the territory. So far no one's ever wanted to kill me, though. But I get plenty of interesting stuff. Shut-up-or-die e-mails, poison-pen letters, anonymous slams posted online with altered photos. I've seen my head on a stripper's body."

"The card and the photos went beyond all of that. And they were delivered to where you live."

She acknowledged that hard fact with a frown. "Which is why I'm here and not there. The station is another matter. But they do make every effort to protect us."

"It may not be enough. It may be time for you to drop the story. Or let someone else do the reporting."

Deke had moved away from the couch by the time she came out of the kitchen. He was close enough to reach out to her. But he didn't.

"Too late now, don't you think?"

"Kelly, don't give these guys more reasons to kill you."

"If they want to try, they will. I don't see how me quitting is going to make them give up."

Deke tried another tack. "If you get a concealed-carry permit, you would at least have a gun. Lieutenant Dwight can speed up the process."

"You and I both know that won't guarantee my safety."

"Just think about it. And go with me to a firing range," he pleaded. "Get in some practice. If you change your mind, you're ready."

"Anything else you think I should do?"

"Besides listen to me? No," he said.

She gave him a stubborn look, but he didn't lose his temper. "Can we agree to keep talking about this?"

"Let's drop it. I'm exhausted anyway," Kelly said, adding quickly with a flash of guilt, "but so are you. Listen, I appreciate what you and Hux are trying to do."

Deke grabbed his jacket, but he didn't put it on. "Is having someone want to take care of you the worst thing that ever happened to you, Kelly? Tell me the truth."

She just glowered at him. His dark gaze fixed on hers again, but she stood her ground. "I don't have to tell you anything." Her voice wavered slightly.

Deke came to her. "No. You don't." His arms went around her and she didn't push him away. Yet she was unwilling to relax. She faced a different kind of danger in his embrace: needing him too much.

His lips brushed the top of her head and his hand began to stroke her hair, parting the silky strands to rub the nape of her neck.

Unfair. He had seized the advantage. A huge advantage. The onrush of physical sensation caused by his gentle caress melted her resistance. Kelly rested her head on his shoulder. "I give up," she whispered. "Just keep doing that."

"Don't mind if I do," he murmured in reply. "But I know damn well you haven't given up."

Kelly lifted her face to his, offering her lips to the strong mouth that claimed hers. Deke cupped her head and drew her against him firmly for a kiss that went further than their first or their second. Third time counted for all with this one. His tongue teased hers, then entered, tasting her deeply. The tender but forceful kiss was nearly unbearable. Kelly responded with her whole body, drawing what she needed and craved from the pressure of his.

A minute had passed before he lifted his head. She touched a finger to the lips that had given her so much pleasure. "No more," she whispered. "I can't think when you do that to me."

"That's the idea," he growled.

Kelly straightened away from him. She

picked up his jacket, which had been tossed aside in the heat of the moment, and handed it to him. If it had been up to her, she would have listened to the voice in her head, sent him packing, and slept in the warm leather that smelled intoxicatingly of man.

"You should go."

Deke accepted the jacket and slung it on a little awkwardly. He chucked her under the chin. "I liked that," he said nonchalantly. "To be continued?"

Kelly managed a ghost of a smile. "Maybe."

"Do you want to go to the firing range tomorrow?"

"Definitely. Even though I'm not that scared. It's weird. I guess I should be."

"If someone is closing in on you, Kelly, he's going to have to deal with me."

Deke bent his head and lifted her chin with a fingertip. A searching, final kiss sealed a silent deal. They were in this together. The details could come later.

Kelly yielded once more to the mouth that sought hers so urgently.

The following afternoon at WBRX, Kelly ignored her phone when it rang, occupied with a hundred things she wanted to get off her desk. The ringing stopped, then started again. With a sigh, Kelly looked at the number without recognizing it and picked up the receiver. She had a feeling that the caller wouldn't go away otherwise. Distracted, she forgot to say her name, going with a brusque hello instead.

"Kelly! It's Natalie Conrad. Just a quick question. I know you must be terribly busy."

"You're right about that," Kelly said courteously. "But ask away."

"Do you remember the young artist I talked to you about? Luc Allen? He does conceptual pieces on death and rebirth."

Save me, Kelly thought. Natalie had taken a call from him at the Buckhead mansion. "Right."

"He's looking for a space, a very large one, for an installation." Natalie coughed. Kelly wondered if she was smoking. "My art-world contacts have not been helpful."

"I'm not sure if I can be."

"Kelly, I must fly back to Dallas to sign paperwork for the new museum, and I don't know when I'll be back."

"Oh."

"I would love to take care of this as soon as possible. I suppose I could call Monroe. He knows Atlanta."

Hint hint. Kelly got it. She told herself that she didn't have to solve the problem, only make suggestions. The largest building she could think of was the old factory she and Deke had visited together. But the second Natalie saw it, she would run for the hills.

"Does the space have to be painted white or fixed up?" Kelly asked.

"No. Luc admires the patina of decay. He wants something gritty with a dash of danger."

Kelly rolled her eyes, glad that Natalie couldn't see her do it. "Well, there's an old factory on the other side of Atlanta," she said.

There wasn't a chance in hell that Natalie would set foot inside it. Kelly was sure of that.

"I don't know who owns it, but I looked inside it once. It's cavernous — I think it takes up half a city block. There's a roof and a floor."

"The other side of Atlanta? Where, specifically?"

She told her. Natalie went quiet. "We would have difficulty getting insurance," she said. "I understand there have been incidents in the area."

Kelly was almost surprised that Natalie had heard of them. The billionaire's widow lived in a bubble.

"That's true. But I guess people would drive out to see the installation. Honestly, Natalie, it's not my area of expertise. That's the only place that comes to mind."

"Just a moment. I'll tell Luc," Natalie answered after a few seconds. Kelly heard a male voice mutter something in the background. It sounded like the young artist was right there with her.

Natalie came back on the line. "He needs to look at it. Thank you so much, Kelly."

"Glad to help. Bye." She hung up. Favor done. Natalie and Luc could take it from there.

CHAPTER 15

Gordon seemed to take up most of the space in the interior of the van. The WBRX vehicle was a mini broadcasting station on wheels, crammed with equipment and trailing cables.

"Looks good so far," Gordon said about the tape. "Want to see it again?"

"Okay." Kelly watched herself take two steps toward the camera and speak the lines she'd memorized. They were at the open area by Gunther Bach's apartment building, taping additional footage. They might need it if they ran out of new developments and had to take the story back in time.

"How's that?"

"Looks good. Thanks for coming out, Gordon."

The burly cameraman shrugged. "No one else would do it. They think a suicide scene is bad luck."

Kelly patted his thick shoulder. She knew

he was on her side. "They could be right. Let's hope they aren't."

"This is a nice neighborhood," he said casually.

Which hadn't stopped him from looking around as intently as Deke before they shot a single frame. Kelly felt safer, working with a guy as big and as ornery as Gordon Lear.

He sat in the swivel chair, fiddling with dials and knobs, whistling tunelessly.

Kelly glanced outside the small window in the door — and slammed her head against it. Seeing stars, she realized dimly that the whole van was rocking.

Thrown out of his chair, Gordon rolled heavily, spreading out his arms to stop himself. The van tipped sideways, then banged down on its axles. It took several seconds for the screeching sounds of metal stressed to the max to die down.

Kelly gasped, holding her head. "What the hell was that?"

"Don't know." She looked down at Gordon, who seemed dazed as he slowly got on hands and knees, then grabbed a built-in shelf to get up.

"Are you all right?" she asked.

"If the van doesn't blow up. Whew." He hung his head, still holding on to the counter.

Kelly moved the door, opening it with difficulty. The shock of the impact had done something to the latch. She stepped outside onto the sidewalk, gulping in air. A few yards ahead of the van was a pickup truck, black but so rusted it looked brown. It had stopped in the middle of the street, smoke pouring out of its muffler. Deep gouges in its sides told the story. They had been sideswiped.

She started to walk to the truck but began to limp. Then she thought better of it and stopped where she was. A guy built like a bouncer was getting out of the truck's cab, trading curses with another man behind the wheel whom she couldn't see.

Kelly turned, relieved to see Gordon slowly exiting the production van. He had been banged around but he was still standing. He walked to her side, eying the man coming toward them.

He had facial piercings and weird hair — a thick, orangey thatch, like he'd done the dye job himself with bleach and henna. His tattered pants were held up with a studded belt. The skull-and-crossbones buckle said whatever else needed to be said about him. He looked half-wild and menacing.

She flinched inside when the man's hand went up suddenly, holding something black.

She let out her breath when she saw it was just a vinyl holder for insurance and registration.

"You have?" the man asked.

Okay, speaking English might be a problem. She would manage, but Kelly was still shaky. She crossed her arms in front of her to control the trembling as Gordon went back into the van.

The man looked at her. "I see you on news."

His voice was gruff but not threatening. Thank God for that. She didn't want to deal with road rage from someone who'd hit them while they were standing still.

"Yes," she said acidly. "And that is a news van. Bright white. Don't tell me you didn't see it."

"Sorry," the man said calmly.

Kelly stepped aside when Gordon returned with a pen and paper, and the two men exchanged information. Gordon made sure to write down everything. She took the opportunity to memorize the plates and other identifiers, as well as the condition of the truck. The other man inside stayed in it, one hand draped over the wheel while he waited for his passenger.

The punk and Gordon surveyed the van together.

"That's a lot of damage," Gordon said wearily. "I have to call the cops."

The punk shook his head. He stomped back to the truck and got in, banging the door shut. The driver floored the accelerator and the truck zoomed away, going miles over the speed limit.

"How do you like that?" Gordon said indignantly, his fists clenched at his sides. Without thinking, he crumpled the paper he was holding. "So much for a nice neighborhood. Unless it means the cops get here faster."

Kelly slipped her arm over his elbow. "Forget it. I have a bad feeling about those guys. They could come back. I don't want to wait around to find out."

Gordon grumbled his agreement. Using the side of the van, he smoothed out the crumpled paper with the insurance and registration information before he folded it and put it in his pocket. "Where's your action figure when we need him?"

"What?"

"That guy with the gun. You know, from the building."

Kelly rubbed her head, which was beginning to ache badly. "His name is Deke. And I don't know where he is right now."

As soon as she figured that out, she would

give him an earful — and the license plate number and description of the truck.

"You okay?" That was the first question Deke asked.

"Kind of rocky," Kelly answered. "But hanging in there. The van is in the body shop. Monroe didn't blow a gasket. But he did tell me and Gordon to stay the hell at home for a day or two."

"I think that's reasonable."

"Did you find out anything about the pickup truck?"

"Stolen. Bogus plates. More to come. Want to go to the firing range?"

"Yeah," she said slowly. "That sounds like a good idea. Let's do it."

As it turned out, there wasn't much he could teach her. Kelly was no novice and she seemed instantly comfortable with the handgun and small-caliber bullets he provided, figuring it would be less kickback for her and more precision. He gave himself the handicap of a heavier gun.

She loaded hers, looking great in goggles and ear protection, then turned to the target and began to fire when he gave the signal. Her stance wasn't textbook, but she hit her targets in the kill spots.

Deke had expected as much. But he was enough of a marksman to want to beat her at it. When they stopped after several rounds, he took a pack of playing cards out of his pocket.

He held the cards up when she set her gun aside. Kelly took off the ear protectors.

"Tell you what," he said. "Let's shoot these. I'll attach them to the big target."

"Okay. With what?"

Deke went back to his duffel bag, unzipping it and reaching in. "With this handy packing tape dispenser I just happened to bring along."

Kelly's eyes narrowed behind the goggles. "Is this a test?"

"Just a little friendly competition. I'm on my last bullet."

She checked the barrel of the gun she was using. "I have three."

Deke walked by as she stepped aside, then she watched him tape a handful of cards to the paper targets.

"Don't want all the little pieces to blow away, right?" He walked back to her. "I'm going to try for the ace."

"Fine," she said. "I'll take the three of diamonds."

They put their ear protection in place and took their stances. They fired around the same time, then put down their guns. Deke could see from where he was that he had hit the large black shape of the ace card near the center. Kelly's card looked a little ragged.

"Go look," she said.

He walked over to the target. She had hit every diamond on her chosen card.

"You're good," he told her from where he was.

"Thanks." Her tone was matter-of-fact. He took more cards out of his pocket and taped them up.

When he was standing next to her, they reloaded.

"Did you ever try tossing cards in the air and shooting them?" Deke asked her.

"You mean from the side? Split them in half? No. Never saw the point of it."

"Oh."

"I mean, if you had to shoot a bad guy, would you do it from the side?"

"If I had to, yeah," Deke said.

"Well, I like to hit a target where it counts."

He was getting the idea. "I wasn't suggesting we split cards. It just came to mind. I saw a guy who could do it on YouTube."

"Really. Do you believe everything you see online, Deke?"

She was teasing but he felt the need to defend himself. "Maybe it wasn't YouTube. Maybe I saw it on the news," he answered.

"That's possible. Considering we make up at least half of what we broadcast."

"Is that right." Deke smiled as he checked his gun. "Why?"

"Because the real news is too freaky to put on the air. You ready?"

"Yeah."

She turned toward the new set of targets and fired off several rounds. Deke did the same. This time she went with him to look at the results.

"You win," Deke said. "You plugged every single card in the center except that one."

Kelly looked at it. "Can I have a do-over and still win?"

Deke laughed out loud. "Go ahead."

They went back and he stood to the side as she took a last shot. "There. I think I got it," she said.

He took the gun he'd given her back and set it aside with his. "Just making sure."

Deke walked out one last time to the targets. The missed card was cut in two. The larger paper targets that she'd used were peppered with shots in the heart area.

He pulled off the two halves of the last card and brought them back to her. "I think you're ready to officially join my team. I'm not sure I should tell them you can shoot this well, though."

Kelly grinned at him. She curled her hand and blew imaginary smoke off her index finger.

When they were done and back in Deke's car, he picked up a call from Hux. Kelly had to wonder if there were two teams, good and bad, keeping an eye on her at all times.

"I'm with Kelly, so I'm putting you on loudspeaker," Deke said. "What'd you find?"

"The registration number you got from Gordon bounced back. That thing was probably forged, and the insurance company doesn't even exist."

For a punk, he'd paid a lot of attention to details, Kelly thought. But then he hadn't been alone.

Hux continued. "Okay, the driver's license number the guy gave Gordon? That belongs to a World War Two veteran who gave up his keys ten years ago."

"Great." Kelly sighed. "I'll take that as proof it wasn't an accident. They slammed into us to get us out of the van. More intimidation, and in broad daylight."

"So be a good girl and stay indoors with the blinds pulled down," Hux said.

"I *think* you're teasing."

Kelly lugged a heavy tote bag filled with folders and a laptop up to her hotel apartment and set it in a corner.

She didn't know why she'd brought work home. The tote bag would be lugged back to the station tomorrow, its contents untouched.

Kelly headed straight for the bathroom and got undressed. Her on-air makeup felt like a mask, heavy and itchy. She swiped off most of it with a makeup remover pad, then turned the shower on full blast and got under the hot, pulsing spray.

She felt a little better when she got out and put on a thick, soft robe. Then her cell phone rang. Probably Deke calling to make sure she was still doing okay. He'd warned her about the delayed effects of being in a crash. It had been her first, so she'd listened.

Kelly answered without looking at the number.

"Hello."

"My dear Kelly. I *had* to thank you."

Natalie Conrad. Just about the last person on earth Kelly felt like talking to.

"What for?"

"You were so helpful. Luc was truly inspired by the old factory you recommended. He's already installed his new piece. We want you to see it before anyone else."

"Oh — I don't think I can. Not right now."

"Have I called at the wrong time again?" Natalie managed to make the question sound insinuating.

"No." Kelly didn't feel like explaining. "I just can't go."

"But you must."

"Sorry. Does Luc have a Facebook page for the installation? I could look at photos."

"I shall ask him. He'll be here soon." Natalie sounded a little giddy. "May I call you back?"

It would have been outright rudeness to refuse, so Kelly said yes. The reluctance in her voice didn't dampen Natalie's enthusiasm. She chirped a good-bye and hung up. Kelly slipped her phone in the pocket of her robe and went into the kitchen to forage.

Slim pickings. Kelly ransacked the empty kitchen drawers for a takeout menu that the previous tenant might have left and came up empty-handed. Nothing. She would have to go online.

Curling up on the couch with her laptop sounded okay. It was warm as a cat and she could read the menus comfortably on a larger screen.

She was settled in and browsing when the chime for a video call sounded. It wasn't someone on her contacts list. Deke was waiting for her to accept his call. She did, a second before she thought about what she looked like.

Kelly was adjusting the wrapped towel around her head when Deke's face appeared on the screen.

"Hey, beautiful."

"As if. With no makeup?"

"Yeah." His smile convinced her.

"Okay. Take me as I am," she said lightly. "So how did you get my Skype contact information? I don't remember giving it to you."

"You didn't. Great handle. KellyBelly is easy to remember."

"I don't know what I was thinking." She laughed. "I guess I was hungry at the time. I'm reading menus right now, as a matter of fact."

"Then I won't keep you." He winked at her. "Eat. It'll do you good."

"I can order online and talk to you at the same time," she said.

"You're a woman of many talents."

"Hang on." She returned to the restaurant page and placed an order, then went back to Deke. He now had a bottle of beer in one hand that he'd gone to get. Sitting down again, he looked relaxed and super hot in a T-shirt that was just snug enough over his broad chest.

"So what's for dinner?"

"Chinese," she said. "Lots of vegetables. And fortune cookies."

He leaned forward. There was that grin again. Irresistibly cocky and sweet. The casual conversation was unexpectedly intimate. He was probably across town in some anonymous suite, but they were face-to-face.

"If you could write your own fortune and have it come true, what would it be?" he asked.

A wild night with a handsome lover is in your future. Kelly didn't say the words out loud, but she sure as hell thought them.

"Oh, I don't know." She yawned behind her hand.

"Stay awake long enough to eat," he chided her. "You've been running on empty."

Kelly heard the muffled ring of the phone in her robe pocket and groaned.

"Who's that?" Deke asked.

"Natalie Conrad again," she said, looking at the screen and letting the call go to voicemail. "She wants me to go view her pet artist's latest creation. I said no."

"Creation as in . . . painting? Sculpture?"

"I don't know. It's installed in that old factory we visited, which I told her about. But I don't want to go back there."

Deke looked interested. "What if I went with you?"

"Since when are you interested in modern art?"

He laughed and took another sip of beer, leaning back in his chair. "I'm not. But I'd like to meet her. I can be Russ Thorn again."

"What? Why?"

"Just to talk to her. Apparently that museum of hers is never going to get built. The money's gone."

Kelly was surprised. "Already? How long has it been since the ball?"

"I don't have a calendar on me. Not long, though."

"And where did the money go?"

"Down the drain. Our Dallas team just found out that Gunther Bach's bank handled the financing for the museum."

"I didn't know that," Kelly said.

"Stands to reason," Deke replied. "She and Gunther were more than pals."

"Yes," Kelly said slowly. "Once."

"And there's something else. Natalie Conrad was unloading art from her collec-

376

tion weeks before the ball. It's amazing what some of that stuff goes for at auction. Tens of millions. Sometimes more."

Kelly thought about the recently removed paintings at Natalie's mansion. She was pretty sure the glamorous widow had said she'd loaned them to keep them safe.

Deke put down the beer and got serious. "So here's what happened. The art was promised to the museum, in return for major donations to build it and slap a name on a gallery or a wing. Now all the important paintings and sculpture are gone. There might be some minor pieces left. But the billionaires got rooked."

Kelly didn't get it. The museum was Natalie's idea, and she'd wanted to honor her late husband. Gunther Bach had to have been acting behind the scenes.

"She can't be the only person in charge."

"No. But the money she raised went into a trust that she controls. The museum board just hired a private investigation firm to find out more. If I ever get the chance, I'll ask Natalie my own questions. You know, turn on the charm. You never know what she might say in an unguarded moment."

"Don't overdo it, Mr. Thorn. She asked if you were my fiancé."

Deke smirked at her through the screen.

"What did we do with that big fake engagement ring you wore at the ball?"

"Around here somewhere. I think I brought it with me. But I'm not going to wear it again." Kelly turned her head when the concierge buzzer rang. "That's the food. Gotta go."

The following afternoon, Kelly and Deke waited in his car for Natalie Conrad to show. The street outside the old factory was deserted as the day began to shade into dusk.

"I'm still not sure I should have agreed to this."

"You're with me," Deke said.

Kelly shook her head. "When are you not totally sure of yourself?"

"Oh, it happens," he answered, drumming his fingers on the steering wheel.

The purring roar of an expensive sports car got their attention. Natalie pulled over in front of them, parking at a clumsy angle.

Deke got out and Kelly quickly followed suit. They walked to the side of the car and Deke opened Natalie's door for her. He stepped back as her flawless legs swung to the curb. As always, she was elegantly dressed.

"Thank you," she said to him. "Russ

Thorn, isn't it?"

"Yes. It's a pleasure to meet you, Mrs. Conrad. I didn't have a chance to at the ball." He helped her out.

"Hello, Kelly," Natalie said when she was standing. She offered an air-kiss. "Don't you look lovely." The compliment was mechanical. "I'm so glad you found the time for us. I have to be back in Dallas even sooner than I thought. Something's come up. The museum board insists that I appear in person."

Deke avoided Kelly's gaze.

Luc got out of the other side of the car and came around. He had starving-artist cheekbones and piercing dark eyes, with unkempt black hair that had streaks of paint in it. He was taller than Natalie, but not by much. And he was a whole lot younger.

"Luc, this is Russ and Kelly."

He spoke only to Kelly. "The space is fantastic. But you knew that, eh?"

"I only saw it once," she replied. "How did you get permits so quickly?"

"No need for that," he answered. "I backed up a truck to the loading dock and went in with my materials and a ladder. No one was inside and no one stopped me." He went ahead, taking long strides. "I prefer to work alone."

Natalie tried to keep up with him as Kelly

and Deke exchanged a look. She and Luc went in together and closed the door behind them.

"Now what?" Deke asked. "Maybe I don't want to know."

Kelly stood close to him. "I have no idea."

Natalie came out in another minute and waved them up the stairs. "Luc says you may enter," she called.

"Ready, Mrs. Thorn?" he said under his breath.

"Don't call me that," Kelly muttered. But she took his arm.

They stopped on the threshold, adjusting to the difference in light. Kelly could hear Natalie's heels clicking, but she couldn't see her. There was some sort of giant mess ahead of them. Luc's disembodied voice came from the darkest part of the space. "Look up."

Kelly did. The artist switched on a huge flashlight. A giant spiderweb of frayed rope had been hung from the beams, snarled around found objects — thrown-away baby dolls with matted hair, plastic bleach bottles, old sneakers with no laces.

"The debris of civilization, straight from the gutter," Natalie said grandly, stepping forward. "Marvelous work."

Kelly looked at her without saying any-

380

thing, then at the installation. She still couldn't see Luc. Then Kelly saw something swinging at the center of the web. A female figure was wrapped in rope and hanging upside down. For a fleeting second, Kelly recoiled. Luc obviously had strange ideas about women — and no talent for anything but hustling rich ones.

"I agree," Deke said. "I've never seen anything like it. Marvelous is the word."

"Luc is an unknown," she said airily. "But I believe in encouraging emerging artists."

He didn't bat an eye. "May I ask what you paid for it?"

So much for charm. Kelly gave Deke a sneaky pinch as a warning.

"Perhaps too much," Natalie replied.

Deke didn't stop. "Will it be on display in the new museum, Mrs. Conrad?"

Natalie moved into a patch of light from the high windows. The effect was unflattering and she seemed suddenly older. Her mouth thinned as she glared at him. Then she collected herself. "What a good idea. Yes, perhaps. In time."

Luc finally showed, walking around the web. "Never. My art belongs here. You bought it, but you don't own it."

"Don't be difficult," she said to the young artist, her voice thin and high. "I expect something for my money."

Deke walked Kelly away and out of sight, but they could still hear the quarrel.

Kelly had a banging headache by the time they made their escape. "Do you believe those two?"

Deke was waiting for her to put on her seat belt before he pulled out from behind Natalie Conrad's sports car. "Takes all kinds."

"I think she's losing her mind."

He smiled slightly. "Natalie Conrad is definitely under a lot of stress. So are you."

Kelly left the seat belt unfastened and rubbed her temples. "You noticed. Do you have any aspirin?"

"Not in my car. Come on, buckle up." Deke glanced over at her. "Sorry I talked you into this. But there was no other way for me to meet Natalie."

"Happy to help," Kelly replied sarcastically.

Deke didn't reply, his dark eyes suddenly intent on the rearview mirror. "Now who is that?"

"Huh?"

Deke swore violently as he pushed her head down. He threw himself over her and forced her whole body below the level of the dashboard.

There was a screech of brakes and spinning wheels. Bullets cracked the side window she had just looked out of.

They both heard the other vehicle speed away but they stayed down for a minute, breathing hard. Slowly, Deke lifted himself. "Stay down."

She did.

"They're gone," he said. "A drive-by. I should have known." His hand moved to her shoulder as he helped her lift up, still breathing hard.

CHAPTER 16

They sat back, stunned, their ears ringing. Kelly brushed the crumbled safety glass into a heap in her lap, dazedly wondering what she ought to do with it.

Deke called Hux first, and then Lieutenant Dwight. "On their way," he told her.

Kelly turned to look at him. "Are you sure you're not hurt?"

He didn't get a chance to answer. Natalie Conrad came out of the old factory, running awkwardly in her high heels.

"What on earth happened?" she called.

"Let me handle this," Deke warned Kelly. "Go for it."

He unlatched his door and got out. "It's okay, Mrs. Conrad."

"It most certainly isn't! Look at that window. Why is Kelly still sitting inside? Is she hurt?"

Deke interposed his brawny body between

Natalie and the car. He caught her shoulders.

"Let me go," the older woman said imperiously. He did but he stayed close to her, anticipating her every move as she bent down and peered at the disintegrated window next to Kelly. "Do you think you can walk, dear? Perhaps she shouldn't try to. I'll stay here with her while you go for help, Russ."

"I called. Someone's coming."

Even in a state of semi-shock, Kelly was well aware that Deke was keeping Natalie at a distance.

"Are you injured, Kelly?" the older woman asked nervously.

"No. Just catching my breath. Please don't fuss, Natalie."

"I'm so sorry." The older woman straightened up, rubbing the small of her back. "Who was it?" she asked. "How did they do it?"

"Two guys, I think. One had a baseball bat and the other had a tire iron," Deke said. "They saw me using my smartphone when I came out and I guess they wanted one just like it."

Natalie frowned at him. "But I thought I heard gunfire. And Kelly was shot at before

— not that far from here. Horrible. Just horrible."

"But you didn't, Mrs. Conrad. Why don't you sit down right there just in case they ran into the factory — and here comes Luc." Deke lifted his head and called to the artist. "Did you see anyone go inside?"

"No. What's going on?" He stayed where he was, looking indifferently at the car.

"I was sure I heard bullets," Natalie said to Deke when he turned to her again.

"You know, these empty lots echo," he said vaguely, gesturing toward the one across from the factory. "Your ears will play tricks on you."

Natalie's agitated gaze narrowed as if she found the idea insulting.

"Hmm." She walked a few steps away and leaned against her car. Then she thought better of it and moved away to sit down on a low brick wall, smoothing her dress under her.

"Kelly, do get out of that car and come here. Russ, perhaps you could help her out."

Kelly scooped up the crumbled glass in her lap and poured it into the cup holder. Then she saw the bullet hole in the center divider. She and Deke had been very lucky.

Natalie Conrad was right about hearing gunfire. Kelly understood that he had his

386

reasons for misleading her. She'd find out what they were the second they were alone.

"You think she set us up?" Kelly asked, leaning in to hear his reply. They were in the hospital cafeteria having coffee.

Thanks to Hux, the mandated exam for Deke in a non-public room had been offered to her as well. Neither she nor Deke had been injured. The attending doctor didn't ask for details.

Hux had returned to the old factory with an officer and driven the damaged car away for forensic analysis and retrieval of bullet fragments. The officer had returned to the hospital with Hux's car and left it in the lot for them on the lieutenant's orders.

"No idea. It's not impossible," Deke said.

Hospital staff in scrubs and doctor coats milled around the open space, picking up food and avoiding each other with fluid moves that made them resemble fish in a giant white aquarium. Kelly looked at them, still feeling strange. The ringing in her ears wasn't entirely gone. The clatter of trays at the trash receptacles bothered her.

"When I told her about the bat and the tire iron, she gave me the weirdest look, Kelly."

She glanced at him absently. "That doesn't

prove anything. You may be taking paranoia too far."

"When you do what I do for a living, Kelly, there is no such thing as too much paranoia. There is a contract out on you. You have been threatened, sideswiped, and shot at. Crude but effective."

"And not Natalie's style," Kelly pointed out.

Deke rolled his eyes. "I didn't hear you say that. I promise never to remind you that you said that."

"It means something." Kelly's expression was thoughtful.

"Listen to me. I've been a freelance agent for ten years. My dad was a cop and so's my older brother, and my other brother is an investigator. My friends are all cops and feds. I have seen with my own eyes that anybody is capable of anything."

She made a placating gesture. "Okay, okay. Calm down."

"I am calm," he insisted, then softened his tone when a man in a white coat gave him a searching look.

"Then let's talk about something else. You got Luc and Natalie back into the sports car pretty damn fast."

"They did that themselves. I told Luc the cops were bound to look around the area.

That was all it took."

Kelly smiled, remembering what she'd asked the artist. "I don't think he had permits for the installation."

Deke shook his head. "Bye bye, Luc. Maybe there's an outstanding warrant on him for making bad art."

Kelly's mind was elsewhere. "Natalie's so nosy," she mused. "I wasn't expecting her to leave just like that."

"Hey, I didn't want her inside the car or bothering you. And I couldn't be sure who'd get to the scene first. Dwight and Hux would have covered correctly, but I didn't want a strange cop calling me Deke Bannon when he asked for my driver's license. She would have picked up on that."

Kelly sipped her coffee. "I wonder where she is now."

"That's the least of my worries. You and I are going to lie low for a couple of days. I'm putting in a request for an armored vehicle."

"Don't be ridiculous. I'm not going to roll through the streets in a tank."

He grinned. "Don't say no yet. What I'm talking about looks like an SUV, but bigger and tougher. Huge front grill, plated sides."

"Right on trend in Atlanta," she said wryly.

Kelly looked directly and confidently into

the camera lens, about to deliver another installment of her ongoing story.

"In the news tonight, there are few clues in the death of Atlanta financier Gunther Bach. And it may not be a coincidence that the spectacular meltdown of the Bach financial empire began only days before his fatal plunge from his penthouse balcony. Millions disappeared. Investors weren't insured. Did money lead to murder?"

She took a split-second pause to emphasize the question and take an invisible breath. The evening news production team had decided not to use the footage Kelly had shot at the scene with Gordon. Just her, full face.

"And exactly what happened in his last hours?" Kelly continued. "A source close to the investigation is about to reveal new details that may shed fresh light on the puzzling case, and WBRX is preparing an exclusive report."

She turned to Dave Maples.

"Thank you, Kelly. Folks, be sure to tune in to WBRX for more on this developing story in the days to come. And now, in other news . . ."

They continued the six o'clock broadcast with practiced ease, covering a variety of stories with a few lines each. None came anywhere close to the Bach story for generating viewer interest. Monroe had bet the promo budget on that.

The source was Deke, of course. Who had promised her more insider info after she promised him to let him know her whereabouts at all times.

Deke watched the broadcast on a small TV positioned over a diner counter. The waitress, an older lady in a dark blue dress and white apron, seemed fascinated. She turned up the volume.

"I just love that Kelly Johns, don't you?" she asked Deke.

He mumbled a yes from behind the cheeseburger he held in both hands.

"She's smart and she's good-looking," the waitress said.

Deke nodded. He was just glad she'd recovered from the drive-by with no ill effects. For a little while she'd had him worried.

"Do you think that Bach fellow jumped like they said at first?"

"I don't know, ma'am."

A portrait photograph of Gunther Bach filled the screen. His bland smile and well-groomed silver hair were prominently featured.

"I can't say I like that face. He looks to me like he cheated people," the waitress said. "He has those strange eyes. Narrow and cold. That's the kind of man who'd order a great big steak with everything and leave a dime for a tip."

Deke suppressed a smile. The waitress had guessed correctly, but the idea of Gunther Bach eating at a diner was incongruous.

"You done?" she asked him. Without waiting for an answer, she took his plate. "Ready for pie and coffee?"

"Don't mind if I do. Apple is fine."

Kelly settled into her couch, leafing through a magazine without reading it. She didn't want to think and she didn't want to watch TV. When her phone chimed, she looked at the number and picked up. "Hey, Coral. What's up?"

"Listen, Kelly, I found something amazing." The bubbly junior reporter never seemed to lose her enthusiasm. But she, like everyone else at WBRX, still didn't know about the drive-by. Deke wanted Kelly to keep it quiet.

"Are you still at the station?"

"Yeah, working late. So, okay, I made a friend at the State Department in DC, and he's been helping me out with the foreign stuff," Coral began.

Kelly smiled, remembering her own sources and other "friends" in government. Extremely useful for background on headline-making news. Never interested in on-screen credit.

"And?"

"He helped me trace the shell companies overseas, and we found a link to Gunther Bach."

Kelly sat bolt upright. "Tell me more."

"It's really complicated and you sound tired, so this is the short version. Bach was a silent partner in the financing for that abandoned building. For a while he owned it outright."

Kelly grabbed a pen and scribbled on the magazine cover. "Got it. Keep going."

"I took about a million notes and now I'm editing them. I can give you a typed-up report tomorrow."

Kelly put down the pen. "Coral, *you* are amazing. Thank you. I can't wait to read it. And listen, one more thing. Have the security guard walk you to your car when you leave tonight. Be careful."

She heard someone else in the background speak before Coral answered. "I hear you. And I will be. But right now, my, uh, friend is actually here with me."

"Ohhh," Kelly said. "Go, Coral. See you tomorrow."

She leaned back into the cushions and thought hard. The connection didn't surprise her. A hidden door had opened. A whole lot of other secrets would come tumbling out.

But they were still no closer to finding out who was trying to kill her. Deke and Hux had hit a dead end as far as the vehicle used in the drive-by. He had been blinded at the crucial moment by its headlights in the rearview mirror, unable to see who was at the wheel.

And he'd told her he wasn't going to pump Natalie Conrad for information. As far as either of them knew, she was back in Dallas.

There were no clues on the street by the factory. No tire tracks, nothing that might have been thrown from the speeding vehicle. An evidence team had retrieved several bullets from Deke's car and submitted their findings to a ballistics database for comparison.

The drive-by still didn't seem real to Kelly. She barely remembered it, in fact.

But the armored car Deke had requested did make her feel safer. Despite his protectiveness, he hadn't moved in with her, but he appeared at the right times to escort her to work and back.

And he always called . . . right around now. Kelly looked at the clock just before the phone rang.

"Updates," he said briskly. "Want to get them over with?"

"Sure," she said.

"Our fingerprint wizard struck out on the card you got and the photos. But the paper expert at the FBI said the card and envelope stock was unusual and made by hand. He doesn't have a sample that's anything like it, and they have about a million samples on file."

"Okay," she said tiredly. "I can't believe getting that card ever scared me. Nothing does at this point."

"That's not good." He paused. "Mind if I come over?"

"No. I'd like to see you," she said. He'd been on her mind all day, at work and everywhere else. She felt herself flush slightly and pressed her lips together.

He was at her door in less than half an hour. His dark gaze sparked with a touch of fire when she looked up at him. Kelly stepped backward, not quite ready for what he might be thinking about.

"Come on in."

Deke surveyed the hotel apartment, as if she hadn't been home for two hours and someone needed to do that. Protective to a fault — but by this point in the investigation, she couldn't complain.

There was a laptop tucked under his arm. "Did you download a movie?" she asked teasingly. "I don't know if I can stay awake that long."

"You could call it a movie. It's a short one." He went to the couch, shucking his jacket along the way and tossing it over a chair. "Give me five minutes."

His tone was businesslike. She would have given him more time than that.

The laptop was set down on the coffee table as he eased himself onto the couch and opened it, touching a few keys to pull up a surveillance camera video.

"That looks familiar," she said, looking over his shoulder. "That's where Gordon and I were shooting the day we got sideswiped."

"It's Gunther's building," he confirmed.

"They have to have good security with all those rich tenants."

"Yes and no. Their system was down that night."

Kelly arched an eyebrow. "Really?"

"Don't get started. Hux is on it," Deke said.

"I hope so."

"This footage is from the building next door, which has even more cameras. Their security personnel reviewed the night's footage at our request and passed it along to us."

Kelly was immediately interested. "Is it something that we could broadcast?"

"Maybe. It's not that clear. And there's no sound."

She sat down next to him on the couch and peered into the screen. Deke touched the red arrow for Play.

"This particular camera is programmed to scan an area slowly. So it caught the commotion afterward but not the actual suicide."

"Good. Not something I want to see."

"The EMTs got there fast. There was a witness, so it was called in right away." Deke pointed to the screen. "There's the police, they talk to the EMTs — business as usual. Now look on the street in back of them."

Kelly saw a long, dark vehicle in the background drive slowly past the first responders gathered around the crumpled figure on the sidewalk. "Looks like a limo."

"Watch."

The rear window rolled down and a face appeared for a moment, indistinct and pale.

"Would you say that was a man or a woman?" Deke asked.

"Hard to tell. Play it again." Kelly studied the grainy tape. "A woman," she said at last. "But I wouldn't swear to it in court if I had to."

"Why is she there?"

"Deke, what she's doing is morbid, but that's human nature."

"She came back for a second look."

Deke replayed the tape once more and stopped on a frame where the face appeared, a white oval with shadows for eyes. Then he advanced the footage farther ahead.

"Look again. Everyone's in a different position. And here comes the same limo again. Just couldn't get enough, I guess."

"I know what you're getting at," Kelly said. "But you can't prove it, and there's no chance of identifying whoever that was."

Deke blew out a frustrated breath. "I don't think I'm the only one who noticed the second go-around. After that the cops cordoned off the street."

"Are the limo's plates ever visible?"

"No." He let the tape keep running. It wasn't high quality and the people on it moved in a herky-jerky way, in and out of focus.

"Rental limos look alike," Kelly said. "I'm no expert on the subject, though. Anything distinctive about that one?"

"Good question. And you're right about rental limos. I would say this one was privately owned. But without identifying the plates, we don't have anything."

The surveillance camera had swung around to a service area on the side of the building where it was mounted, where there was nothing of interest. Deke paused the video.

"That's it."

"Interesting. But not conclusive. I don't think we could use it," Kelly said. "What's your next move?"

Concentrating on the investigation was only semi-effective. Being so close to Deke again was getting to her. They'd had to sit side by side to look into the laptop, their thighs nearly touching. Every time he shifted position, she moved fractionally sideways. It didn't matter. His body heat reached her. He would have to be across the room for her not to notice it.

"We didn't talk to every building manager in the neighborhood. There may be other footage of the limo. A neighborhood like that has plenty of surveillance."

"That's true. And WBRX is going to do more on Gunther Bach's suicide. Viewers are hooked."

Deke looked up at her. "Did any tips ever come in?"

"No. We didn't start a hotline. Maybe we should."

"I'm for it," Deke said, raising a hand.

"It's getting a tremendous amount of buzz. I think *Vanity Fair* is looking to do a cover story on the case. Ordinary murders don't get that much reaction. We run them for a day, maybe two."

"Bach was a big deal," Deke said.

"We're still circling around the story."

Which was a polite way of saying that Bach's death was a chance to spin conspiracy theories that didn't even have to be factual. Or so Monroe Capp had said. Kelly didn't share everything about her job with Deke, any more than he did with her.

"I noticed that when I watched your broadcast. A little bit of truth and a lot of speculation."

"That's what keeps them coming back for more," Kelly said.

Deke shut down the laptop and closed it. He clasped his hands in front of him, looking up at Kelly standing on the other side of the table.

"So you still think it's a good idea to stay with the story? Does it have to be yours?"

The blunt questions took her aback. "I'm not handing it over to Dave."

"Someone wants to kill you. You survived shootouts one and two. Going for three?"

"Deke —"

"We need new evidence. It's not out there or we're not finding it."

Kelly shrugged. "Coral found out something interesting, but I don't know if it would help," she said. "She just called from the station. She's tracked down definitive information that links Gunther Bach to the abandoned building. He owned it outright for a while."

Deke was caught off guard for a moment. He didn't say anything.

"Now that he's dead, it may not matter," Kelly said. "And when he was alive — well, I don't think that was him in drag and a red wig in the car at the shootout. The first shootout," she corrected herself, her voice brittle. "But I guess he could have ordered someone to stalk me."

"Maybe, but —"

"Wait. I haven't finished. I'm not going to back down or hide."

"I'm not saying you have to do either. But

you're putting too much on the line," Deke insisted. He stood up, as if he was taking command.

"Such as?"

"Your life."

"Oh right. You told me once that you were my goddamn guardian angel. And I do appreciate everything you've done, more than you'll ever know. But I am sticking with this, Deke. Believe it or not, it keeps me sane. I feel like I'm fighting back."

Deke got up, but he didn't move far from the couch. He stood near it, hands jammed in the pockets of his jeans. *Stay there,* Kelly willed him. It was easier for her to be tough when no one got close.

"The body count is too high," he said stubbornly. "We're getting nowhere and we've followed up on every single lead ten times over."

"Have you?" She took a deep breath and composed herself. "What about the woman who escaped? Maybe the redhead should be on the list of possible suspects. Why limit it to men?"

"As far as the woman who disappeared, the search for her is ongoing," he replied tersely.

"Hope she doesn't turn up dead." She hated the sarcasm in her voice, but the words were out. Deke would just have to deal with it.

He hesitated before saying more. "I'm not going to speculate. Are you going to air the new information about Bach?"

"Yes, when we know it's solid. I haven't read Coral's report. She's still typing up her notes."

"I hope she has a bodyguard," Deke muttered.

"Apparently she does," Kelly tossed back. "My guess is that he's not in your league, though."

"You're missing the point, Kelly. Maybe these guys won't stop with you."

She folded her arms across her chest. The gesture was more self-protective than stubborn. "I wouldn't put anyone in harm's way."

"Then don't put yourself there either."

"I'm not giving up on the story!"

She knew her face was flushed with anger. She could barely control it.

"It doesn't take much to detonate you, does it? Okay. Have it your way." Deke turned around and slammed out.

CHAPTER 17

Kelly closed the cover on the report. "We're getting somewhere, Coral. This could have been enough to indict Gunther Bach for financial fraud."

The younger woman laughed a little ruefully. "Too bad he's dead, huh?"

"From what I know, plenty of people would have loved to make that happen."

Coral took a heavy folder from Kelly's desk. "I got that impression. This holds about a million articles on Atlanta society, including all the scandals." She put the folder on top of a stack, with her copy of the report on the top and her laptop on the bottom.

"Monroe wants to continue the series on Bach. Your research is exactly what we need," Kelly told Coral. "The complete autopsy results haven't been released. In the meantime, we'll use a lot of this."

"And Fred Chiswick will boil my contribution down to one sentence. If I'm lucky," Coral complained.

"You get your name on the credits," Kelly assured her. "That's what matters most."

The material in the overstuffed folder hadn't been digitized — the station's budget shortfall had temporarily halted the switchover. Clippings and photos and press releases bulged out. Inevitably, the folder began to slide and an avalanche of stuff scattered to the floor.

"Oops!" Coral bent down to collect it all.

"Let me help." Kelly gathered handfuls of press releases and put the yellowed newspaper clippings on top, picking out a photo. "Hello. There's a familiar face."

It was a black-and-white snapshot of Natalie and her late husband Harry standing next to Gunther Bach at some charity extravaganza.

"Who's that?"

"Natalie Conrad. Widow of a billionaire, patroness of the arts, and all-around pain in the neck. Possibly a former flame of Gunther Bach."

"Oh. Can we work her in to the story?"

Kelly set aside the photo and put the other collected items back into the folder, then looked under her desk for a box to put it in. "Please don't. If I never talk to her again, that would suit me just fine."

She took two pairs of high heels out of the cardboard box and handed it to Coral. "This should hold everything."

The junior reporter got the folder back into some semblance of order and looked at the photo. "She's very glamorous. When was it taken?"

"Years ago," Kelly said. "She still looks good. I'm not sure if she's had plastic surgery, but it's safe to say she's into Botox and collagen. Maybe I can find a more recent picture of her."

Kelly looked through the folder again. "Here we go. Holy cow. I was at this party."

"Are you in the photo?"

"Unfortunately." She handed it over quickly. "Look at what I was wearing. I had to borrow a jacket with monster shoulder pads from June Fletcher. And here it is. It came back to haunt me."

Coral laughed and studied Natalie's face. "I see what you mean about the lip collagen. Too pouty. And too much Botox. Her face looks like a mask."

"I guess we all get to that stage eventually," Kelly said, putting her work space to rights. "You know, wondering if you need a tuck or a full lift, and obsessing over wrinkles. I confess to both. I haven't had anything done, though."

"Don't. You look great," Coral insisted.

Kelly gave her a wry smile. "Required maintenance comes with this job. Sorry if I sounded catty, but you get in the habit of studying other women to figure out how they deal with getting older."

"Oh, shut up," Coral said. "What is that saying? Don't mess with Texas."

"How'd you know I was from Texas?"

"Word gets around. Listen, thanks again for the chance to research this. If you need anything else, let me know."

Kelly nodded.

Deke walked into the diner where they had agreed to meet. Kelly was waiting for him in a back booth. That resolute attitude he was beginning to know so well showed in her straight posture and squared shoulders.

Their eyes met, green versus brown. Even from near the door, he saw the faint flicker of uncertainty in hers. Deke smiled. He wasn't going to revisit the argument and had said as much when she'd finally called him. Other things were more important.

He still had to protect her, and he was man enough to swallow his pride, along with a decent hamburger.

Deke slid into the booth across the table

from her, setting his laptop on the red vinyl seat.

"I'm hungry. How about you?" Briskly, she handed him one of the two menus the waitress had left on the table. They exchanged small talk, then ordered and ate.

When there was nothing left on the table but their coffee cups, Deke opened the laptop. He positioned it with the back to the main area of the diner so that only they could see it.

"What do you have?" she asked.

"A lot of new stuff," Deke replied. "The forensic accountants are dismantling Gunther Bach's companies and picking through a mountain of spreadsheets and cooked books."

"Where did all the money go?"

"He spent a lot of it. But there should be about a hundred million left when all is said and done."

"In cash? Stocks and bonds?"

"Bach liked to be liquid. He got out of real estate before the market collapse, including unloading the building where the shootout was. Cash instruments and cash are a big chunk of what's left."

"Cash as in real money?"

"Exactly. It takes up a fair amount of physical space. He had to rent a private vault to store it all. Anyway, we're going to use some of it to set up a sting in Dallas."

"Oh?"

Deke grinned. "Hux is handling it. He loves to do things like that. We still have orders to sweep up everyone we can. Our sector chief is angling for a multiple indictment."

"I still think you should go after the biggest guy first, but I'm not in charge," Kelly said.

"Never thought I'd hear you say that."

Kelly ignored the comment. "So how does the sting work?"

"The team chemically tagged fifty thousand in bundled bills from Gunther's stash and hid it inside shiny new washing machines in the back of a truck. We'll let word leak about the transport. We want the truck to get hijacked and driven to the border. It won't go across."

"How big is the truck?"

The question seemed to amuse him. "It's a semi. Won't fit in a smuggler's tunnel."

"Good visual."

"It's a great trap. The tagged money is the bait, and we can lock the doors of the truck's cab by remote. Our driver will get out at a truck stop and leave it unguarded."

"Let's assume the hijackers have guns.

What's to keep them from shooting innocent bystanders if they think they have to blast their way out of the truck stop?"

"We replaced the windshield and side windows with the bulletproof stuff. They won't want to draw attention to themselves, though."

Kelly shook her head, impressed. "Sounds like you thought of everything. But you can't make anyone steal it."

"It's not that hard, Kelly. Our informants get the word out that a cash shipment is heading southwest. The bad guys take it from there. Greed never made anyone smart."

"I don't know about that. Gunther Bach was."

Deke stopped talking when the waitress approached with a coffeepot for refills. They both thanked her and the conversation resumed.

"I was about to get back to him," Deke continued. "As of now, all his personal and corporate bank accounts are frozen."

"Did the IRS do that?"

He nodded. "After the fact. Believe it or not, he died without a will."

"That takes away a classic motive for murder," Kelly said.

"Which leads me to think that he wasn't

expecting to die. Someone got to him when his guard was down."

Kelly gave him a troubled look. "I feel like that's what's happening to me."

"I wish we knew more. At this point we just don't."

"Forget it. I can't think about it too much."

Deke agreed to that silently, looking back at the laptop.

"Back to Bach," he said. "Seems like more than one bank manager was well paid to avoid due diligence when it came to identifying the holders of certain accounts and verifying where the deposits came from."

"Repeat that in plain English, please."

"Put dirty street cash in with legitimate money. Mix well and launder thoroughly by churning through different accounts. No one knows where it came from when it's all clean."

Kelly nodded. "Also a good visual. Thanks. Can I pass that along to the graphic designer at WBRX?"

"Be my guest."

Kelly leaned her elbows on the table, bracing herself for the question she didn't want to ask. "While I'm on the subject of Gunther, whatever happened to the autopsy results?"

"The cause and time of death are established. He was dying when he went off that balcony, but he was still breathing. The high level of the tranquilizer in his system wasn't enough to suppress vital functions and it didn't kill him."

"Any new theories on who did it?"

Deke pulled up a different document on the laptop screen.

"We still have one more person to interview in his building. Frances Berry may have been the last person to see Gunther alive."

"She didn't kill him."

"It does seem unlikely. Here's her driver's license info. She's sixty-seven and she gave her weight as one hundred and five."

"That sounds about right," Kelly said. "So why —"

"She's away. Indefinitely, according to the building staff. She had her mail held, stopped all regular deliveries like newspapers, and gave her kitty to her housekeeper."

The image of the elderly woman who'd been rebuffed by Natalie Conrad came back vividly to Kelly. "Something's wrong with that picture."

"That's what we think."

"Oh boy," she sighed. "Everything is happening at once."

Deke shut down the laptop and closed it. "Hux might have an update on the evidence analysis for Bach's apartment. I'm going to call him from my car, not here."

"Can I listen in?" she asked eagerly.

"So long as he okays it. I can put the call on speaker."

They got up and Deke left several bills to cover the tab, adding a generous tip. The waitress spotted it from three booths away and smiled.

"You made her day," Kelly said.

"They work hard." He pushed the glass door open for her as they exited to the parking lot.

He helped her up into the armored vehicle. No one gave them a second glance. It did look like an SUV. Deke called Hux, who picked up after several rings.

"What do you want, Bannon?"

"Just checking in. Kelly's with me. She can hear you."

"Hello, Kelly."

"Hi."

"Listen, Hux, is there anything new? How about latent prints from Bach's place?"

"The process is not instantaneous," the other man grumbled. "Did I ever tell you that when I was a rookie, I had to walk ten miles through snow to get to a database?"

"No."

"Only it wasn't a database. It was a lousy filing cabinet. Are you listening?"

"Yes, we are."

"I'm talking about a lousy filing cabinet stuffed with index cards. We matched maybe one print out of a thousand if we were lucky."

Deke rolled his eyes for Kelly's benefit. "I take it you haven't matched anything yet," he said to Hux.

"No. I'll let you know if and when we do. Hey, you going to the dinner for the sector chief?"

Deke hesitated, looking over at Kelly. She seized her opportunity.

"Can I come?" she asked Hux.

"I'll see if I can wangle an invite. That okay with you, Dekey boy?"

As if he could say no at this point. "Sure."

Deke smiled at Kelly when Hux conveyed the date and time. "Got that?"

She was entering it in her smartphone. Hux said good-bye and hung up.

"Where is it?" she asked.

"Don't worry about that," Deke said. "I'm doing the driving."

"Right."

"Don't tell anyone," he said.

"I know the drill," she assured him.

On the specified evening, Deke came up to get her at the hotel apartment, a dry-cleaning bag slung over his shoulder. He was wearing the battered leather jacket and jeans that looked clean.

"Yes, I have to change," he said when she looked at him from the other side of the open door. "You look nice."

"Thanks. Come on in." She was wearing a dark brown, belted dress with a huge faux tortoiseshell buckle. The color showed off her blond hair, which was smoothly combed over one shoulder. She'd decided on a rich caramel shade of cream shadow that brought out the green of her eyes.

Boldly, he pressed a kiss to her cheek, then headed for the bathroom as if he lived there.

Kelly smiled to herself. She wouldn't mind helping him change out of his usual dark T-shirt into something ironed and crisp. She could even help him button it up. Nice and slow.

There was the faint sound of plastic and rustling tissue paper as he removed a fresh shirt from its dry-cleaner hanger.

Not yet, Kelly told herself.

Deke opened the door of the armored SUV

for her and helped her up onto the running board, which was conveniently wide.

"I didn't know they built these things for women wearing high heels," she said.

"We had it customized. Just for you."

"Ha ha."

He closed the door with a chauffeur's flourish after Kelly got in, swinging her legs into the footwell. Once he was inside and the doors locked, his arm went around her shoulders. Kelly half turned into his embrace and parted her lips for a kiss she knew was coming.

It was tender but brief. Kelly lifted her head and pressed her cheek against his, soothed by the strong hand caressing her back. "Is there a way we could do this every night?" she murmured into his ear.

"Hmm. Wouldn't mind." He kissed her again and took a little longer about it. Then he stopped. "I have to bring you home right afterward, though."

She sighed and straightened, pulling at her dress. "Look at us. Necking like teenagers in a parking lot. Sorry. I got carried away."

"Hey." He touched her chin to make her look at him. "Don't apologize."

The dinner was attended by several members of Deke's team, and there were other teams at different tables in the restaurant. Kelly knew that the financial fraud task force was big, but she hadn't expected to see so many people tonight. There were no civilians besides herself, as far as she knew.

She studied faces when the waiters removed the appetizer plates and bustled around the table. They looked just like regular people you would see at the mall. Tall, short, thin, plump, and everything in between, in a range of ages. There were more men than women, but at least a third of the agents were female.

A waiter refilled her water glass and Kelly leaned away from him, brushing shoulders with Deke. Something about the moment of contact drew discreet looks, though no one made a comment. She sat up straight, thanking the waiter, who continued around the table.

"So, Kelly, some of us have been following your reports on Bach," said the sector chief, Doug Hightower, a thickset man in his fifties with thinning hair and bright blue eyes. "Good job."

"It's a complicated subject." Kelly smiled at him.

Hightower had made a point of talking to her just before they went in to dinner. He'd told her to contact him if she ever needed more information, then added with a chuckle that he probably wouldn't give it to her.

"You nailed it, though," said another agent, whose name she didn't know.

The arrival of their entrées halted the conversation and the table talk soon turned to the food, which was excellent. Kelly started in on her fajita-seasoned steak and Deke did the same.

She looked around again, only half listening as Deke and the agents talked shop with the chief. Another guest returning to her table caught Kelly's eye and smiled.

Kelly nodded and smiled back, wondering why the woman, who was probably past sixty, looked so familiar. With a start, she remembered where she had seen her before.

She waited for a lull in the conversation and lifted her head to talk to Deke in a low voice. "That woman over there — who is she? I know I saw her at Gunther Bach's memorial service."

Deke looked that way and grinned when he turned back to Kelly.

"That's Frankie. I meant to introduce you to her before we came in, but I couldn't find her in the crowd."

"That would be because she's only five

feet tall."

Deke rose, leaving his napkin on the table, and took Kelly's elbow when she did the same. "Excuse us, people. We're going to table-hop."

"Don't take too long," his boss said jokingly, "I can't be held accountable for missing desserts."

Deke steered her across the room and filled her in. "Frankie is an agent. She was assigned to our team eighteen months ago. We needed someone next to Gunther Bach and she was perfect for the part."

"She's an agent? What a hoot." Kelly waved to the older woman. "I never would have known."

They reached the table and Frankie got up, standing to get a hug from Deke. "I'd like you to meet Kelly Johns," he said, pulling out an empty chair for Kelly when Frankie sat down and finding another one for himself.

"I know her name," Frankie said with a touch of amused exasperation. "And we've met before."

"I can't believe this," Kelly said. "I may have to do a story on you some day."

"No thanks. I'm two seconds away from retirement and I'm looking forward to peace

and quiet," Frankie said with mock stern-
ness.

"Frankie's seen it all," Deke said. "Okay,
true story: She helped nab a mob boss in
Brooklyn once outside his favorite diner.
He'd been tailed that far and Frankie came
up to him when he left, asked him to — get
this — help her cross the street to the hair
salon. He couldn't say no to a sweet old
lady. We slapped cuffs on him after she was
safely inside."

Frankie laughed. "Nothing to it. What a
blast."

"So do you use your real name?" Kelly
wanted to know. "Frances Berry, wasn't that
it?"

"I got that last name off a jelly jar. Frances
is my real first name, but I go by Frankie.
It's Frankie Goodlett. And it's very nice to
meet you again, Kelly."

They stayed and talked for a while until
the desserts came out of the kitchen, held
high on trays to scattered applause, followed
by urns for coffee and tea on wheeled carts.
A white-haired gentleman came over and
sat down carefully between Frankie and
Deke.

"Just in case," he said to Kelly. "I don't
want him putting the moves on my wife."
He winked at Deke.

"Are you an agent too?" Kelly had to ask.

"Long retired. I started with Wild Bill at the OSS, then went covert in the Cold War until the USSR broke up. So I switched careers and became a crossing guard."

"Kelly, about half of what Tom says is true. I'm going to leave it up to you to figure out which is which." Frankie gave her husband a kiss on his wrinkled cheek. "Tom, this is Deke's friend Kelly Johns."

"From WBRX?"

"The one and only," Frankie confirmed. "What kind of cake do you want, honey?"

"Any kind that I don't have to stand up to get."

Kelly was charmed. Obviously the Goodletts had been together for more years than she'd been alive. And they still had it going on.

CHAPTER 18

The following day, Kelly settled into the backseat of the WBRX town car, giving the driver directions to the post office. She'd had her mail held when she'd left the rental condo. It had been a while since she'd bothered to pick it up.

The driver waited at the curb in a yellow zone while she went in to the low brick building and came out again, holding a rubber-banded bundle. Kelly tossed it into the backseat and got in.

"Where to?"

"The station. Thanks."

She sorted through the items, setting the junk mail and catalogues aside and leaving the bills unopened. There was an envelope from the building manager of her rented condo.

Kelly opened it and took out a form letter, reading it as the town car whizzed through the Atlanta streets.

Dear Tenant:

We are asking all residents to move their cars into alternate accommodations, as the parking garage is long overdue for necessary maintenance and repair. The contractors will begin on the top floor and move down from there. Residents with vehicles on the top floor received e-mail notification in advance, confirmed in this letter. Cars must be moved by . . .

Kelly read the date. Tomorrow. It was a good thing she'd picked up the mail today. She picked up her smartphone and scrolled back through dozens of e-mails, stopping on a message with no subject that she hadn't bothered to open. There it was. The condo manager liked to send out e-mail blasts to announce trivial improvements. This was major.

But Deke still hadn't looked over — and under — her car. No way would she get into it until he did. The drive-by had left her more wary than ever.

"Skip the station," she called to the driver. "I need to stop somewhere else first."

"I got nothing else to do," he said cheerfully.

Kelly gave him the directions. Then she

took out her smartphone and left Deke a message. If he could meet her there before she was scheduled for hair and makeup later in the afternoon, both issues would be taken care of.

Deke called back almost immediately. "Kelly — I don't know how that slipped my mind. Sorry."

"No harm done. I haven't gone near the car or the condo since I left."

They agreed to meet at the garage in forty-five minutes, enough time for him to grab some gear. Kelly asked the driver to pull into temporary parking by the building's entrance as she stayed in the car, waiting for Deke.

Through the glass, the doorman acknowledged her with a tip of his hat, but she didn't recognize him. There had been other changes during her absence. Large urns filled with flowers stood by the side of the doors. A uniformed employee was polishing the brass framework.

It was a nice building, but it was never going to be home again. Kelly didn't want to go up to the condo. She hadn't missed it.

She read through new e-mails while she waited for Deke to show. The driver turned on the radio and low, soulful music drifted back to her.

There was a quick honk. Kelly looked through the rear window. The armored SUV was behind the town car. She gave the station driver instructions to wait and got out to go to Deke.

He was leaning over the passenger seat, pushing open the door for her. "This won't take long," he said. "I have to get back. There's a follow-up meeting on the cash sting with the truck."

"Let me know how it goes."

"You'll be the first. It's turned into a media stunt," he said, pulling away and driving toward the ramp to the parking garage. "Sorry I can't give you an exclusive."

"Not a biggie. We'll run a story on it anyway."

Deke slowed and rolled down his window when a fair-haired young guy in a security guard uniform approached the SUV.

Kelly looked in her purse. "I need my building ID. That's how residents get in and out of the garage without the valet service."

"Here comes the guard."

"Hi, Curt." She found the ID and gave it to Deke, who handed it to the guard to examine.

"Hello, Ms. Johns. Is this a new vehicle for you?"

"No. It belongs to my friend. I'm here to —"

A blaring horn behind them captured the guard's attention.

"Excuse me." He returned the ID to Deke and moved away to talk to the impatient driver.

"We can go up," Kelly said. "The ramp's on your left."

Deke was looking intently into the rear-view mirror. "Okay."

He turned to get a better look at the car behind them, a luxury model in silver.

Kelly did too. "Is there a problem?"

"I was thinking I'd seen the driver before. You can't now. He flipped down the sun visor."

Kelly faced forward. "Fancy car. He can afford to live here. He probably forgot his ID."

The silver car backed up in response to the guard's energetic wave and drove over to the side.

Deke turned the steering wheel and took the SUV up several connected ramps, coming out on the roof. There were only a few vehicles. Kelly's car had a lot of room around it, but he parked several spaces away.

Deke held out a hand. "Keys please."

"You can use the remote to unlock it and

426

pop the hood and trunk." She singled out the main key and handed him the whole ring.

Deke did all three from inside the SUV. With the hood and trunk open, the car looked disabled. But there was no one around to notice that or offer help.

"Stay here," he said, grabbing a duffel bag filled with odd gear.

Maybe it was overkill, Kelly thought to herself. But she was grateful that he was checking things out. She watched through the window as he went to her car, using a wand thingy to inspect it from below. Then he inspected the engine and went around to the trunk.

Deke saved the interior of the car for last. The wand touched the Lone Star decoration hanging from her mirror, making it swing. He bent down to reach under the seats and into the footwells.

"Not getting a beep," he called to her.

She got out and went over. "What is that thing?"

"State-of-the-art sensor. Almost as good as a trained dog." He put it back in the open duffel bag.

The stack of file boxes on the passenger seat caught Kelly's eye. "Would it be okay to put those boxes in the SUV?" she asked.

"I'd rather not leave them in the car if I'm going to put it in a public garage."

"Sure." He went around and got two off the top, leaving one box for her. They got them squared away and Deke handed her the ring of keys and the remote.

"I should warm up the engine," she said. "Sometimes it dies on me. I've been meaning to replace the battery."

Deke waited by the back of the SUV as she walked over and shut the hood and the trunk. She went around to the passenger side to retrieve a few more scattered papers and put the key in the ignition, relieved to hear the car start. She walked back to him.

"I forgot my purse," she said. "It needs a minute or two anyway."

He seemed to be listening to the engine. "Runs rough," he commented.

"Guess this is my chance to get it serviced." Kelly went around to the passenger side of the SUV, reaching for her purse as Deke climbed into the driver's seat and shut his door, rolling up the window.

She straightened and looked at him. He opened his mouth to say something but she didn't hear it. In a split second the shock wave from the bomb hit, rocking the SUV. Deke reached over and grabbed her, hauling her in.

The air shimmered with sudden heat. Acrid dust billowed out toward them, stinging her eyes and searing her throat. Deke was coughing too hard to speak.

Kelly was able to think straight for a few seconds more and dragged her seat belt twistedly over her shoulder, clicking it somehow. Through his window she caught a glimpse of the fireball that engulfed most of her car. Thick black smoke curled out of the hood, rising higher and faster by the second. She scrambled to slam the door on her side as Deke turned the key in the ignition and jammed his foot down on the accelerator.

They were halfway down the top ramp when the car exploded above them. The force of the blast slammed them into a retaining wall. There was a thud inside. Momentarily stunned, Deke stared at her, his eyes unfocused. Then with an effort that was half animal strength and half willpower, he forced the wheel to turn and pulled away with a screech of tires.

Kelly had nothing to brace herself with. She clutched the seat belt as the armored SUV sped around the curving ramps, going faster as he reached the ground floor.

Ahead of them was the entrance to the parking structure, but there was no sign of the guard. Deke gunned the engine and raced out, forced to brake against his momentum when he saw people up ahead. Not all of them were looking up at the roof. Several were crouched around a motionless figure on the asphalt who was staring at the sky.

Gasping for breath, Kelly glanced toward the group and realized it was the guard. She saw his mouth open and a trickle of blood ran down the side. His eyes closed, then opened again. He was alive. Maybe not for long.

Deke had already slowed. He swung over and threw the gearshift into park. "I'll do what I can. Don't get out."

Kelly heard a distant siren begin to wail.

Deke rubbed his forehead, then winced and lifted his hand. A bruise almost hidden by his hair was purpling. Kelly knew better than to mention it. He wouldn't care.

Lieutenant Dwight had brought them to the station and into a private room where Hux met them. The armored SUV had been left at the secured scene for inspection by the bomb squad.

"There must have been a tail on the WBRX car from the time it left the station," Deke said. "This guy likes to make sure he's done his job. If you hadn't gone to your car, he would have found another way to eliminate you."

"Sick bastard probably gets a kick out of seeing his victims get hurt," Hux muttered.

"I never noticed him." Kelly looked anxiously at both men.

"Don't blame yourself," Hux assured her. "The bombing was in the works for a while. We spoke to the condo manager. The letter and the e-mail were both bogus. The wild card was when and whether you would return to the apartment."

"And I did."

"No question that your stalker is patient and a professional," Hux said. "Ex-military would be my guess. The bomb squad said the materials and probable mechanism indicate it. Simple but effective. The bomb wasn't on a timer and he didn't have to set it off remotely. The heat of the engine would do that. He knew his stuff."

Kelly shook inside. "But not that my car takes forever to warm up. I got lucky."

"You saved your own life when you walked away," Hux said. "The guard almost bought it. The driver of the silver car hit him head-on trying to escape. We're getting complete statements from the witnesses now."

He looked over at Deke. "You okay, pal?"

"The medic said I was."

"And he told you to get a recheck before tonight," Kelly reminded him.

"Later. Not now."

She had expected a reply like that, but she looked at him with concern, then turned to his partner. "Hux, do you know where the guard was taken?"

"I can find out."

Hux pulled out his smartphone and texted somebody. She and Deke were silent. The soft chime of an incoming answer echoed in the room.

"Atlanta General. He's still critical," Hux said.

"Can you take us there?" she asked.

"Say when," he replied.

Deke stood up as if every muscle in his body ached. Kelly knew how he felt. Terror had been followed by a strange stiffness that she fought against with every step. But they had escaped with their lives.

The nurse at the front desk of the ICU ward was polite, but she made it clear that only family members were allowed past her.

Kelly looked down the wide hall. Outside a room stood a middle-aged woman with the same fair hair as Curt, and a younger

432

one who was probably his girlfriend or wife. They seemed to be keeping vigil. A doctor came out and spoke to both women. The three of them went in together.

She looked up at Deke, who put an arm around her shoulders as they walked back to the elevators. His reassuring hold conveyed emotions neither could voice.

"One way or another, we're going to get the bastard," he said quietly. "But you have to stay out of the line of fire. That's an order."

CHAPTER 19

An older officer led Deke and Kelly to a room that had once been someone's office and closed the door after himself when he left. The unused office was furnished with a scratched metal desk and two oak swivel chairs. But it had what Deke had requested: a bulletin board.

He tacked up a Wanted poster. "Work in progress," he said. "What do you think?"

Kelly didn't answer right away. She walked closer.

"It's a composite image of the driver," Deke said. "But all the witnesses agreed it was a good likeness."

The poster had been reproduced in color. Kelly looked at the face of the man above the big letters that spelled out WANTED. The dark blue birthmark that tinged his skin from his neck to under his jaw was so noticeable that she almost didn't recognize him at first.

Silently, she confirmed other details. He had a piercing gaze and black hair. His features were coarse. The written description fit, too: He was massively built, tall enough for his head to touch the roof of his car. He had thick fingers and a chunky ring on his left hand. Kelly remembered neither, but then she hadn't seen his hands.

"Oh my God. I think I saw him at Natalie's house," she said in a low voice. "I thought he was the landscaper."

"What?" Deke was taken aback.

"When I went there after Bach's memorial service, he showed up outside at one point. She excused herself to go talk to him and left me alone. I didn't think anything about it — the grounds of her Buckhead house were really overgrown. Then they got into an argument that I could hear through the window."

"Jesus, Kelly. Why didn't you tell me?"

"I didn't know there was anything to tell. I couldn't understand what they were saying. Although I did think it was weird when she slapped him."

Deke seemed to be about to say more, then decided not to interrupt.

"He just stood there and took it. He was huge. This description fits." Kelly handed the poster back.

"You mean he didn't react to the slap?"

"I don't know. His back was to me. Then he turned and happened to see me through the window. I remember not liking the look in his eyes. Natalie came back a little while later."

"And then what?"

"I left. I didn't see him around and I didn't see a third car. It was strange," she admitted. "But Natalie is just so theatrical — and she treated the house servant like dirt too. I just wanted to get out of there."

Deke absorbed the information. "That birthmark didn't make an impression, I take it."

"He was wearing a scarf."

"So our suspect knows Natalie Conrad." Deke leaned against the metal desk. He was both thoughtful and angry. "I'm thinking we should pay a call on her."

Kelly looked at him doubtfully. "Didn't she say she was going to Dallas?"

Deke nodded. "Yeah. But not when she was coming back. We gotta get on this."

Kelly rose and collected her bag. "If you need me to, I could pick him out of a lineup. Count on that."

Deke straightened. "I meant Hux and someone else when I said *we*. She thinks I'm Russ Thorn."

"And she thinks you're my fiancé," Kelly said firmly. "If you show her that poster, she's going to know that I connected the dots between her 'landscaper' and our car bomber."

"I don't have to show it to her, and the poster hasn't circulated beyond law enforcement yet," Deke pointed out. "But we do have to talk to her. I'm thinking they should bring along a SWAT team."

"She might not appreciate that. Try something a little more subtle first."

Deke went over to her, but she stepped away from him. "Please, not now," Kelly said. "I'm just not up for it."

His hands stayed at his sides and he didn't try to follow her.

"Sorry if it sounded like I was pissed off with you, Kelly. I wasn't. After the drive-by, I shouldn't even be surprised."

"That makes two of us."

"Come on. I'll drive you to WBRX. Don't tell anyone about this."

Several hours later, Deke called her.

Kelly had thrown herself into work. Her businesslike hello was unemotional. "What's up?"

"Lieutenant Dwight decided against displaying the Wanted poster for the general public until someone can talk to Natalie. The cops have it, we have it, and everyone's looking for him."

"When is she coming back?"

"We picked up her name on the passenger list for a ten P.M. flight tonight from Dallas to Atlanta."

Kelly made a note of it. "You're not meeting it. Who is?"

"Hux. She doesn't know him from Adam and he's not the kind of man she would even look at. But we can't arrest her. Basically, he just wants to see if she's traveling with anyone else from our rogue's gallery."

"Good enough," Kelly said.

She fiddled with her pencil. If Natalie was tangled up with the bomber, she must have had something to do with the drive-by. The thought made her feel sick. Especially when she remembered Natalie's hovering concern after the fact, when Kelly had stayed in the car amid broken glass and bullets, with only Deke to run interference.

He was there when she needed him, in ways she never could have imagined. As far as what else Natalie might have done or was planning to do, he was definitely not paranoid.

"Saw your broadcast, by the way." Deke's calm voice interrupted her racing thoughts.

"You seem to have recovered."

"I'm a nervous wreck."

Deke didn't get into it. Kelly was grateful. "The hotline graphic looked good," was all he said. "Anybody call or e-mail yet?"

"Lots of people. Coral and Fred are sorting through the replies. No telling what's valid and what's not at this point."

"Keep us posted. What else is going on over there?"

Kelly shook her head. "I hate to say it, but Monroe could hardly contain his excitement, once he was sure I was okay and no one else beside the guard was hurt. He personally donated a chunk of money toward the medical bills."

"Decent."

"You can't keep a car bombing off the news, Deke. It's a huge story."

"Is that because it involves you?"

She frowned. "Yes. And you. You're a hero around the newsroom."

"Just don't mention my name on the air."

"Never have, never would." A sudden thought struck her hard. "Deke, if the bomber saw you and he knows Natalie, your cover is totally blown. Russ Thorn has to disappear."

"I know," he said. "Nothing I can do about it."

■ ■ ■ ■

Kelly had a glass of wine once she was home. She fell asleep on the couch with her clothes on, waking after midnight when she finally heard her smartphone ringing inside her purse. She squinted at the screen. Three missed calls, one after another. Deke.

He hadn't left a text or a voicemail.

She called him back. "I know it's important," she said.

"Yeah. A highway cop just pulled over some monster guy who fits our description."

Someone was talking in the background. Deke talked back. "What? Say that again? Got it. Silver car, different plates," he said to Kelly. "Driving erratically, may be drunk. The officer got him cuffed and he's waiting for backup."

"Deke —"

"This could be it, Kelly. Just wanted you to know."

Someone else called to him. Deke hung up. She knew next to nothing and she wasn't in the game. For once, Kelly didn't mind. But she wasn't going back to sleep.

The line of speeding cruisers ate up the highway, turning off onto a parallel road that wasn't lit. For his own safety, Deke was in the passenger seat of the third car back. The laptop mounted on the dash gave off a faint blue glow that illuminated his face.

Lieutenant Dwight was at the wheel. "Hope this doesn't turn bad."

"Who's the officer?"

"Good guy, from what I heard, but still wet behind the ears."

"A rookie?"

"Not quite. But not that experienced either." Lieutenant Dwight slowed when the first two cars pulled over and flanked the highway patrol car. Their doors opened and more cops in tactical gear scrambled out.

Ahead, parked crookedly on the wide shoulder of the road, was a silver, late-model luxury car that fit the Wanted poster description in every detail except for the plates.

A huge, black-haired man lay facedown on the gravel by the rear bumper, motionless, his thick arms behind his back. His wrists barely met. The cuffs were taut.

"I count four guns pointing at his head. I think he got the idea," Deke said.

"Let's hope so," was the lieutenant's terse answer.

The arresting officer came over when he and Deke got out of the car. His dark uniform showed the signs of a scuffle when he moved through the beams of several sets of headlights.

"You guys can take it from here. He almost had me."

"How'd you get him down?"

The officer held up a nearly empty bottle of vodka with a long straw in it. "This helped. It's why I pulled him over — I saw him drinking it. He got out like a good boy and then he went for me."

Methodically, Dwight walked around the prone man, his shoes crunching in the gravel. "Lost his balance, did he?"

"Yup. He fell just like that. I made my move."

"Any ID on him?"

"I was going to look in his pockets when I saw you guys coming down the road. Have at."

Hux and Deke were sitting with Kelly in a quiet restaurant in Atlanta a few days later. "His name is Konstantin," Hux said. "That's it. First and last. No driver's license and no passport or other ID, but he says he's Russian. Been in the city for about a year. Doing odd jobs."

Kelly glanced at Deke. "Like landscaping?" she asked Hux.

442

"I don't think so. Even though he looks like he could pull a tree out of the ground with his bare hands."

"How'd you get him to talk?" Deke wanted to know.

"Konstantin hasn't said much yet. But he wants to. His attorney isn't against it."

"He's lawyered up already? That was fast," Deke said. "Remind me not to ask for a business card. If I ever need a criminal lawyer, I'm pleading the Fifth."

"They're angling for a plea bargain. Apparently Konstantin doesn't want to be deported at the end of his sentence."

"If he lives that long," Kelly interjected.

Hux acknowledged that.

"What did Interpol say?" Deke asked.

"He's a wanted man in Russia. They don't fool around over there. He evidently prefers an American prison, a shorter sentence, and a ticket to a nice, warm country at the end of it."

"So much for justice," Deke muttered.

Hux shrugged. "It is what it is. He's facing a charge of attempted murder, since it looks like the guard is going to make a full recovery."

"Don't forget aggravated assault and vehicular assault and the bombing," Deke pointed out. "And there may be more than one killing we don't know about."

"Which all has to be proved," Hux said. "Just as a side note, Konstantin may have done some enforcing for the money-laundering ring around Atlanta. And did I tell you that truck got stolen, Deke?"

"No."

"Dallas has the hijackers under lock and key," Hux said.

"More power to them. This is bigger."

"Yeah, looks like," Hux said casually. "The DA will add it all up when the time comes."

Kelly twirled a french fry in a small pool of ketchup. "You know Natalie Conrad is paying his attorney, right?"

"Someone has to," Hux said.

He didn't bother to ask how she knew that, and Kelly didn't explain that she'd heard it from Monroe Capp. If the crime wasn't too heinous, her boss made a point of befriending criminal lawyers who needed to put a positive spin on cases they were handling. In this case, he must have called in a big favor to get the information.

"We'll get something out of it. Lieutenant Dwight is going to be on the other side of the table. By the way, Kelly, he said you could watch through the two-way glass."

"Seriously?" Her green eyes lit up with excitement.

Deke shook his head at Hux.

"There are two conditions," Hux went on. "That you don't reveal any information until and if Dwight clears it for release. And that you tell no one about being in on this."

"I keep hearing that. The answer is always yes. I consider myself sworn to secrecy in advance."

"Dwight wants that in writing." Hux smiled blandly. "He said you'd understand."

"Okay to that too."

"Why is he even allowing her to be there?" Deke asked.

Hux looked at him and then at Kelly. "I think you should ask him yourself, pal. I'm just the messenger. Please don't shoot me."

They had a day to decompress before Konstantin's interrogation. Only Lieutenant Dwight wasn't calling it that, now that there was a lawyer involved.

At the appointed time, Kelly showed up at the police station early, going in the back way, through a metal detector. She signed in and followed the crew-cut officer who was waiting to escort her upstairs.

He found her a seat in the room behind the two-way mirrored glass. She made herself comfortable, assuming she wouldn't be alone there. But for a while, she was.

Kelly watched Konstantin enter, guided by an officer and followed by his high-powered attorney. The interview would be taped. She kept an eye on the TV monitor as well.

The lawyer was in his sixties, fit and well-dressed. His heavy-set client was wearing an orange jumpsuit that was a little too big for him despite his size. The blue birthmark seemed darker and more obvious under fluorescent lights.

He was handcuffed. As a courtesy, not behind his back. But a chain extended from the wrist cuffs to a heavier cuff on his leg.

Shackled, Konstantin still exuded menace. His steady gaze moved over the bare room and then fixed on the camera. Kelly shifted in her seat, unable to shake the feeling that he was looking directly at her.

She looked back through the two-way glass, avoiding the TV screen that transmitted the cool hatred in his eyes.

Konstantin took a chair and slouched in it. His lawyer whispered something that Kelly couldn't hear and he sat up straight. But he didn't stand up when Lieutenant Dwight came in with a colleague. The other officer moved outside and stood by the door.

They got right down to business.

"Lieutenant, you're aware that my client is interested in a plea bargain."

A weary look came over Dwight's lean face. "Let's talk first." He let the attorney continue.

"We're looking for a reduced sentence, Lieutenant. I believe my client can help you put more than one killer behind bars."

"Go on."

"Konstantin." The lawyer turned to the huge man, who was slouching again, massive arms folded tightly across his chest. "Can you tell the detective about the shootings at the abandoned building? Three people died."

"One, I knew. Not the others." Konstantin looked at the floor. "Pyotr came to this country before I did."

"Let's move on," the lawyer interrupted smoothly.

"No. I will tell him."

Lieutenant Dwight managed to look encouraging. "Go ahead."

"I was in that building on an upper floor. I saw the whole thing. All the people."

Which meant he had seen Deke. And her, Kelly thought.

"Who else was there?" Dwight asked him. He did all the questioning. His colleague seemed to be a listener.

Kelly noticed that the lieutenant kept the focus on details that were directly related to the crime. He didn't seem interested in Konstantin's life story, not that the thug was telling it or even looking for sympathy. But she supposed Dwight would get around to that too. Eventually. A lot of seemingly miscellaneous things could become part of a strong case.

"A news team with a camera," Konstantin said after some thought. "There was a blonde who talked for them."

"Do you know her name?"

For a fraction of a second Konstantin hesitated. "Kelly Johnson. No. Johns. Kelly Johns."

"Anyone else?"

"There was another man on the floor below me. He looked like an agent, I thought. Not a policeman."

A muscle twitched in the lieutenant's jaw. "Did the man see you?"

"No."

"Did the news crew see you?"

"No. They ran away. When the shooting stopped, I came down."

"Where was the agent?"

"In front of the building talking on the phone. He didn't see me. I found the blonde's press pass, stuck it in the fence, and shot at it."

"Why?"

"If she came back for it, she would know to stay away."

"What happened to the pass?" Dwight asked after a moment of thought. "I don't remember seeing that on the evidence list."

The man lifted his massive shoulders. "I don't know."

The lawyer harrumphed. "With all due respect, Lieutenant, this pass is not important."

Meaning, Kelly thought, that it wasn't information he could trade on behalf of his client.

"If you say so."

Dwight took a moment to glance at the few notes he'd made on a yellow legal pad. Kelly noticed the lawyer reading them upside down.

The lieutenant looked at Konstantin. "I feel like I missed something. Miss Johns saw you at Natalie Conrad's home, arguing with her. Exactly what is the connection between you and Natalie Conrad?"

"We know each other a long time. She was the one who —" Konstantin lifted his hands as if he were testing the cuffs.

The lieutenant's body tensed visibly and his colleague's hand went to the holster on

449

his belt. With a shrug, the prisoner settled his hands in his lap, concealed by the folds of the baggy jumpsuit.

"Keep your hands where we can see them," Dwight said. He tapped the metal arch bolted through the table.

The lawyer nodded and the man complied, moving his hands up to his chest. The awkward position made it look like he was praying. Until his hands curled into fists.

"This is a preliminary conversation, Dwight," the lawyer reminded him. "Not everything is on the table. Konstantin, do not answer further questions about Natalie Conrad unless I tell you to."

The lieutenant looked at the lawyer with obvious disgust. "Okay. Let's get back to Kelly Johns. She received a card with pictures of herself. Someone shot those too. Did you do that, Konstantin?"

He shook his head. "I delivered the card. I didn't know what was in it. Some fool in the lobby let me into the building. There is always one, eh?"

Dwight made a note of the reply. "And later, there was a drive-by shooting in the same neighborhood as the building. Were you involved with that in any way?"

Konstantin only shrugged.

"Do you need me to repeat the question?"

"No," the prisoner said sullenly. "I heard you. I was not involved."

Kelly was picking up a rhythm to Konstantin's answers. Sometimes he lied. Sometimes he told the truth. The idea was to keep the interviewer off balance — and coming back for more.

The officer at the door came in to clear away pizza boxes and soda cans. The men in the room had stopped to eat after two hours. Konstantin was allowed one free hand to eat pizza. The other was cuffed to the table.

The young officer who'd escorted her to the room had brought her a chilled bottle of water during the break and asked if she wanted anything. Kelly was too tense to be hungry.

The second round of the questioning took a different tack, once both of Konstantin's hands were securely cuffed again. The lieutenant was an expert interviewer, but the thug across the table was tougher.

It was a toss-up as to who was winning. But Kelly sensed the balance of power shift when Lieutenant Dwight changed the subject abruptly, tired of Konstantin's evasions.

"What about Gunther Bach?" he asked.

"Who?" The prisoner's expression barely

changed.

"You know who I mean."

Konstantin gave the lieutenant a sullen look. "He jumped off a building. He died. It was on the news."

Dwight looked at him steadily.

"Who cares? People would line up to throw rich bastards off buildings if they could," Konstantin added.

The lawyer shot his client a quelling look, then turned to Lieutenant Dwight. "You know, this may be enough for one day. I think you have an idea of how Konstantin can help you."

Dwight shook his head. "Actually, I don't."

"But you will. There is more. Of course, you and I both know my client is going to do time. We just don't want it to be hard time. I'm sure we all understand each other."

"I have to talk to the DA," Lieutenant Dwight said levelly. "As you say, this is preliminary. Let me get back to you."

Kelly was stunned. A young sergeant opened the door and came in, looking through the glass to see everyone standing in the interview room. "Is it over?" she asked, frowning in disappointment. "Darn it. I heard this was going to be good. What'd they say?"

"I can't repeat a word. Sorry."

"Oh, well." The sergeant gave her an odd smile. "Someone said to ask you."

"Who?" Kelly looked at her, puzzled. Then she suddenly got it. "Did Lieutenant Dwight send you in here?"

"Yes, ma'am. He doesn't trust anybody."

The sergeant winked at her and left.

CHAPTER 20

Deke and Kelly had turned the unused office at the police station into a temporary conference room on the case. They'd been at it for hours. The bulletin board was covered with sticky notes and photographs and diagrams.

"One more time," he said. "The balcony railing hadn't been touched. Gunther Bach did not kill himself."

Kelly sighed. "Konstantin could lift you over his head and throw you. But there's still no proof that he or Natalie had anything to do with Bach's death."

"Not yet," he said. "Although the evidence team went back again — I stopped by the lab to talk to the tech."

"Oh?" Kelly asked with interest. "What'd they find?"

"They missed some prints under the lip of the kitchen counter and a few in the bathroom. Some were Bach's, some were his housekeeper's. Her alibi checked out."

"And the others?"

"There was just one we couldn't identify. Not in any database."

"A tantalizing new clue has emerged in the mysterious death of Gunther Bach," Kelly said in her anchor voice. "An unidentified fingerprint hides a secret. Join us at six for more."

"Stop it. We don't know anything solid."

"Look, it's not like I want to spin the story," she said. "Konstantin isn't going to walk out of jail, and thank God for that, but he didn't act alone."

"Kelly. Juries want facts. We have to have physical proof of a crime before we can even arrest her."

Kelly just looked at him. "How much do you have to know? Dwight keeps telling me that there are three main reasons for homicide: sex and money and control."

"That's true. Now apply them to this case," Deke challenged her.

"Bach was her lover."

"That was a while ago," he countered.

"He controlled her money."

"Not for long." Deke looked back at the laptop on the metal desk and touched a key to keep the screen from going dark. "There's a piece of the puzzle that's missing. I feel like it's just out of reach."

"If Konstantin really confesses —" She stopped herself. "I couldn't believe it when he started to talk about his connection to Natalie. Why? Natalie paid for his lawyer."

"Interesting question. But a confession is still not evidence. Basically it's his word against hers."

Kelly began to pace. "I'm beginning to think that's what you and I sound like."

"No. I'm on your side. Konstantin is ready to betray her, for what it's worth." Wearily, Deke ran a hand through his dark hair.

She looked at her watch. "It's getting late. Let's move this to my place. I'd like to order in and keep going."

Kelly peeked through the sheers behind the heavy curtains that blocked the light. The morning sky was gray and covered with clouds. She stepped away from the window, walking noiselessly on the thick carpet.

Deke was sacked out on the couch. His arm was thrown over his eyes and the blanket she'd given him had slipped off his chest, revealing the crumpled polo shirt he'd slept in.

Kelly was beyond tired. She hadn't slept at all.

Before he'd dozed off, Deke had set her

up with encrypted passwords to databases she'd never dreamed of being able to get into — and added that the passwords changed every twenty-four hours.

Kelly had made the most of the opportunity.

She shook him awake. Deke sat up, running his hands through his hair.

"Why am I still here?" he asked her.

"You dozed off," she said. "I want you to look at something. I found interesting stuff on Natalie Conrad while you were sleeping." She didn't mean it as a dig, but he seemed to take it that way.

He managed a smile at her reply. "What the hell."

"I'll make coffee."

"Thanks." He stayed on the couch but he sat up. In a few minutes, Kelly returned with two mugs. Deke drank some of his and set the mug aside.

"Okay, show me."

Kelly brought over her laptop and set it between them on the middle cushion of the sofa, tapping keys to open different files on the screen.

"Check this out. And this. And that."

Deke's eyes widened as he gave a slight shake of his head. "You're a kid in a candy store. I hope you confined your research to

Natalie Conrad."

"Of course," she said indignantly.

He seemed dubious on that score. But he read through everything she showed him. Kelly kept tapping the arrow keys, her coffee mug in her other hand.

Deke didn't seem impressed. "I don't see anything incriminating."

"Natalie is desperate for a reason. She's almost broke, Deke."

"So?"

"She was the sole trustee of the museum money. Where is it? She zeroed out all these accounts."

He looked at the relevant file again. "They're in the US. Did you find anything from foreign banks? I know she has offshore accounts in the Caribbean and Switzerland."

"I'll find them."

"Just so you know, Kelly, being broke is not a crime."

"No, but it could be a motive."

Deke shook his head.

She wasn't going to quit. He didn't know that she'd saved the best for last. Kelly opened another window. A credit card statement appeared.

"Here we go. One of many," Kelly said. "Natalie has a lot of credit cards. But this

458

one seems to be set aside for her car, airplane tickets, stuff like that."

"I got it." He yawned. "Transportation and travel."

"Exactly," Kelly said. "It looked routine. Except for one little thing."

Deke glanced at the file again and his eyes narrowed. He lost his bored look and leaned toward the laptop. He scanned the statement twice just to be sure.

"A limo company in Atlanta billed her on the day Gunther Bach died," Kelly said. "She was supposed to be in Dallas."

"Yeah. I spotted that."

Kelly sat back, looking very satisfied with herself. "Does that answer a big question?"

"Maybe," Deke admitted. "But we'd have to track down the driver for that car and that time period, and confirm that it was Natalie Conrad in the car, and about a thousand other things. Interesting lead, though. Good work."

"I'm sure you would have found it eventually," Kelly said. "Now what?"

"We do all of the above. Give me a few days." He looked up when she bounced to her feet. "Calm down. If that was her in the limo, all she did was look. That's not the same as being at the crime scene in Bach's apartment."

Kelly sighed with exasperation. "But we might be able to put her near it at the right time. Deke, I could write the prosecution's opening statement using just this."

"Don't."

She lowered her tone. "Ladies and gentlemen of the jury, Natalie Conrad returned that night for only one reason. To find out if Gunther Bach was dead."

"Guess what, Kelly. You aren't going to try this case on the six o'clock news."

Kelly glared at him. "I wasn't planning to. But I don't understand why you're not excited."

"Solving this case is going to take months. You're getting ahead of yourself," Deke said.

"As usual," Kelly retorted. "That's how I get things done."

"Dial it down, okay? Natalie Conrad is still in the clear, legally speaking. One little thing like that isn't going to put her behind bars."

"Thank you for that brutally honest opinion," she said acidly.

"Sorry. I know it's early for a reality check. But you didn't find the magic key."

"At least I looked."

Deke ignored the childish dig. Kelly was ashamed of making it, but she was too tired to apologize.

"We have more work to do. A lot more if Konstantin decides to shut up. Dwight is going to have a tough time breaking him as it is. He might not ever be able to do it."

"I know that, but —"

"You have to have something concrete to get an arrest warrant. Meaning evidence that places her in Bach's apartment before he was found dead."

"I didn't want to ask Frankie at the team dinner, but I guess she never saw anything," Kelly said. "You never did say."

"No. On stakeouts, either you get lucky or you don't."

"Got it."

Deke waved at the credit card statement on the screen. "Without other evidence, without a prior warrant, a judge would be likely to call this an unreasonable search and seizure, in clear violation of the subject's constitutional rights."

"Thanks for the civics lecture." Kelly got up and moved to the kitchen counter with her empty cup. "Too bad. I'm impatient, I admit it. Wouldn't it be great if *she* would confess? Just saying."

Deke got up and stretched. "Lunatics do it all the time. She could take responsibility for every crime in Atlanta for the last ten years and it wouldn't matter without corroborating evidence."

He went over to the window and pulled the curtains open. The sky was lighter, but not by much. Kelly stared out the window, as if the answers were out there floating around like clouds.

"What if there were some way I could get her fingerprints?"

Deke chuckled. "How? Pretend to be a manicurist? She might figure out who you are."

Kelly scowled at him.

"Collecting evidence is not your job."

His unequivocal answer hung in the air between them. Kelly didn't meet his gaze as she shut down her laptop, staring into the screen until it went black.

"You and I still make a good team, Kelly. But we can't work the same side of the street."

Kelly didn't answer. She closed the laptop with a decisive snap.

CHAPTER 21

Deke didn't ask for details of the next interview with Konstantin, and Kelly didn't offer any. She guessed Dwight had already briefed him.

Keeping her mouth shut was an interesting sensation. She hadn't spoken to him for a couple of days. He'd finally called her.

"Are you not talking to me?" Deke asked.

"Isn't that what we're doing?"

"You're so quiet. It makes me nervous."

"Just thinking."

"Here's the deal," Deke continued, "based on what Konstantin has said so far, Dwight thinks he can drop a few hints to Natalie Conrad that would get her into the station for a private chat. Just him and her."

"Really." Kelly was irked. Deke had not only been briefed, he knew something she didn't know. "What's that going to accomplish?"

"Dwight might get somewhere with her.

He's good with women."

"He must take lessons from you," Kelly said dryly.

"It's tomorrow. Can you make it?"

Kelly pretended to be blasé. "I think so. I have to go to WBRX tonight, though. Coral needs help with the Gunther Bach story. And Gordon wants me to help him edit our exclusive interview with the security guard's mom. Curt's doing better but he's not out of the woods yet. Viewers are really rooting for him. We set up a fund for the donations."

"That's great. How are you doing?"

"About the same," she replied. "I jump every time I hear a loud noise and I still don't sleep too well."

"We got the bastard."

Kelly was silent for a moment. "But not the bitch."

For a miracle, Deke didn't start lecturing her. "Be patient."

"Not my strong point, Deke."

"You need to work on that. Anything else?"

Yes. I miss you. She wanted to say it. She bit the words back.

"No. Thanks for calling."

"You bet. See you around."

It was a relief to retreat to her office. Kelly

leafed through the material Coral had collected. "You must be working night and day."

"Just about. What's going on with you?"

Kelly chose her words carefully, keeping her promise to Lieutenant Dwight in mind. "Okay, you know who Natalie Conrad is and some of the back story with her —"

"Yes," Coral said avidly.

"It's possible that she's involved somehow in the Gunther Bach case."

"Ooh."

Kelly hesitated. It seemed unfair to even hint at Coral taking on more work, but the junior reporter-slash-assistant was so eager.

"There is one fingerprint that hasn't been identified at Bach's apartment," Kelly began, then stopped. Was that fact on the forbidden list? If it wasn't, it would be.

Coral made a note of that on the outside of a file folder. "Anything else?"

"No. Maybe I shouldn't have brought it up."

"That's okay," Coral said. "Listen, are you sure you're ready to come back to work? Some of us have been wondering —"

That was a red flag to a bull. Kelly snapped out of her mood.

"I'm here, aren't I? That's all I have to say. Bring me up to speed on WBRX. How did you all survive without me for a week?"

Deke joined her in a first-floor waiting room at the police station a half hour before Natalie Conrad's scheduled arrival. The lieutenant's coaxing had worked.

"I assume we're not invited," Kelly said.

Deke nodded, glancing out the window at a scattered mob of media people. "Dwight warned me not to show my face. I guess I should get out of here. She might not come in the front of the building, though."

"I can understand why."

"Any WBRX reporters out there?" he asked.

"Maybe. That's not something I have control over."

Deke studied her for a moment. "Granted. But Lieutenant Dwight might think differently."

"He can think what he wants," Kelly retorted. "That happens to be the truth."

He nodded, looking out the window again. "Hmm. That looks like a national news van. I didn't know Natalie Conrad was that important outside of Atlanta and Dallas."

"Don't forget Paris and New York and Moscow and a few other cities you may have heard of."

Deke raised his eyebrows. "Well, Dwight

is going to be wearing kid gloves. She won't get treated like an ordinary suspect."

"Is she officially a suspect?"

"Natalie Conrad is now a person of interest," Deke hedged. "But I doubt he would say that to her face."

"Does he really think he can get her to talk?"

"He has his doubts. Apparently he couldn't talk her out of bringing her lawyer."

"Who is it?"

"Gerry Boudreaux."

"He's expensive."

"Like I said, she's not that broke." He snapped his fingers. "Hey, I forgot to tell you the latest. We got an internal customs report from ICE. Her European representative was stopped at Heathrow with paintings taken off their frames and rolled up. He tried to get through customs without declaring them, and it turns out they were valuable."

"We know she's selling art. He must be taking them to foreign auction houses on her behalf."

"Apparently he didn't say. Maybe he stole them from her. The rats could be deserting the sinking ship."

"I don't feel sorry for Natalie Conrad."

"Let's stop talking about her for five

seconds," Deke replied. "Maybe we could try for a whole hour."

Kelly understood what he was getting at. She thawed a little. He seemed to sense it.

"Want to head upstairs to our office?" he asked. "I'd like to be behind a closed door before she gets inside the building."

A stir on the sidewalk outside the window got Kelly's attention. "Wait a sec. I think that might be her. Maybe she is coming in the front. That's not her sports car, though."

It was a recent luxury model, black and sleek, but anonymous somehow.

"Must belong to Boudreaux," Deke said.

"Good guess. I think you're right."

Kelly was fairly sure that Natalie was behind the closed window. Was she the only one who thought so? The media mob didn't rush over.

Large sunglasses hid the woman's eyes, but Kelly knew Natalie well enough to recognize her with them on. She stared at her through the glass. A memory nagged at her. Then it hit.

For a moment, peering out from the window of the black car, Natalie Conrad's face had looked exactly like the face of the woman in the red wig.

"That's incredible. I just had a flashback to the shootout," Kelly said. "That was her in the car in the parking lot."

"What?"

"I've never seen Natalie in sunglasses. They aren't the same as the ones she wore that day, but they're just as big."

"Sure you're not seeing things?"

"Not completely sure," Kelly admitted, looking again. "But it's not just the sunglasses. Natalie's mouth usually doesn't look that tense."

"Could be a lot of reasons for that," Deke observed. But he was curious enough to move behind Kelly and take a discreet look on his own.

Kelly stared harder, hoping the reflections hid her. It was hard to tell because of the sunglasses, but Natalie seemed to be looking at the milling reporters on the sidewalk and not at the police station building.

"I know why her mouth looks different," Kelly said suddenly. "I remember thinking her lips looked too full at the ball. Sort of blurry. Too much collagen will do it. She must have had an injection right after the shooting."

"Maybe so." Deke seemed unimpressed. "Which is proof of nothing, except that women notice stuff like that."

The black car pulled away. No one outside followed it. "I'm not going to argue the point." Kelly really wasn't that sure. "Let's get out of here."

They turned a corner and stopped at the vending machine to get a couple of bottles of water. The young female sergeant Kelly had met the previous day said hello, stopping to chat.

The sound of high heels got Kelly's attention.

Natalie. She was going the wrong way if she was heading for Lieutenant Dwight's office.

The older woman stood stock still, her gaze fixated on Kelly. She whipped off her sunglasses. "If it isn't Kelly Johns," she said in a strangely composed voice. "Dwight didn't tell me you'd be here."

"I was just leaving," Kelly replied.

"Why? You might be interested in what I have to say to him."

Kelly hesitated.

"I came to talk to Dwight as someone who truly knew Gunther Bach. There are rumors going around that I don't need to repeat. Hurtful, untrue rumors." She smiled thinly at Kelly. "I'm sure they've reached you. Perhaps you even ferreted them out."

Kelly gave a slight shake of her head. "I don't know what you're talking about."

Boudreax, a powerfully built man in his

forties, hurried up, looking daggers at Kelly. He spoke to his client. "Mrs. Conrad. Please."

"Don't interrupt. I'm chatting with Kelly Johns."

Kelly took a step forward, trying to edge past Natalie. The older woman blocked her way.

"Lieutenant Dwight is waiting for us," the lawyer said.

"Then he can wait a little longer."

The lawyer put a restraining hand on her arm. "Don't plead your case in the halls, Natalie. I told you not to."

Natalie whirled to face him. "Get your hands off me, Gerry Boudreaux. Do you want to see yourself on the news?" She jabbed a finger at Kelly. "She can help you with that."

Had Natalie gone off the deep end? It sounded like it.

"Not now. Not here." The lawyer again.

Gerry Boudreaux's good advice probably cost a thousand dollars per hour, Kelly thought, judging by his suit and shoes.

Natalie chose to ignore his comment. "She came to my house. She pretended to be sympathetic. I was too distraught to tell the difference. Such a sad day. And I had an unexpected visitor. She overheard a quarrel.

471

So unfortunate."

The venomous undertone in the other woman's voice made Kelly hold up both hands in a peacemaking gesture. "No, I didn't."

"I remember differently. I had my suspicions at the time. And now . . . what are you doing here?" Natalie advanced on her, her high heels clicking sharply against the floor.

"I really was just leaving," Kelly said. She sensed Deke move behind her, a clear message to the infuriated Natalie that he had her back.

Natalie's dark green eyes glittered with rage when she glanced over Kelly's shoulder. "I've seen you before. This man is not your fiancé."

Half-crazy. Possibly certifiable. But not stupid. Kelly didn't answer.

"You lied to me about him too. He must be a detective. The damned police and the reporters are all in bed together. And to think I thought you might be my friend."

That was taking it too far. Kelly began to edge away. There was nothing to be gained by arguing with someone this angry.

Natalie snapped open her Hermès bag and took out a handkerchief, pressing it to her mouth. "I feel sick. Gerry, take me home. There's nothing to be gained by talking with Lieutenant Dwight. He'll probably feed every word I say to this whore."

"Actually —" Kelly began, then shut up. Measured footsteps echoed behind her.

"Excuse me." The lieutenant brushed past her. "Mrs. Conrad, I can see that you're upset. I want to assure you that our interview will be entirely private."

"I don't have to talk to you, Lieutenant," Natalie snapped. "I came in because I hoped I could clear my name and — explain a few things. But that's impossible."

She turned and stormed out. Her lawyer followed her without a backward glance.

Dwight turned to Kelly, his anger showing in his eyes. "Thanks for blowing the interview," he snapped.

"I didn't mean to. I just happened to be standing here when she appeared."

The lieutenant didn't seem interested. He strode past her and back into his office.

"Deke. Talk to him."

"Later. Over a beer."

"No, now," Kelly insisted. "I played by his rules. You know I did."

"I'll tell him that. We'll get her one way or another."

"How?"

Deke lowered his voice so that only she

could hear. "Konstantin told us last night that she was behind everything, starting with thieving on a colossal scale."

"What?"

"She used to belong to the mafiya. They think big."

"That can't be."

Deke kept going. "You got in her way. You were the only person who actually saw her at the scene of the shoot-out. Then there were the threats to you. Gunther's murder. The drive-by. The bomb. She did the planning, he carried it out. They really have known each other for years."

"No," Kelly whispered.

"You may have been the only person who ever caught her in the act."

"But I wasn't even trying."

"Do you think she cared, Kelly? And by the way, Gunther Bach didn't steal her fortune. She took him for all he was worth. She's had years of practice. Natalie's brilliant at what she does."

"She's delusional. Or you are."

"None of the above. It's the truth. She only seems broke. The majority of her assets are overseas."

"Why did Konstantin confess?" Kelly asked.

"Because she fired his lawyer and told him

to get a public defender." Deke lifted his shoulders in a shrug. "But guess what. We still don't have corroborating evidence."

"I was wondering why you didn't follow her."

"No warrant."

Kelly heard her phone ring inside her purse. Automatically, she reached in and looked at the screen. "My assistant," she said. "I'm going to take this."

Deke walked away. Kelly found a niche and stepped into it, avoiding the curious looks from police station staffers who'd overheard some of the confrontation with Natalie.

"Hi, Coral."

"Guess what," her assistant began.

Kelly wasn't exactly in the mood to play games. "Just tell me, okay?"

"Where are you?" Coral asked.

"Downtown at the police station."

"Perfect. Okay, after you left I did some thinking and I realized Natalie probably had dual citizenship."

Kelly didn't know one way or another. "And?"

"I called my friend at the State Department, and he did some investigating for me. Natalie not only has dual citizenship, she has a US passport and a newer Russian passport, which is biometric."

Lieutenant Dwight came out of his office and walked in the other direction, without looking at her. It was enough to distract Kelly.

"What?"

"It has an embedded microchip with her personal and biological data."

"I'm not following you, Coral."

"A lot of countries issue them. The US does, too, but only includes a full-face photo in the chip. The Russian microchip holds an official record of Natalie Conrad's finger-prints."

Kelly began to pace. "That's not possible." Deke would have known about something like that. On the other hand, he didn't work for the State Department, which was a world unto itself.

And he didn't know everything.

"My friend called in a favor — a big one. By the way, you can't go public with that, Kelly," Coral warned her.

"God, no. Never."

"But long story short, I have ten clear fingerprints belonging to Natalie Conrad. So the cops and the feds can rule her out or, you know, arrest her."

Kelly almost dropped the phone. "Ah — how soon can you get here?"

"Twenty minutes?"

"All right. Meet me in the police station parking lot. Northeast corner." She hung up.

For what it was worth, she wanted to actually see the prints before she handed them over to Dwight. If they were the real deal, the lieutenant would take it from there.

Kelly walked quickly through the hall and used the stairs to exit to the first floor. She didn't know where Deke was.

The officer manning the metal detector looked up as she went past. Kelly nodded to him, not waving because her phone was in her hand. If Coral needed directions, she had it ready.

Once outside, Kelly stopped rushing and breathed a little more easily. She walked toward the northeast corner, which had fewer cars — hers was closer to the building — and shade trees. She'd picked it thinking she and Coral would be less conspicuous.

A car entered the lot on the other side, stopping at the security gates when the guard leaned out. Kelly craned her neck to see the driver, then realized it was a man. She kept walking, looking in her purse for her glasses so she could get a good look at the fingerprints. Kelly's hand closed around the glasses. She stuck them into a side pocket of her purse, distracted enough to stumble.

She looked down at the pavement, which was smooth. Then she realized that she had been shoved.

A hand seized her arm at the elbow, precisely pinching a nerve that made her lose her grip. Shooting pain ran up her arm and she dropped the purse.

"Turn around," said a soft voice. Whoever had ambushed her had the advantage of surprise. The hand tightened and she was whipped around.

Kelly found herself staring at Natalie Conrad.

The older woman's face was streaked with mascara, as if she'd been crying. Her eyes were red and her gaze glittered with malice. A little too late, Kelly realized that Natalie's other hand held a gun.

She backed Kelly against a black car. "Reach behind you. Open the door — yes, the back door. And get in."

Kelly guessed it was the lawyer's car, but where was he? Her hand fumbled for the door latch. Natalie let go of her long enough to step back when Kelly opened the door, then delivered a blow to her midsection that made her buckle. Her head banged against the frame of the car as she was shoved inside.

Natalie's violence was skilled, relying on speed and the ability to unbalance an adversary.

Kelly's head snapped back when Natalie hit her under the chin with an uppercut from the gun. "All the way in!"

Stunned, Kelly managed to drag her legs over the bottom frame of the door, hitching into the middle seat. Something warm and solid stopped her. Not something, she realized. Someone. The bulky body made no protest. Kelly guessed that it was Natalie's lawyer. Shot dead. She felt something wet under her hand. The seat was drenched with blood.

Natalie slid in and closed the door. Kelly was trapped between a dead man and a homicidal woman.

The gun was inches from her face, held tight. The arm that Natalie had gripped still throbbed, the hand weakened by the nerve pinch. Kelly's other arm was constrained by her awkward position. Still, she could move it.

Natalie stared into Kelly's eyes, her face twisted with deranged fury.

"This will be easy," Natalie murmured. "But so unnecessary. You seem unable to take a hint, Kelly."

Let her talk. Kelly barely listened. By fractions of an inch, she began to free her arm.

The gun in Natalie's hand shook. "But you have had everything. You would not understand."

Kelly was sickened by the self-pity that began to creep into Natalie's voice.

"I knew you were following me right away. Trying to get a story. The rise and fall of Natalie Conrad." She clutched the weapon so hard her knuckles turned white. "I sent Konstantin after you time after time — oh, I was a fool. He was looking out for himself."

Her heart racing, Kelly kept calm. Natalie seemed to soften for a second. Then the older woman steeled herself again. A hard look came into her eyes.

"I'm not going to rot in jail. You are my ticket out of the US. When I am safely away, I shall take your life."

Natalie wasn't delusional. She was completely demented. But she still seemed to know how to handle a weapon.

The safety was off. Natalie's manicured finger tightened on the trigger, backing up her threat. Kelly jerked her arm free and knocked the gun up and out of Natalie's hand. The bullet went into the roof of the car, the force of the shot deafening them both. She yanked the gun away from Natalie, who cried out and fought to get it back, clawing at Kelly, going for her eyes.

Kelly hung on to the gun with one hand and slapped Natalie's hands away with the other. She pushed her back toward the closed window with all her strength, banging Natalie's head once. Then twice.

Unconscious, Natalie slumped, and Kelly let go of her.

The door latch opened noiselessly when she reached behind Natalie for it. The weight of the other woman's body was enough to open the door. Breathing peacefully, Natalie tumbled halfway out onto the asphalt of the parking lot.

Kelly reached between the front seats and gave the ignition key a quarter turn. She leaned on the horn. Again and again.

In the distance, the guard at the gate turned to see. Then a brawny male body blocked her view. Deke looked into the car. A moment later, he straightened and yelled to the guard to call an ambulance.

He bent down, shifting Natalie and looking her over quickly. "She'll live. Are you okay?"

She had never been so glad to see anyone in her life, but it was still a stupid question.

She didn't answer it. Kelly handed him the gun. "Careful. The safety's off."

"On you or the pistol?"

"Just help me get out of this car!"

He offered her his arm. She pushed it away and clambered into the front seat to avoid Natalie's prone form. The lawyer groaned when she kicked him.

"Oh my God. He's alive. I thought she killed him!"

Deke had already opened the front door. "She tried to. I think we have what we need to go forward, don't you?"

"Shut up, Deke. Just shut the freaking hell up."

"I love you too."

"I didn't say —"

"Get out by yourself." He was going around the car to the other side. "I have to help Gerry."

CHAPTER 22

Here we go. Kelly was ensconced on the sofa in her condo. The evening news show had already begun. But Dave Maples was alone on the set, looking straight into the camera.

"More on those headlines later," he said affably. He glanced toward the empty anchor chair next to his and back into the camera. "If you were wondering where Kelly Johns is tonight, we have an important announcement to make."

"Pause for effect, Dave," Kelly said. He did.

"As we all know, her incredible series on the international criminal ring based right here in Atlanta garnered local awards and worldwide attention. To recap."

Another pause.

"The case started with three murders at an abandoned building and a mysterious woman who escaped the scene. She turned out to be the mastermind of a financial fraud on an unprecedented scale — and an accessory to murder and other violent crimes. Natalie Conrad's trial is ongoing. Her henchmen are jailed. WBRX brought you the story. Kelly Johns reported it. One year later, she's up for a national Emmy. Congratulations, Kelly. I know you're watching. Folks, we'll be right back after the break."

Kelly clicked off the TV. Her phone was flashing with a text from Deke.

Delivery. The box won't fit under your door. Go look.

Long-stemmed roses, maybe. Or chocolates worth craving. Tickets to a concert at the Fox Theater. A peach pie. She ran through the possibilities until she heard his knock.

Kelly opened the door. Deke stood there, holding out a small velvet box.

"Marry me?"

The lid opened at his touch. A gorgeous diamond solitaire set in platinum sparkled against white satin.

Kelly's eyes widened. "Are you kidding?"

Deke grinned. "No. So say yes."

"Out here in the hall? I don't know, Deke."

He snapped the box shut and put it in his pocket. Then he bent down and scooped her up into his arms, kicking the door shut behind them.

She told him the truth, the whole truth, and nothing but the truth in a single word.

"Yes!"

ABOUT THE AUTHOR

Janet Dailey's first book was published in 1976. In the twenty-seven years since, she has written over one hundred more novels and become the third largest-selling female author in the world, with 325 million copies of her books sold in nineteen languages in ninety-eight countries. She is known for her strong, decisive characters, her extraordinary ability to recreate a time and a place, and her unerring courage to confront important, controversial issues in her stories. She lives in Branson, Missouri.